To Barbara with love
Robert

A SHARD OF GLASS, (ANWEI'S DIAMOND)

by

ROBERT PIERPOINT OGDEN

ISBN: *9781784072094*

Author's e-mail: robertpierpointo@gmail.com

Cover photograph by Annabella Proudlock©

To my wife and family

With thanks to Stephanie Thornton for her encouragement and professional advice. Thanks to 'Mango' for inspiring the Cameroonian scenarios and to Hilda Borkum for helping with the South African sequences.

With thanks also to
Shirley May for her meticulous proof corrections

"Without the encouragement of many others, I would have given up years ago"

Description

After the massacre by Biaffran soldiers in her native Cameroonian village, Anwei and her childhood sweetheart escape to Douala separately. She is left behind while, Jason, selected by accident, goes to England to study. While he is away she has an affair with an English forester who returns home ignorant of the seed he has planted.

Anwei is rejected by her village for having a *matis* (mixed race) baby, and nearly dies on the road back to Douala. Djarli is adopted later in a dramatic scene by the natural father and his English bride becoming Charles who is educated in England to the level of first MB medical degree but in his gap year takes a trip with *Medicins sans Frontieres* to the Congo region.

Coincidently he discovers his birth mother and together they mount an expedition into the Congo jungle to claim her inheritance, a remote village, known to contain extremely valuable minerals in the form of coltan and carbon nano-particles but presently inhabited by lepers. With the aid of a band of misfits including a Catholic missionary escaping child abuse in Ireland, some Cape Coloured fishermen, a Texan ship's captain and an unsavoury apartheid-born South African they seek to make their fortunes. A naïve Australian female journalist almost gets them all killed but their expedition is finally saved by the genius of a convicted Welsh physicist and an old Jewish diamond expert.

Brimming with emotional encounters and violent conflicts, this African story is a truly exotic and sympathetic human experience with well constructed and exciting plotlines and absolutely believably flawed characters.

Table of Contents

Part 1: The Origins of Charles

1

In a sleepy corner of Cameroon near the Nigerian border, the Harmatan was blowing hard from the north. For about three months from November to March, this Saharan wind turns the grass pale yellow and dislodges the flaky leaves from the trees. As the sun beats mercilessly down through the dust, the ears, eyes, and mouths of the people become parched and they spend their days listlessly hiding from the red-tinted sun in the huts whose natural fabric becomes eerily brittle. The lush greenness and the sticky wet mud is banished for these months and life takes on a new aspect as the Fulani cattle are moved south to graze on the spent cornstalks, fertilising the soil before the burning of the excess grass prepares the ground for the planting in the early rains.

Around Christmas, nearly a term after their joining the fifth form, at the school shared by their villages, Anwei from Santambu and Jason from Chomba had come to know each other intimately. They had made fumbling love a few times, he clumsy and rough and she cautious and scared, preoccupied with the thought of bursting condoms, AIDS and worse. Their mores were a mixture of old tribal custom, preachy prurience, common sense and carnal attraction. She remembered how such things had been explained to them at school with all the sympathy and delicacy of a hell and damnation sermon. The loss of her maidenhood was quick and perfunctory, without pleasure or pain and without physical satisfaction, but awakening in her a deep emotional need and a new joy. On Jason's part it was more like a lusty duty and a rite of passage, awakening in him new needs and pleasures. In spite of this they became closer, sharing in the fear and excitement of all young lovers.

Their friendship had cooled for the month of their school football championships when Jason was entirely devoted to practice and the matches themselves, spending all his free time with his team discussing tactics and professional football and their local and national heroes. Although the girls wanted to be part of it, the boys kept them at a distance and let them know that football was a male thing and the girls were there to admire them, support them and worship them if they wished, but they had nothing to offer to the arguments or discussions. Their school team went on to win. Jason was the goal scorer in more than half the matches and he gradually became more bigheaded and unapproachable. This left Anwei unhappy, no longer being needed as part of his life but still having a strong desire to be with him. She watched him play and he always smiled at her but these gestures became more perfunctory, merely a means of conveying to his teammates that he had a convenient and desirable "GF."

2

It was on one hot day that catastrophe befell their quiet communities. Nothing unusual had been happening as burning hot days followed baking nights and the women struggled with the cooking, tended to the children's needs and kept house while the men went off to cut wood, hunt bush meat, collect the palm wine and lazily drink the afternoons and evenings away.

A grinding of Landover engines heralded the unwelcome arrival of a raiding party. They were from across the border in Biafra, lost and foraging for food. At first they were polite as they entered the village, toting their rifles but smiling at the people and calling them "brothers and sisters against tyranny", but their demands became a burden as time went by.

On the third day they started fooling with the women and pushing the local men about. The pubescent daughters were sent away to neighbouring villages. Soon resistance started and anger filled the air. In the evening Ngola, who was Jason's senior half brother, was shot as he fought with a soldier who was molesting his wife. The doctor was sent for, but perhaps fearing questions from the authorities and reprisals from the soldiers, he delayed and arrived three days later. The time allowed sepsis to set in and the wound to the lung had irrevocably sent Ngola down a painful path to death. As he coughed up blood and pus, his face was distorted in agony, his body racked with the effort of vitality but after twenty-four hours his body gave up the fight and he collapsed, drowning in his own fluids.

The doctor wrote the on death certificate "septicaemia of the lungs," explaining to the simple villagers that this was the technical term for what had happened and the bullet wound was incidental and unworthy of mention, and if he did mention it, lengthy enquiries but no help would follow.

From then onward bitter resentment was festering in the hearts of all the villagers of Santambu. The chief of the village drew the heads of the families together in a very brief and secret meeting and asked them to send a message to Fon Chom, the chief of Chomba, to request that the remaining women and children could all be sent there. And so in the dead of night, when the soldiers were dozing at their posts, the women and children crept away. Most went to Chomba, while others went further afield to relations in other villages.

3

It was on the fifth day of the occupation of Santambu that Jason, his senior brother, Bukani, and three other boys from Chomba crossed the road and went down the path past Santambu to the river to catch some fish. It was a dry, cloudy morning, but it brightened up later, and as the wind dropped away completely, it became oppressively hot in the mid afternoon.

The boys had been working for a few hours, in turn casting two nets a way upriver where a wide bay formed a warm water pool. This fruitful fishing ground was regarded generally as reserved for the villagers of Chomba, while other pools downriver were used by the Santambu men and boys. After they had been fishing, two at a time with the small cast nets for about four hours, they had taken a reasonable catch and were making their way back along the river. Approaching the junction with the path leading around Santambu and home, they heard sounds of coarse laughter coming from a clearing by the river. Peering through the undergrowth, they saw five soldiers in the process of stripping off their battle dress, preparing to cool off in the river.

Their dialect was unfamiliar but the boys heard a few words of pidgin they recognised, such as "officer" and "freedom" said over and over. The boys thought they might be saying, "Why fight for freedom if your officer won't give you freedom to relax in the hot afternoon?" They said it over again one to another with affirmative grunts as if to add justification to a dubious proposition. "Uh-huh, we fight for freedom. Tell the officer we must be free to wash and be cool. Uh-huh." They were a patrol. They were bored with days of plodding the riverbank encountering nothing. They had no leader.

The soldiers had carelessly stacked their assault rifles in a vague attempt at military order, but none had the sense to stand guard over them and now they were naked and slipping and sliding in the soft mud toward the river. The place they had chosen was well-known by the locals to be too steep and slippery for easy access. The soldiers learnt this as they crashed into one another until they saw, fifty yards further down, a better place with a small sandy beach. With much shouting and gesticulating, children again since they were freed from their heavy kit and uncomfortable clothes, they made their way clumsily down to the sandy cove.

Jason, untouched by their childishly innocent antics, started to feel a red haze of hatred smother his rational thoughts and become a burning need for revenge for the death of Ngola. He sat quietly as his pulse rate subsided, gaining control. The others were all frozen to the spot, perhaps having the same feelings or just catching the mood from Jason.

In the pockets of their scruffy shorts, Jason and Bukani had several small lead weights. They were the size of a medicine bottle cork. In fact the plug which formed the mould from which they had been made by Jason's father was such a cork. They each had a wire passing through, looped to attach to the periphery of the cast net.

Jason looked at the weapons and turned one of the weights over in his fingers. Later he was to have no recollection of how he had arrived at the plan, but he suddenly knew what they had to do.

He led the other boys forward toward the rifles, and taking a weight from his pocket, he tried it in the end of a barrel. The tapered end fitted in up to about halfway. A round pebble drove it in flush. He twisted off the excess wire and showed his comrades.

Each took a rifle and did the same until they were all plugged. They tamped the ends to try to disguise the appearance and replaced the weapons as untidily as they had found them. They withdrew to the undergrowth and observed the soldiers. They had stopped fooling and playing around and were lying peacefully in the shallows talking in low tones, occasionally grinning and laughing.

"My God," said Jason, "what have we done?" The elation of the recent action had given way to fear.

"I know what it's called. It's in military history. We've spiked their guns," replied Sanjo academically.

"Yes, what now?" demanded Jason, now very nervous and unsure.

"We have to get them to fire the guns before they find out. Otherwise we've wasted our time," said Bukani, a year and a half Jason's senior. He was usually quiet and thoughtful, but in this time of real danger was taking command.

"How?"

"Are we sure all the plugs are securely fixed?" asked Bukani slowly.

"Yes," the others said in unison.

"So we have to make them react."

11

"How can we do that?"

"Scare them," Bukani answered.

"What with?"

"Acacia pods, fire, noise, and running away," he said as a smile spread slowly across his face and he pulled matches and two bent cigarettes from his pocket.

"You see their uniforms; they've been lying in the sun. They are dry. We set them alight. Then we make a fire over here and load it with Acacia pods. While they are worrying about the clothes, we set light to the acacias and they crack, crack like machine gunfire in the distance. They will go for their guns. We will then run from here across there so they see us. They will shoot and kill themselves with the exploding bullets."

The boys were silent, each in his own way coming to terms with the enormity of the task. They were all very frightened and inclined to slope off and forget it. But they could not. The deed was already half done. There was no backing out. For sure if they walked away, the soldiers would come to their village and find them, identify their father from the weights, and shoot them all. None of them could think of a better solution and all feared the last act—that of breaking cover and running while the soldiers aimed and fired the guns.

They could see one of the soldiers standing up as they peered through the bushes. He was talking with the others, urging them to get up. There was no time to waste.

"OK, I will go," said Bukani. He slipped across to the uniforms, put them together in a pile, and lit a match. Thin smoke began to rise, almost invisible in the brightness of the sunlight. He threw their canvas and rubber jungle boots on the pyre and the smoke began to blacken. The other boys collected twigs and the pods from the nearby bushes. Bukani returned and they waited. They could see the soldiers now sauntering back, their stark bodies gleaming as the droplets of water rolled down their smooth dark skins.

A deep roar came from the man in front as he saw the fire. He was a giant and the boys' hearts jumped as the sound reached them. Fear made them all feel sick. Bukani signalled for silence. The soldiers' oaths were fierce, but the spectacle

12

was fine to see: five naked men in bright sunlight, dignity thrown to the wind as they danced around beating the remains of their uniforms against the ground in hope of extinguishing the fire. Bukani thrust a lighted match into the tinder-dry kindling.

The soldiers were angry and fearful of what could happen to them now they had lost their uniforms. The cracking pods were not as loud as the boys had hoped.

Bukani thought quickly. "Ohi, ohi, Nigerian rhinoceros, put the fires out if you can," he shouted. The soldiers heard the jeering tone. They recognised "Nigerian rhinoceros." As predicted they went for their rifles.

"Now!" shouted Bukani, and the boys broke cover and ran away down the path. There was an explosion of noise behind them as three or four rounds of cheap lead bullets jammed in the barrels and they burst. The guns, set to automatic fire, disgorged themselves in random directions. Bullets flew everywhere.

Sanjo was not the last of the runners. He fell in front of Okwane, caught by the ricochet of a stray bullet. Blood was oozing from his right thigh.

"Stop!" shouted Okwane. "Help me with Sanjo."

They all turned. There was an eerie silence. The explosions had stopped. They could see fifty yards away the results of their work. The head of one soldier was facing them, eyes open, mouth and cheeks flapping, appealing for mercy without words, half his face hanging off like a charred steak. He must have shouldered his rifle. As the others were all disembowelled, they would have shot from the hip. There was movement—the fitful jerking they had all seen in a downed bird or a monkey knocked from a tree with a slingshot. The movements subsided. A light breeze from the river brought the stench of the splattered guts to their noses, and a new fear assaulted the boys: the fear of death itself, so close.

They lifted Sanjo and at a half trot made it back to Chomba, skirting Santambu and avoiding any contact with the occupying soldiers.

As soon as they arrived at the outskirts, they stopped to get their breath and make a plan.

Bukani was confirmed as the leader now. No one else wanted the job.

"We cannot tell the truth," he spluttered. "There are too many people in our village now. The women and children from Santambu are here. So we need a story for Sanjo's leg."

Sanjo had perked up a bit and tried to walk.

"It's not hurting much," he said bravely. "Perhaps it's just a flesh wound. Say I fell from a tree onto a spiked branch below." They looked at the wound. It was not large, like a hole in the flesh, quite neat.

"OK, we'll get Magdalene to see to it."

So they took him to the rudimentary little clinic, one of the few brick buildings at the edge of the village.

Magdalene was a part-trained nurse. She had been working in Douala but had come home to marry. Her job had been taken from her because she had been late back from the five days she had been allotted for the ceremony. She had settled back in the village as the reception nurse at the clinic. A doctor came twice a month, and she did first aid and dispensing in between his visits. She lived in a room at the back, and her husband, who had a labouring job in Douala, would stay with her from time to time, and she would then become pregnant again.

The boys piled in and dumped Sanjo down on a chair.

"He cut his leg on a branch."

Two naked, potbellied children came and peered at the scene with wide-eyed curiosity.

Magdalene, preoccupied with preparing food for her brood and the squawking voices coming from a transistor radio, asked no questions, and seeing the wound to be a typical small puncture, she cleaned around the hole and placed an absorbent dressing over it.

"You boys, always getting hurt," she tut-tutted but spent no time wondering what it was all about.

The boys dispersed.

4

The sky was beginning to redden in the west, and before Jason had made it to his compound, darkness had fallen and the village was lit with small nightlights by each hut. His mother was busy supervising the cooking, which the senior sisters were doing. Anwei was there with Julu, his younger sister, Anwei's age. They were sitting on stools and together they were platting the hair of another younger sister and chanting quietly to themselves a little rhythmic song.

"God is good.
Jesus loves us.
The birds in the sky,
God is good.
Jesus loves us.
The fish in the river,
God is good.
Jesus loves us.
The cattle in the field,
God is good.
Jesus loves us.
The snake in the grass…"

Each child took turns to furnish the last line, not repeating one they had before, and laughter burst out when someone forgot and made a repeat. The chant would start again. Usually the game ended early with a repeat. But sometimes it went on through "the captain in his ship," "the pilot in the plane," "the queen in the palace," and when it had been going on long enough, someone could say, "God in heaven," to signify the end.

Jason swung the small net bag of fish into his big sister's hand and hailed his mother respectfully.

"Oh, eh. Jason. Where you all been? Late on now." Jason smiled at her and she turned to look closely at him. The smile was forced. She recognised the tension in his face.

"You all right? You look scared."

"No, Mother, just tired, Sanjo had an accident. A branch stuck in his leg. We had to carry him all the way home. Nurse Magdalene cared for him."

"Oh, so she'll be round later scrounging for this and that for the children. What did she do for him? Did she use any medicines?" she asked, gauging the general level of benefit that would have to be given to the nurse in exchange for services rendered.

He looked over at Anwei. She looked back, slightly worried, but continued with the rhythm of their game.

He and Bukani shared a hut. Bukani was not there. He had gone off to be with some of the other older boys. Jason hoped he would not drink beer and start bragging about this afternoon. He took off his baggy shorts and with a small towel round his waist made his way to the men's washhouse. It was just a concrete pad surrounded by a woven wall. There was a large pump with a long, curved lever. A few tin cans served as scoops. Jason returned to the hut feeling cleansed and fresh and smelling of strong carbolic soap. Dressed in a thin robe, he wandered over to the cooking area, took a piece of charcoal-roasted fish and a bowl of maize porridge flavoured with sweet potato and spices, and sat down alone. Anwei came over to him.

"You are welcome, Anwei. Are you settled?"

"Oh. So you will speak to me, great man," she teased.

"You were busy," he said flatly.

"We are settled. My mother is not happy. We will not burden you long. The soldiers will go. God will care for us." She put her hand on his wrist. He did not react except to raise his face to hers. Their eyes met long and deep.

"I must rest and you are occupied with all these children." She acknowledged the polite dismissal with a nod and withdrew, leaving him to his troubled thoughts.

On his mat he twisted and turned, with the memories of the day's adventure torturing him. He had thought up the crazy plan. He was responsible. He had caused the trouble. And now he worried about the reprisals. The soldiers would attack the village. And then the nightmare returned as visions of the broken bodies writhing on the ground, trying in vain to regain the lives they had so recently been enjoying. He slept fitfully.

5

Jason awoke fully, unable to lie down any longer. The village was quiet except for the groans and snores of the sleeping inhabitants. The blood rose in the back of his neck and he felt his face burn with guilt. He should warn the headman that the soldiers would come. No, he daren't; they would send him to the soldiers to confess and he would be shot instantly. He rationalised: The other soldiers would see just an accident. The patrol had been playing a silly game. Why else were they naked and shot to pieces with their own guns? When he tried to lie down, his head hurt. When he stood up quickly, he was too dizzy. He stood up slowly. The dizziness subsided. He took a few steps outside and wandered away from his hut. The twinkling of the stars, usually his friends, made him feel intensely alone.

A soft hand gently took his. He turned and Anwei's slender warm arms wrapped around him. Her lips were soft and warm, her mouth fervent and her active little tongue burrowed between his lips seeking companionship. A rush went through his body as he relaxed. She sucked gently on his lower lip as they parted from the kiss. They said nothing as he took her head in his arms and held her close to his chest. He felt tears well up behind his eyes. He did not know why. He released her and they started to walk toward his hut. They entered and he placed a stick across the door, a code between him and his brother to say he needed privacy. Anyway, he did not expect his brother back that night.

He put two mats together and gently laid her down as she shed her wrapper. He dropped his clothes in an invisible pile. She took his head in her hands and placed her mouth over his. He rolled back, not in rejection, but in a comfortable gesture and she, placing one slender leg over his, put her head in the cup of his shoulder and waited for him to take the lead from her.

"Oh, Anwei," he murmured, "today has been a very terrible day. We have done a most evil thing. I think God will not forgive us. You comfort me, Anwei, but I think I am a dead man. They will kill us all."

Anwei's day had been difficult. She'd had to adjust to her new surroundings and fit in with the workings of another household. There were the younger children to look after and her junior sister had been criticising her all day, working off her own fears and frustrations on Anwei. She had been planning this moment all day, filling her mind with delightful thoughts to distract her from the carping. She had watched the compound closely to see if Jason would appear, planning, if he did not, to slip into his hut, praying that his brother would not return.

She would now listen to his story and let him lull himself into a compatible mood, but as the story unfolded, she became more and more alarmed as she realised that the danger he spoke of was no exaggeration. Fear began to grip her again. She heard the whole story. At the end of it they held each other tight, her head firmly against the hard muscle of his shoulder. Very, very gradually she felt him relax. His arm pressed her more gently and she regained a little freedom. She was aching slightly from being so long in one position. She shifted and he lay flat again. Her right hand had been all this time pressed between her breast and his chest. Now she moved her fingers and gently entwined some of his springy chest hairs, slowly moving her hand downward until she took the soft, warm deadweight of his penis in her open palm. She was breathing faster now.

"Oh, Anwei, forgive me, forgive me. I am not sure for what yet but I am frightened for tomorrow."

"I forgive you. Tomorrow will come tomorrow but tonight I will care for you." And she moved up and kissed him very deep and long. In her hand she felt the stiffening heat of his shaft. As she broke from the kiss and knelt astride his thighs, she took it in both hands and it seemed to have a being of its own, an energy as it hardened and grew. She rolled onto her back and as he came with her she raised her heels to his shoulders and opened her body as wide as she could for him. She gasped as he entered. He was gentle and slow, unlike their previous urgent, unfeeling couplings. They kissed and caressed and moved together, turning over this way and that in a whole *Kama Sutra* of playful physical adoration until, after an age, in a plethora of urgent thrusting from him and a deep uncontrollable twitching vibration of her hips, they moved, united in a momentous prolonged rush heating her spine and threatening to burst her head. For the first time she was sensing the full all-embracing satisfaction of a grand orgasm beginning to rise in her.

Now, she thought, *I will know my man.*

But that was not to be. A split second before the climax of their magnificent copulation, a sharp and loud explosion shook the ground and air. Jason missed his stroke and Anwei moved so they separated, she screaming as he tried to manage the spewing and splashing of the semen erupting from his engorged penis. He felt a pain in his spine he had never felt before as he collapsed, flaccid, onto the weeping body of his lover. There were more explosions and gunshots coming from the direction of the river.

She felt his strong arms so tense round her, becoming a terrifying crush. Each, in their own way, knew what was happening. Cold tears streamed down Anwei's face. Tears of remorse, of frustration, of fear and of the love so recently painfully interrupted. She was aware of the tension in every muscle of Jason's body and she was aware of cold sweat and congealing sperm between them. Their bodies separated and he rose silently. He lit a small night-light, splashed himself with some water from a plastic bottle and selected from the hanging rail a pair of khaki, military-style shorts and a heavy, rough, black T-shirt. On his feet he wore a pair of brown plimsolls. She knelt to tie his laces.

"Anwei, you are good for me. You will be mine if you wish it. May God care for you. I must go." He ran his strong hand across her head, the tight curls passing through his fingers.

With her head down and just audible, she murmured, "I wish it, Jason Kalango. I wish it."

6

The other men of the village were forming a crowd in the main clearing by the chief's house. There was coughing from the few smokers and questions abounding. No answers. When Jason arrived, he went to Bukani and the others, forming a small group around a flat raised stone. They stared at the ground, avoiding the looks of the others.

The Fon came to the stoep of the bungalow. Behind him was Jason's father, often called upon to advise the chief. He had obviously woken the Fon this morning to brief him on what was happening. The chief raised his right hand to reveal that his robe was twisted, hastily donned.

"Kinsmen," he hailed them. "Bolengo Mbengwe Kalango will address you."

Jason's father came forward to the edge of the boarded veranda.

"Brothers, we do not know what has happened, but we need to find out what the soldiers have done in Santambu. We need to approach the village silently. We shall need to keep the numbers to a minimum. We shall form four patrols of four men. Each party will have a leader trained in military or police work. We have four such men here, Arthur, Igbei, Nanui and Manfred. Choose your men. Do not choose your blood brothers or sons to be in your own patrol. We have only four pistols and very little ammunition."

The last two commands and the statement about ammunition made the gravity of the situation clear to everyone. To many the mere existence of guns was a surprise. Each of the boys of the ambush burned inside with guilt and fear; perhaps if there had been more light and less excitement, their discomfort would have been noticed.

As the leader, this cool and damp morning, Bolengo had managed to discipline the villagers to act in unison to identify the threat. He went with Manfred's patrol.

The four groups took the four paths that led from the main road to the village of Santambu. When they saw the smoke rising from the clearing, they feared the worst. As they approached they heard the growling of engines and more random shots. With the grinding of gears the engine noises trailed away as the vehicles left the village toward the ford in the river. Bolengo and Manfred's patrol entered the village and the stench of destruction assailed their nostrils. They stopped for the other patrols to arrive.

"The school is burned down. The headmaster was beaten, but he will live. We sent him back to the village with two of our men," reported the leader of the party that had circled to the south.

The other men, including many from Santambu, had heard the news and followed the patrols. They entered Santambu village to witness the carnage. Behind them crept the women. Most of the huts were reduced to ashes. The bodies of the fifteen Santambu family heads hung by their feet from the joists of the chief's bungalow as the flames licked around them. From the state of the bodies it was obvious they had been beaten persistently through the night. Dried blood streaked from abdomen to neck, their heads covered with blood and skulls broken. There had been little need to shoot them. But the soldiers must have felt it necessary to use their guns in an act of finality.

The men started to cut the bodies down and lay them on the ground while teams of youths formed to try to extinguish the flames with buckets of water from the river.

Jason came forward in the first group after the patrols and saw the body of Bolo Sojenji suspended by his heels, his face in the throes of agony, his body horribly mutilated, blood everywhere. He cut him down before Anwei arrived and threw some water over him to wash away some of the hideous blood.

The Santambu women came forward and sobbed and wailed over their husbands and fathers. Some of them had been abused by the soldiers and were weeping in pain and disgrace. Their sorrow was deep because the suffering of their men was so plain to see. A few Santabu men who had been missed by the carnage were sitting around, listless and dazed. Litters were made and the Chomba men carried the bodies back into the shade of the bush while the younger men were set to dig graves. A runner was sent to Bamenda to fetch the doctor and the priest.

At first Jason was able to join in thoughtlessly with the activities of the group, but gradually he was haunted by guilt

21

concerning the origins of this chaos. He feared for his life in case it ever became known what had caused this massacre. His nerve broke at the height of the activity when everyone seemed to be busy. Anwei caught his eye as she was wrapping the body of her father, and he dropped his gaze in shame as he slipped away to Chomba. He entered their hut and found Bukani was sitting on the stool, staring at the floor.

"I have money," Bukani said flatly. "We will go to Douala. We cannot stay here. We are disgraced and the Santambu men will kill us when they know. The other two will go to Yaounde. We have discussed it. Bring everything. Leave nothing."

As the weeks passed, the villagers united to try to clear up the carnage. Bodies were buried and the huts were being rebuilt in Santambu. Some white foreigners passed through the ruined village and took photographs and wrote a lot of notes.

Anwei's widowed mother was unable to look after her any longer. The girl was another mouth to feed and not a great help. School fees were out of the question. Her sister, Lulahlu, stayed to help to care for Balenga. So Anwei was sent off to her aunt in Douala, who said she might be useful around the pharmacy and there was a salary involved. It was made plain that most of this was to be sent directly back to her mother each month and Anwei would be allowed the minimum for necessities.

So it was that Jason's and Anwei's adulthood had started. Separated by tragedy, they each went to the big city.

7

Jason and Bukani slunk away from the villages like jackals with their tails between their legs and heads down.

For the first twenty miles or so they had taken jungle paths, emerging onto the main road around the junction south of Bamenda, where they found transport toward the coast.

The two young men rode in a cramped minibus for seven hours. During this time they slept fitfully and talked idly with the other men and women crushed into the small, hot and noisy space. They found out from their fellows that there was well-paid work on the new bridge being constructed over the river. It would be hard labour, carrying stones, making up boarding for pouring concrete, assisting with making cement and so on. They arrived at the place called Bonaberi where there was a ferry to cross the river to the main city of Douala. When they unravelled themselves from the uncomfortable van, they saw the activity of excavation and building going on. It was a wild scenario. Never before had they seen so much happening in one place at one time. There were men pushing wheelbarrows, others with pickaxes, carpenters sawing and hammering wood, and it all seemed to be carrying on in spite of a small wiry white man who was darting around from one group of workers to another.

They could see he was a madman from his expressions, throwing his hands up in horror, slapping the back of his hand on his knee, shrugging his shoulders and grimacing. At one moment he seemed to be throwing insults at one gang; the next he had his arm round the shoulders of a worker, smiling and joking. But his radiant eyes caught their attention—they were a most brilliant light blue in dark sockets, widely set with a broken nose over a large, black, bushy moustache. His moustache seemed to do all the talking, shouting and laughing. Most of the workers were wearing French *bleus*, the jacket with the sleeves removed or no jackets at all, and trousers in various states of disrepair and cut off at all levels from ankle to crotch. The little white man wore a bright blue suit in new condition, making him stand out as the man in charge.

Suddenly he was standing in front of the two newcomers. "*Bienvenu mes gars. Ongleesh ou Francais?*"

"English," they said a little self-consciously.

"Ah! You are ze two zey send from ze ozzer side?"

Bukani hesitated to answer but made an expression that said, *So what if I am?*

Suddenly another man broke in.

23

"*M'sieu Ettienne, je cherche m'sieu Ettiene, si'l vous plaît.*"

"*C'est moi. Et tu, mon ami?*"

"*J'arrive d'autre côté. Mon collègue, voila Gérard, et moi, Joël.*"

Gérard was small and obviously weak and old.

"I sent for two men, big and strong for ze boulders."

Ettienne turned and faced Bukani, who was six inches taller than Jason.

"OK, English, what do you call yourself?"

Bukani answered.

"I have another job for the old one. I need some men here who can lift those stones and move them to the riverbank. If you're not already on the payroll, then you can come on now if you wish. If you are already being paid, jump to it, *tout suite.* But I have nothing for the boy."

Jason smarted under this insult but smiled back a polite, "*Merci, M'sieu.*"

Bukani gave the money and their bags to Jason and stripped off his shirt, pleased to have the chance to earn money so soon.

"I will go into town and find a place and come back this afternoon." said Jason.

Jason went down to the waterfront and brazened his way onto the company's pontoon, which made regular trips across the river with men and materials and as many hitchhiking locals as it would hold. He was burdened with the belongings of both of them and he needed to find some place to stay. This was not usually a problem in the villages, but now he began to realise he would have to pay. He talked with one of the labourers, who said there was a village where all the casuals lived outside the camp of the permanent employees. He was told to walk up the hill away from the town about half a kilometre, go past the iron gates with the security guard and through a gap in the wall down a path and he would be there.

The concrete streets were unfamiliar. They were treacherous even for those used to such things, but as a country boy, he found the hidden holes frightening, imagining great rats living there ready to dart out and bite him. He was unused to the traffic that seemed to rush past at frightening speed, vans and minibuses stopping suddenly for people to jump out and more to get in. He was impressed with the girls who seemed to have beautiful clothes, some in very short skirts, very provocative and immoral. Perhaps these were the dirty girls his mother had warned him about and the boys at school had lusted after—girls who enjoyed endless loving. His mind wandered until he nearly tripped on a loose stone. He stopped to get his bearings. Yes, he was on the right street, according to his directions and had not walked too far. He quickened his pace and decided to look at the ground more carefully so he wouldn't fall or trip. The bags were beginning to be uncomfortably heavy.

8

He came to a magnificent pair of metal grid gates painted gold and set in a bright white-painted wall along the left-hand side of the road. He thought it must be the entrance to some sort of palace and knew it to be true when he saw white women with bright pink legs sticking out from under mini dresses, bright yellow hair long and blowing in the breeze. He saw neat grass flat as a table, with strange white huts on wheels in straight rows and little stone pathways between. Children with the same reddish skin and yellow hair wore dazzling white cloth hats. They were surrounded by many brightly coloured objects and were tended by motherly black women in flowery dresses. He took in the whole scene in an instant like a photograph as he passed the gate and then nearly walked past the jagged hole in the next section of grey wall.

The path through the gap was well worn and ran down the side of another block-work wall topped with barbed wire and broken glass. It was a puzzle to him, since he was not used to walls, that he was not in the fine compound with the strange pink alien humans he had just seen. As he descended the path, the rough hedge on the right became scrappy and broken, and he was able to see the camp he was seeking.

A wooden open-sided shack blocked his way. A very large woman with a fat round face was staring at him from a rough wooden table to which her elbows seem to be attached.

"You are welcome," she said without changing her tired and bored expression. "I don't know you. If you have just arrived and wish to enter, you pay me now. Three francs."

Jason was unsure. A thin man standing behind the woman raised his eyebrows as if to say, "That's how it is, brother, take it or leave it." And then he grinned, waiting to see what the green country boy would do.

"My brother and I. We need a room, a place to sleep."

"Better go to the Hotel Meridien," said the thin man, smiling at his own joke. Jason had no idea what he meant.

"Pay me and I will tell you what to do," growled the woman, shifting her buttocks on the thin wooden bench dangerously bowed under her weight.

Jason was not happy, but it had been a long walk uphill and then down to this place and there appeared to be roofs of some sort here. He dug deep into his shorts pocket and came out with the leather purse in which their precious money was stored. Counting out carefully three franc coins, he paid the money. Her fat hand quickly covered the money and it disappeared.

The skinny man waved his arm vaguely onward and said, "Ask any woman. You'll probably have to pass right through to the other end of the village."

Rounding the shack Jason followed the path downward. On either side, at all angles and built of a mixture of planks, plywood, beaten oil drums, and corrugated iron, were sheds and shanties from framed huts to lean-to shelters.

Inside and in front of these crude dwellings, women were busy tidying, washing underwear and sheets and carrying water up the paths. A few had children around their heels but most were young and unburdened. He could see they were from all tribes. Some he thought were very ugly, being small and stumpy or immensely tall and much blacker than the women of his people. Some had long noses like white men and were fair in colour. Many languages were being spoken, from the singsong, clicking tones of the forest people to the guttural growl of the lighter long-nosed ones. As he passed through the first group, the women took not much notice, looking up, perhaps, but not smiling.

Entering a lower area, he was greeted occasionally by a smile and uncertain greetings until the village seemed to open up onto scrubby open land littered with broken stones and tree stumps. The huts were fewer and not substantial. Women were leaning or squatting and not so busy. They smiled and greeted him, but he did not know their dialects until a girl caught his eye. She was familiar, so he walked over to her and she greeted him. She was older than he.

"You are welcome. I know your face. You are Jason from Chomba. I am Bernadette from Santambu. Your senior sister is my good friend. What brings you to this terrible place?"

Jason did not want to tell the whole of their story, so he related their journey down and simply said they were looking for work and Bukani had been hired and now he sought a place to sleep.

"Maybe I should help you," said Bernadette. "Have you eaten? Let's go and find something to eat."

Outside some of the shanties, the women had placed small pieces of food and some sort of drink. These things could be picked up and paid for with a few centimes.

They took some fried groundnuts and yams, and Bernadette led off to a place where rotting logs provided seating.

She ate in big mouthfuls, chewing hard and swallowing quickly. Looking more closely he could see she was thin and drawn and her clothes were very poor. He handed her the sugar water and she drank.

"This place is bad. Many of the men treat us very badly. I want to get out, but I am owed money and it is promised to me."

He was so pleased to have found a kindred spirit that he hung on her every word.

"Why are you here?" he asked.

"I came to the city with one of the older boys," she said. "He said he was going to make a fortune. I don't know whether you know what was happening in our village back home, but my father's house was full of hatred. I think Daddy caused fighting between his three wives. He used to exaggerate their faults and play them off against each other. He would go

27

for weeks without visiting any of them and then he would accuse them of things and cause them to fight. I think now he was equally evil to all of them, but at that time I thought he just hated my mother because I was her only child. The other two women had several and they in turn caused the children to compete and fight.

"I had no brothers or sisters to support me, so they picked on me more often," she went on. "In the end any promise of change and I would have gone. I gave myself to Thomas when I was young. I needed someone. I enjoyed his warmth and his body was a comfort. But of course, when we got here, he could not make things work for him. He was clever at school and did not wish to work hard labour. He got a job at a bookshop, paying very low wages, but the proprietor offered him a bed in his house over the shop. There was no place for me, so he just said, 'OK, you get on with it.' Then I met a man who works on the project. He took me a few times and then became bored, but I found out that this place offers a chance for us single women.

"If you can find a decent man, he will be making good money on the bridge. The women help a man build a house and keep it for him. I have a place for a house over there. I have to defend it against the other women. But it is there and I have some plywood and some timber. You can find it around or you can buy it from the docks or from an evil dealer in the village who steals money from you when you deal with him."

Jason was surprised by the long and sudden outburst from this senior girl. Then he realised she must be hungry as well, probably been without food for a few days.

"Those fried nuts are good and I am very hungry," he said. "Let me get some more." With this he left her and walked over to the vendor's hut and bought nuts and hot yams and spiced meat. He laid it all out on paper on the log.

"She insisted I try all her things. I am sure I cannot eat all this," he said.

Bernardette looked up at him. Her expression was a bit hard but not unpleasant.

"Is your brother's name Bukani? I know him, he was a year ahead of me," she said. "Will you help me build my house and then you and he can stay here tonight?"

Jason had no choice and he did not want a choice. This girl was good. He did not find her attractive like Anwei, but she was practical and strong and sensible.

"We have a little money," he said. "I can buy some wood or whatever we need."

She smiled for the first time. He noticed one of her teeth was broken off jaggedly. Suddenly she closed her mouth. "I fell and hit a rock," she said, tight-lipped. And then she smiled again. "Little brother."

So they set to work. They went to the dealer in secondhand timber at the camp, and he sold them more packing case ply and four-by-two timber, rusty nails, and a hammer with a short handle for an exorbitant amount of money. They laid plywood on the ground. Bernadette had seen these huts built before, so she told Jason what to do, and he banged nails in while she propped up the panels until they had a small shack about twelve feet long by six feet wide. It was a start. It could grow.

"How will you find your brother? There are thousands of workers down on the project. If you wait until closing time, you will not find him among the rest. It will be better if you go now.

"I know a small path that takes you down there quickly if he is by the ferry. If you give me money, I will buy food for Bukani." Jason gave her much more than would be needed for a meal. "I will buy some mats to sleep on. And some sacks for our heads," she said.

Jason arrived at the riverbank in about ten minutes, an hour or so before the night fell and the whistle blew to stop work.

It was not hard to meet Bukani as he jumped off the pontoon. He looked fresh after his first day, while the others looked bent and tired.

"Such work," he said. "Like the harvest time but ten times as hard. I haven't seen rocks like that before. They come from a mountain fifty miles away. Can you imagine bringing stones fifty miles? They say we are taming the river by building a stone bank here, and then the French will build a bridge way over the river so people do not have to travel all the way round or use boats.

"The men say there are machines to do the work we are doing, carrying these stones, but they are all on the wrong side of the river. Look at those yellow things there. They are monsters. Maybe they won't need us when they move those animals over to the other side."

And so he went on, so full of his day's experiences.

"The big man is from further north still. His tribe had elephants to move trees. But the elephants died a year or two ago due to a curse from another tribe, who were cutting trees in the same forest so his people were going hungry. They tried to buy machinery, but the dealers sold them bad trucks, which broke down. None of his people could fix them. He said to me, 'You want to make money, learn about machinery. You can fix machinery you won't go hungry.' He has to work to pay off the debts of the tribe."

He put his earthy hand on Jason's shoulder.

"So, little brother, where are we going to sleep? You got any money left for food?"

"I met an old friend of yours. She remembers you from school. She's a friend of Josephine, our senior half sister. Bernadette is her name."

"So what do you have to do with her?" Bukani looked displeased.

"Oh, nothing, except she's making you a meal and we built a house this afternoon, strong and good; small, it's true, but we didn't have time to build a palace. We will make another room tomorrow, then we can sleep together, and she can sleep on her own. She'll cook and we can both work. I think she was hungry."

"Look, brother, we don't need a woman to look after us. I suppose she gave you a story about how tough it is in town and how she's been mistreated. Well, that is her problem. She came here with a man, Thomas. I did not like him. When she was with him, he was halfway decent, but she was arrogant; 'Look at me,' she was thinking. 'I got such a clever man,' and they

30

would strut around all puffed up and proud." He paused. "Tell me more," he said, wishing for more details of his half-remembered crush.

"She's good and strong and wise. She knows how to live. What do you or I know about the city? Perhaps she can find me some work."

"They're laying people off at the project: all those under twenty. Something like 'shurance.' You know what that is? Anyway, if you don't have one of those identity cards they gave us last year and you're not over twenty, you can't work there. Now boys are looking to find other jobs. Not easy for you because at least they have met people, and who do we know?"

They were walking up the narrow path in a long single file with the other men from the project. At a place where the path rose steeply to another level, they found the fat woman on a wooden chair with the thin man standing behind. All the men slipped her a few coins, which she put in a bag between her knees. Some heavy, muscular, younger men were sitting around looking as if they just might become involved if necessary. They were smoking *Gitanes* and talking among themselves. When Bukani reached the woman, she said, "I know that boy; he's paid. Who are you? You the brother? Three francs." Jason paid the money and it tumbled into the bag with the other coins.

"Who's that?" Bukani asked.

"I don't know. The fat one must be the boss-woman here. Those big boys behind her must be her sons. The thin one looks evil."

They trudged on until they saw Bernadette. She was smiling and joking with another young woman in a shack nearby. She was looking very smart with her hair neatly tied back and a new dress with a bright flowery pattern.

Jason saw there had been a transformation since he had left. A bright-coloured curtain hung across the entrance, and the area in front of the hut was swept clean. Bernadette turned from her companion and smiled at the two men.

"Bukani, you are welcome. Jason fixed up this house and I would like to cook for you both."

She led them across the area to the doorway and gestured for him to enter. He looked inside and in the gloom saw three sleeping mats on the plywood floor and a small shelf with a few personal things laid out. There was a mirror on one wall and a crucifix on another. Each sleeping mat had a sacking pillow.

"We have candles for now. Maybe we can get a kerosene lamp later. I have a place for a fire and I've cooked some groundnuts. Would you care for some beer to celebrate?" Outside was a little bench and the boys sat down, leaning gently against the wall. She appeared with a chipped plate and two stained teacups. Next she went to the little fire burning between two large building blocks and took off a tin can. Holding it in a cloth to prevent blistering her hand, she poured some baked nuts onto the plate. She brought out a jar of beer from the shack and poured some into each of the cups as the boys held them out.

"Our first meal. Hey, little brother, you are quite a builder," she said, giving all the credit to Jason.

"No, Bernadette, it was you who told me what to do."

She folded her long legs and squatted before them, smiling shyly at Bukani.

"It's good," he said, noticing her damaged front tooth and her half smile. "You have made a home for us. I thank you for your good work," he said stiffly. Bukani had still not warmed to the idea of this woman intruding into the relationship between him and his brother, but he was willing to concede that she was practical and cheerful. He tried also to forget the absurd regard he held her in when they had been at school.

"You men sleep on that side. I will squeeze into the corner," she said. "I have not done a real meal. We will have to get food from others. There is plenty but you need a little money."

When they had each had a little beer, they stood up and wandered away from their new abode. In fact food was not so easily obtained at this hour, and they had to go all the way out to the street to find Lebanese vendors with barrows who sold them samosas and roasted yams.

"Very expensive," said Jason, and he held back his appetite as his big brother ate to restore his energy. Bernadette also held back but took a long drink of water.

They were sitting on the kerbside with their feet in the gutter. Bukani was in the middle. His mood had changed and he was relaxed after the food. He smiled at each of them in turn.

"I seem to have a family," he said.

Out of the corner of his eye, he saw Bernadette bite her lower lip as she lowered her head toward the pavement and clasped her hands tightly together as if in prayer.

"Tomorrow I will seek work," said Jason. "I am sure I will find something, maybe in a government office. I am well educated to A level."

"Yes, my brother, you are right." But the next two weeks would prove him wrong. There was no work to be had.

9

Jason wandered the town, ready to try anything. But he soon realised that however clever he was, he needed contacts and introductions to make any progress in a world overcrowded with hopeful youngsters.

He looked forward to returning to his happy little family every evening after another fruitless day. Bernadette was a good and efficient housewife, and Jason helped her put up another room. When Bukani got paid for the first time, they bought enough plywood for a sloping roof and some tar paper, which would keep the rain off. Some two- by four-inch timber and some broken concrete building blocks served to raise the floor off the ground. Jason became quite skilled with a hammer, straightening the bent nails and hammering them in true. The shack became a two-room bungalow. The boys slept in the back room while Bernadette slept in the general day room.

On the narrow stoep, they would sit out on a bench in the evenings. Bukani would drink a bottle of beer while Bernadette served some roast groundnuts or crispy fish as a prelude to a staple meal of pap and gravy. They felt like royalty as they watched the other people doing much the same thing in their own way. Life was good even if the roof leaked in the rain and the rats could be heard at night under the plywood floor.

For light they bought a hurricane lamp and for cooking a kerosene ring and a couple of pans. They all enjoyed this Spartan domesticity. It was a new experience of interdependence. Jason saw his brother slowly soften toward Bernadette. One day he even said something towards reconciliation.

"Bernadette is a good cook and tidy around the place. I am glad you found her. She's not so arrogant now." And occasionally Jason thought he caught them smiling at each other.

He determined even more to find himself a job as he was beginning to find this new friendliness between the other two slightly odious. However hard he tried, he always came up against the same obstacles: too much competition, and the others in line always seem to have something he lacked, usually an acquaintance at the establishment. Clutching his certificates he even went to see Thomas at the bookshop, which was to play such an important role in his later life.

"Jason. How surprising to see you in Douala. I always thought you might be a bit of a stay-at-home boy."

"No," said Jason. "I came down with Bukani to find some work."

"How's big brother? I remember he was rather quiet."

"He's very well, thank you. He has a temporary job on the bridge project just until he finds something better."

"That sounds like our Bukani. They tell me the pay is very good there, but the work! It's just like slaves on a chain gang. Are you looking for work too? I'm sorry, you cannot work here. The boss has all the people he wants. Did you do well at school? A levels, all that? You know I failed mine. Damn examiners only let a few through each year."

"I suppose I was lucky," said Jason, smiling shyly and looking at the floor. "You know Bernadette? She lives with us, cooks and cleans. She knows the town.

Thomas hesitated before he spoke again. "Did she mention me?"

"In passing; she said you parted company."

"How is she? You know, I did what I could for her. The truth is this job doesn't pay very well," he said under his breath. "But I have a good prospect here. Very interesting people come here: learned people, politicians and some businessmen and some of the white people. There are chances. Sometimes people from the British Council come for books on local topics and reports.

"Here comes my boss. Take a book off the shelf and look at it. You should go to the British Council on Commerce Road. They sometimes help boys with good education go to university or something like that.

"Greet Bernadette and Bukani. Perhaps we will meet soon. We villagers must stay together. Perhaps we should have a village meeting. I know some more from our area. I go to the big Catholic cathedral for mass and we sometimes meet outside afterwards."

10

Jason left, little knowing the portent of this meeting. Commerce Road was long and he had no idea what he was looking for, but lacking any other destination he wandered in the right direction, helped by passersby. There were older houses and from time to time more modern concrete buildings. One such imposing building had a large badge on it stating STANDARD CHARTERED BANK and then below it BRITISH CONSULATE in medium-sized lettering, and rather obscurely, BRITISH COUNCIL.

The building was forbidding, with a man inside who looked like a soldier in dress uniform he had seen in picture books. Taking a gulp of air for courage, he climbed the six steps to the entrance and pushed on the glass door. The soldier glanced up and waved. Instinctively Jason took the envelope with his A level passes out of his shirt and waved them at the man. There was a loud growling noise from the glass door, which made Jason take a step back, but the man waved for him to come forward, so he pushed again on the door and it gave way.

"Good morning, sir," he said boldly and smiled. The soldier was sitting stiffly behind a large book on a small table. His uniform was of good dark-blue cloth and had white ropes and gold stars on it and large brass buttons down the front. He had a military cap, which was placed by the large book. Jason thought he must be very important, so he bowed.

"Master, I have come to seek your advice about my further education. I have my credentials here."

The great man consulted his book. "Kalango," he said roughly.

Jason recognised his name and was amazed that the man knew it.

"Yes," he said.

"Sign your name here."

Jason found he was shaking slightly, but he took the pencil proffered to him. He hesitated. He had developed the usual flowery illegible type of signature beloved of adolescents: several upward jerks and a succession of meaningless ellipses and a final squiggle.

"Take the lift to the third floor." The man pointed to a lobby a few steps higher. Jason went there and waited. Suddenly a hole appeared in the wall and a smartly dressed lady came out, pushing rather rudely past him without giving him any greeting. Another soldier, this time in a shabbier uniform with rubber sandals on his feet, looked at him and said abruptly, "You, you come or go. Come go up or down. Going up now." This city language sometimes puzzled him, all these words about moving: 'come', 'go', 'go up', 'go down', 'gonna come', 'come-go,' not like his own dialect, which was more about being, feeling, seeing and hearing.

This man made it clear that whatever he wanted, Jason better get into the little space with him. It was light inside and there was a row of buttons on the wall. The man stuck his finger on one and the wall closed behind him. He nearly panicked when there was a jerk.

"See you no come go in lift before. Very automatic. I press the button, go up to second-third-fourth floor."

Jason gathered his thoughts and blurted out, "Third floor."

"Bri'sh Council: Education, culture, song-an'-dance, grants, scol-chip," said the man importantly and at that the wall opened again, and the man said, "You go past the second. Very smart. Go left, see the 'ception."

Although Jason had read about all these things—tall buildings, elevators, receptionists and so on—the real thing was a lot different from his imaginings. By now he was exceptionally alert as his senses were assaulted by the very bright lights, the startling colours of the red carpet and deep blue wall of the passageway. At the end behind a wide desk decorated in bright shiny metal was a white woman with a large amount of straight yellow hair. His step faltered for a moment as he realised she must be the receptionist.

"Oh good, at last. You are a bit late, but never mind. We have your passport and visa all fixed, and the driver will pick you up now. He's waiting for you. You will pass by your residence and pick up your bag as you requested, and he will take you to the airport. Now, Hussain has your ticket to London and passport. You will be met by Mrs. Frankish, who will take you to your lodgings in Reading. She will give you the first instalment of your grant money. Now, you did get your A level certificates, didn't you? They are most important. Better check them." She held out her hand.

Jason was very confused but began to realise he was being given some sort of opportunity. He would hand over his certificates, and the whole thing would cease there and then. He held out the papers and a bell rang at just that moment. The strange woman picked up a thing looking a bit like a shell. Jason thought this must be a telephone, and sure enough she spoke into the shell. He opened the top sheet and the lady smiled at him and gestured for him to put them back in the envelope. A small smart black lady appeared and grabbed his hand in a friendly but urgent manner, tugging him down the passage to the lift. This time it went down a long way and a

37

smell of petrol permeated into the small space. When the wall opened again they were in a dimly lit place full of cars.

A man wearing a similar military uniform with white gloves was there and the lady spoke hastily to him. Finally she turned to Jason and said, "Go with him."

The man looked him up and down suspiciously and said, "Where is your residence?"

Jason thought fast. He had seen on the front of the big gold gates **"BRIDGE PROJECT RESIDENTIAL COMPOUND"** in both English and French.

"I am staying by the residential compound of the bridge project."

"You may sit in front," said the driver, reading Jason's mind.

The speed of the car startled Jason but the quietness amazed him more and it felt cold inside. It seemed to glide like a bird, except when it slowed down to negotiate the potholes where the road was broken up by the rains. The driver appeared to do nothing. Jason wasn't really sure if he was driving except for his occasional flamboyant turning of the steering wheel. The man in his soldier's uniform made himself appear very important and authoritative. He blasted the horn at anything in front as he pushed mercilessly through the traffic. Jason began to recognise the road.

"Stop here," said Jason, and he threw himself out of the car along the road by the wall and ran down the path. At the table where the fat woman sat, he dodged round without paying and raced through the shanties as women raised their eyebrows and clucked to one another over their washing. He rushed into their own shack and leapt across the dayroom without seeing Bernadette in the dim light.

As he was throwing various things into his bag, he felt her presence and glanced up to see her leaning on the side of the entrance to the back room.

"You must have hit the jackpot, little brother, rushing in without greeting me and now packing. Where are you off to?"

"I think I have hit the jackpot," he gasped. "I think I am off to England. I think I am going to go to university. But never mind, I have a car and driver waiting for me in the road."

He stood up. The bag was bulky and heavy enough to make the right impression. She smiled at him.

"I am happy for you and I wish you the best of luck. I will pray for you, and I will tell Bukani of your good fortune." She took his left hand warmly and kissed his cheek.

He was not at all surprised that she took the news so calmly. This was already beginning to be a topsy-turvy world for them all. She had been the verge of starvation waiting for some turn of fortune and it happened. Now her new young friend was going to go to England, that strange green place full of white people wrapped up in sombre heavy clothing they had all seen in pictures: red buses bigger than a house and buildings towering above the earth. The world just seemed to get bigger and bigger, and they were all beginning to be a part of it.

"I think I am going to the airport now. I will go in an aeroplane. If it's all a mad dream, I'll see you tonight and tell you all about it."

He slung his thin leatherette jacket over his shoulders and made his way quickly up the pathway. At the table the fat woman was surprised to see him again and let out a sort of yelp as the thin man growled an insult. He was pleased to leave them behind. The driver folded a small newspaper as Jason approached the car and with a long-suffering expression told him to put his bag on the floor, not on the seat, behind.

By now Jason's heart was pounding, sweat was showing under his armpits, and he began to feel embarrassed that his body was causing an odour in the enclosed car. The chauffeur sniffed almost imperceptibly and cracked his window open. Then he picked up a small tin can that hissed and seemed to make the car smell sweet.

At the airport a wiry little man with Arabic features met the car. As Jason climbed out, he thrust a little green book and a long flimsy paper into Jason's hand and said, "Passport, tickets, change planes in Paris. Don't get lost. Come this way quickly, we are late, but I have made sure you will get on. Put your bag there."

A smart-looking but bored girl checked the passport and ticket, giving him a boarding card as his bag disappeared alarmingly down a chute. By now Jason was moving automatically, led by efficient people in uniform until he was sitting in a large comfortable seat between another young man and the small round window. He was no longer reasoning about his surroundings, just taking these bewildering new sensations in. He had completely lost control and he left God to take care of him.

And so it was that Jason Kalango became Jensen Kalango, successful candidate for a British Council Grant to study a three-year degree course in an under-subscribed red-brick university. To the British authorities the boy was of the right age, identified by a blobby passport photo showing black curly hair over whites of eyes and toothy smile. Another Cameroonian who was privileged to be given a British university education. No questions were asked about certain inconsistencies like spelling of the names and date of birth, because the college clerks who were perfunctorily processing his papers knew that in Africa the spelling of names varied and no one registered the birth of a child until it was sure to survive, leading to uncertain and conflicting dates of birth. And who cared anyway? There was a quota of student places to be filled. One clever African is much the same as another.

11

It was on the day after Jason's flight from Douala that Anwei arrived to take up the offer her aunt had made for her to work as her assistant. She had hoped she might find Jason, who had vanished as if into the air. She yearned for him at nights, although by day she was worried for his safety after he had suddenly disappeared on the day after the massacre.

A few months after arriving, she had come across Bukani, who had told of Jason's good fortune and given her an address to write to in England, which he had obtained from the British Council. She had been overjoyed with his success and had determined to keep in touch, as she burned with the memory of their last night together. In her laboured handwriting she scribed long and passionate letters that he answered occasionally with short notes explaining how things were in terms she found hard to understand.

"A man pushed me on the tube in London the other day and said, 'Black boy, go home.' The skinheads are the worst. They have yellow-white skin and shave their heads. They wear rings through their ears and noses. Their jeans are narrow and filthy and they wear things called bother boots on their feet. If they weren't so nasty, they would be like clowns. But they are violent to all black people for no reason at all."

She could not fathom out what part of Jason's anatomy had been assaulted and what sort of white man would have a ring through his nose.

Time passed slowly in the boring city. Her main relief from sitting behind the counter all day were her visits to the sprawling shantytown to see Bukani and Bernadette. She began to enjoy it there as the people amused themselves with music and singing to pass the time. Bukani had bought himself some drums and was a good singer.

Bukani and Bernadette decided to get married. If they all been back home there would have been a great celebration with hundreds of guests from the area around. As it was, Bukani was frightened to send a message back to the villages in case it provoked a violent response. Not enough time had passed since the massacre and their ignominious departure. They were city people now, but they were conscious that Bernadette might get pregnant at any time and their fugitive status had heightened their need to conform to the Church's teachings regarding marriage.

The wedding was a small affair involving a hodgepodge of project workers from the shacks and their wives and girlfriends, all from different regions and tribes but all refugees for one reason or another. Lost souls in the big city, they made enjoyment however they could, and a wedding was a great excuse for a good party. It was a great day for them all and a release from the grinding work and meagre expectations.

The pharmacy where Anwei worked was small and untidy. It was owned by a fat Lebanese. There were two of them behind the counter. Marie France was her superior and her aunt. She was about twenty years her senior, unmarried, with a degree in pharmacology. Everyone who knew her wondered how she had got a degree because they knew she was dull and found the simplest problems difficult. Anwei carried her aunt at the pharmacy, doing the stock control, the expenses and profit accounts, and the taxation and wages. The owner had appointed her aunt. He had fantasized about making her into his mistress years ago, pestering her and loading her with favours. But she had been wary and avoided his advances. She had also avoided the advances of all sorts of more eligible young men, preferring the comfort of eating and sleeping until one day, too late, she had sadly accepted that by winning all the little defensive skirmishes, she had lost the war and all chances of matrimony. Mr Fathi, working his way through a stream of more willing country girls, had lost interest in her but let her continue to work with him at the pharmacy.

By the time Anwei had joined the staff, Marie-France had grown fatter and lazier. Anwei was sharp, though educated only to secondary year two. Between them they convinced Mr. Fathi, who had other business interests, they could manage the shop, and so he came by less frequently. The shop did a slow trade and paid little but they were both too dependent to demand more.

Their normal routine started at seven in the morning and finished at seven in the evening. At lunchtime they slept in a small room at the back amongst boxes of stock or, if they had money, they might go out for a snack around the corner or to do private errands in the town.

Jason was coming home! He had written to Anwei to say he had finished his studies and was urgently coming home. She was overjoyed at the prospect of going back with him to the village or anywhere else than this dreary life in the pharmacy.

12

In June Jason returned. He had been found out. Unfortunately his small-town secondary school had not been up to the educational standards required, and the headmaster had manufactured the pass results he required to maintain the government assistance his school so desperately needed. Jason, due to his prowess on the football field and his confident personality, had been selected to be the recipient of A level certificates in maths, higher maths and physics, in which he had not shown talent nor interest. He was on an enforced repatriation flight due to the unwinding of the charade that had placed him on an aeronautical engineering course at Reading University in place of a hapless but brilliant student of a similar name who had been hospitalised in Douala on his departure day due to being run over by a truck.

As he settled into his seat near the back of the plane from Paris to Douala, he was aware of a stunning young woman in the seat across the aisle. He smiled as he looked round and she smiled back. Their contact was broken off by a large lady with several bags made variously of polythene, paper or cloth, and three small children with their little backpacks of toys and their eyes wide open, taking in all the unfamiliar sights. As the family settled into the row in front, he sneaked a few glances but by then the girl was engrossed in an important-looking folder.

As the flight progressed through the drinks round and the meal, although he had no opportunity to make an opening, he remained conscious of her presence and hoped she noticed him. At last as the movie was about to begin and she put her folder aside, he leaned over and ventured, "You look very busy. Have you been studying in Europe?"

"Oh, I have. I am in my second year at Oxford." At this point he noticed the superior quality of her clothes and her superb shoes. He was slightly put out by her response, not because it was delivered in a way to belittle him, but because it was just a fact that Oxford was superior to Reading, where he had just been removed from his degree course.

"Are you enjoying England?"

She looked at him and smiled. "I am very lucky. My dad bought me a cottage in Abingdon, and I live there with a few good friends. It takes the rough edges off the difficulties."

"Like what?"

"Oh you know, student halls and digs, putting up with the other students, eating chips with everything. We have a marvellous cook we took from Yaoundé. She goes to market in Reading every week and buys most of the things we need to feel at home. She cooks us beautiful meals so we don't have to feel homesick. Dad's a diplomat. We are very lucky."

Jason's eyes fell on the middle seat next to her, which was empty. She saw the direction of his gaze and with an almost invisible shrug, she said, "I'll budge over, so we can talk.

"I've been in England for about nine years on and off," she said. "I went to school near Goring. A place called Queen Anne's. There were a few Africans there, not many. My best friend there was a Nigerian. We had a big fight when we first met. You know, sort of nonsense really. They had to pull us apart. We were going tooth and nail. I really hated Nigeria and although my father was a diplomat, he was not able to hide his feelings about Nigeria either. I suppose I picked up some of his vibes. Anyway, we treated each other warily for about a term— you know, avoiding each other. I was not happy that first year. I never seemed to be able to get on an even footing with the other girls. They were either condescending, patronising or they would shun me. I think my defence was to be a bit aloof. Anyway, one day a group of girls had me cornered and one shouted, 'You're such a stuck-up black bitch, but you're just a spade, like all the bloody bus drivers in London.'

"I was clenching my teeth, holding back tears of absolute desolation, when Doria Matenko came flying round the corner, her eyes lit up her face set in fury. 'Come on, you stuck-up little Cameroonian, let's beat these pink-faced idiots till they scream.' And so she and I, who were both pretty big and strong for these girls, laid into about five of them until they all ran away hurting. When we were done, we looked at each other and laughed and giggled at the fun we'd had. Anyway, we got respect from then on, and many of those girls became our friends too. You know how it is.

"What surprised me when I first came to England was that these people are so much like us and yet so many seemed to hate us, and then as soon as I got to know anyone, they immediately turned into truly good friends. I had such kindness

44

from some and was still being despised by others. I would really worry about racist remarks. You know, it burned me up inside some days and I could not sleep. Then I realised everyone was doing it to everyone else. The Pakistanis and the Banglas came in for it, but so did Jews, Irish, the French, and anyone else. In the end I joined in. Nobody seemed to mind."

"What happened to Doria?"

"Oh, she's around. My dad's a snob. He won't associate with people 'like that.' Her dad's a businessman and my dad thinks he got started on the proceeds of bank frauds and scams. They certainly had lots of money and didn't mind showing it off. Doria wouldn't talk about it much. Dad said that sort of African brings all Africans disrespect."

He told her how he had nearly starved to death in Reading. "I never want to eat another Marmite sandwich or drink another bottle of milk in my life!"

She laughed.

"I was going to do aeronautics but changed my mind."

"Oh," she said. "What now?"

"I don't know. I want to be a politician," he said, hoping to impress her. "We really need some good people in politics from the Anglophone side of the fence. The Francophones seem to have everything their own way at the moment." She turned to look at him directly and they smiled at each other; when she turned away she was quiet.

And so they chatted and snoozed. He found out her name was Victoria Namuji. At one point her father came by and sat in the seat he had vacated. He introduced himself as Dr. Amoko Namuji and talked for a few minutes.

After her father had gone, she told him, "Daddy gets a seat in first class, of course. Sometimes I can too, but now too many people seem to be able to travel first and there are no spares."

At Douala there was the usual scrum in the baggage hall, but Dr. Namuji took the time to shake his hand and say good-bye, pleasantly telling him to get in touch and giving him a business card. "You seem to have made a good impression on Victoria."

Jason was very surprised, as this would not normally be expected from a Cameroonian father but he supposed that the doctor must have become westernised in his travels; certainly Victoria impressed him with her clear English accent and her self-confidence.

Anwei was at the airport to meet him. As they came through customs, she could see through the glass panelling he was full of animation and excitement with a girl he seemed to be escorting. There was a brief meeting with an older man, they all seemed to be saying good-byes, and then the man and the girl were picked up by a male servant, a driver in a smart white safari suit, and their baggage was taken care of by more people. She saw Jason collect his small bag from the carousel and make his way to the exit. She pounced on him and grabbed his hands firmly.

"Jason, thanks to God you're back. I've missed you so much. Thank you for your letters, they filled me with hope. Where will you go now? You can come to my place. I have a room—comfortable but not big."

Jason was at a loose end. Here was an offer not to be refused, so he let Anwei take him back and feed him up and give him many nights of happiness. He spent his days wandering listlessly about, thinking only of Victoria, while at night he stayed in Anwei's small room. They made love energetically, she with the intense love of the reunited, but cruelly, he was bored with her and her mean little home; compared with Victoria, she no longer seemed to be so attractive. Subconsciously he was spoiled for the ordinary life in Douala. Albeit a failed student, he had seen possibilities, a whole new life, a different civilisation. He was besotted by his short contact with Victoria, who became the embodiment of that other life and an opportunity to grab at it. Her bright conversation and animated beauty crowned it all.

Early on the fourth day, he could bear it no longer He made an excuse and said he might be back. Anwei was not fooled and without tears bade him farewell, knowing he was going after the rich girl she had seen at the airport. He took the bus to Yaoundé.

13

The day after Jason disappeared, Anwei was walking along the pavement rationalising her fate, trying her best to sort out her emotions and trying not to be consumed by her fury against Jason. As she rounded a corner on the muddy sidewalk, a shocking sight faced her. A white man was kneeling on the ground, gasping and crying out in pain. Without thinking she went forward and saw immediately what had happened. His left ankle had gone between two concrete slabs over the storm drain, and he had fallen to his knees in the dirt. Anwei instinctively bent to help him. In the days when Mr. Fathi had still been interested, he had insisted on Anwei doing a basic first-aid course. After the stranger had extricated his leg, Anwei had been able to administer dressings and a bandage to cover his grazes from the contents of the tiny first-aid kit always present in the bottom of her plastic market bag.

"You saved my life," he exaggerated, looking directly into her eyes and smiling broadly.

"Oh, it was a little cut, that's all," she replied like a mother to a small boy.

"You think so? You didn't feel the pain!" he said, changing his expression to stage agony.

"You never cried out. Don't think it was so bad."

"I've been trained to resist pain."

And so the banter continued until he had asked her out to dinner at a small place called King Bell, where they could hear local jazz.

That evening, in the dim light of the candlelit restaurant, while he listened to the subtle variations of the music, he observed her closely. Her skin was very richly brown and her complexion was perfect. Her nose was not quite straight and the wide nostrils were finely shaped. He had read a little about the physical characteristics of the African peoples, and he tried to place her in a tribe as they ate slowly. They talked a bit about music, but she did not have much knowledge even of local musicians. He asked her about her life and she told him she was "OK", working in the pharmacy, and that she would eventually marry a boy she had known in school who was now away.

When the plates were cleared, he could see she was getting restless. He turned to her across the table.

"You OK? Music good?"

"OK," she said, but with a pout. The pout that saves a thousand words in expressing a kind of limited disapproval. Then she followed it with a toothy smile that said, *I am happy. You are here, what more could I want?*

But Bertrand realised the evening was losing its sparkle. He signalled to the waiter and paid the bill.

"I'll take you home," he said.

"Oh, no, no, why go home now?"

"You're bored."

"No, no, not bored. We go nightclub, dance, and you drink whisky," she said in a rush.

So they took a beat-up yellow taxi from outside and went to the San Pierre, the only club he could remember the name of.

The dance floor was crowded. The girls were almost all African, ranging from short and fat to startlingly tall. There were sudden flashes from white teeth and eyes. The men were a mix of Europeans, Middle Eastern and a few Africans. As they danced, he began to notice that Anwei shared an elegance of movement and an articulate rhythm with many of her sisters moving like reeds in a breeze on the crowded dance floor.

The music was recent and loud, African and American with infectious beats, and soon they began to dance as one as they swung and gyrated to the raucous melodies. After about ten dances, he soaked with sweat and she still cool and serene, they wove their way through the crowd to the bar. Bertrand recognised some of his German and French operatives perched on stools, with girls draped over them or standing earnestly discussing angles of cut, gradients of roadways, power and abilities of various big plant machines and the other paraphernalia of the timber extraction business. As a field accountant he was not absolutely at home with these lumberjacks of the tropical rain forest, but one of them recognised him and immediately admired Anwei, and while still leering at her, poured Bertrand a large whisky and Coke. He offered it to Anwei first and she took a small sip.

"Whisky very bad," she said, "make me do bad things." Her eyes lit up with mischievous fire. "Have a drink, dance some more."

A tall, slender girl with an outrageous henna-coloured Afro came up quietly as Anwei turned to Bertrand.

"This my sister, Lotus." Lotus smiled and shook hands with the circle that had spontaneously formed about them. Some of the men seemed interested but most let the situation pass and continued with their own agendas. Other girls wandered over to the party and made small talk from time to time, smiling and joking in a pleasant and attractive way. Most had missionary school education and with strict parents and large families had a childlike charm about them.

Anwei turned to Bertrand. "I go with Lotus for girly talk. You stay here, drink whisky, and talk man-talk with your friends."

She was gone.

14

Bertrand was then treated to a story from a corpulent lumberjack who was drawing the crowd's attention as he continued a typically Teutonic tree cutter's tale of woe.

"Oh, Helmut, he ate the local bush meat. He got into terrible trouble with diarrhoea. He was in the jungle with his gang. He was so much hurting, he forgot everything, dropped his pents, and got in the way of a falling tree. Huh, nearly killed him, but funny! Ha, ha, ha!

So there was Helmut his pents round his feet. *Sheissen*, you should have seen him! Fet, ha! I am fet but he is fedder. The treetop was all round him. Anyway this monkey came down with the tree, poor beggar, jumped at Helmut, who was trying to stand up and grabbed his testicles, you know, his balls, as you say. Don't know what he thought it was. Helmut- nuts, ha, ha, ha. Bedder then monkey-nuts, ha, ha, ha. Anyway, he squeezed and Helmut let out this terrible roar, 'Aaahhh,' and the monkey tried to get away, but he wouldn't let go.

"Helmut had to go with the monkey. Well, next they were on the road. Oh my God, there's Helmut running along the road and the monkey jumping up and down in front of him, pulling him along by the balls. But Helmut was a scout, *jah*, and he remembered his knife in the sleeve of his bush shirt, so he pulled it out and went for the monkey, *yah?* Bloody monkey jumps away, and Helmut lost his balance, and the knife takes a great slice out of his foreskin. Ha, ha, ha, so now he is a Chew, ha, ha, ha. A Chew with diarrhea, ha, ha, ha."

So grinding on, one fat German about another. The listeners were full of whisky, and knowing Helmut to be a bully and a braggart, all took a personal delight in his misfortune.

"Anyway, he went home to his vife, end you know he alzo hezz a girlfriend, no? Very beautiful *fraulein* in Weisbeck," he said in lowered tones. "Ha! First available flight, ha, ha. So, vot's se point? Peeder all in bandages, left nut size of coconut, ha, ha. Can't do nuzzing for ze vife nor ze bloody *geliebte*." This brought more laughter.

Bertrand knew the story to be partly true as he had taken the unfortunate Helmut down to the Polyclinic. He also knew the story was all round the town in one form or another. He had been waiting in the clinic near the nurses' station and had been privileged to overhear a snippet of their interpretation of the incident.

"Poor man," said a young female voice, "he must be in such pain."

"My, oh, my, such an evil world," said a deeper-voiced, more mature woman. "What you think he doing with monkey anyway? These white men. This is why we got AIDS problem. Too much wickedness."

"No, no, not so. Man had an accident."

"I don't know. It's not natural. You tell me, girl, how's that happen?"

"Oh, you just got a bad mind. You not very professional. That's the truth."

15

Bertrand was becoming aware that Anwei had wound her left arm in his right, had put her cheek against his left shoulder and was stroking his thigh with her right hand. She was tall and she was 'light' in that her proximity and intimacy were not imposing or hot, but feathery and gossamery. She was immensely feminine and he was aroused.

"Want to follow you home," she whispered deeply. And she looked up at him with a wide smile. He said nothing. She turned her face down and tightened her whole body almost imperceptibly.

After months of enforced celibacy, Bertrand made love like a raging bull. He was absolutely self absorbed, saturating himself in physical sensation as they made love over and over again. She, on her part, deeply hurt by Jason's defection, threw her whole self into the act, her body exacting sensational revenge. They took no precautions. They had said almost nothing until they were lying enfolded and exhausted on the crumpled bed at six o'clock the following morning.

Anwei had turned over and closed her eyes again when she felt Bertrand sliding out of bed and heard him busy in the bathroom. She was warm inside, and as she lay there she was able to imagine the contours of his body against her own. When he kissed her lightly and left her, she made a definite decision not to go to the pharmacy. They were never busy. Marie France would be there and a small lie about being ill would satisfy her incurious aunt. The bed was delicious. The sheets had been crisp when they had entered it and they still had a wonderful clean smell to them. The pillow was encased in a thick linen cover and was not spongy like the foam she was used to but soft and supple. She was not going to foreshorten this taste of paradise, which might never come again.

She floated gently in and out of sleep for an hour or so until she heard bustling in the kitchen somewhere down the passageway. The sun streamed in through the window and her head felt light and airy. She was happy. Not just content but something a lot better. She sat up, and then throwing off the covers, she went to stand in front of the mirror.

White man held me here, she thought, looking at her shoulders. Suddenly she felt silly as she caught sight of her pubic area. *He entered me here*, she thought, and jumped back under the covers on the bed. She hugged herself and smoothed her body with her hands from her breasts to her thighs. She kicked the sheets down and smiled until tears came to her eyes. "Bertrand, Bertrand. Huh. Darling Bertrand, *cherie, m'amour, je t'aime.*" She screwed up her face, held her breath, and was just about to let out a little subdued scream when she heard the latch of the door click. She pulled the sheets up to her chin and shut her eyes.

"*Ma'moiselle?*" said a deep female voice.

"Yes," she said abruptly, trying to adopt the right tone but not knowing what would be appropriate.

"*Herr* Bertrand, he has gone to the office and won't be back till five. I will look after you. You may shower. I can give you a meal and you may go."

Her accent was slightly Germanic. Anwei opened her eyes wide and saw her black face was square and regular. She was a big woman and Anwei preferred to stay in bed until she was gone. Then she stole into the bathroom, peed in the pink toilet, and climbed into the bath for a shower. This also was a luxury. Lots of beautiful hot water cascaded down her body and disappeared musically down the plughole. She helped herself liberally to shampoo, which she did not put on her head, but foamed up in her pubic bush and smothered all over her body. It all smelled nice and felt good.

As she dried herself on the large, soft, white towel, she was glad she had worn jeans last night. They look good in the morning, not like a skimpy rayon dress. She had carefully laid them on the chair after she had hesitantly taken them off while Bertrand was in the bathroom. She scrabbled around for her frilly nylon panties, which had not been so carefully removed. She jumped into these and her jeans and yellow cotton blouse, slipped on her shoes, retied her hair, and ventured tentatively out to meet the maid in the distant dining room. The large mahogany table was laid out for one.

"You may sit there. I am Hedder. I will give you what you want," she said.

Anwei got the impression that Hedder knew what was best for Anwei. She was pleased because she did not want to have to make choices. She was not used to all the paraphernalia.

"You will eat porridge with sugar and bananas, yes? And you may drink tea or Milo or water."

"Oh yes, why not Milo?" she said hesitantly and smiled in submission to her guardian. The big woman put the things on the table and let out a great sigh. It was not unsympathetic, but there was a hint of a maternal judgement in it. Anwei could hear a radio quietly playing in the kitchen as Hedder disappeared to start clanking around with dishes and plates.

After she had finished eating, she took the plates into the kitchen, where she found Hedder ironing white shirts.

"I will go," she said.

Hedder turned and seeing the plates, frowned.

"You take care, girl," she said, not unkindly, and went back to her ironing. "What you doing is your business, but be cautious."

16

Bertrand came back to an empty flat that evening. He had been busy all day and had not had time to find out about Anwei. As he had entered the office that morning, he heard that three new foliage strippers had arrived on the docks unexpectedly, but the cutter heads were missing and he'd had to track them down to a separate shipment, which would arrive in a few days. He had then had to meet government officials about the new tracts granted in the last few days. These meetings were a cross between a wild tennis game and a diplomatic negotiation. There were always hidden agendas. They all amounted to much the same thing, support for an official or a village project, but each item had to be subtly uncovered, addressed and then dealt with at the least cost to the company, achieving the highest level of goodwill amongst the officials. The game involved a high level of concentration and now, after a regular flow of these sessions, Bertrand felt he was beginning to understand the African mind and the rules of the game.

He had come home at nine, shed his clothes, flopped down on the bed, and slept until midnight.

When he awoke, he missed her acutely. She was present everywhere, clothed, naked, smiling, grimacing, pouting, talking her cute pidgin, wiggling to the music, and making love. She was just a phantom. He walked into the bathroom, and her silky, curved body was in the shower; he could hear her voice. Alas, in reality there was silence.

He did not know how to contact her. Anyway it was too late. He showered and stood, drying himself, not knowing whether to get dressed again or go to bed and sleep. After his short nap he was not at all tired. He dressed and then did not know where to go. He had not been going out much. He had a few fairly staid friends who would go to restaurants on Fridays or Saturdays or form fours for bridge occasionally. Quite often he would sit in his apartment reading, first technical stuff or accounts and then a fast-moving novel until he felt tired enough for bed. Tonight he needed to break old habits.

Nervously he gravitated to the only place where he thought he would meet some acquaintances. He told the taxi driver, *"San Pierre."* He would have a few beers, listen to some tall stories and jokes with the boys and then come home to bed.

The place was a lot quieter than the previous night. A few of the die-hards were at the bar and some girls were dancing together on the floor. One or two European men, now not hidden by the crowd, were looking rather ridiculous gyrating to the tinny-sounding music. The barman looked bored. Bertrand asked for a beer and was presented with a pint glass with a handle marked with the Lion brand badge. Two of his lumberjacks were arguing about the recent bonus, neither satisfied but for different reasons. He perched on a stool and turned toward the floor.

"Where' you girlfrien'?" demanded a perky little nymph with straightened, highlighted hair. "Me, I'm Juliette. Your girlfrien' leave you? Not coming tonight? I am very nice dancer.

Please, may I have a drink?" She held her hand out to shake in a tactile overture.

He tried to turn away rudely but couldn't. At the back of the room in the darkness, he thought he saw the flash of a henna-coloured Afro and a skinny girl leaving by a small back door.

"She's too tired today," he said without thinking.

"Oh, you had too much fun, not so? I like your girlfriend. She not come here before," she said, and then, "Why you not want to dance?"

Bertrand took a long draft of beer and relaxed mentally, bringing his consciousness down to earth and the earthy. He caught the spirit of the moment and smiled. The girl was quite pretty and cheerful so he sat with her and let her go through a whole repertoire of inane small talk while he thought about Anwei.

"You not listening," she accused and as quickly as she had appeared, she vanished. He felt a hand take his from behind him and Anwei's cheek brush against his.

Anwei's day had been strange. She had left the flat about eleven o'clock, suffering Hedder's disdainful expression with equanimity. It was a fine morning, not yet too hot, so she walked to the pharmacy. Marie France was obviously ready to give her a sharp rebuke, but her instincts held her back as she saw the confident smile in Anwei's eyes and the smart jeans. This was unlike Anwei's normal diffident behaviour.

"Uh-huh," she said. "And where's this girl been all morning all done up for a party? I think maybe she didn't sleep between her own sheets. Yes or no?"

"Auntie, what you thinking? Didn't you ever have some fun?"

Although Marie France kept up the questions, Anwei was determined not to dilute her fragile memory by sharing it. That would come later when disappointment needed to be offset by bravado.

The day seemed to drag on until at seven they shut up the shop and wandered off to squeeze into shared taxis taking them each in opposite directions to their small rented rooms.

To Anwei, her room in an old wooden house, which had seemed so adequate up until now, looked small, cheap, and shabby. She noticed a cockroach disappearing under the bed, something that would not have bothered her before and the bed, wide and hard, that was too low and the tired, greasy-looking rattan furniture.

She felt a great need to clean. She peeled off her jeans and top and hung them carefully in the curtain-fronted wardrobe. She took a wrapper from her drawer and tied it round her waist. Bare-breasted she set to. She filled her plastic bucket with water and added detergent and started with the chair-covers and the cane armrests of the sofa and armchair. Then she moved to the exposed parts of the floor and scrubbed hard, creating a cleanliness she had rarely seen before. The windowsill followed and the small cooking ring in the corner and the steel tray beside and the Formica splash board behind. Then she went to the bathroom, and stripping off the wrapper and panties, she ran the shower while she used a big rough old scrubbing brush to scour the tiles of the shower tray, the small square sink, and the cement floor. In the yellow glow from the dim light bulb, there was not a lot of difference apparent, but it made her feel good, and the application of some bleach made a fresh smell. By now she had worked up a good sweat so she sat on the hard tile floor of the shower and let the tepid water cascade down through her hair and face onto her body while she soaped herself liberally.

Her hair gently kinkled as the water diluted the straightener. It felt wonderfully free, though she knew it would look all bunchy and uncontrolled when she saw it in the mirror. She'd wear a ribbon tomorrow and have it straightened again on Saturday with her friend and neighbour.

All this she had done for Bertrand. She felt him sitting in the armchair while she did the floor and imagined him standing in the doorway as she cleaned the windowsill and wiped down the shelf; and she was sure he was behind her in the shower as she scrubbed on hands and knees. She was pleased to be naked for him, and once or twice she had caught herself pursing her lips for a kiss.

Now she was sitting on her bed cutting her toenails. She knew she had attractive feet. She was proud of her body altogether; people said she was beautiful, a Fulani perhaps. Her feet were slender and her ankles strong. She found some blue nail paint in a sampler she had borrowed from the pharmacy and just for fun, she painted her toenails and then her fingernails. She found silk culottes, actually rayon. She put them on and lay on the bed while the varnish dried. His face stared down at her from the saggy fibreboard ceiling. His eyes were blue. She hadn't noticed before, and his straight blond hair hung down toward her. The image vanished as she heard the clack of some hard shoes in the alley outside. Her outer plywood door scraped on the floor as it was pushed open, and in came Lotus.

"Oo la la! Look at your hair. You been through a bush backwards? Why you here all alone anyway?" She swept in, snatched the only tumbler from the table, and filled it from a Coke bottle of water. She took a drink.

"You don't have enough fun. Should be, you come along with me."

"No, no, I'm happy here. I been cleaning my room."

"That what the smell is?"

Lotus sat down on the bed beside her friend and stared away at the wall.

"Guess who's in the San Pierre."

Anwei felt her heartbeat rise.

"So?"

"Your nice boyfrien' Bertrand."

"What's he doing there?"

"He's just drinking beer and talking." Anwei felt a pang of fear and Lotus sensed it.

"Maybe dancing."

"Who with?" Anwei asked just too fast.

"Who cares?" teased her friend. "You?"

"Oh well, maybe a little."

"Enough to come back with me?"

"Like this? Look at my hair all over the place, all bunched and sticking here and there. What will he think? I come through a bush backwards?" As Lotus turned, their eyes met,

57

and they fell into screams of laughter, smacking each other's hands and embracing each other with a light kiss on the cheek.

"Oh, sista, I think you gonna go with me," Lotus said joyously.

"How so? Not possible," she said deeply.

"Here, let me," said Lotus, and she knelt behind Anwei taking handfuls of her thick curly hair and tying it successively in bunches with ribbons.

"Now you, girl, get decent; put on some breastwear. Just look at your toenails and fingers! You were going anyway; just waiting for me. Not so?"

Lotus dropped behind Anwei as they entered the nightclub, and as Anwei's eyes adjusted to the darkness, she recognised Bertrand and saw the little sprite with highlighted hair. They approached from behind Bertrand's left shoulder and the smaller girl's eyes met hers. Anwei's expression narrowed to a glare of furious force, which melted the girl on the spot. Anwei heard her say something to Bertrand as she scuttled away. Anwei took his hand, which was cocked over the back of the barstool. There was an instant of annoyance as he acknowledged the disappearance of Juliette, who had begun to amuse him, before he turned and saw Anwei.

They smiled and kissed lightly on each cheek.

17

In the next six weeks, they spent as much time together as his job would allow. It was his task to visit the sites up-country to sort out financial, technical, and personnel problems as they arose.

Each in their own way knew they were living in a fantasy. Anwei sometimes remembered Jason and yearned for his smooth muscular black body and the ease with which they could laugh and joke in pidgin or Hausa; and Bertrand sometimes found himself imagining a very warm bed in a very cold room with some beautifully perfumed and gentle blue-eyed English blond. What they both enjoyed was the contrast.

So Anwei enjoyed the elevated status and the luxurious way of life, and Bertrand came to realise that he had been lonely before her intrusion. Her joyous companionship enriched his life. They both enjoyed the sexual experience rendered all the more exciting by their physical differences. His white hairiness was at first godlike to Anwei. Bertrand, on the other hand, was amazed that all his prejudices about black women disappeared as he marvelled in the silky beauty of her chocolate complexion. He adored her childlike expressions, her natural courtesy, and he soon learned how to deal with pouting objections and her occasional glared demands.

Sometimes in the morning, he would wake to see her brown, smooth, perfect high cheeks with her eyes shut and a look of complete serenity, and he would be overwhelmed with a sense of deep longing and adoration. When stirred she would automatically roll over into a position of submission and then open her eyes. As time passed their physical satisfaction was ever better and their affection deepened to love.

However, there was no doubt he missed the familiar conversations he might have had with his own kind. The talk between him and Anwei was fun but unsubstantial. He and she had little in common other than their recent experiences. He soon tired of endless stories of her family and the trials and tribulations of village and city life faced by basically primitive people. He had found them fascinating at first—a real insight into another way of life—but they soon became mundane and reminiscent of Coronation Street or any other working-class soap opera. Occasionally she mentioned Jason obliquely. She made out he was a cousin, but Bertrand was sensitive enough to her phraseology and mood to know that he was more than that. Anyway, Jason was away somewhere and seemed to be set to remain there for many months.

Subconsciously or sometimes overtly, Bertrand was glad about Jason, an escape route, someone to take over responsibilities, perhaps. He was spending more time at the squash club with his male compatriots, making excuses to her about business meetings, but actually propping up the bar and covering familiar ground in sport and politics. So it was not so hard to open a conversation in the form of a reality check with Anwei.

"It is coming up to June," said Bertrand sadly, but rather abruptly, one evening. "I have to go back home."

"I think you going to take me with you, not so?" Anwei answered with a great big grin.

"Not this time, my love."

"You ashamed because I'm black. All those white people won't like me," she said, curling her lips down at the ends of her wide mouth.

Bertrand lost his patience, felt a passing anger, but turned away to hide his expression and keep his mouth firmly shut. Recovering, he turned and said, "Perhaps I'll send for you after a few weeks."

"Huh, maybe," she pouted, and then she smiled. "OK, good," she said, as though closing the deal. He loved the way she could suddenly change her mind.

There is a beach six miles west of Limbe, the old slaving and timber port on the Atlantic Coast downriver from Douala. The sand is a dark chocolate, the uniquely coloured ancient effluvium of the active volcano that lights the sky at intervals. The air is warm and moist in the late afternoon and the fine sand has a soapy quality. It was here that Bertrand and Anwei came for their last weekend together, splashing and laughing, teasing and kissing, teaching swimming, learning swimming in the warm sea on a scorching hot day.

As the sun sank down over the ocean, they sat in the gentle surf basking in the reddening rays and the spume. Bertrand spread soft brown grains over his arms and thighs, and Anwei smoothed it away with gentle motions of her slender fingers. Nothing more was necessary for a perfect moment.

Their close communion was exciting. They were a long way from the beach café and saying nothing they rolled lazily in the sand as the sea receded. Quickly the equatorial sun disappeared, leaving a moonless star-studded sky like a sparkling dome. They made love silently, as the wavelets broke around them, slowly and effortlessly climaxing as smoothly and gently as their surroundings—no crescendo, no puffing, but just the gentle rhythmic climb to ecstasy and a mutual carnal rush. They lay entwined in the balmy air on the cooling sand for a happy eon afterwards, listening to the dull beat of the distant jukebox and the tinkling splashes as the ripples curled and broke in the windless night.

They had a short distance to walk to their chalet at the run-down resort hotel where after some fun chasing the cockroaches out of the bathroom, they showered, soaping each other and caressing some more.

Sleeping that wonderful sleep of the satiated after several more copulations, they were woken as the volcano puffing and roaring in the background made a sharp explosive crack, like the biggest fireworks ever heard or a shell exploding nearby. They rushed out to the veranda at the side of the chalet, but they were only able to see the distant spurts as white-hot magma shot skyward. Occasionally the breeze carried the roar of more explosions desynchronised by the distance.

"Oh, I'm so scared," she said, creating an excuse for Bertrand to enfold her in his embrace, take her inside, and distract her from her fear with yet another love-making.

In the morning a fat French woman was haranguing the clerk at the checkout about cockroaches in the bathroom. As they passed, they giggled and joked about the stupidity of the white people, a favourite theme now—a theme Anwei loved as it gave her a confidence about her humanity she had never erstwhile had in the presence of whites.

That afternoon Bertrand and Anwei had been up the mountain road to get a bit nearer the volcano and had seen the stupid foreigners. They were barging their way through lines of humiliated policemen with arrogant protests, risking their lives by trekking onward up through evacuated villages. "What good can these people do? They just look and take photos. This is our mountain and it is angry. Why, maybe it's all these ugly tourists in their coloured shorts with their fat white bottoms hanging out." She suddenly stopped and giggled. "You think I'm rude? These are some of your people, but you're not like them. They are stupid!"

At this point Bertrand felt utterly alienated from his own kind. He was sure she was right. This was an angry mountain, a mountain about to spew enough magma to envelop everyone for miles around. What business did these ridiculous people have probing around, arrogantly tempting fate? He was beginning to see life through her eyes, to see the white man in a different light: arrogant, foolish, demanding, insensitive, confident, and altogether too quick for the imposed sloth of the tropical heat.

At the end of the week, she saw him off at the airport.

"I go to my village, see my mum," she said.

"Good, be sure to greet her from me and give her a nice present from us. You choose. What would she like?"

"She likes French perfume; you bring some back, please."

They held hands and she massaged the soft pad at the base of his thumb as they talked. She held back tears masterfully as he left her at the departure barrier. He had given her a decent wad of local currency, which should see her through the next several months, paying the rent and buying the small luxuries to which she had become accustomed. He felt a great emptiness as he turned abruptly away, and she wandered listlessly through the crowd toward the bustling taxi queue.

18

Abandoned by both Jason and Bertrand, Anwei felt a desperate need to return to her roots in the village. Memories of Bertrand slowly faded over the next months as she settled back into village life. Her sister began to accept her into the family again, especially as she was able to buy things for their children to take to school and help to pay the fees. Anwei did not realise it, but she was buying her way back into the village. Her mother had been able to consult a real doctor in Bamenda and had been able to purchase modern medicine for the pains that had made her life a misery for the last five years.

It was not long before Jason was dumped by Victoria, who found out he was rejected from Reading University and was in fact a poor village boy with no advanced education. His handsome body was hers for a couple of months, but as his conversation was stilted and ignorant, she found she could not take him anywhere without her friends teasing her about his evident lack of general or particular knowledge, even about football, which he professed as his great passion. It also became embarrassing that he had no money, so Victoria had to pick up all the bills at expensive places where he would never have gone except with her.

For the next three months Jason refused to accept the rejection and took a job in Yaoundé. He barely survived but spent his free time pestering Victoria, phoning her and barging into cafés, clubs and other public places where she would be innocently passing time with friends. She made several attempts to warn him off but unfortunately for him, her father heard of the problem and engaged an agency to "discourage" him.

Fear of physical assault drove Jason back to the village. He arrived two months after Anwei, who by then was aware of being pregnant and naturally needed a father for her unborn child. He accepted that the child was his and agreed to tell everyone they were a couple to be married after the birth.

Anwei became a celebrity with all the women, and the men took her seriously as the betrothed of one of the most promising young men of the nearby village. She glowed with all the respect she was receiving, and Jason felt very much elevated in the small community in which they moved, keeping up the charade of his high educational status. There seemed to be no lasting memory of the massacre and certainly nothing to connect the boys with the brutality of the soldiers.

As the months passed, the rains fell, and the ground became a sea of mud for days on end, Anwei began to feel the burden of her pregnancy. In August during the worst of the rains it became obvious to her and her mother that she was approaching full term. There was great rejoicing in the family and everyone was pleased that she would be doing so well for her betrothed. Jason was proud and strutted, saying he was so happy that God had proved them to be a good match and shone his light brightly on them.

19

Jason's old hut was now occupied by two younger brothers, but they had made room for him. When he came in, they plied him with questions about the aeroplane, the big cities and the shows. Had he seen London Bridge and the Empire State Building and the Queen? Did he have lots of money now he had been to Europe? He was enjoying the attention and giving fairly straight answers when he heard a kerfuffle going on outside. Half whispers. "Anwei" several times and "Jason."

"Johnny," he said to one of his brothers in the dark, "go and see what they are talking about."

When he came back he said, "It's about Anwei. She is in labour for a baby. It's very big and may be twins. They say you should know. Are you going to marry her?"

"Even if she has twins?" piped up the other boy, Sunny. "You don't want twins. They say they are the devil's children."

"The preacher says twins are special, but I think they are unnatural."

"They used to hide twins in the jungle and let the ants eat them."

Jason was hardly listening to all these myths enjoyed so much by his younger brothers. He had heard them before and knew they were old superstitions.

He dressed in his suit trousers and flip-flops with a loose shirt over his shoulders and made his way through the huts to the village square, where years ago the people had met to form patrols to go to Santambo. Now he would go alone, except he noticed Sunny and Johnny were with him.

"I brought this torch," said Sunny.

"Good, then switch it on and we will see the path more easily."

"No!" said Sunny.

"Ah hah!" said Jason casually, guessing the reason.

"Maybe someone over in Santambo can lend us some batteries," said the hopeful Johnny.

So they trod the path toward Santambo, so well-known to them all, in darkness.

Jason began to appreciate the miracle that was taking place and even started to think about praying and thanking God, whom he had ignored for his time in England, where he could not imagine God being at all. It seemed more like the devil's domain, a continual struggle for survival and success, with no respite except for a casual affair with a shrill, vapid, thin, pink girl who seemed fascinated by his beautiful physique and his smooth black skin.

As the trio made their way toward the bungalow, there was a commotion going on. Sisters seemed to be everywhere sitting around or standing and talking twenty to the dozen about the past experiences of every mother in the world. There were no men to be seen, and Jason and his young brothers felt out of place until Balenga, Anwei's mother, came out.

"Oh my, oh my, but she'll be all right. She's early, I think. My goodness, when were you here? Oh dear, maybe not. But you are a beautiful pair. You will have fine daughters and sons." Turning to the younger boys, she went on.

"I know these boys. They are your brothers. I have some orange juice and some biscuits. Find a seat. Hey, you girls," she yelled at the sisters and cousins, "come on. This is the husband. Show some respect."

Three of the younger girls moved sluggishly to the side and then wandered off into the darkness.

Jason sat and the boys took places on either side. There was groaning from within. There were interminable pauses when nothing was happening. Jason sat with dignity as other sisters, cousins, aunties, and so on wandered in and out of the house with little excuses to give Anwei something or to take a message.

When Anwei heard of his presence, she sent a message of thanks to him for coming. As he sat there, trying to look serious and important, he began to have feelings of great love for this girl now going through agony for their benefit. He knew it was her duty to do it and that, as a woman, she must bear the pain. But he was affected by an emotion of great depth. He began to feel a sense of duty and devotion toward

65

her. He would not go so far as to forsake all others, but he swore to himself that he would never deprive her of his attention, love, money, or anything else that was his to give.

He began to imagine the future with several sons running around with him in a spacious field or even gardens, kicking a football as he had seen fathers do in England or visiting a zoo, perched on his shoulders. He even imagined shy little girls with their hair platted in patterns done up in pretty dresses, ready for church. Church. He hadn't been for a long time. Perhaps he and Anwei had better smarten up. They couldn't have children who weren't regular churchgoers. They would have no chance in the world.

The night wore on and the short dawn lighting the sky through the big trees reminded him of a terrible dawn a long time ago. His nose caught a whiff of a cooking fire and the whole horror was refreshed in his mind. He looked down at the smooth heads of his brothers who had succumbed to sleep, resting their heads on his lap some hours earlier.

His mood changed and just as he was beginning to feel that enormously deep pleasure of being alive and part of a new day in a wonderful world, there was a scream from within. A rumbling crash of furniture was followed by some good old-fashioned country curses from Balenga.

Groans of grotesque profundity followed and then more screams and then it stopped.

Jason heard deep breathing and then the cry of a child.

"There is another!"

"No, no, no!" Then, "Oh! God have mercy! Look, hold it up, shake it. It's no good. This little one hasn't made it."

"Well, it's not twins after all."

"What's wrong with the other one?"

"What do you mean?"

"Well, look at the colour."

Then in a deep whisper from Balenga.

"My God, it's white. It's a fine boy, look. But he's as white as a missionary."

"The girl looks a nice healthy colour," ventured Anwei's big sister.

"But she's dead," said Balenga with finality.

66

"The boy must be an albino," said the sister.

There was a loud and deep clearing of the throat from Balenga. Then there was silence.

Jason was not sure whether he had been awake or asleep. His eyes closed and he fell forward onto the boys' heads, crashing them together. They awoke together and both sneezed at the same time, wiping their broad noses generously with the backs of their hands and returning to the sitting position, blinking life back into their half-closed eyes.

"What's this place?" asked Johnny.

"We're in Santambo," Jason answered. "You two run back to Papa and tell him I have a son."

"I'm hungry," said Sunny.

"And cold," added Johnny.

"Go, you boys, someone will give you something," scolded Jason.

They ran off but he saw their pace slacken before they were out of sight. They would smile and charm some porridge from someone by telling of the happy event.

Jason shivered slightly in the cool of the dawn. Then he was not quite sure what to do next. It was obvious that mother and child were sleeping. He expected the proud grandmother, Balenga, to announce the birth to him so he could go and strut and boast a little to his friends around the little coffee kiosks. All he could hear were the gentle snores of Balenga and the calm breathing of Anwei. He decided to peep in. The single chest of drawers was spilt over the floor, and one of its drawers was split and broken, with clothes strewn over the rough mat. In a crude box lay a dark baby, and in the arms of Anwei, just visible, was another pale-looking baby. He coughed to get attention and immediately Balenga came alive. Her eye sockets stretched so wide, they threatened to drop their bleary contents on the floor.

"Oh my God, Jason," she said, standing up and blocking access to the bed, both visual and physical. "You are a lucky couple, a very beautiful boy."

She saw his eyes go to the crude box crib. "No, not that one. She died. Good luck. You did not want to have twins.

Cover it up. Never happened. Only her big sister and auntie know about that one."

Jason was shocked at the inert little bundle in the box, but he could not keep his eyes off it.

"There's a spade behind the house. Give her a burial. Then no one knows. No bad luck or evil spirits to displease. Pray to Jesus and all will be forgiven. Only the trees will see. Go to the burial place out back."

She placed the dead baby in a polythene bag and handed it to Jason.

"You come back and meet your son when you have done this."

The spade cut silently into the soft earth, and it took no time to get down about four feet, which seemed very deep. He was not sure whether to leave the limp little bundle in the polythene bag. As he was thinking, he read "Jan Smuts, Cape Town, Duty Free" and a picture of a bottle of Johnny Walker whisky emblazoned on the side. It suddenly struck him as blasphemous and a tear came to his eye as he gently covered his dead daughter with earth.

And so it was that the granddaughter was buried almost directly on top of grandfather Sojenji because as Jason left, he nearly tripped on a rough wooden cross that he saw in the dawn light had "Sojenji" roughly engraved upon it.

When he returned, Anwei was outside in the early sun and holding their only baby, their son, very close to her. He was wrapped tightly from head to toe in white embroidered swaddling clothes with just his tiny face showing. Proudly she showed him to Jason. He was thrilled now, easily forgetting his earlier gruesome task.

"He's rather white, or pink."

"All babies are like that," she said blithely as if she knew about all babies.

She engaged his eyes in a wide, warm engulfing smile and induced in him an emotion of joy so intense he was speechless.

"Say you are happy and proud. Say you love us deeply," she pleaded.

"Anwei, I am happy and proud and my love for you is eternal," he said and kissed her cheek, leaning over the baby and catching the unfamiliar scent.

"What shall we call him?" asked Anwei.

This had to be decided by the family who had consulted widely. They had chosen to honour the boy with the mother's family name and his own.

"Djarli Sojenji Kalango."

20

Tigman, an old football friend, had always been suspicious of Jason's departure after the massacre; intuitively he had sensed Jason's extreme fear.

One evening when Anwei and Jason were walking in the village, Anwei carrying her baby, Tigman, surrounded by brothers and friends, greeted them.

"I am happy for you two with your little white man."

It was said with an expression of cold politeness. Anwei kept smiling, but burned inside with anger and shame as the words "white man," not heard or uttered for months past, had reminded her of Bertrand. She had felt tears rise in her eyes and forced them down as Jason answered his greeting. She dared not look up as Jason quietly said, "Thank you, Tigman Ogukwe," and holding his head slightly higher than normal, led Anwei past.

But for Jason this had been a cutting insult that he had heard too many times over the last few weeks. As he lay in bed at night separated from Anwei as is the custom during the first months of nursing, it nagged at him. But why was this child so pale and white? He had consulted the nurse, Magdalene. She had rolled her eyes and sucked her teeth, frowned and grimaced, but all she had managed to say was, "You know, these things happen. By the grace of God he's a strong boy and you will be proud of him." Jason was satisfied for about an hour after this explanation, but he started worrying again.

What he wanted to do most urgently was to talk to Anwei about this question but the circumstances contrived to make this almost impossible. By the ancient custom they could not sleep together during this time and during the day Anwei was never alone, always attended by a flock of young girls and other nursing mothers. When they did have a chance to walk out there always seemed to be more urgent things to discuss, such as what he was going to do for a living and where they would live.

These questions also had been troubling Jason who was beginning to realize that his absence from the village had left him without a place in the community. Anwei had given him half the money she had received from Bertrand in the dutiful way of a faithful wife. He came to the conclusion that the best way of solving one of these problems and avoiding the other question was to leave the village and head for the city.

Jason went to see his father down at the workshop. It had expanded with the purchase of a small lathe, standard drill, thread cutter, pipe bender and creaser, along with several other machine tools. He now had five apprentices, two of whom were his own sons and the rest nephews. One of Jason's half sisters was installed at a desk behind a big upright typewriter and a pile of exercise books. In the yard another sister presided over an assortment of goods for sale.

"Markessa and Elivera look after payments. We take about half in cash now and the rest in barter. We always have too many eggs and vegetables, so we sell them off here to make a little more cash for things we need. She also types letters for people; certificates, CVs and small contracts. I fixed up that old typewriter and she learnt from a book. She's very fast now."

He told Jason that he and the boys were getting well-known all around for fixing pumps, pipework, and valves, and making frames for pumps and engines. Recently, one of the apprentices had started fixing simple things on motorcycles, cars and trucks. Bukani was training as a mechanic and would join them soon.

"That's where the money will be. Anyone who runs a car can afford to pay good money for repairs, and they have to be done: no choice. I am also sending Ogwe to technical school in Bamenda to learn these things properly."

There was a bustle of activity as his brothers and the others hammered and drilled and welded the metal into useful shapes. He felt a bit left out in his white shirt and lightweight trousers, in contrast to their black shorts and patchy singlets. There was noise coming from the engine behind the mud wall at the back of the workshop.

"Diesel is expensive. That thing never stops all day, drinking all the time." And Jason noticed the long shaft running across the roof with the leather belts driving the various machines.

"Twenty-five horsepower; it drives the shaft and the welder," his father said with pride. They walked a little way from the shop and sat on some old truck tyres.

"Father," said Jason formally, "I think I must leave the village."

"But you have only just arrived after so many months away. And your mother is so proud of you and filled with love, especially as you will give us another grandchild. We can find a place for you here for a few years. Then a man with your education will be required, and you will be given a real job and respected by all, and I will be very proud to be your father."

Jason realised this was a long speech for the old man, who was not used to talking in long sentences, normally giving orders and instructions in a quick staccato.

"Douala and Yaoundé are where the opportunities are. I am ambitious to be a politician, have power and influence. Even in Bamenda nothing serious happens. The people just vote as they are told and the Fon's appointees or some powerful cadre man gets the job."

"What's so wrong with that? We have stability and peace. We don't want riots and confusion."

Jason did not wish to argue nor would he dare be so impolite to his father.

"Yes, Father, this suits us here—"

His father cut in, "But now you have seen the world, you want to change it."

Jason smiled shyly and lowered his head.

"You broke my heart when you ran away," his father continued. "Now you break my heart again because you are the best educated of all my children, but your education may well make you unsuited to this village life. I suppose you are used to town ways, money, cars, and such things, but these cities are dangerous places. I was in Douala, and I saw plenty of wickedness there. So you must be careful. You must attend church regularly and do as the preacher says. You must not cheat but always be true and you will succeed."

Jason knelt before his father in a gesture of absolute submission.

"God bless you, Father, your patience will be rewarded. I have always regretted the pain I caused as a boy. You must forgive me."

"I have always believed there was more pain than was evident. Whatever it was, I forgive you now and wish you well in your endeavours."

Jason's heart swelled with joy as he backed away from his father, bowing in reverence. He still had the problem of Anwei. His elation gave him the courage to ensure the matter would be dealt with. He meant to lead her gently to the subject of the baby. Was he normal and OK, or was he maimed or an albino?

He walked over to Santambo at a time when he quite often would visit to take her for a stroll on the dusty main street. There was the usual chatter around her mother's house, but this evening it seemed more shrill and argumentative. Anwei was sitting quietly on the veranda, leaning against the wall feeding Djarli, his little pale face contrasting with her dark breast. Her mother and aunt were in hot argument.

"You don't know what you're talking about," he heard Anwei's mother say. "Many babies are pale and they get darker; then they are normal after a few months."

"You mean cooking in the sun. Huh!"

"You make me so angry. You insult us. Look at his eyes now. They were blue, now they are green and they will soon be brown. Many of us have brown eyes, not black."

"Yes, but his skin."

"His skin is beautiful."

"He'll have nothing but trouble, you see, scabs, itching." The aunt looked up and saw Jason. She was embarrassed. "Oh Jason, I was just admiring your son."

Jason smiled without feeling. Anwei looked up, appealing for his support.

"What is this?" he said. "What is it they are saying?" Looking down at her, he saw an expression of complete devastation. She was absolutely exhausted.

Then in a very small voice, she said. "They are right. He is a white man's. He is a white baby."

Both the older women turned immediately on her. "No, no, no," they said in unison.

"I didn't mean that," said the aunt.

"How is that possible?" said her mother. "No, no, not my girl with a white man." She was more horrified than if it had been the devil himself molesting her daughter.

"Mother, he was nice. He was kind, and Jason had gone, left me for another woman. Now he will go away forever."

Jason felt a throbbing in his head. This was his worst suspicion and he was ill equipped to deal with it. His mind slowly turned over the words and recent events.

"The money," he said dully. "The money was his." Jason was overcome with humiliation. "How can we Africans ever hold our heads high if we continue to take the tidbits the white man throws us, and our women soil themselves for money?" He was shouting. The women all turned to him, surprised at his impolite outburst.

"Oh, it was not like that. I did not do it for money. He was kind. We had happy times, good times. You had gone to see your rich girlfriend in Yaounde. I did not think you would come back. I had no idea I was pregnant until three months had passed and when you came back I was sure and proud that it would be your baby. Jason, I have loved you since we were children."

Jason looked at his woman. Her mother and aunt were sitting on either side of her on the small wooden bench. Her face was streaked with tears. Her eyes were shot with blood. Her mouth was turned down and she was on the point of breakdown. She was still beautiful, but desperately sad.

73

The realisation came home to him with a hammer blow; his girl-child's chances had been usurped by the more vital offspring of a white man. By a remote chance they had shared her womb, but the other man's foetus had survived, while he had been obliged to bury his child, dead on delivery.

"Everything was so easy when we were young. Now it is all so complicated and I cannot work it out," she appealed.

Jason was silent and from where Anwei was sitting, his gaze was pitiless.

"It is simple," he said. "I am leaving for the city. I don't know if I shall return. I may send for you if I want you. I am not happy with you. I will see how I feel after some time away."

Anwei bowed her head in shame. She knew he had the right to abandon her. She thought maybe he did not want to keep the tainted money however much it would have made his life easier. Perhaps he still felt a shred of love and pity for her, even after the revelations of her past.

Jason turned and walked away. He did not remember ever having been so unhappy. But the confusion of the last few months was gone, and he felt as though a lead weight had been lifted from him, only to be replaced by a knife stabbing at his heart.

Jason left town. He had his father's blessing and he had divested himself of his responsibilities toward Anwei.

21

After Jason left, there was cold emptiness in Anwei's heart. Her sister and cousins were good but everything slowly became difficult. Anwei increasingly found herself moving from a position of respect to the role of the poor relation. People did not know how to treat the white baby. There was a mixture of reactions from the villagers. Some of the younger women were jealous of the fair-skinned boy and became spiteful. The men gradually became supercilious and talked amongst themselves in the beer hut. Her mother and sister were loving and supportive but the very curiosity of their expressions hurt her as if she were the mother of a freak. She became more and more sensitive to the remarks of all the village people concerning her baby and his origins.

One misty, silent morning, very early, before the village was properly awake, she slid out of her mother's house and walked with her baby in a sling on her back down the dewy path to the road. It was a bad season of the year to travel, the last month of the rains. And no sooner had she reached the road than a heavy downpour assaulted her.

She had a pair of good shoes on but, unused to wearing them, she soon felt the blisters being raised on the sides of her ankles. She stooped to take them off and carried them for a while. She must have made about two miles before she became aware of some of the problems facing her. She had to stop to feed the baby, who was making his hunger known vociferously. As she sat there, she felt more wretched, lonely and defeated than ever. She still could not understand why Jason had been so cruel and careless as to leave her. But he was a man and had to make his way in the world, while she was a woman expected to care for the child, whatever the conditions. There was almost no money left. Possibly there was enough for a meal or two but none for the other important things.

After two days of tramping through the mud, she had only made about twenty kilometres. With no money she could not get a ride in a van, so she collapsed in a heap with no idea as to where she was. She began to shiver violently, unable to keep warm. The rain was streaming down her, over her head and down her neck. The cooling effect was hurting her with a pain that added to her complete mental agony. Her baby was now her only reason for being alive, but at the same time he was the reason she was having such a hard time, so love was tainted with anguish; her heart was split between the profound affection of motherhood and the hatred of the burden weighing down on her.

Her agonised peace was shattered by a roaring of machinery. It made no difference to her immediately but the noise began to impose yet another aggravating lance in her consciousness.

The truck was a lumbering behemoth. The three men inside were sweating liberally in the smoky cab. It was a Berliet log-hauler tractor unit. It was being taken into Douala for a much-needed overhaul. The low ratio on the twin axle drive was not functioning. The three men inside were looking forward to two weeks in Douala, boozing and whoring, meeting old pals and lying in the soft brown lagoon sand.

They had been singing to the growl of the engine to keep awake in the humid heat of the morning. Their journey had been long and wet. They had been on the road three days, sloshing through mud axle deep. Their rations were about used up and the two bottles of whisky were gone. They still had twenty five litres of boiled water for drinking and about ten gallons of rainwater for washing. The cab was cramped, with suitcases stuffed behind the wide right-hand seat. They had taken turns with the demanding job of driving. The power steering was stiff from lack of lubrication, and the clutch had to be disengaged every time the vehicle started gaining speed in the muddy slime of the bush road.

Jens was at the wheel. Lothar was snoring against Helmut, who was vigilantly spotting dangers in the road for Jens.

"Look there, Jens!" he said as he saw a brownish wet-looking mass by the road.

Just before the wheels would have splashed a sheet of brown mud over the bundle, Jens brought the truck to a halt, brakes snorting. A wide-eyed black face emerged from the bundle, and they perceived that there had once been bright colour in the brown cloth that wrapped it. There was some more movement and they realised they were looking at a woman holding a pale-looking baby. Lothar woke up, and as the truck was stopped and feeling an urgency, opened the door and climbed down to the road. His big boots splashed in the mud as he landed almost on top of Anwei.

"Do you speak English, sir?" she asked him, rising awkwardly to her feet, holding Djarli out in front of her.

"Mein Gott, das, was ist dieses?" he exclaimed, surprised. "Yah, I speak some."

"Please, sir, I am trying to arrive at Douala. I have walked a long way. I have been sleeping. My baby is very needy."

"Do we have room?" he shouted over his shoulder, urine splashing into the overflowing ditch. The question was rhetorical as they were in good spirits and full of rough gallantry, so they made space in the crowded cab and hauled Anwei and Djarli up.

Anwei was unused to the stench of diesel and sweaty white bodies, and at first she was overcome, holding her dirty cotton wrap to her face. The roaring of the engine was frightening after the silence of the muddy road. She was wondering what these men might do to her, but she was sure she would have died if she had sat in the mud any longer, so she bore the stink, the noise and the discomfort.

They had to shout.

"What's your name?" yelled Lothar.

She shouted back against the racket.

"Annie," he repeated "What's your baby's name?"

"Djarli."

"OK, Charlie," he said.

He had run out of conversation. He spotted the water bottle.

"You like some water?" He held the bottle toward her.

She took a swig and wet her finger to feed Djarli, and then held the bottle gently to his lips. He drank a little and then spluttered.

As Anwei handed the bottle back she had tears in her eyes, too emotional to say thank you. He got the message louder than if she had shouted. Lothar was embarrassed that such a small kindness should have such a profound effect. In the rough and tumble of his daily life such things were taken for granted. Then he glanced at the baby. He was puzzled by the baby's obvious paleness. What was this starving girl doing with a white baby, abandoned by the side of the road eighty kilometres from Douala?

The truck lumbered slowly into town in the afternoon, making slightly better speed as the road changed from mud to a broken hard-top and then to a tarred surface. By this time the three men had changed shifts three more times. Anwei's presence in the cab had become irksome but they were generous fellows and as they passed along the lower dock road, they saw Anwei beginning to recognise the place. They stopped, gave her a handful of money and wished her on her way.

With the money she obtained some milk for Djarli and some food from vendors for herself. As it started to get dark, she staggered into a filling station. Finding a space in the crowded forecourt under the flatbed of a semitrailer, she lay down next to some other abandoned women and their children. Her sleep was disturbed by more violent dreams and brightly coloured hallucinations. Three day's lack of sleep and food had taken its toll.

As daylight came, her mind returned to normal and she began to think logically again. She found that she was down in the dock area. The place stank of cut timber, diesel fuel and rancid palm oil. Her place on the ground was greasy so her clothes were soiled. She felt, for the first time, totally filthy and unkempt. She really wanted to die. As the sun warmed her body, she gained a little energy and started climbing up into the town.

The streets began to be familiar. She recognised the road where she had worked a year ago. The buildings on either side had the same off-white appearance, but between them was the blackened shell of the pharmacy. No sign of her aunt or the proprietor.

In her weak condition, she was not able easily to comprehend the scene. The shop had been her place of work for two young formative years, and to see it burnt out, just a blackened shell, was a terrible shock. She sat at the kerbside and stared blank-eyed and numbed by what she saw. There was no future and now it seemed no past.

An old man who had occasionally run errands for them in her previous life came and sat next to her.

"You look done in," he opened without looking up. "I haven't seen you for a while. What is it, boy or girl?" he asked, looking at the pathetic bundle at her breast.

Without focusing her eyes, still staring ahead, she said, "Boy."

He coughed and spat. Without showing much interest, she asked, "What happened here? I used to work here, remember?"

"Burnt out by jealous wife, they say."

She was so tired that she lost the gist of the exchange and fell asleep right there on the sidewalk. As the afternoon waned and the heat of the day passed, she woke. The old man was still there when she awoke.

"I suppose you don't have any little jobs for me now," he joked.

She smiled at him and asked him what had happened in the meantime.

"When you left, people gradually stopped coming to the pharmacy because that fat woman was so rude. I don't think she knew what she was doing. People came back complaining: short of pills, wrong medicine, overcharging, there was no end to the arguing. Seems only you knew how to run the place, and when you left, she did not know how."

Anwei grunted to acknowledge his remarks.

"Anyway, the boss came back to run the shop, and then the trouble started. It seems he was partial to a well-covered woman, and when his old passion was rekindled, she flirted with him until they finished up spending time in various hotels. I know, I have contacts everywhere in the city. She was renowned for having the same loud manners as he. Anyway, the wife found out and had a gang burn down the shop. She meant to kill the fat one, but she had gone home and the husband was stocktaking. The fat one came back in the morning, screamed, and hasn't been seen around here since. Anyway, he got badly burnt, the shop was destroyed, and the wife has to look after her man for the rest of his miserable life.

"Here," he said, handing her a greasy-looking package. "I was lucky while you were asleep. That shoe shop, they sent me out for food. Of course I got some for myself. Then they gave me what they didn't want. So take it. You look as if you need it. There's even half a bottle of Coke."

22

Anwei went to the area where the camp had been to try to find Bukani and Bernadette, but it was not there. Bulldozers had levelled the ground and there was no sign of the shacks. So she and her baby formed a team for begging. To her this was a last resort and had to be a stepping-stone to better things. The misery of begging and the danger of being picked up by a beggar's pimp was in her mind always, but to eat and feed the baby, she had to try.

"You! I know you," a strong deep voice said behind her in the market two days later early in the morning. She turned to see the large frame of Hedda.

"What you got there?" she asked as she folded back the scruffy cloth covering Djarli.

"*Mein Gott!* This is his? Well, you better be quick, *fräulein*. He is leaving this afternoon. He's been here about a month. You might catch him at the airport. He didn't contact you? No, of course not, he brought his new bride with him. Look, I have a plan: Come with me to clean yourself and the baby and get it wrapped in a clean, white swaddling cloth. I have one from long ago. Herr Bertrand is departing on the three o'clock flight and he's busy until then. You catch him at the airport and get him to give you plenty of money. Yes, money every month to look after this baby. You do as I say. I had the same problem a long time ago, and I was not so lucky. You catch him at the airport and make sure he pays."

Anwei was overawed but also saw the chance to give her baby some hope, to be saved. He had already nearly starved to death with her on the road. By the time she had arrived at the airport in a fresh new wrapper and top, with Djarli wrapped up nice and clean, she had resolved to hand him over for a new life in Europe with Bertrand. It was the best opportunity Djarli would have in life. She would have to make a new start to her own chaotic existence here in Cameroon; the baby would have a better start with his natural father.

23

Bertrand went to England with mixed feelings about Anwei. The last long weekend with her had stirred deep emotions in him, but at the same time he realised that to marry such a girl from such a different background would lead to many difficulties. It bothered him that it might just be racial prejudice. No, it was a kind of fear based on the racial difference. It was a sort of assumed incompatibility. Their affair had been sudden, unexpected and completely spontaneous. She had her roots and he had his, and importantly, she had Jason, her beau. He stuck with his theory that she would be happier with Jason in the life she knew. Taking her to an alien environment and forcing her to live a new life with unsympathetic people would be a cruelty. Yes, he thought it through, but was still uncertain. He was not stimulated by anything except her enormous physical attraction. Apart from this they had no common ground in culture, education or ambition.

His parents had a large house in Buckinghamshire. His father's retirement posting was in London. He was a petroleum engineer with an oil operator whose main interests were in Borneo. The posting involved occasional trips to Brunei and Sarawak, which his mother thoroughly enjoyed.

For the first week at home, Bertrand did nothing except to lie around the house or garden and walk down to the pub, where he gradually made friends with the rest of the community. His father was absolutely tolerant, knowing the stresses and strains of working on foreign postings, but his mother, who had nothing better to do, would say things like, "Why don't you call up John Grosser? He was such a good friend," or "Phoebe Parker (poor girl, always known as Pee-Pee) should be still around. Why not give her a ring?" Bertrand would just say, "What a good idea," and recline with a newspaper or magazine and dream a little of Africa and Anwei.

Bertrand was given a desk in the London office as support logistician to the world operation. He was required to procure equipment, ship materials to locations, and help with the human resources function. It was a great insight into the workings of the corporation, as he was also deputised to the directors as a sort of general assistant and played host to foreign business associates. He loved it. He did occasional short trips to European offices. His weekends were free, but he knew he was also on notice for another district manager's job anywhere in the world.

24

Gradually over weeks the memories of Anwei faded and Bertrand started to get involved in distractions such as playing tennis on Saturdays with the members of the Great Hall Tennis Club and taking an interest in other village events. It was at the tennis club that he met Sophie. She was someone he'd known slightly as the younger sister of a great childhood friend, Benji Bennet. They found themselves sitting out watching a game in which neither player was good enough to win nor quite bad enough to lose. Each game involved a series of deuces with the advantage passing back and forth almost as frequently as the ball crossing the net.

"My God, these are tedious players," he growled under his breath.

"Actually, they are all very tedious players and this is a thoroughly boring tournament," remarked the girl from the other end of the short bench.

"Sophie," he exclaimed. "I was searching my head to remember your name. We were tiny kids when we last met. You were just a little item always under Benji's feet."

"And you were an enormous curiosity and a fearsome bully. I was awed and frightened of you at the same time."

She was blonde and clear-blue-eyed, and he remembered her for only one regrettable incident when he was eight years old. He'd hit her rather hard. He'd been busy piddling in the Bennet lavatory, wondering whether he and Benji had time to go up to the grange on their bikes when he noticed a small girl standing next to the bowl, staring intently at his willie. Wide-eyed, she had simply said, "Can I watch?" And then he had hit her without thinking and pulled the chain and left, but that night he had been kept awake by a turmoil of very strange and shameful thoughts. Their age and gender difference had kept them apart ever since. Now he noticed her smile, her dimples, and a certain sad maturity in her eyes.

"Anyway, how's life after Roedean? You did go there, didn't you? I thought your parents were rather grand. Your dad had one of those big imposing Rovers that doctors had."

"He was a doctor," she teased. "He called himself doctor, but he was a PhD in mathematics, hence those diplomatic jobs sorting out the economies of emerging countries."

"Yes, I remember you disappeared to the Far East suddenly. I missed Benji. We used to go on adventures together up at Robin Grove. We used to hope we would run into Robin Hood. We played all the parts of his merry men, shooting our homemade bows and arrows."

"Benji's inside," she said flatly.

"Inside where?" he exclaimed stupidly,

"Inside. I mean prison. Oh shit," she said. "I keep telling myself it's nobody else's business and then I keep blurting it out."

"What the hell did he do?" he said as he turned to look her full in the face.

"Oh, it was all too awful. He got Daddy put away as well. You can't imagine the problems it all caused, and Daddy thinks it is what caused Mummy's strokes, and finally when she died, he went all to pieces and now I look after him and live up here in this boring place full of boring little boys who are estate agents and farmer's accountants or solicitors and their hideous wives, who spend all their time rushing around in their Honda Civics. All the intelligent young people have gone except for the yobbos and no-hopers who spend their time boozing or shot up." She was crying now, tears streaming down her cheeks.

Bertrand's interest was raised. He had suspected there was something a bit more interesting about this girl than her mid-blonde hair and her blue eyes. So this was it. Her family had been broken asunder by some awful event.

He stayed silent. There was nothing he could say that would not sound trite or be inappropriate.

"It was drugs," she said and then wiped her face with her handkerchief and straightened her back. Smiling, she said, "It's OK. I survived. Poor Benji's the one suffering. I visit him. He's completely broken. He's done about three years now, and he has another three to do before he can get parole.

"He was rather a sensitive boy. Of course, I didn't realise it. He was my big brother, my protector and comforter. When he hit me, I always knew it was my fault and promised myself to do better next time. I always sought out his approval. Silly, really. Anyway, it started at school. You know he went to Winchester? There was a great scandal there but he was not involved in that. Some of the boys were expelled in his year, but not he. At the time I just thought he wasn't part of it, but later it seems he was just lucky and slipped through the net. He got in touch with some of the boys who were caught, just to try to supply them, I imagine. Most of them have jobs in the city or are making fortunes overseas: moved on, grown up. Now I dearly wish he had been caught then. But who knows? It might not have made any difference.

"Poor Daddy, he wouldn't believe the signs he was seeing. I was up at Newcastle, and Benji was hanging around the house answering calls on his mobile and dashing off in his little Peugeot, occasionally working in bars for petty cash, he said, paying no money to Mummy and slinking off for days or even weeks at a time. He seemed to be bright and normal most of the time, but he had a strange unbalanced lifestyle. You know, dirty trainers and designer jeans and silk shirts. Sometimes he wore heavy gold chains. Mummy said they were chrome, but they weren't. They were that dark colour of twenty-two caret gold.

"Can't blame Daddy, really. He was commuting to Whitehall at the time. It all came to a head in April seventy two. Daddy had some leave left over and took a two-week break at home. No holiday had been planned, so he started to do some gardening and a project for a pond and fountain—you know—what they call a water feature. Benji was supposed to help but he was away on a trip—probably literally.

"Daddy was in the garden with some local chaps digging the pond when Benji phoned. He asked Daddy to go up to his bedroom and get his shoulder bag from under his bed and bring it to the pub in the village. He said if he wasn't there, never mind just to leave it in the shed in the car park and he'd get it later. Afterwards Daddy said he had been angry and slightly suspicious but mostly just miffed that his son should use him to run errands, but he'd innocently thought he might have a pleasant drink with his son this sunny afternoon. He didn't know the pub was being watched. He went in hoping to find Benji and stopped for a half pint. He said he did not feel comfortable in the pub. Everyone was on edge.

"He saw some obvious strangers there, but he was not a frequent visitor himself, so when Benji did not appear, he drank up his beer in silence and left. He dropped the bag in the shed in the car park and he was immediately arrested! Can you imagine! They charged him there and then and took him into custody. He was an hour in the local police station and then they took him up to London. They didn't listen to a word he said nor did they let him phone his solicitor until twelve hours later at midnight from the cells in Hammersmith. Mummy was out of her mind. The car had been found at the pub and of course, Benji was nowhere to be seen. There were about two hundred grams of heroin in the bag and Daddy had been arrested as a trafficker.

"He didn't know anything about the bag, but the police just assumed he was lying. And because it was slowly dawning on him that Benji must be very deeply involved, he was not very forthcoming under questioning for fear of getting him into further trouble."

Bertrand looked at her, concerned. She was drawn and tired.

"Anyway, to cut a long story short, he was remanded in custody for two months while his solicitor and accountant had to show where every penny of his money came from and how he spent it. He was finally convicted for withholding evidence and obstructing the bloody police. His Queen's Counsel, the most bloody expensive lawyer there is, only managed to get his sentence reduced. He was in Belmarsh and then Ford prisons

85

for about two months. When he came out he had lost his job and his pension. He sold the big house and bought a horrid semi in the village.

"Then it was Mother's turn. She had a stroke and while she was making wonderful recovery, she had the big one, an aneurysm and internal bleeding. She died in his arms as he was trying to teach her to walk again. He blamed himself for pushing her too hard, but the doctor put him right and said he should not blame himself and try to relax. They prescribed antidepressants and he seemed better, but he went downhill physically. He lost his will to exercise and wouldn't work around the house, that horrid small house. He didn't complain but I knew he hated it. He saw himself as a failure after being a big man, popular, powerful..." Tears were choking off the flow of words. She coughed and straightened her head. A wan smile spread across her face.

"Just about that time Benji was sentenced. There was no saving him. The barrister did his best but the police had collected evidence going back over four years. He was an addict and a skilful courier. They had evidence of him in Thailand, Pakistan, California, Amsterdam...anywhere where deals are done. He had a large amount of money in various banks and was dealing on his own account. They had fourteen people at his level and a whole lot of street runners, some of whom had squealed on him as being the contact man, the bagman. They call it Queen's evidence."

25

"Daddy tried to recover, but I just watched him lose weight and fall into despondency," Sophie said. "He began to lose his memory and even wonder drugs didn't have any effect. Money drained away on cures and drugs until I called a halt to the whole sorry business, and now I just look after him. It is a chore but at least he is hygienic and self sufficient in many ways. He reads the paper and raves about the government and how it was in his day. He has a few old pals who come to visit from time to time and they snooze amiably after I have done steak and kidney pud' or some such served with stout." She paused and wiped her eyes with the backs of her hands.

"Oh, I am so sorry I've gone on and on without a break. You must be awfully fed up hearing all this bad news. I just had to unload. I don't suppose you'll ever forgive me." She looked down at the grass and then suddenly with a radiant smile she said, "Would you think it terribly forward of me to ask you out for a drink? My treat. For old times' sake. You know I really want to go to that new tapas bar in Mayfield. It's probably terribly common, but I was told they serve some very good Rioja."

"Yes," he said, "but you must let me do some of the talking."

"Promise. I'll pick you up in the Rover Vitesse Daddy was about to replace when everything blew up."

It wasn't long until they were regarded as an item by the locals. Yes, the locals were a pretty boring bunch on the surface but they found a few like-minded people in the bars, pubs, and restaurants. Mostly they spent time exploring the villages and towns, walking for miles. Bertrand had a tonic effect on her father, who perked up every time he came round. He would quiz him about his life in the jungles and forests. Sophie would be busy in the kitchen or around the house bringing them coffee, pleased she was released from inconsequential and argumentative conversations with her dad.

Bertrand noticed how clear he was in his memories of his past career from the Far East to Whitehall, but not at all clear about the recent past. He hardly ever mentioned his wife or son. Benji, if mentioned, was frozen in his memory as a small boy of thirteen or so, not a grown-up college student or a layabout in his twenties, and his wife a gay young thing dancing the Charleston and Black Bottom at High Commission balls. The big house was not mentioned at all. He just revelled in past glories when he had exciting adventures and more recently when he had some power. He mentioned all sorts of politicians, media men, scientists, and other friends and acquaintances, and some heads of foreign states who had at one time or another been personal friends. He began to assume

Sophie was his wife, although he always made a special effort to call her by her correct name.

One very rainy day the old man had a frightening accident. He completely lost control of his bodily functions, creating a horrible mess in his chair, and in his attempt to hide the mess made everything worse, soiling the carpet and half the furniture. Bertrand and Sophie had been out, and when they came home in the afternoon, they found him lying on the floor of the drawing room fast asleep in his own mess. Sophie screamed, thinking he was dead, and Bertrand had to stop himself from panicking or retching. He phoned 999 for an ambulance and the crew was excellent. The ambulance was well equipped, and the paramedics managed to get the old man up and into the ambulance without creating more mess or getting anything on themselves. Sophie went with her father in the ambulance. When they had gone, there was an oppressive emptiness in the house. In the silence Bertrand set about cleaning up. He was not used to work of this kind and diluted masses of disinfectant in water and washed everything in sight. The result was a house stinking of pine essence and feeling damp. He shoved the clothes left behind in the washing machine and took a guess at what cycle to use.

At home that night he read the letter from his firm giving him notice of his next posting to Jakarta in three weeks' time. He was told to get inoculations and to go to London to get his visa sorted out. He realised he needed to make a decision about Sophie. He knew he had fallen for her as never before and their few nights together had been wonderful. It had been his mother's rather stiff attitude to "soiling your own nest" and the fact that Sophie was on call most of the time in her home that had restricted the number of times they had managed to spend the night together, but she was an enthusiastic and humorous lover and he had become besotted.

26

She phoned from the hospital at seven and he went straight over to collect her in his mother's car.

"They don't know what's happened to him," she said as she got into the car. "They think he has lost some major part of his brain function. You know, basic things like bowel control. He looks a mess. He's babbling and incoherent. He seems to be fighting sometimes but other times he just goes into a coma. It may be temporary," she said rather hopelessly. "When he's fit, they'll give him a brain scan or something."

For the rest of the journey back to her house, they travelled in silence. There was no more to be said about her dear father.

"Thanks for clearing up. It must have been awful," she said with a thin smile as they sat down at the kitchen table. "He'll be all right, I suppose."

"Look, Sophie," he started, "I know it's not a good time…"

She looked at him as if to say, "No it's not a good time, so shut up."

He stood up. "More coffee. I'm afraid the house stinks of disinfectant now, and perhaps I've ruined the carpet."

"It's not your fault," she sobbed. "It all goes back a hundred years when we were in Jakarta. Oh, that day began a chain of events…I must sleep. I've been up all night and am almost falling over. Let yourself out and call me this afternoon." As she stood, she turned. "At least I have you, the only hope in a hopeless world. You are my friend, aren't you?"

As she sobbed her heart out, he held her and supported her up the stairs. "Let me help you up to have a good hot bath." He only thought of her distress. There was no lust for her naked body floating in the steamy water. He was now the nurse. After her bath he tucked her into bed and left.

27

The next morning Bertrand made a determined effort to get to Sophie before she was up. His evil intent was to get into bed with her—an opportunity not to be missed while the old man was safely away in hospital.

As they were relaxing with coffee after a leisurely carnal morning, he popped the question.

"Look," he said, "I did not have a chance to tell you yesterday, but the dreaded posting has come through: Jakarta."

"What about Jakarta?"

"My posting," he said. "Well, I know it's not a very romantic moment, but would you come with me?"

"What do you mean, go with you?"

"Well, will you come as my wife? Will you marry me?"

"Oh, my God. Jakarta. Well, of course I'll come with you. But what about Daddy? I mean he's ill in hospital."

But not for very long. That afternoon the message came through that he was to be discharged from the hospital, as the doctors were not able to do anything for him. Bertrand and Sophie went to help him make the transition from the hospital to a nursing home specialising in the severely disabled Alzheimer's sufferers found by the welfare officer. They said it was impossible for him to be discharged home because he needed twenty-four-hour care. They found him a good place.

Sophie was looking forward with mixed feelings to going to Jakarta. It was going to be their honeymoon, albeit a working one. She knew it from her childhood. She had enjoyed being a post-colonial daughter. The family had left rather too late for comfort during the communist riots of 1965. She remembered the tiled floors of a large concrete house with a high-pitched roof. It had enormous rooms with open sides leading to wide verandas where she and her brother would sit with their mother while she read them stories after lunch. She could feel the hard wooden seats of the rattling bus riding to school in the cool of the morning through the smoke of the city. She had loved the smells of the damp dust, the hawker food and acrid garlicky odours of cooking fires. They would sometimes buy chewing gum, one unwrapped piece at a time, from the boys who ran up alongside the bus, reaching up to the glassless windows. They had gone to the English school where all the children wore neat red-checked shirts and blue shorts or skirts. It was an ordered life full of sunshine, parties by swimming pools, Coca-Cola, and potato chips.

Her memories were all happy until the end of their stay. Their amah had been a beautiful and calm girl; she was chubby, brown and warm, quiet and shy, with a tactful and silent way of imposing her will on the children. All Sophie's memories were of an idyllic life shattered by horrible events and an extreme change of surroundings. She was able to face up to it now, but for months and years afterward she had suffered nightmares and weeping fits when she had sudden flashbacks.

Their house was in a wide but quiet road to the southwest of the main city. Father was collected for work each morning in a limousine with a uniformed chauffeur. Mother used the less salubrious family car to take them to swimming, parties and sports activities.

Amah had a room in the house but she also had family and perhaps a boyfriend in the town. About twice a week she would say good night at seven, having put the children to bed, and slip out to get a bus. The following morning at five o'clock, she would arrive and go to her room, appearing as any other weekday morning bright as a pin at half past five to get the children to school. Only one morning it did not happen like that.

The whole family was woken by a scream. Something in the voice must have alerted them, for after they heard it, they all found themselves standing in a huddle on the wide veranda. Father was the first to move.

"I'd better go and see what it is," he said. "Maybe an accident, someone needing help."

"Should we really get involved?" Mother pleaded, not wanting her husband to get caught up in all the troubles and then, "My God, what have I said?" She placed her hand over her mouth to stop herself, and then said, "Of course, darling. Let me come with you. They may need some first aid."

So they dressed in the first clothes to come to hand and Mother took her first-aid kit, a stylish number in a zipped leather case with a list of contents inside the flap, and they went out into the street. The children followed in nightclothes, barefooted. Their father stopped, frozen by what he saw. Mother screamed and fell forward onto her knees leaning against the wall. Sophie did not scream. Her eyes glazed over.

"My God, it's Josephine," said Father. His voice had been dry and barely audible. Sophie could remember the lump in her throat preventing her from breathing so that she felt she would suffocate. She also was kneeling in the dusty road. There was their beloved amah thrown against the wall of their house, like a rag doll. Sophie had torn her eyes from the sight of death only to find herself staring at the strewn contents of the broken black plastic handbag: a wooden crucifix by a lipstick tube, a large hairbrush for brushing through Amah's luxuriant long black mane, a gold-hasped diary with a broken lock, a bent and dented toothpaste tube, small school exercise book, and a pair of red knickers in a polythene bag.

She turned again and saw her father crouch to feel the twisted neck. It was broken, the head to the left and to the back, forming a fatal angle. Her clothes were torn open, exposing the black nipples on her brown breasts. Worse than anything she had ever seen was a reddish-brown stain growing like spilled paint on the skirt of her blue flowered dress. There was an opening movement of her legs, and her skirt rolled back slowly above the knees.

Her father was staring into her eyes, and her mother, recovered by now, was feeling her chest as if to pump air into her. She saw her mother's hand drop to the hem of the skirt and push it slightly back. There was a gasp of disbelief from all around as the veined tonsure of an unformed baby showed from under. Sophie's mother had picked up the child, pulling on the cord, which had broken, shocking her even more. "Jesus, God," her mother had said in a thin voice that sounded like a genuine supplication. But there was no life in it.

Sophie had never seen her mother crumple so completely. She had lost all her stiffening and was leaning like a collapsed tent, half against the wall and half against the dead Josephine, holding the bloody lifeless foetus close to her breast as if the heat of her body and the warmth of her feeling could revive it.

Sophie remembered her eyes had been dry, wide-open staring at the unfolding scene when her brother began to sob.

Their father had turned and she had never seen such sadness in his face. She saw tears in his eyes, and then she saw no more as the lump in her throat was released with a great spewing of vomit. Tears gushed from her eyes.

He held his great hands out toward his children and their mother and he managed to choke out, "Go inside. We have seen enough. God rest her soul," he whispered. Then turning to the crowd, he asked, "Who saw anything?" He was answered only by blank stares from the motley crowd of dull-eyed onlookers turning and shuffling, unable to do anything and wishing not to have been there at all. Sophie's mother, having somehow come back to life, had laid the foetus to rest in the lap of the murdered amah. She took the children's hands, leading them into the house.

The family never spoke of this event. It was as if each had different versions of the same awful nightmare and could not bring themselves to burden one another with the details.

The sad bustle started. There was the visit from Josephine's parents and the funeral arrangement. Their father had not gone to work that day and seemed to be home a lot the following days. The packing up began. Boxes were everywhere, and they all had to make choices about what they could take and what had to be abandoned. Their mother said all the things they left behind would be given to the needy children, to their friends, or to the children of the servants.

In the daytime Sophie was temporarily distracted from what she had seen. But her beloved Amah haunted her nights in a repeating nightmare, as a broken and unwanted toy, and she, Sophie, was the one who took her from the toy box and flung her against the wall. When a baby screamed somewhere in that virtual place, she would wake up. Sophie would crawl into her bigger brother's bed, and they silently hugged each other till they slept.

Something very profound happened to him, and although she sought comfort in his stronger, bigger presence, she was aware he was no longer the joyous, ebullient big brother she was used to. He stopped teasing, and what's more, he completely stopped being nasty and bullying her when no one else was around. She was both pleased and sorry for this lack of attention. They had gone on sleeping in the same bed frequently until they had arrived back in England, and they both cried in their dreams.

That was a long time ago, but the nightmare still destroyed her nights in times of stress, and she thought it had done worse for Benji.

Curiosity and a strange need to purge her memories had excited her when Bertrand had proposed going to Jakarta, and so she had been shocked to the core when Bertrand came in one evening to announce he would have to go back to Douala for a six-week period to relieve his successor, who needed urgent treatment in Paris.

28

"Where the hell is Douala anyway?" she sulked. "Goddammit, I got all psyched up to go to Indonesia, and now suddenly it's Africa."

The tantrum was short-lived as he knew it would be, but all the same Sophie had a strange apprehension concerning Cameroon; she was not sure why but was aware it had been a phase of Bertrand's life from which she was completely excluded. She was not exactly fearful of skeletons jumping out of cupboards, but she felt apprehensive. At first she contemplated delaying the marriage until after he returned, but that filled her with a worse fear that he might change his mind or come to some harm before they had time to make their grand statement to the world. But as it would be a great adventure to go Africa, she was, at the same time, elated.

The wedding was a quiet and mostly uneventful happening. Her father had roused himself from his exile at the nursing home and in a confused way had managed to make an attempt at "giving her away."

A continuous stream of jobs, small and large, imposed themselves upon the happy couple over the next few weeks.

Not only were they preparing to take themselves off to a new way of life, but they also had to do various things for her father. Fortunately he had a good solicitor, and the estate agent dealing with the house was reliable and managed the business efficiently. With the excellent nursing home, they were able to make a "lifetime" deal using the remains of his savings and the proceeds of the house sale. They discussed going away, and the matron of the place assured them he would not notice their absence. The routine activities of the home would soon have a therapeutic effect, and they should visit in six weeks and see the improvement. Bertrand's mother was both solicitous and interfering, which raised the tension but also helped them as she dropped gems of wisdom in between carping irrelevancies.

Sophie had found it particularly hard to say good-bye to Benji, who had come to rely on her visits for his basic sanity and hopes for the future. He had turned nasty toward the departure time and tried to be manipulative. But it had dawned on Sophie that he was manifesting a cruel selfishness, and after a tearful farewell she convinced herself she was no longer his keeper nor perhaps even his friend.

All of this they accomplished in two weeks of continuous activity until at last they were actually going for the flight. They had a flaming row at the check-in desk: the row they had managed to avoid all the time that Sophie had been the second female in the Dormand household, when every evening both of them had collapsed into bed too tired to make love more than perfunctorily or eat a proper meal or relax with a drink—just the two of them.

While Bertrand's back had been turned returning the airport trolley to the stack, Sophie had been approached by a fat woman wrapped in the bright colours of Africa, with three bright-eyed clinging children, and Sophie had agreed to check in for her two large, plastic-wrapped bundles.

As the bundles went through the weighing machine with their baggage, Bertrand exploded: "What the fuck is going on?"

"Darling, we've got about forty pounds of our allowance unused. This poor woman—"

"What bloody woman?"

Of course the woman was nowhere to be seen. The check-in girl was occupied on the phone. He moved her away. "Never," he shouted, painfully restrained by the public surroundings, "never accept parcels and cases from these people."

Suddenly she saw the sense in what he said.

"OK, I messed up. For Christ's sake do not shout at me in a public place. I just won't stand for it. And don't ever swear at me like that. How was I to know? I've never been to bloody Africa."

"Are all these yours, sir?" The girl looked doubtful but who was she to challenge this smart-looking couple.

"Yes," said Bertrand uncompromisingly.

As they settled into the wide business-class seats, they both relaxed at last. Their fate was sealed. For the next six hours, at least there was nothing either had to do or could do except to accept glasses of champagne, canapés, meals, movies, and sleep. He turned and smiled.

"Sorry," he said. "It's not important but occasionally people have been stung. Your 'mama' was probably just bringing back some designer goods to trade or to give to her many relations. It's not any sort of big deal, and I suppose we should help if we can."

"I'm excited," she replied, ignoring his apology. "But completely whacked." They kissed and sipped their champagne.

Her time in Douala had not been a great success. She found herself marooned in the apartment, fortunately close to the Akwa Palace hotel, which was nice enough and had an excellent French cuisine, a good pool and an adjoining casino. The main snag was the other clients who were mostly oilfield. Not really rough, but still men away from home, and she had to fend off various advances. Sometimes approaches she might in other circumstances like to have followed up. She swam lengths in the Olympic pool three or four times a day.

For Bertrand, the work was tedious. Jean-Paul, his successor, who had been gone for two weeks, was halfway through reorganising the filing systems and had hired a new secretary who was fluent in French but lacking in English. He was obliged to communicate in French, which he was finding irksome in spite of his essential competence. He wanted to make a trip up-country with Sophie to give her a tour, but the rains prevented this. Douala had virtually no culture and he began to realise that all the social life he had enjoyed in the past was work-related and with expatriates of his ilk, who like him rotated out every year or two; or his activities had related to Anwei. His successor had created a social circle of French flavour and although these friends were politely welcoming, he did not slot easily into Jean-Paul's place. He and Sophie ate in the hotel and went out a couple of times, but he found himself, after so short a time, an outsider with no need to make potential longer-term acquaintances.

He and Sophie were happy enough. It was a honeymoon after all, and an absolute contrast to the mess they had left behind.

Jean-Paul returned on time looking pale but fit, hinting mysteriously that he had had a major trauma (unnamed) but had heroically survived. After a week working together, the time came for Bertrand and Sophie to return to the UK for a three-week stay before going to Jakarta. They were both rather pleased that their stay was over and Africa would be behind them.

29

It was on the concrete apron of the airport, white-hot, foot-blistering hot. Bertrand would never forget the slap, slap, slap of her hands as she pleaded, "Boss, darling, he your baby son, look very fine, very beautiful."

The baby was wrapped in a dazzling white embroidered cloth, swaddled like a biblical infant, and the woman had placed him out in front of her at arms' reach as an offering is made to an angry god. She was kneeling with her chin near the ground, her slender hands still beating the concrete rhythmically. Her voice was now deep, and she was chanting a groaning song like a mantra

When his vision returned to normal, Bertrand was appalled as the line of her body became absolutely familiar. The image in his mind was of her naked and silky and black, with her long elegant fingers stretched out across the soft pillow of his bed, and the mantra was of pleasure and ecstasy rather than pain and sorrow; but the curve of her back and the position of her knees and feet were the same: Anwei.

The child's little cheeks were puffy and his big green eyes alive and eager. Bertrand was unable to move. He had stopped dead, and the passengers behind him piled up and then dispersed, leaving him and Sophie, who had been ahead of him and turned back, together with the wailing woman. She had ambushed him from behind the corner of the building, where the baggage handlers were now finding comfortable, shady ledges for their afternoon sleep.

Bertrand's heart was beating uncontrollably. He saw Sophie bend down. She lifted the baby and moved toward the woman. "Do you know her?" she asked over her shoulder.

"Yes, I know her," he said flatly without expression.

"It's your baby?"

"How the hell would I know?" He did not mean to sound angry. It was just the tension of the moment. He had been in control, organising their departure, rearranging all the travel arrangements to the Far East, and now he was lost. Who was in charge? What was his position in this?

She knew. "He's beautiful," she said quietly.

Bertrand did not answer. He was looking round like a man in panic. Anwei had stopped chanting.

"Sir, darling Bertrand, sir. You will take him with you. On plane. To Londe. Give him school and good life. This no good here for matis baby. Fine in Pareh, Englan'. He grow big and strong. Very fine white man. He is Djarli Sojenji, his name is so." Her face lit up like a tropical sunrise, and he remembered the love he had felt for her only a few months ago stirring in his pounding heart.

Sophie was still holding the baby in her pale freckled arms, and Anwei turned the beam of her smile toward the duo.

"You take care my baby," she ordered the young bride, the smile now morphed into a serious frown.

"Yes," said Sophie, "I shall."

It was that simple. Bertrand felt like an observer at an auction where a bargain had just been struck by two other parties.

They then had to contend with an officious little airline clerk who was relishing the chance to bully the embarrassed expat couple.

"We want to take the baby with us," Sophie explained as if they were dealing with a slightly awkward souvenir.

"No, not possible, no ticket and no passport."

Bertrand was beginning to wake up to his situation. The most difficult problem, the baby, seemed to be over without any explanation necessary. Sophie had adopted him and, satisfied, Anwei had gone, melted away into the white heat of the day.

He pulled out the boarding passes. He flapped them on the back of his left hand. He was trying to think. The panic was passing and he realized he was in no position to make a fuss. The alternative was to either dump the baby on the hot concrete and board the plane as if nothing had happened—and he knew Sophie would hold that against him for the rest of his life—or to face up to the responsibility. He could not understand her actions. Anwei was gone, placing all her trust in them. A life was at stake. A life he had started and known nothing about and yet was part of him.

Fortunately theirs were full-fare transferable tickets and they had been bumped up to first class.

"Please take me to Mr. Johnston," he told the clerk.

He had passed any number of his labour force through this airport, and Brian Johnston, the station manager for British Caledonian, was a business friend and squash partner.

"We can't travel," he said when Brian appeared, rather obviously carrying his briefcase, ready to depart for a late, convivial, lunch and siesta.

"I know it's a bit late, but can we get our tickets back and go tomorrow or the next day?"

"It's no problem, old fellow. We'll have to sort out immigration. I can fix that; give me your passports. I'll get it done tomorrow. Your baggage is first class: easy. Anton will get that back through customs." Bertrand was impressed with this efficiency but was aware that Brian was obviously puzzled and amused at his bizarre predicament: new wife, brown baby, sudden cancellation of trip home. What was all this, he was probably wondering, too polite to ask but already constructing a story for the bar of the Panther Club, where he would go for a submarine sandwich and a couple of pints of lager.

"We will go back to the flat," Sophie said.

"No we can't do that. We handed it back to the landlord and he said he was starting the workmen early tomorrow."

So they had gone to the Harbour Imperial Hotel as the Akwa Palace was full.

30

After her long journey and the emotional stress of the hand-over, Anwei was drained. She slunk away to a corner in the shade, curled up, and slept like a stray dog. She awoke to the rattle of baggage trailers and the shouts of the handlers as they prepared for the arrival of the evening flight. There was nothing left for her. She had given up her baby instead of benefiting by him. She had an overwhelming desire to see Bertrand and ask to be taken along to England with him, but she feared for the son she might never see again. If she caused trouble, he might just give her back the baby and refuse to take him back to Europe, or the woman may have changed her mind.

Anwei wandered back into town that evening and found Hedda. "You may stay one night, but my boss will be back tomorrow," she said.

Anwei's frame of mind had not improved after her fitful sleep; it was still blank.

Bertrand acknowledged that Anwei had to be tracked down so she could sign the adoption papers. He knew Hedda would be the link.

Anwei had gone back to her to seek advice about her next move. Hedda was not happy about the adoption but was persuaded it would be the best for Djarli Sojenji.

When Bertrand and Sophie had had come to see her, she acted as Anwei's mentor and she struck a hard bargain for an allowance for Anwei, harbouring bitterness about her own past experience and knowing that Bertrand was well paid.

Anwei complied with all the paperwork required for the adoption, and Bertrand set up a bank account and a regular payment system for her. The amount was small compared with his salary, but Anwei was happy as she would be able to afford her rent and some comforts.

"We must call him Charles," said Sophie as they went up the steps to the Consulate Office of the High Commission "but he also must keep his African name, Sojenji. We will register him as Charles Sojenji Dormand."

Anwei was satisfied.

31

Charles loved his adoptive mother, Sophie, who had always been attentive to his needs and sometimes smothered him with love and affection but "the parents" sent him away to boarding school before his seventh birthday. He had been deeply upset and had felt profoundly rejected at the time and resentful later even when he acknowledged that children are sometimes just packages that have to be shelved for their own good and general convenience or expediency.

About an hour after the bewildering good-bye to his tearful mother he had hooked up with a couple of other young hooligans and started his new life. Before supper he was introduced to the head of his dormitory, a boy called Fraser, a Scott. There were three new boys.

"You squirts do exactly as I say, d'ya ken. Y'll get a wet towel round y'r arse if not."

Charles was the only coloured boy in the school with a thoroughly European name and white parents, clear upper-middle class diction and the accompanying confidence. There were some Indians of different colours, one extremely black and rather frail and one chubby brown Muslim boy who was an exceptionally good wicket keeper. Among the other boys were the usual startling blonds, fair, dark and freckled gingers. They were all inquisitive about each other, enjoying their differences, their talents and humour, often screaming with laughter at silly little rude jokes. This was a time when emotions could get intense.

Not being stupid, but ignorant of the mores it was not long before Charles transgressed by helping himself to some illicit chewing gum belonging to an older boy. A severe beating up taught him a lesson not soon forgotten. It was not the last; it seemed that everywhere he went and whatever he did in the first two terms he was treading on someone's toes, straying into their territory or simply doing something not generally acceptable. His essential ebullience was thus beaten down and for the next term he was dulled into submission.

His life in the small prep school was a complex mix of love, hate, fun and misery. Relationships with the other boys would change quickly while always seeking out stability and some sort of continuity to take the place of the parental love absent so suddenly. It is plainly impressed on new boys early on that the masters are the enemy and that the law is enforced by the biggest and most brutal boys. No one is to suck up to staff or to seek favour or the most near fatal transgression to "sneak". The problem was to know how to be nice at all. A blue-eyed blond with an angelic smile was likely to be thoroughly beaten if he was caught being civil to some unsuspecting master. Only in this way could the eleven and twelve year olds maintain their dominance over the little squirts. Here boys learnt about hierarchy. First born or only children, found it hard after they ceased to enjoy the protection of their doting, indulgent mothers. Those with younger brothers and sisters whom they may have bullied and dominated for years found themselves having to kowtow to bullies themselves.

The masters were another kind of hazard. Frustrated men who wished to form meaningful contact with the boys they hoped to educate were thwarted by the mischievous antics of the bright or the dull acquiescence of the dim; some were driven to violence, and others to misplaced affection verging on paedophilia, hopefully repressed, and others resorting to alcohol and slow disintegration.

A few masters excelled and became the ideal father figures sought by their developing charges. So it was with a certain Mr. Hopkins who was the sports teacher who recognised that the dispirited and beaten down Charles could play rugby.

Charles very soon gained the nickname "Soddy" as his middle name Sojenji became known. His lustrous curly black hair and his smooth complexion and ready smile made him attractive to all and especially to one blue eyed bouncy squirt called Billy Tiley who arrived the year after Hopkins discovered Charles's rugby potential. Charles had grown by this time into a reasonably fast, muscular and brave player for the school seconds. Billy, younger and quite small but even braver was tried out as scrum half and then made his place in the team as full back proving that bravery in low tackling was invaluable. He trained hard to kick long and sure and soon gained a secure place in the first team along with Charles.

Billy and Soddy soon became inseparable although they were in different years. After rugger games the boys went to two primitive baths to remove the mud. The two were in the habit of wallowing long after all the others had dispersed adding fresh hot water to the muddy soup remaining. What they talked about Charles could not remember but they chatted back and forth incessantly. It seems all this time together was not sufficient because they took to meeting at night in the tank room at the top of the old mansion which was the school house and chatting away there or sharing the earphones of Billy's cassettes player. As time went by they discovered it was more comfortable for them to share Charles's bed for these meetings. Mutual enjoyment of Radio One and close bodily contact was the basis of a rather innocent association where they professed their love for each other. They were only eleven and twelve and they discussed everything from exciting times abroad swimming in clear blue tropical seas, sailing dinghies, shagging gypsy girls, climbing mountains, shooting rapids and rugby tactics. They were happy.

32

Neither seemed to be upset or bothered when Charles moved on to Brookham Manor, a minor public school where he went through the whole initiation process again. Being a naturally ebullient and cheerful boy with a strong streak of independence and a growing belief in the rights of the underdog he came to the attention of the self important prefects. Their duty it was to ensure conformity to all the petty regulations and customs of the school. Charles was well able to outwit them in deceit and cunning but they always seemed to assume, without evidence, that they had been duped. When they managed to get him on some minor or trumped up misdemeanour they hit him with the maximum force, no doubt, justifying their brutality with the self righteousness so prevalent in the bullying psyche.

His early career at this place was mediocre but he managed to do well at certain studies. In rugby he made the seconds as his interest waned in his third year. He became fascinated by the processes of biology particularly in relation to the human body. It had a lot had to do with one of the teachers he encountered. As with many adults who follow a profession they can point to certain teachers who enthused them in the subject most important to their future development. So it had been with Charles and with a certain Mr. Smith. Smith was an unfulfilled medic who, by default, had trained as a school teacher. He did not have the mental capacity to win scholarships and his humble background, whilst not allowing his parents to support him in the pursuit of his ambition to be a doctor, left him with several disadvantages including a thick Birmingham accent which the snobbish little toffs he tried to teach would mimic mercilessly, embarrassing him at critical times. He had strayed into the private school system through a mixture of dogged egalitarian idealism, good nature and contrarily a misplaced respect for the upper classes and even a desire to join them.

33

Charles considered his first two years at Brookham an emotional void but at fifteen he discovered girls. Suddenly like a flower in a meadow he seemed to be attractive; no longer gangly, mop headed and uncertain he was an olive skinned Adonis. As boys of his age do he took care of his appearance, dealing immediately with the occasional zit, brushing his hair into lustrous waves, pulling his shoulders back, and even creasing his trousers into impressive sharp edges. His first beautiful experience was with a rather frail and petite girl, Veronica, who would walk with him on Sundays after church. They had met at the village fair where he had been part of the school gymnastic exhibition allowed loose after their display with a couple of pounds of pocket money to buy ice cream or, if they could manage it, cider. She had shared a plastic cup of cider with him and become giggly and infatuated at the same time. There was also his best friend's sister a couple of years his senior who took him for the same age as he seemed to have a natural talent for very deep and satisfying kissing.

Having no interest in cricket in the summer term, Charles joined the thriving Sea Scout crew who would spend a couple of afternoons a week pulling a heavy old whaler up and down the river, a glorious unsupervised excursion in the summer sunshine. It was an opportunity to smoke cheap cigarettes huddled under a stiff tarpaulin, the oars forming tent posts. Occasionally there was a special treat for the boys of the Scouts to take out an old motor lifeboat. On one such occasion, on a holiday afternoon for Ascension Day, Charles was the skipper of the boat as they motored happily up the river. Out of sight they produced bottles of beer and "butts" to smoke in a leisurely fashion while cruising. They spotted a gaggle of girls in severe navy blue uniforms on the towpath and, perhaps lightheaded from the beer and tobacco, Charles maneuvered the boat smoothly to the bank and offered the girls a cruise complete with beer and smokes. How could they refuse?

At sweet sixteen Julie was an accomplished flirt. She immediately spotted the most advantageous spot to pose herself crossing her shapely legs over the edge of the wooden engine cover. Convent girls have a reputation to defend and she was well able to do that with her deep blue eyes and high cheekbones and ready laugh. Charles and she were each leader of their small group. It had been she who had persuaded the more reluctant of her little gaggle to accept his offer. An adventure on the river would spice up a boring afternoon walking on the towpath doing nothing very much. They all took a swig or two of the beer and a puff of the boys' ciggies. Charles made several shy eye contacts with Julie and blushed as he searched his mind for things to say that would not sound crass or might even be funny. But who cared? They were busy imprinting shapes and colours gestures and smiles into each other's minds. What was actually said was not important unless it was objectionable. He was impressed by her demure, smiling acknowledgement of his remarks. She was conscious of his apparent command and confident humour. They found common ground after a few shy moments: the nuns and the teachers at St. Agnes's were a good source of ridicule as were the masters and instructors at Brookham. So before the joy of the party evaporated in a very close near fatality they began to feel wonderful hormone-driven joy and magnetism.

The happy occasion was lost in a split second. No one except Julie really noticed it happen, and she only because of the pain of a graze on the side of her neck and a sudden cool feeling as her cape disappeared from her shoulders.

"Where's my cape? That hurt, you bloody thug." She shrieked, looking directly at Charles. There was no sign of the garment but the noise from the motor had changed. A regular clunk had added itself to the faster vibration and noise of the engine. Immediately Charles dived for the throttle and the gear lever, disengaging the propeller and idling the engine. Looking down he saw the evidence. Wrapped tightly round the prop shaft in a solid ball were the remains of the cape. There was a gasp from everyone on the boat as the reality of what had happened dawned on them.

"My God, you could so easily have been killed. The clasp was unhooked wasn't it? Saved your life." said Susie, who was sitting next to her on the engine box. "It might have been me look mine's done up. If mine had been caught it would have strangled me!"

Julie was obviously shaken but it had all happened so fast she had not had time to be frightened.

"Your neck is bleeding. The clasp must have scratched you as it was pulled off you." said Charles.

A rusty first aid box yielded a small sachet of surgical spirit and some cotton pads and Elastoplast adhesive bandage in sealed packets. Tenderly Charles attended to the small wound. The girls all disembarked, on to the bank of the river, amid rather stilted goodbyes. Charles jumped over with them and took Julie's hands in his.

"Terrible," he said.

"It's OK," she replied. "I'll say someone stole my cape. Of course I'll be in trouble, but I'm not dead and you aren't on a manslaughter charge."

"Why are you so cool?"

"Because I met you, silly. You saved me now you've got me for life. You'll have to really kill me to get rid of me now."

"Don't say that. I am going to have nightmares anyway."

"Write to me: St Agnes's, Julie Runcorn. We'll meet again for sure. We must make it happen."

34

Charles was speechless and absolutely bowled over. He did not have nightmares but fantasies ranging from rescuing Julie from marauding monsters, climbing mountains with her, sewing her up after tragic accidents and lying with her on white beaches in obscure places. He managed to conjure up all the features of her face and dreamt of kissing her beautiful soft lips. In fact it soon became impossible to avoid the image of her face from crowding out other thoughts.

He wrote several letters until he got round to posting one. It was answered immediately. In fairly mild terms it stated how much she had enjoyed meeting him. She was surprised he had actually written. "Boys tend to say things and not do them." She would like to see him again but the convent school was "like Fort Knox most of the time and they were treated like the gold bars: not to be let out." However, would he and Steve like to scale the wall, clamber over the roof and come and see them in the dorm? To Charles this did not seem to be a silly idea. The school encouraged plenty of physical pursuits and he was superbly fit from circuit training and long country runs. Scaling a mere fifteen foot high wall would be a manageable task worth planning. He and Steve got to plotting. It was clear from her letter that they were expected to enter through a window which would be left open for them.

They knew getting caught would be letting themselves in for immediate expulsion and perhaps criminal charges. What would they do once inside? Being boys of a certain age their thoughts turned naturally to the warmth and comfort of soft nubile young bodies and deeds only imagined and illustrated in porn magazines. Enough incentive to make a serious attempt: After all, they were the brave types that would conquer Everest given the chance.

With these overwhelming motivators Charles wrote back to Julie asking for more details and received a detailed plan of the roof top, the letter box which would give them a lift-off to the wall and instructions to bring a rope about ten feet long and clear sketches of how to make it into a loop with four or five knots for foot holds.

In his next letter Charles asked how she knew all these practical details. She answered that her dad was merchant navy captain and had made her and her sister learn all sorts of knots and their uses. Incidentally she added that the wall had brick piers built into it which were capped with terra cotta pointed pyramids which would guide a well thrown rope loop over them and there was one conveniently near to the pillar box, shown in the diagram.

The boys hunted high and low for a rope of the right type and found the junior school tug-of-war rope, long forgotten in the bottom of a sports gear locker in the old abandoned changing rooms. They cut off the appropriate amount and set about creating the requisite ladder by tying double twisted reef knots about half a metre apart downwards from the three meter loop. They tested it out on a wall in the school and it worked from ground level up to a height of about ten feet.

They practiced their descent over the roof of the classroom block passing dangerously close to the housemaster's bedroom. They reckoned he would be gin-sodden by one o'clock so planned their escape for one-thirty sharp.

The expedition was a success, in the sense that they made it into the convent and the dorm but it did not come near to the boys' fantasies of a sexual initiation. The boys were sweaty and dirty in their track suits and the girls were wrapped up warm in their flannel dressing gowns and winceyette pyjamas. They were all shy and reserved. They talked about the adventure of getting there and how clever the girls had been to map out the route and how much the girls admired the boys for being so gutsy but after about half an hour it dawned on them all what a dangerous predicament they had created. None of them even considered any further mischief. The route had to be reversed with minimum risk. None of them could face the consequences of discovery. Fear was to be the new motivator. So the boys pecked the girls on their cheeks squeezing hands and planned their escape. Except for the surprise of a light coming on and a small window opening as they descended, they encountered no hazards, no bobbies on the beat nor panda cars looking for missing persons so they managed to get back to their own dormitories on the other side of town without incident.

Tired though they were the next morning, it was with the most enormous satisfaction that they grinned almost continuously to each other. They knew they had achieved something. Charles was pretty sure he knew, from his point of view, what it was. Two days later it was confirmed. He received the most effusive letter from Julie asking if she could come over and see him the following Sunday as she had worked out a scam to go to a church hall concert with two friends as part of her classical music studies. She and her companions would be trusted to take four hours out of school. She would not be accompanied to the vestry if he would meet her there. So began a lifelong bond.

35

Julie went overseas to her parents in Bombay for the summer and Charles went to join his in Brazil. They wrote a few passionate letters but the post was slow and they did not have access to email.

The autumn term began and Charles and Steve started training for the rugby seconds both having a good chance of making the first fifteen.

To keep their skills up, as they called it, he and Steve planned a series of night time expeditions or 'creeps' for the next few weeks. Charles was caught. He dislodged a slate just outside the housemaster's room. As the slate crashed to the ground the sash window of the bedroom shot up and Mr. Grantham, bleary-eyed but fully awake was staring into his face. Ever sarcastic: "Coming in for a cup of cocoa, boy?" he asked. "Get yourself in here, Dormand. I've been after you for while." When Charles was inside the window, the master led him through the bedroom which stank of stale alcohol and in to his day room or 'study'.

"Sit down." The master sat at his desk while Charles perched opposite on a hard chair. "Well, you've properly stuffed yourself now. No more caning. You'll be before the head in the morning and possibly expelled. Where were you going? No clandestine assignations, I hope."

"I couldn't sleep, sir," Charles said, trying to look innocent, perched on the edge of the chair.

"So you decided to risk your life and disturb the peace by crashing around on the roof, dislodging slates and causing mayhem."

"That was an accident, sir."

"Ah, you did not want to wake me up at this ungodly hour! So you were making some sort of *rendez-vous*. Who with?"

"With whom? Sir." Charles said without thinking.

The housemaster's eyes nearly popped out of their sockets.

"Sorry, sir. Nobody,sir. I needed fresh air, sir."

"Well, never mind. You nearly met your maker and you met me instead. Are you satisfied? The headmaster will deal with you in the morning. Go back to bed and let me go back to sleep."

Charles started to rise from his chair and could not help noticing the master's eyes go directly towards the cabinet where all the boys knew he kept his supply of gin.

As it happened the headmaster, "Crabby" Crabtree, was not inclined to expel boys for harmless pranks especially as he had, the previous term, received a phone call from the Mother Superior of St. Agnes's with an absurd and pleasingly uncertain enquiry about boys possibly visiting her girls at night. He had not followed up the enquiry and knew he had to treat Charles's misdemeanour as inconsequential in case further investigation revealed some seriously bad behaviour leading to expulsion. He needed to avoid unwanted attention from the press, always sniping at the private schools of the wealthy. He therefore stripped Charles of all his privileges, demoted him from junior prefect, immediately promoting another boy and giving him ten hours of detention and four hours of outdoor chores every week, thus spoiling his chances of making the rugby firsts. He instructed all his teachers to load him with study tasks, essays and reports to fill all the detention hours and he put Mr. Grantham in charge of assuring Charles complied. The housemaster was not at all pleased with this arrangement so he did everything possible to make Charles's life disagreeable.

36

Charles's first reaction was pure rebellion. He messed up his assignments, failed to show up at appointed times and became generally unmanageable around the school until "Bumble" Smith took him aside one day, sat him down and like a Dutch uncle coaxed him into seeing the positive side of his predicament.

"This is your chance to get ahead. With all this study time you could be getting the four A grades you need to go on to university." He pronounced the word with a horrible emphasis; a bitter reverence. "You want to be a doctor; carry on like this and you might get a position as a porter, worthy as that would be but not so satisfying. If I cannot persuade you to change your attitude I will personally be very disappointed. Let me tell you why I am teaching chemistry and anatomy in this place."
Suddenly his tone changed and Charles thought he saw a tear in the master's eye. He was angry. Smith looked up at the lanky sixteen year-old. "You bloody spoilt brats don't know you're alive. Your parents have money to burn and you waste it. Well, damn you. You pull yourself together and get on with the task. If you change your attitude you might make an excellent medic, save lives, gain respect and a good standing in life. Don't throw that away, Dormand, you little bastard."

"You're right, sir,"

Smith had calmed down and was acute enough to detect a nuance in Charles's reply.

"What, then?"

"I am a bastard, legally"

Smith paused for a moment non-plussed and then burst into laughter. "Jesus wept, full of surprises, you are." He spluttered. The relief to both of them was immediate and profound. Charles joined in the infectious laughter giggling almost uncontrollably. He realised subconsciously that he had never seen this dapper and mismaligned little man laugh before. Soon real tears rolled down both of their cheeks.

After several minutes Smith stopped suddenly and said very sincerely, "God bless you, son. Don't hold it against yourself. History is full of *enfants natureux*, (pronounced the Brummy way) boys and girls who have risen to the top. Promise me you will do it too. Will you do it?" He held out his hand in a rather stiff gesture of friendship. Charles took the hand shook it gently and as Mr. Smith turned to leave the classroom sat down, put his head on the desk in front of him and sobbed the deepest sobs ever.

He felt as if the encounter was a cleansing of his soul. From then on, he threw his whole being into his work and, in the trials, got straight A plus grades. Mr. Smith never mentioned the incident but there was a new and powerful bond between the two of them.

Charles was happy again: it was clear from the letters he received from Julie that she adored him or at least she adored the images of him she had imprinted from their brief meetings, and they managed to meet more or less legitimately two or three more times that term.

His friendship with Mr. Smith grew stronger almost into obsessive love as they revised his subjects and explored the internet for knowledge. One day completely unexpectedly while they were going over some tricky chemistry process Smith turned to Charles and said, "You know, Charles, I have come to terms with not being a brilliant man. If I had been given the chances you have, I may have become a mediocre doctor and been a lot better off. Helping you has made me realise the great satisfaction being 'just' a teacher can bring. I see my job differently. If I can help a few like you to get through your teenage years and make into a decent career I will not feel wasted."

"Thank you, sir," was all Charles could manage.

37

Of course, Bertrand was overjoyed when Charles received his pass slips showing four straight 'A' plus grades: all that he needed to go on to Exeter to study medicine. Keen for his son to progress as far as possible with whatever medical studies he wanted to go for, he financed him fully through college for his MBBS, B.Sc.

It was in the early part of his third year, as he contemplated the testing period of exams, that Charles went into a stress related deep depression. For reasons only known to psychologists, he became obsessed by the life changing remark he had made to "Bumble" Smith: Life-changing because the run-in with his favourite and beloved pedagogue was what caused him to get a grip on his life, take his studies seriously and motor on through A levels and entry interviews. He had turned instantly from an unruly teenager in to a swat. The crucial remark was, of course, his admission to being a bastard. His father Bertrand had explained his origins to him a year before: How Charles was the result of a loving relationship with an African girl called Anwei and how Bertrand had had to leave her, not knowing she had conceived, and had married Sophie; how Charles had been born in a village in upcountry Cameroon and nearly died on the road to Douala; how his adoptive mother had immediately responded open-heartedly to his impoverished birth mother's request to adopt him. Then his father had said to him, "I am very proud of you as my son." Charles, taking all the information into the hard drive of his brain, had seen no reason to take action or tell anyone. It was just not very interesting.

In his deep depression all this clutter came swarming to his mind. He resented greatly that his African origins had been repressed. He was thoroughly europeanised. His olive skin, deep dark eyes and curly hair were more pronounced now he was gaining his manly persona. He needed to find his mother and explore his African identity. This unresolved problem was adding to his general stress level. He took to flopping down in front of a small portable television all day, not really watching letting feature after feature pass by his eyes. His father had told him about his name Sojenji being that of his mother's family. Through the fog of his distress he formed an unplanned resolution to go to Africa to find his mother.

It was by chance that he was informed by a TV program that it is quick, easy and cheap to change one's name by deed poll. That was the next step he would take. He informed the university authorities and his parents in a badly worded letter that he was to be known as Charles Sojenji from now on and his previous name of Dormand was no longer to be used. That done he concentrated anew on his studies.

When he went home for Christmas he found his father, far from the gentle and benign parent of old, was furious.

"You are throwing everything we have done for you in our faces."

"No, you and Sophie stole me away from my roots. You abandoned my birth mother. What happened to her? You left her to starve or be enslaved. You don't even know where she is, do you? Typical big white boss man: get the native girl pregnant and abandon her."

Bertrand's anger subsided as he managed to put his son's words into context. He knew he might have done a better job of informing Charles about the circumstances of his birth, the fact that he had done his best for Anwei; how Sophie had her own reasons for being so anxious to care for the baby offered to her in the sweltering heat at the airport, how Anwei had suddenly disappeared after a couple of years and he had not had time or the freedom to pursue her; how he was sure she would have found a way of life which would not involve him anymore; a thoroughly African way of life in Douala. Now he had to face up to the view of this angry youth standing over him. He opened his mouth to speak but Charles had left.

It was six months later when Charles came home with his finals results and the invitation to his graduation ceremony. Father and son were one again.

"Thanks, Dad."

"No," he paused, "thank you. You make me so proud. Go and show your mother and apologise to her for your behaviour during the year. I told her it was exam nerves and she believed me, but she was hurt when she guessed what it was really all about."

115

38

Later that week Charles proposed to his father that he put the books aside and do something practical and if it were medical all the better. He had made enquiries about *Medicins Sans Frontieres*. They had offered him a place in Democratic Republic of Congo. An opportunity to do some real field medicine seemed ideal in spite of his father's misgivings about entering a chronic war zone known to be rife with bands of terrorists and war lords. Little did they know how it would change his life.

Julie was no less apprehensive. She was nearing the end of her training as a nurse, no doubt a choice of career influenced by Charles's medical ambitions. She realised there was no holding him. There was a tearful parting and she was worried she might never see him again. The preparations were all made and Charles set off first to France for the training course, compulsory for all new recruits.

Part 2: Krels's Story

1

It had been a grand day. They had made bows from strong saplings in a stand near the muddy hole and cut some arrows. The bows had been long and had taken all morning to make. They had made straight arrows from a bamboo nearby and feathered them carefully. Bontong had taken the lead all morning showing Joaquim "Joe" Krels how to split the saplings and tie the gut taken from a broken tennis racket. Joe had taken some heavy nails from the farm workshop to insert for the tips.

The morning was rounded off perfectly with a bathe in the cool water of the pond they called the Pig Hole, a favourite with them going years back. They had splashed and played and dived in from the bank. They dried off in the sun before donning their clothes and making their way back to the worker's galley to get simple food.

They had gone stalking in the afternoon and brought down a small buck, proudly bringing it back to the farm to show Joaquim's father. That evening after eating with the house cook in the kitchen, they had stayed in Joe's room reading comics and chatting. It was the precursor to a disaster.

Bontong was supposed to go back to the quarters at nine, according to Krels Senior's rules, but these were often ignored, and Joaquim's parents were out on the stoep drinking brandy with friends from a neighbouring farm. It was getting pretty late.

"I have a gun," said Joe.

"Yeah, for real?"

"Of course for bloody real, man."

"OK, OK."

"Right."

"Are you going to show me? Where'd you get it?"

"Won it in a bet at school. It's up there."

There was a loose plank in the varnished boarded ceiling running along one wall, creating a hiding place for the small collection of secret items a fourteen-year-old boy wishes to keep to himself.

"Right then, let's get it down," said Bontong. "I want to see this. You got ammo?"

"It takes five millimetre, come."

They both stood up on the antique Dutch chest that had been against the wall for the fifty years of the bungalow's life. Their shoulders were just below the ceiling line. There was a gap in the boards of the next room and the light coming up drew their attention. Bontong signalled silently, pointing with his eyes.

There, lying on the bed was Joe's sister Avis, his senior by a year and a half. In her left hand she held a small photograph, and the other was beneath the thin sheet, reaching down between her thighs. There was rhythmic movement. The boys were hypnotised; they had never seen the like of this before. She started moving her hips more, and dropping the photo, she moved her left hand to her breasts. Her mouth was forming a tight purse: Joaquim recognised the expression she always used when concentrating hard to do some intricate task. Her eyes closed. She then rolled over onto her front and with a few violent gasps came to rest with a great deep exhalation of breath.

The gun forgotten, they climbed down.

"That's how girls do it," said Joaquim uncertainly.

"Yes, but Avis…I mean…white girls do that?"

There was silence.

"Here, feel this," said Joaquim, and smiling mischievously, he took Bontong's right hand and placed it on his trousers, through which could be felt his erection.

"Man, this too," said Bontong. There was a short intense silence. Their embarrassment was broken by Bontong.

"Look at that moon. I'm going to get caught for sure. I'll be dead meat." He sloped off toward the veranda door. "The dogs will bark and the old man will beat me."

His bare feet padded silently over the beaten earth of the compound.

The next morning Bontong showed up late.

"Hiya, Joe!" said Bontong.

"You're late," said Joaquim, "we've missed our chance at the river."

"My dad had me do some chores. He must have heard me come home last night. He was angry, but I think he's given up on the beatings."

They stood apart, awkwardness showing in both their attitudes.

"What we did last night...," said Joaquim.

"Hey, brother, you know, if you ever want to, some of the girls in the compound...well, you know, they get to fool around sometimes. Man, they like it."

"Forget it," said Joe, his expression hardening to disgust. This was forbidden territory. Both boys knew it. To Joaquim it was exciting but so far out of reach he should not even contemplate it.

"Forget it, Bo." He smiled easily to soften the offence. "Hey, Friday, bazanga! I'm gone." It was easy to announce it now, in contrast to the more disturbing subject just avoided, but he had been dreading the day all through the summer. On Friday he was to go to Greenswards Secondary College for boys in Bloemfontein.

2

In December 1987, after two uneventful years during which Joaquim had demonstrated, along with a small gang of malcontents, his unsuitability to the indoor life and academic pursuits of a city boarding school, he had returned home to his parents to find major changes at the farm. The bungalow had been fenced round, excluding the old farmhouse or "the quarters." Trees had been cut down, and many of the paddock fences had been removed.

"What's all this, Pa?" he'd asked as soon as he saw his father.

"A few changes." His father looked drawn and old and was not smiling.

Joaquim had gone to his room. He hated the way it was in the house now with iron gates over all the bedroom doors and bars at the windows. Last year his father had reluctantly agreed with Mr. Kaesle, the insurance broker, to have the place secured.

He joined his father on the stoop.

"I have bad news. You've seen the results. We've been foreclosed," Krels Senior said when Joe joined him. The father gave his son a glass of beer.

"It's a bloody disaster. But it's my fault. That's what upsets me so much. That nice Mr. Kaesle got me wound up on such a deal, I was to retire a millionaire. Now I am made to feel lucky that I can live in my own house. Anyway, I had to sell off the land, or rather the bank did."

"All of it?"

"I managed to save the old village and this house with the yard and the garden. The new farm manager will live in a small bungalow over there on the site of the old quarters. The blacks had to go back to the village. This will all be arable. These new people have got no idea, but they sold all the livestock on a low market. I got land deeds made out for the villagers, but they squabbled amongst themselves, so I had to help them subdivide it. They then accused me of stealing their birthright."

"No pleasing them. But Pa, our family has owned this land for a hundred, two hundred years. How come the bank can take it away?" Joaquim interjected.

"Well, the truth is I screwed it for me and your ma, and I screwed it for them as well. Kaesle promised me an easy retirement on an enormous pension. I had money worries as the price of beef was on the floor. After all the good news he told me about investing in derivatives, he said the farm had to be used for security on the loan used to secure some sort of financial instrument. 'No risk,' he says. 'The banks never foreclose on farmers, whatever happens.' All that changed because he and a crew of buggers just like him had sewn up a lot of farmers and the banks had no choice when we failed to keep up repayments. The Corporates saw their chance and with the same money bought us up cheap, and now the arable crops are going in all round us. The cattle all went for dog-meat and corned beef at rock-bottom prices. The big machinery moved in destroying all the fences and trees.

"All the boys and servants feel betrayed. None of them will work on the farm or in the house at the moment. They're all in a big sulk. Your mother is cooking and managing here." He stood up to get a couple more beers from the fridge in the corner of the veranda.

"It's extraordinary that a storm in a little corner of Southern England can ruin me and send businessmen from New York to Tokyo to the wall. It was in October. By November I knew I was broke and up to my neck in debt to some bank in the US with assets in Hong Kong, worthless. I had to look on a world map to find Hong Kong. Turns out it's a tiny island near China. I thought my money was in London. But never mind, London was just as bad."

Joaquim had not paid much attention to the newspapers, but no one could fail to have heard something of the crash that had sent stock markets plunging in London and round the world. It would not have affected his father except that he had hocked the farm to get into Hong Kong derivatives, becoming a paper multimillionaire in three months. He had lost it all in three days when the market took three stepped drops and every geared security, bond, and leveraged investment dropped five to ten times as fast, mocking the fall-back provisions and making rash gamblers out of timid shopkeepers and prudent businessmen all round the world. And here was a stolid Boer like Maartin Krels in amongst them.

"So what now?"

"Well, look, your results at school—"

"I know Pa, not good. And all that on top of this."

"Stick around until your call-up. Do that for the country. God knows we need it. That de Klerk looks like he'll give the whole lot to Mandela. Where de Klerk's coming from, I don't know. A black president is what we might have. What is happening? A woman prime minister in UK and now this Mandela, who is a known terrorist.

"Anyway, whatever happens someone has to keep law and order. When you come out of the army, you could join SASS and really make a difference."

He paused to light a cigarette.

"The fact is, my boy, your ma and I can just about get by if things don't get worse, but your school fees, man, do you know how much that costs?"

Joe was pleased but was not too quick to show his father. There was a little capital to be made here.

"If necessary I can leave, Pa, that's OK."

"We'll see. Right now, those contractors are a bit short of help and they need someone to operate a digger. I said you might be interested. They will train you. Our boys aren't working, and the firm would only take one if he was fully trained already. Pay's not bad and it will give you some pocket money. I think you will be knocking down the old house so they can put up the new one. The surveyor said the timber's rotten and the families ruined everything else."

So Joaquim settled down to a Christmas holiday of enjoyable vandalism on the old three-story Dutch farmhouse. The servants stayed away from the family, which seemed to be a relief to his parents who, without the responsibilities of the farm, found the domestic work a therapeutic distraction.

But things were scarce. Nothing in the house was renewed or repaired. His mother had started cultivating the one-acre garden they had salvaged from the farm, keeping chickens for eggs and a few sheep for meat and a couple of cows saved from the herd. They bought groceries in small quantities, and items like beer became a luxury, not a habit. Joe spent some of his money on such luxuries, and his father soon got used to accepting gifts of beer and cigarettes to supplement the meagre amounts he was allowing himself out of the housekeeping budget.

On Christmas Eve a tall, lean man known as Vincent, who had been the senior stockman, came to see his father. He was polite at first but it was plain to see he was on a mission. The conversation was becoming heated. Vincent and Maarten were both standing. Joe saw Vincent start to wave his arms in great gestures. He smiled. He knew this man, Bontong's father, and had loved his display of arm waving when he became excited or frustrated. Usually his words emerged through a half smile in expectation of a good-hearted counter argument, but tonight things looked different. Joe walked over and stood beside his father. Very uncharacteristically Vincent did not even greet him.

"We don't have the bonus, and then we don't have Christmas food for the family. Look at you, baas. You lost nothing. You still got your nice house, good food. Even the little baas working and getting good money. We go down the old village and try to move in with the old parents. No food, everything primitive. Big wire fence all round. We are just trash now. Yes, I tell you, trash. Boys have all gone to the town. Not much work there except to join gangs of skollies. Girls, I worry about the girls. Keep screaming, 'What's happening to us?' Babies all hungry. Girls threatening to go into town at twelve, thirteen, fourteen. You know what happens to them?" He lowered his tone and looked to the ground. "You know what happens to them," he repeated as a statement, more like a shameful accusation.

"Go," said his father, now angry, "leave. I have done all I can do and I have said all I have to say."

Vincent was stumped. He had said his piece. He had lost. He was angry. The white man was dismissing him. Joaquim Senior was too weary, too ashamed. He'd fought hard to keep the village from the bank. He had made sure the well and the pump were also kept for the villagers. Now they wanted more and he knew their demands were fair.

Vincent put his soft hat on his head. "Yes, baas, thank you, baas," he muttered almost inaudibly.

Slowly he stood tall, all his six feet, and stared hard at the baas. Maarten felt acute remorse for the power he had inherited and misused, but he had been trained from early childhood never to weaken. They stared at each other for a full fifteen seconds.

"*Amandla ngawethu*," (power to the people), Vincent finally said quietly and deliberately. He backed off without breaking eye contact during the retreat of two metres and then turned and, stiffly erect, walked away.

"Arrogant bastard. All you've done for those people over all these years and they want more. Kaffirs always want more," Joe said and handed his father a beer.

His father hated to hear Joe using such a word, but he was too beaten to correct him.

Their dinner that Christmas Eve was quiet and stilted. Avis and their mother cooked a large cockerel and some festive items. Maarten opened a bottle of red and another of white wine, but the dinner was mostly silent. Joe and Avis seemed to drink most of the wine, as their parents were too inhibited to drink more than their first glass. When he went to bed, Joe thought of the encounter with Vincent. It might not be seriously threatening. He had seen him angry many times, but he had always appeared with a smiling face and a will to work the next morning.

They went to bed in silence after having said good night with formal familial kisses.

3

Joaquim was awoken by the loud crash of the grill on his bedroom door being slammed shut and chains being wrapped round the bars to tie it shut. Harsh voices in whispers were giving instructions in the village patois, Swahili, Afrikaans, pidgin, and local words. He understood snippets.

Bare feet smacked on the tiled floor. There was more crashing as the various gratings, designed to keep intruders out, were being secured to imprison his parents and his sister.

They had moved on down to the large living and dining room, probably four or five of them.

"In here, get all this shit out. Hey, always wanted to drink from these."

"Idiot!" said another voice, and there was a metallic crash. Joe thought it was probably the shooting trophy he had so proudly won this year.

There was a lot of noise from the dining room and kitchen. They were eating and drinking.

"Here, beer," said a voice. "Brandy," said another.

He could hear the fan of the fridge; the door was open.

"Hey, get this milk. The babies want it." There was a crash. "Imbecile! Look at the mess."

"Put those tins in the wheelbarrow."

"We can take jewels. The whites have jewels and money."

"The safe will be behind a picture. I've seen it on the bioscope." There was a splintering of wood and tinkle of glass as pictures were ripped off the walls and thrown down.

"No safe."

"The baas's bedroom."

He heard them leaving the lounge area and entering the passage. There was a crash and the noise of the telephone bell striking the floor and then the dull purr of the dial tone.

"Don't want the bastards from the police coming here."

Joe heard the rattle of chains being ripped off one of the grills.

There was a scream as his mother was pacified, and the old man shouted, but was silenced quickly. There were more noises of destruction as the men searched for the nonexistent safe.

Joaquim could do nothing. The bars on his room were tied tight with the chain, and he could not reach through to loosen the knot without being heard or seen by the raiders.

He knew not to shout. They would beat him or kill him if they became aware of him. So he bit his tongue and tried to control his anger. He wanted to know who they were, but he'd been off the farm for some time save for a couple of two-week visits and could not recognise the voices. The men were leaving his parents' room. He withdrew deeper into his own room and flattened himself against the wall.

"What's in here?"

"The girl. I told you."

"The chot you fancy."

"Just a white girl."

"You're going to get your cake tonight."

Joaquim heard the chains being ripped off the grill next to his. He heard screams and then, "Get out, no, no. My God, not you, Bontong!" And then he recognized the deeper tones of the same voice. It had been two years since he had heard his friend speak.

He climbed up on the chest to hear more plainly what was happening, and he looked down into her room. They were pinning her down on the bed. She had stopped screaming because there was a broad piece of cloth over her face.

He saw Bontong from behind; he was taller now. Joe could see his face from the side. It had lost its boyishness. The rose-petal mouth was now a harder gash, and the skin was of a rougher texture with a slight growth of beard. He could see Bontong was frightened. The trusted guest in the house where the boys had spent all those many years together was now being faced with a harsh choice. Joe could only see part of his sister. Her flesh was waxy white in the light of a candle brought from the other room. She was tied with webbing normally used on the farm for restraining cattle. They had splayed her to the wooden posts of the heavy oak bed frame. One of the men turned to Bontong and shouted at him in words Joe did not understand. Then he seized him round the neck, and the other man pulled his ragged jeans off him. They jeered at him, but Joe could see that Bontong was partially excited but still afraid. Then the men started to make more encouraging sounds, and the words they spoke were more gentle and persuasive.

Avis had stopped struggling and the atmosphere in the room seemed to electrify with tension. There was a quiet period of perhaps a minute during which Bontong was staring directly at the girl on the bed. Joe was frozen. He saw the naked man-boy climb onto the bed and start caressing the white body of his sister. His hands molested her breasts and her crotch and returned to his genitals, massaging himself into readiness. Joe nearly panicked and gave himself away. His right hand moved and he felt a hard metallic object. The gun! It had been forgotten all those months ago, and now furiously ashamed he remembered why.

126

He hefted the small pistol in his hand: a 'handbag' gun. His left hand found the ammunition. Expertly he loaded the weapon, taking care not to make a noise. It was a two-barrelled type like a Derringer. He now had a view through the planking of the rise and fall of Bontong's tight muscular buttocks. On the pillow he could see the reddish flame of his sister's wavy hair and the boy's black hands grasping a sheaf of it. He aimed below the nape of his neck. He noticed idly the fat that had developed there in the last two years. He pulled the trigger. The report was earsplitting, as he had discharged the weapon near to his face. He looked down. The scene was confused. Bontong had rolled onto the floor, and his sister's mouth was a mass of blood. He aimed again this time at the chest of the boy and squeezed the trigger.

From one side of the frame of his view, he saw a movement. One of the men had a gun. Joe dropped off the linen chest, dived across the room and hid in the massive mahogany wardrobe. Through the door he heard the men come out of the next bedroom and approach his. There was a shrieked discussion. They would have to spend time unchaining his grill if they wanted to get him. They were now very frightened and agitated, so they decided to run.

Joe's heart was racing and he was very confused by what he had seen. He was sure he had shot Bontong the first time. The blood on Avis's body must have been his. But why on her mouth? Something about the line of her mouth was not right. He began to fear that the bullet had passed through and killed her.

Now the men had gone, he needed to get to his parents.

He left the wardrobe and attacked the chains on the gate. It seemed to take an age to undo the series of random knots but at last he managed. He wanted to avoid Avis's room but the grill was open and the door behind it ajar. He entered. He went to his sister first and felt her neck for a pulse. There was a weak throb but she was not breathing. Her mouth was a mess and he saw that the bullet had knocked some teeth out and penetrated the palate. Her tongue was swollen. He untied the webbing straps and rolled her body on its side and put his finger into the mouth cavity pushing the tongue forward and down. There was a sudden inhalation of breathe. Then she went into a violent spasm of coughing. He did not know what to do next. But when the spasm was over he thought she would be safe. He looked at Bontong on the floor. The candle threw a wavering pale light on him. There was a pool of blood by his chest and no movement. A feeling of contempt came over Joe as he as he kicked the grinning face to see if there was life and turned to leave.

What he found in his parents' room was completely devastating. His father was lying face down on the rug, red blood mingling with the background of the Persian motif. He went to him and knew immediately he was dead. His mother was crumpled in the corner. She was alive but unconscious. Because of her position she was snorting slightly as her head rose and fell on her chest.

Tears swelled to his eyes in grief at his father's death and the sight of his mother lifeless and ugly, with her face bloodied and distorted in pain. He stood and looked around listlessly. His head was excruciatingly painful. He focussed on the phone lying on the tiled floor of the passage. The cover with the dial was broken and torn away from the metal base. He walked over and slumped next to it and, remembering a trick he had learnt at school in the city to make a connection without putting coins in the box, held the receiver rest tight down for a count of ten and lifted it. The dull buzz of the dial tone returned. Painstakingly he tapped the numbers for the police station. After ten rings a bored voice answered.

"Leipsville Police, Sergeant Dutoit."

4

Four weeks later, having seen his mother admitted to a mental institution and his beautiful sister's face patched grotesquely back to functionality, he sat in a lawyer's office.

"I have known your father since we were boys. He was a fine, honest, and diligent man. You know your father was a rather stubborn man also. He was determined he would get the family back into solvency on his own. He refused help from his friends in the lodge and quite frankly he was very unfriendly when we tried to do anything for him. I regret that the deal he made with Growth Farms left him only with a lifetime lease on the house. From their point of view it was quite generous because the price they paid to clear his debts was over the market value of the property.

"In other words, Joaquim, all I can say is that the Church will take care of the funeral expenses, as your father was a faithful and generous parishioner, but after that there is nothing. Dr. Hoek has agreed to complete your sister's treatment at no cost, and your mother will be taken care of by the private pension and the government. Oh, and by the way, there will be no criminal charges. The police accept that you were defending yourself and your sister, Avis, in a raid. If they catch the others, they will probably take care of them also, you know the way we do things here."

So it was with Joe. He left the office dazed and made directly for the National Service recruiting office.

5

"They might put a Kaffir in the bunk next you."

"You couldn't trust the bugger not to shaft you in your sleep in one way or the other."

"The bastards can't fight. They're always thinking of raping the women."

"You wouldn't want to rely on him in a jam, for sure."

"Ag, man, fuck it I'm not staying in this bloody army any longer than I have to. What next? There'll be Hottnot officers."

"Now, that just isn't possible. You know they can't think tactics. Anyway, what white man is going to obey orders from a *dronkie*?"

"Shit, that de Klerk's giving in. There's no point in having a bleddy army; where's our biggest enemy? Come on, be honest. The enemy is all around us."

"Send the whole stinking lot to the homelands, Lesotho. Freedom's what they want; they'd be free to live their way, Make that *cont* Mandela king." There was a pause. Joe Krels took over in a more serious tone:

"I had a good friend, a Zulu, taught me to hunt with a bow, fight with sticks all sorts. I loved my friend, you know." Krels looked up as he gained the full attention of the mob around him. "Bastard raped my sister." Then he fell silent; a dull vacant expression crossed his face and slumped through his body.

"What happened to him?" Jan asked without much interest.

"I killed him," Joe said sadly.

"Oh Christ," said someone near the back. "What a country."

"It's simple; them or us."

"It's not just black and white. We can't trust the *Khakis*. The pass-whites hate us more and SASS makes us mistrust everyone."

"That's because even among us there are some liberal *khaki* scum."

"SASS is the only chance we have to get the liberals under control and the Bantu kept in their place; admit who's boss, enforce superiority," added Joe.

There was a man called Robinson lying on a bunk in the middle of the dormitory, reading. "What superiority?" he said quietly.

"Knowledge, civilisation, power," said one of the mob automatically.

"I've been listening to you planks for an hour carping on, not looking for a future, holding on to your mythological nonsense. You know what the blacks say about you boers? You've been found out. Your stupidity is only out-matched by your arrogance. But what is worse is that we get hauled through all this shit with you. No one from this Police State of South Africa is free to travel the world. No one is free to associate— not just the Bantu. I can't move about without a permit, my uncle is imprisoned in his house. South African passport isn't worth the paper it's made of. Is this normal? Americans and

Europeans laugh at us incredulously when they aren't crying out for the rights of the coloureds and the Africans. We are the detested race here and everywhere: why? Because of that fascist, Verwoerd, and the sadist, Vorster, and the SP. You care nothing for the Africans."

Before he could go any further, he was interrupted.

"Africans, what do you mean Africans? We are the Africans here. We own this land. We have been here twenty generations. You bloody *souties* don't know half the story. Fuck off out, *doos*, before I puke!"

Robinson suddenly was tired and slightly frightened by the hornets' nest he had stirred up. He knew there was no winning; even if he was able to physically beat every one of them, he knew they felt "their" apartheid was a necessity to their survival and could not be challenged, so deep in the psyche was it etched.

"I'm hungry," he said over his shoulder as he sloped off to the canteen. He was in retreat but it was not a real escape; as the cool night air hit him, he knew he would meet trouble on the way back. He would probably live, but he'd be punished yet again, beaten in the dark or the shower.

Joe Krels was boiling slowly inside. He knew there was some truth in the words of this pommie bastard but he could not admit anything. He knew he had been betrayed by his best childhood pal. He knew firsthand the violence committed. There was no yielding to liberal bullshit; give the enemy an inch and he'll take a mile. He had proof. This great change in South Africa was to him an obscenity. It just could not be allowed. His race would be submerged or annihilated; the wisdom of the forefathers would be lost; no more flaxen-haired beauties, just brown skins and black curly hair. He knew it. For some reason, no doubt the work of the Devil himself, the superior white racial characteristics were often swamped by the savage features of the primitive in the *bruin- ous*. Winding himself up tighter than a clock spring, he got to his feet, not seeing the other soldiers as they parted to let him through.

It was dark outside but across the quad he saw Robinson standing outside the canteen, chewing biltong with a Vimto in his left hand, reading notices on the illuminated notice board.

He stopped for a moment and felt bile rising in his gullet. He could never remember afterwards: Did he walk, march or run across the gap between them, and from behind did he grab the T-shirt of the unsuspecting Robinson, tightening the thin material across his windpipe and unbalancing him? But, yes, as his head fell back, Krels remembered punching his face with a vicious right fist. There was a crack as the victim's nose broke and he tumbled backwards on to the tiled steps.

"At least you're on your own." spluttered Robinson from the ground before a boot in the ribs took all his breath away. Another boot to the head finished the prone man off. Robinson said no more, ever.

Joe Krels was required in the O/C's office the following morning. Standing stiffly to attention, he was wondering how much he had to admit.

"This note was found pinned to the notice board near the body of one of your fellow soldiers, Robinson. What do you have to say?"

Krels read the message. It was simple: *"Krels did this, I cant say for frite of the bros doing me in."*

"Bullshit," said Krels. The officer raised his eyebrows.

"We can't allow this. Whatever I might think about liberals infiltrating the army, we can't have any kind of free-for-all." He paused thoughtfully, pencil poised over a printed form. He screwed up the note. "OK, I am giving you leave to discharge yourself early. Normally, you would have fifteen months to serve. You will apply on compassionate grounds, quoting your mother's condition as the reason."

"What do you know about my mother, sir?"

"Don't worry, man, we know all about you and your origin. I have been notified from above that they were always worried about your character and now we realize that was correct. You will follow the instruction I have outlined." He reached forward to give Krels the form.

"Return this before twelve hundred hours, filled in and signed. You will be off the camp by sixteen hundred hours with your back pay and your civilian kit."

So Krels was discharged without court-martial. Officially, Robinson died of accidental injuries.

SASS would not take Krels after the unofficial character report reached them. A year earlier they would not have been fazed by the killing but they had received recent instruction to reduce their violence and recruit more wisely. He had a friendly interview with the recruiting officer, who had to refuse him, but suggested Joe go up to Johannesburg to see his friend in a private security company. "Plenty of scope for your talents there," he said as Krels left the room.

6

Joe Krels did not visit his mother in the institution nor did he contact his sister. He wanted to forget all that and get on with the next phase of his life.

Security Africa was not so fussy about background and not privy to his unofficial record. The phone call from Agent Coster was enough of a recommendation. And to get a part-trained soldier on their books instead of the usual college dropouts and ex-cons was a treat.

"Right," said Francks, a large man with a bushy moustache and a polished bullet-shaped head. "What about the jungle? We have a new contract at a mine in the Congo, pretty dangerous territory. It's a good contract and we are paying high bonuses."

Krels, looking surly, said nothing.

"I wouldn't offer this to just anybody, you know. It's your training: six-week jungle warfare and survival course, four weeks special hand-to-hand combat, two weeks basic field communications. You've been busy. I know you didn't finish your service, and I know you had some sort of problem, but my good friend Coster says you are loyal and tough."

Krels perked up, his ego somewhat restored now he realised he had talents to sell.

"Right, give me the gen, I'm yours."

And so after a week's general induction and the fast-track issuance of a passport and visa, he was flown up to the Congo in the company's weekly flight to Kinshasa.

Krels was issued an Uzi pistol and a uniform, green instead of khaki. He soon learned that a few of the guards had bought black-market Kalashnikovs from itinerant vendors for the equivalent of two days' pay. The main advantage seemed to be that the 7.62 ammo was available in unlimited quantities, while the Uzi ammunition was carefully rationed by the management. Krels fitted well into the way of life and after a time bought his own AK. His willingness to go on patrols outside the camp was noticed by a bunch of geologists who had devised an interesting plan to explore beyond the reaches of the camp in their time off.

7

"Look," said Bjorn, "it's quite simple. We need protection. You are a soldier and have guns. Look after us and we'll pay you."

To Krels it was a no-brainer. He wanted some action, not like many of the others who were content to sit in a guardhouse and grow fat and lazy.

Armed with his issue Uzi and his Kalashnikov, he would accompany these mad Swedes into the jungle to do their research. He was not very aware of what they were up to, but overhearing various conversations, he became convinced they were out to make a fortune from some mineral or other—nothing obvious like silver or gold, but some obscure muddy stuff.

These expeditions were fine for several months. The location was some sort of village in a hollow, the result of thousands of years of digging for clay. Hovels were lodged in the sides of the big hole in which lepers dwelt. These lepers were workers digging out the clay, and some were potters making pots and other objects. They had primitive wheels but many were shaping the object with their bare hands. Krels knew nothing of this process but he was smart enough to admire the skills and perseverance of the deformed people who were creating beautiful things from the varicoloured, translucent material.

After a while he began to find his way around the village, often away from the geologists, who were absolutely absorbed in their quest.

On one of these expeditions, while the geologists set up their primitive equipment and got to work analysing the soil dug from their boreholes, Joe Krels wandered around the compound, no longer shocked and horrified by the deformities of the broken victims but amazed by their cheerful greetings. One young boy, perhaps fifteen years old, came up to him on bandaged stumpy legs.

In faltering English the boy said, "Hello, Mr. White Man, have you come to dig up this place we call our home?" Joe was confused by this remark. "I guess you are geol'ist going to take our min'rals, but this is our only way to get money. We need money for medicines and painkillers. You come to our shop and see what we make." The boy put out his hand, also partly bandaged but Joe instinctively backed away.

For a flicker of a second, he saw the shadow of disappointment pass across the boy's face. With an inexplicable feeling of mild guilt, Joe allowed himself to be guided by him.

"What's your name?" he asked.

"Herault," pronounced the boy, something between *hero* and *halt*. Joe could not relate to it. They trekked downhill on a winding path. On either side were the hovels of the afflicted. Some were smartly decorated with cloth curtains, having tables or stools in front, but others were like the dens of wolves or dogs, rendering the most basic shelter from the rains.

The shop was a rough wooden hut. There were some civil service desks and tables serving as counters to display the wares. The objects were a revelation, pure art, sensitive lines. The material was coloured clay ranging from bright orange to deep blues.

"Our problem is firing, that is our problem. We cannot collect wood outside the compound because if we are caught, the Mai Mai will kill us. That is our problem; many people have been killed looking for wood for the charcoal burner. So we are obliged to buy wood. That is our problem."

Joe looked over the objects on display. Many had religious significance, some of which he missed, but he could appreciated the smooth lines, beautiful curves, and subtle blending of the colours.

Joe was beginning to feel emotionally hooked by what he was seeing when unexpectedly a gruff Irish voice interrupted his thoughts. "What do you think of our little souvenir shop, young fellow?"

Joe was stuck for words as he was feeling his eyes swelling with unshed tears.

"Nice," was all he managed to reply as he turned to see the speaker.

Blocking the crude opening to the shack he saw a priest, an old man to Krels, wearing a faded cassock and a cracked reverse collar. Over the blue eyes was a high forehead, balding, with a skullcap perched on the crown. He was smiling encouragingly.

"So, my friend, you are part of the gang who's going to make us all rich. God knows, these people could do with a little extra money even if it only paid for the wood they are forced to buy from the tribes nearby. It might put a plate of meat in their hands once a week, or provide some more morphine and antibiotics."

Joe was tempted to accept the elevated status conferred on him, but something prevented him from lying to a priest.

"Sch, man, or is it Father? I am a security guard at the mine. They bring me along for their defence. I don't mind. They pay me overtime. I don't know what I'd do if the Mai-Mai attacks, but what else to do in this bleddy jungle, man? Heh, Father?" Joe paused, slightly embarrassed by his outburst. "Are you in charge of these lepers?"

"Paddy Driscol is my name. Come over to the chapel. I have some rather special tea over there."

Joe was about to refuse to drink tea with this strange priest in a leper colony! What had life come to? It was not an image he could easily live with.

The tea was strong and herbal.

"You'll be wanting sugar or even milk, I expect? Well, regrettably there is none. I'm truly sorry to be such a poor host! Still, there are worse things than no milk, eh, young man?"

The priest passed Joe a heavy cup made of subtly blended coloured clays. He noticed Joe's interest.

"Beautiful, isn't it? The people make them here. It's an ancient tradition. Only the lepers make them now. The rest of the locals have either been killed or recruited. These clays are special. We don't know how they formed these wonderful colours. I suppose it's some anomaly in the minerals around here. Your colleagues think there's some sort of chemical property in some of these clays. They want to make us all rich, or so they say."

"Very fine, father. Why's this place here in the middle of all the fighting?"

"The Mai-Mai won't come here through fear. They fear almost nothing, least of all violence and venereal disease, but leprosy cuts very deep into the African psyche, deeper than syphilis or even AIDS."

"Same problem in South Africa. You're wasting your time here, Father. You can't win with these people. Bloody savages. Sorry, Father, but you know what I mean. Why bother?"

For the next few weeks, Joe would talk with Herault and Father Driscol and a strange reclusive man called Kevin as the geologists beavered away with their instruments and laptop computer. As he walked the perimeter, he noted a few of the features of the terrain and subconsciously absorbed the contours. By the road out stood a broken sign with the letters "asa" still visible.

Part 3: Charles Meets Krels in the Congo

1

Charles was suddenly awake. There was an explosion in the distance, and another nearer. The incessant coughing of the patients formed a background growl to the now regular crashes. *Oh, Christ, mortar bombs*, he thought.

Tentatively he sat up on his pallet with his knees in front of him and his stockinged feet on the canvas tarpaulin, the only barrier between him and the damp vital earth. Without thinking he put on his rough pale-blue smock and heavy drawstring trousers and reached for his boots, pulling them up hard by the draw straps.

A grenade exploded nearer and he heard screaming from a tent nearby. His tent mate, Jouffroy Coumier, was not in his bed. Charles had to go see who needed help. His emergency field backpack was at the end of his bed. With a single well-practiced movement, he hoisted it on to his back and then as he was regaining his normal balance, his ears were split by an almighty explosion so near that a spray of dirt landed on the sides of the tent. He dropped to the ground, a reaction to the noise and his defensive combat training. There was a white hard hat with a big red cross back and front somewhere among the dirty clothes and boots in the corner of the tent. He found it and pulled it hard down on his head, tightening the chinstrap.

His pulse was running fast and adrenaline was sharpening his senses. He needed to get out. A blinding flash put all the camp lights out. He blundered through the entrance of the tent. There was a predawn glow in the small area of sky visible through the treetops. He turned away from the camp to relieve himself. His need was great, so he did not take more than a couple of steps beyond the perimeter ditch. The ditch was to clear the water quickly during tropical downpours and they were strictly prohibited from urinating, defecating or throwing rubbish into it. He was still not sure why or how they were being attacked but he wanted to get himself together before joining the others for a rescue or evasive operation. Suddenly he was picked up bodily from behind and thrown into the air. He was only conscious of pain in the back of the legs and then a sudden impact to his face and no more.

"You, Red Cross, over here. Stay with us, you might live." He heard the familiar tones of South African English, spoken by one probably more fluent in Afrikaans, but speaking staccato English, the lingua franca of commerce and war. Charles looked up. His benefactor's face caught the light from the fires around. It was heavy featured, red skinned and sweaty, sporting a three-day growth and surmounted by an unruly mop of blond, wavy hair. The eyes were pale even in the dim flickering light.

"Looks like you took a hit. That ditch there is excavated. Man, I guess you were lifted with the dirt from the bank. Good thing you had that pack on. Bet your legs hurt a bit. I'm Joe Krels, this is Hani." Krels grabbed the pack and hoisted Charles to his feet.

"These black bastards are all round us," he growled, "and they're armed with grenades and mortars."

"Maybe we can make it out to the river and edge back to camp," said Hani.

They were both carrying assault rifles in their hands and had Uzi pistols holstered across their chests. They had no packs but had magazines hooked into their webbing belts. They had army fatigue trousers and dark T-shirts. They stank of stale sweat and cordite. Krels let Hani's suggestion hang for a few minutes while they both swept the trees and the clearing with straining eyes like radar seeking a target.

"Nothing," said Hani.

"Ja," said Krels. "Follow him, stay in front of me. Let's go."

Charles did as he was told. They half crouched in that uncomfortable mode of soldiers. The Afrikaners ported the assault rifles in their left hands, and each in his right hand held a long bayonet knife with a wrist cord. Charles tried to get comfortable with his heavy first-aid bag. The run was punctuated by stops every one hundred paces. The two men would turn their backs to him and in perfect silence as they all held their breath, they would do their scanning routine again. Soon the ground began to slope downward. Charles could smell the dank odours of the river. They had been following a jungle footpath. Now Hani led them down another path, perhaps paralleling the river.

Without warning they came upon a tent. It was in jungle camouflage of a modern lightweight Terylene fabric, properly staked out. Charles reckoned it was a two-man tent. There was another larger tent adjacent, forming an L shape.

2

"Claus is inside. He got two bullets. He's a bleddy pain in the arse, but we need him. He's a good navigator."

"I'm not a surgeon," said Charles. "I can do some first aid. I am really just a medical student on a gap year. I'm not even a fully trained paramedic."

"What's in your bag? Instruments. You've seen all this stuff done, right? We aren't asking for a beautiful job like Groote Schuur Hospital. We want Claus fixed up so we can get him out. He's got a bullet lodged in his chest. Another one is in the muscle of his arm nearby."

Charles knew he had no choice, and anyway he had some basic training on rubber sheeting, sewing up cuts he'd made with a scalpel. He needed a little time to gather his thoughts.

"OK," he said, "Yes, I can do something. I haven't done much of this before, but it's what I am hoping to be trained for."

"Right. Tell us what you need."

He realized immediately he had gained the Afrikaners' full attention and even, he thought, only the simple respect one affords a craftsman.

"I will try the arm this morning and the rib this afternoon. I will give him a big dose of hydrocortisone in the arm now and start antibiotic injections. Have you pure water?"

"Swiss filter, about one litre, and I can make some more," said the fourth man, whose name was Fokko.

"I have only six self-contained ampoules of Xylocaine for the pain. I think I should do the arm without anaesthetic because the rib job may need a lot. Can you manage that, Claus?"

So Charles started the risky process of field surgery for the first time, almost untutored and definitely ill prepared. He took the water and added hydrogen peroxide. The arm was a mess. The bullet must have been a ricochet. The flesh was torn away under the bandage. Claus screamed.

"For fuck's sake, my God. It was OK just now. Ahhhr, now my fucking ribs are hurting. Jesus, I'm only a sodding security guard. I didn't sign on for this,"

"Shut up while I clean it up. It is a mess. I need you to keep still," he said with a new authority disguising his uncertainty. There was dirt and there was dead tissue, the most dangerous. He sloshed in the liquid and asked for more water.

"You saw me add the peroxide. Please, add about the same amount."

Fokko did as he was told. Using two pairs of forceps, one holding a gauze swab, Charles lifted out the dead flesh and the debris as Fokko poured more of the peroxide into the wound, foaming the blood as it emerged from the newly severed vessels. He worked his way deliberately in towards the base of the wound. Claus was holding himself rigid against the pain.

"Fokko, this is not working well. He must relax. Have you got alcohol?" Charles asked quietly.

"Gin," he said, proffering a dented hip flask.

"Give him gin. All of that if it's full," he ordered and relaxed his grip. His right leg was stiff from sitting on it and his arms ached from holding the instruments. He stood and felt the blood entering his leg again. He looked out of the tent.

142

Hani and Krels were there relaxing on a tarpaulin. Two small black women were with them. They were bush women, very black, unkempt, bare breasted, their lower parts wrapped in faded and thin cotton print. Idly he recognised them as forest people, pygmies, but he had a job to do, so he turned back into the tent.

The gin had the necessary effect. Claus was relaxed and the bullet was uncovered easily and extracted with the forceps. Luckily, no arteries had been severed, so after more cleansing of the wound, Charles sewed it up rather roughly, bandaged it, and told the unfortunate Claus to sleep off the effects of the gin.

Fokko handed Charles a plastic bottle of water. "Don't drink it all at once. The bleddy Swiss filter is hard work." He handed Charles a small survival biscuit.

"How are you doing, Claus?" He looked pale and grunted, "I'm OK, doc. It feels a bit better."

"This afternoon I will use the Xylocaine so it shouldn't hurt so much. You'll have to lie on your side out here and I'll get Fokko to hold you down. We'll have to do it outside so I can see a bit more clearly."

Everyone took the opportunity to rest and doze.

With the patient in a foetal position, he gave three injections of the anaesthetic in the areas around the wound and removed the rough dressing of torn clothes and cotton wadding. It was a long gash like a ploughed furrow, terminating in a big black bruise. The oedema was reduced by the hydrocortisone, but still the skin was soft and pappy around the wound. Suddenly he was unsure. He had worried his way all round this procedure as he lay unsleeping on his mat during the morning. He had picked out the bullet a thousand times before he finally drifted off to sleep. But here he was under the rustling trees, faced with the flabby skin and an open wound and a bullet buried who knew how deep, and he was overcome with a dread. He was rigidly holding the scalpel.

"OK, Charley?" asked Fokko.

"Yes," he said flatly. "I want some more coffee, sweet, please."

He put the scalpel down. It wasn't what he needed next. The second coffee, overloaded with sugar, had a good effect.

Working efficiently with scalpel and forceps, he opened the furrow and delicately removed the dead tissue and cotton fibres, making his way steadily to the point where the wound tunnelled into the blackened soft skin under the right pectoral. Then reversing the scalpel, he cut from underneath the skin to enlarge the passage. The skin opened up readily, too readily. They hadn't told him in class that would happen. How would he close the wound? Cross that bridge when it comes. He saw the bullet. It was not deformed this time. It was between two ribs, with the blunt end toward him. He selected a pair of larger locking artery forceps and went for the bullet. He closed the forceps around it and locked them. He pulled. There was no yielding. He needed something to open the ribs. In his mind he saw a nicely drawn picture in his first-aid manual showing a retractor holding an opening between two bones. There was nothing in his bag like that.

"Look, Fokko, I can't force the ribs apart. What have you got?"

"Leatherman tool?"

"Is it clean?" asked Charles. "Oh, never mind. Wash it in water and then in the concentrated peroxide."

Fokko did as he was told.

"Right, try to insert it just to the left of the bullet. That's it, flat side the ribs. OK, when I say so, I want you to rotate it so it opens the gap. His lung is just the other side so don't let it go in too far."

Fokko's big, rough hand in the overstretched rubber glove gripped the tool, and steadily he exerted pressure.

"OK, twist gently." The gap opened very slightly. There was an awful scraping of hard materials as Charles withdrew the bullet: a sound to put your teeth on edge. He sloshed some peroxide into the vacated hole, dabbed it with gauze, and tried to close it gently. The skin had taken on a blubbery texture and was still holding itself stubbornly apart. Fokko held the skin flaps together while he attempted to sew up the edges. It looked like a pretty poor job, with much of the epidermal layer exposed. He finished up, covering the wound with a dry dressing, and bandaging with wide Elastoplast.

"We'll eat now." Fokko held out a mess-tin with some soupy stew and a chunk of hard, black, dense bread.

"You can sleep in here with us," he said. "Then if he gives any trouble, you'll be on hand. The other tent will be all grunts and groans."

Charles could hear the deep voices of Krels and Hani speaking in a language he didn't know but supposed was Afrikaans. Coarse laughter interspersed with short sharp remarks. When he went out to pee, he noticed the two women had moved in closer and were in the arms of the men, looking like happy ugly children in the fading light. There were empty mess tins and another hip flask on the tarpaulin.

During the night he slept fitfully. Claus groaned in pain as he woke and slept sporadically, and the grunts and screeches from the next tent drew his attention and conjured up horrible images in his mind. The following morning as the sun slipped through a few gaps in the overhead canopy, Charles washed his face with a splash of water from a hollow in the tarpaulin and asked if there was any breakfast.

"The best: biltong, survival biscuits, and coffee, and as many bananas as you can eat. The women bring them in."

There was a survival pack in his medical bag but it was just water and biscuits. He did not want to use them or share them. He accepted the food offered. In the late afternoon, the two women had suddenly appeared silently at the edge of the forest. They stood with eyes downcast, each carrying a rough cloth bulging with green oranges and bananas. Their heads were shining with an oily preparation, which had straightened out their curls into wavy coils held apart with coloured string.

"Well, look what we have here," said Joe. "Fruit! *Com, liefling,*" he leered. One of the girls looked up and smiled nervously and advanced, proffering the bag of fruit with outstretched arms. Hani emerged from the tent and the other girl moved forward. She did not smile but looked frightened and apprehensive. Hani reached for the fruit and peeled a banana. He poked it at the girl in an obscene gesture and at last she smiled.

"Ah, she's not still angry at me after all." He turned to Charles, "Boy, oh boy, these girls are something ugly but they like to *pomp* and they like money. They keep coming back for more. Here, have a banana; you've earned it. Juju, peel the man an orange," he said, turning to the girl.

She evidently understood and took a great patch of peel out of an orange with her large white teeth and continued to peel it with surprisingly dainty fingers. Then the girls squatted placidly side by side at the edge of the tarpaulin, watching the men eating as if watching a feature on television. Charles was touched by the simple gestures of these gentle creatures and the trusting look in their eyes. He had to agree they were not attractive. Their faces had a pushed-in appearance somewhat like a bulldog. There were virtually no bridges to their wide noses, and their mouths were broad with protruding teeth. They were young, so their breasts were nicely firm and their skin was silky, but lightly peppered with small crusty pimples and odd lumps. Their shins were scarred and their broad, bare feet were rough and gnarled for girls so young. He reflected that life must be very hard for these people eking out a living from hunting, gathering and very basic agriculture.

"How old are these girls?" Charles asked naively.

"Thirteen, fourteen, fifteen: who knows? They probably don't," answered Hani.

"Who gives a shit?" interjected Joe Krels unpleasantly and Charles noted the crude callousness of his tone. He felt that Krels begrudged them any humanity other than warmth at night and willingness to be a plaything. Their ugliness, blackness, smallness, wide-eyed innocence, placidity, courtesy, and broad-grinned joy were all to be tolerated or ignored and subjugated to his physical needs.

As darkness fell they supped on another soupy stew made by Fokko. This time he had added some pilchards and anchovies to the basic gravy and the whole thing could, with a stretch of the imagination, be likened to bouillabaisse.

"Man, this is outrageous," said Joe with an expression that left the group guessing whether this was an extreme compliment or an outburst of disgust. Anyway, he ate it without smile or grimace, as did the rest of them.

Charles slept fitfully in the tent with Fokko and Claus. Claus groaned in pain from time to time as he rolled over, trying to find a comfortable position. The grunts, groans, giggles, and panting from the other tent prompted Fokko to shout "For Christ's sake, you animals, go rut in the deep jungle," bringing Charles fully awake just as he was acclimatising to the ambient noise level and floating off into oblivion.

3

In the morning they woke with the dawn. The girls hung around busying themselves, uselessly trying to be of service. They were nervous at the changes in the camp routine as the various items were packed and the tents collapsed. Charles saw Krels hold up some money in a gesture to the girls. Then it went back into his pocket and he walked off down the jungle path with them following happily. Charles did not see this as significant, just pay time. Although he was slightly sad for the girls, he was pleased to see Joe was actually going to pay them.

Mother Nature called him to the latrine pit dug some fifty paces from the camp. As he approached, he heard sounds over to his right. It was Joe's harsh voice and the girls screeching incomprehensible arguments. Suspecting it was probably dangerous, Charles made his way slowly and quietly towards the sounds. There was a raised scream, very short. It could have been mistaken for the screech of a bird or animal. He heard a deep thudding noise. When he got nearer, he saw Joe's black T-shirt through the trees. He was standing, panting slightly, with the military field shovel over his right shoulder. Nothing would stop Charles's curiosity now. He arrived at a small clearing and saw what he had already guessed. The two girls lay on the jungle litter. Their necks were both twisted out of shape. Dark maroon blood was pumping from both the necks. He ran forward.

"They are still alive."

"Their necks are broken like wrung chickens. There's no saving them." Joe said it like a bystander giving a final, regretful verdict on slaughtered chickens.

"You did this?" Charles asked needlessly.

"Birth control," said Krels flatly. "Couldn't let them whelp my offspring here."

Depressingly the whole monstrous inevitability of the situation became clear to Charles. Joe's logic was inhumanly unassailable. What chance would a white boy or girl have out here in the middle of the forest? And how would Krels feel knowing out here somewhere was a son or daughter of his? So he had taken the situation in hand and murdered the potential mothers of his and Hani's infants.

"I'll bury them," he said as he cut the ground with the pointed murder weapon.

Charles couldn't take his eyes off the bodies. They were no more graceful in death. Their coiffed hair was obscene as the curls tangled with the twigs and liana on the jungle floor, and ants had already started to crawl over their young chests and into their mouths.

"This is the bit I don't like," Krels said, as if trying raise some sympathy for the pain of labour. Charles realized that Joe had just implied "This is not the first time, more like a routine chore."

Charles sat down on a fallen tree. He looked at the pale brown skin of his forearms. *My mother was black. She was like these two. What has been her fate at the hands of barbarous white men?*

"Look, Joe, this is too bad," he said lamely? "You've just committed murder. These were human beings."

"Be real, man. These are savages. They live like pigs. You know what they eat. They dig for truffles like pigs, with their bare hands. I've seen them, man. Anyway, what's it to you? Suddenly you a Kaffir lover? Hey, you look bleddy black yourself. Look in the mirror, boy. I see it now. What are you? I suppose you're some sort of bloody mongrel. Africa's full of them. Well, fuck you. You misbehave and you'll be the next." He threw the spade down. "Here, bury your ugly sisters."

Charles acknowledged that over the last couple of years his boyish looks had hardened somewhat, and his African

148

features were beginning to show up. The colour of his eyes had darkened until they were almost black, and his hair was curling tighter. As Krels moved away, an anger Charles had rarely experienced before began to colour his vision, and he leaped for the spade. But as he reached it, reason returned as he saw Krels's right hand brush across the pistol clipped to his belt; so he simply set to the dreadful task of burying the dead girls. Krels watched as he dug methodically.

"Five feet deep for pygmies, ha, ha," he joked.

From an attitude of tragic indifference, Charles became consumed with hate. Krels did not notice Charles's eyes narrow and his face redden as he slid the bodies into the hole. Krels grabbed the spade and scooped the soft soil back over the tangled corpses. When he had finished, Krels stood straight, shouldering the shovel.

"Next, fill in the latrine. Hey ho, hey ho, it's off to work we go," and he did a few little march steps like the dwarfs in *Snow White*.

"Give me that," said Charles as for a second time the crazy notion crossed his mind that he might indeed slaughter this monster with the same weapon that had just demised the two pygmy girls. When it was in his hand he hefted it but realised he needed better odds than to take on a man who was probably trained in unarmed combat as well as being armed. Nevertheless, the resolve to kill was forming firmly in his subconscious.

"I was on my way there. I can cover it in afterwards."

As he started to shovel the dirt into the hole, he could not help seeing amongst the turds and tissue images of the shattered bodies of the two primitive girls. With successive scoops of the friable earth, he said some prayers.

4

By the time everything was packed up, they each had to carry twenty-kilo packs. This was in addition to the guns and ammunition. Krels gave his Uzi to Charles with brief instructions on how to use it.

"Don't forget, keep the safety on all the time and flick it off like this when needed. Learn to be quick at that and it will save your life."

The other men had Kalashnikovs and pistols of various types. Charles noticed Krels had a dark brown canvas bag, a bit like a document case. It had a double strap going across the left shoulder and round his waist like a satchel. This was obviously fairly important to him, as he did not pack it in his rucksack. They had a plan to trek back towards the edge of the city of Kinshasa where they could find a flight out. In the jungle they could make about fifteen miles a day if they worked very hard. This would mean ten or twelve hours of gruelling yomping. Because they could not go in straight lines they would actually make good just a little more than half this amount.

The mining camp the South Africans had left behind was just outside Kasangulu, south of the river they were tracking and about seven miles southwest of the mighty Congo River. Their only hope lay in going toward the main road and chancing that the people they met would see them as neutral or friendly. They were short of rations but had a few items they could use as trade goods for food, ranking these in order of usefulness. Highest ranking were weapons, machetes, Swiss army knives, maps, compasses (three army pattern), and torches and batteries. After this were the water filter, mess- tins and cups, and the solid fuel cookers (two). Groundsheets were very important, but as the rains were holding off, it was decided that the tents could go, just keeping the flysheets. Then they took stock of what was left and they made a long list of items from toothpaste to novels, all of which could be offered in exchange for food. They also had money, which in the villages could be used to reinforce their persuasive powers.

Krels and Hani had made pouches from the pockets of a dead soldier's uniform, which they suspended inside their underwear. Here they kept their passports and the high denomination money, while in their belt pouches they kept small change and their company ID cards.

Krels realised that Charles had the most tradable commodity in his medical knowledge and his field pack. He made sure Charles's Red Cross helmet was clean and bright and took the camouflage covers off the light grey hats of the others. He and the others put white T-shirts on, and they all carried their guns unobtrusively. Half of the first day was lost with the packing up. This was poor military practice and made Krels nervous. However, when they started to walk, they made good progress at first.

Charles's need to kill Krels was becoming an obsession. He thought about it with every step he took through the mushy dank undergrowth. Every bent branch lying on the forest floor looked like the broken, twisted body of one of the pygmies. As they passed people on the paths, he saw the girls' features in every smiling tribal woman's face. He was suffused with a need to avenge the entire womanhood of Africa for Krels's crime. But by late afternoon they were all exhausted and found a place to pitch camp off to one side of a fairly busy jungle path still running parallel to the small river. Claus was confident they knew where they were and they laid out the groundsheets and pitched the two tents in a spirit of brave optimism.

As they settled and prepared to eat their meagre rations, they became aware of a meaty stench in the air, and looking up, a slow drift of thin smoke could be seen through the trees.

5

"Maybe there's a village where we might get a couple of chickens." Hani was busy opening tins and lighting the cooker, preparing to knock up more stew.

"Hani, you stay here. Why don't I take Charlie-Red-Cross? He can work some white man's magic while I bargain for some goodies," Krels said, smiling. "Let's go, Charlie, or are you too bushed?"

Charles paused for thought; he was frightened and he felt the adrenaline raising his pulse rate. But he knew he had to go.

"The promise of barbecued chicken is just enough to get me off my backside," he said. Taking a bearing on the smoke, they searched around the light bush until they spotted a path, somewhat overgrown, going in the right direction. Krels led with his assault rifle at the port in his left hand. Charles followed with the Uzi in his right hand, safety catch on. After about fifteen minutes the ground beneath them began to clear, as the forest litter had been taken for cooking fires. Soon the path became hard packed as they came to the edge of the village.

The smoke was rising from the ashes of the huts. They were nearly burnt out, with the bodies of the villagers half protruding from the ashes. Some heads, some feet, all lifeless. The stench was horrendous as the gentle breeze blew the smoke occasionally in their direction.

As they looked there was a movement near the middle of the village. A dog ran towards them barking accusingly, and then a bent old man hobbled into the village square. Three infants clung to his legs. Beyond him, they saw two old crones. As the women saw them, they began to argue in screeching tones. The old man stamped his bare foot and said one short word. The crones shut up but the three children let go the old man's legs and started bawling in unison. The old man came on towards them, his staring eyes penetrating their very souls.

As he neared them he started waving his arms and haranguing them, spitting and cursing. And then suddenly, as if a switch had been turned he stopped and going on one knee he touched his forehead in salute and proffered his right hand holding the wrist firmly with his left.

"He's seen the red cross," said Joe Krels. Charles went forward and shook his hand.

"OK, get up, old man. Who the hell did this?" he asked futilely.

"Blacks on blacks: they kill their own kind, like cannibals," offered Krels, not sensing the universal irony of his remark. "Look, some of these women have been raped."

He prodded one of the female corpses with the barrel of the rifle. "She must have been good, eh, Charles? Still, you would know, eh, your people, savages."

Charles was fascinated and horrified at the same time. Nothing had prepared him for the carnage he was witnessing. The stench of burning and suppurating bodies was awful. The nauseating tone of Krels's comments was not penetrating his mind. He tried to concentrate on the old man, the only sane action he could take.

"What can we do about these old people and children?" he asked.

"Nothing," said Krels. "Absolutely fuck all. They will die or survive with or without our help. If they can make it to another village still intact they may survive, or maybe somebody will find them, but why should we do anything? There'll be no food here. The soldiers will have looted every last morsel. We'd better get going; otherwise we'll get caught up in this mess. There's bugger all for us here."

Tears were streaming down the face of the old man as he instinctively understood the purport of Krels's words. The women who had moved up slowly behind him started to wail and the three infants continued to bawl.

6

Krels and Charles turned away and the noise stopped. Krels ducked his head through the sling of his rifle in the style of a revolutionary, evidently less fearful and more comfortable. After leaving the clearing, they walked a few paces. Charles realised he had been distracted from his mission to kill his companion. He was relieved but his subconscious was screaming at him to take some sort of action. He was shaking. Krels stopped.

"Boy, oh, boy, all that death and destruction makes you want to piss. Charles, watch my back." Like the half-trained soldier he was, he turned his back on Charles and slipped his arm through the sling to open the fly of his fatigues.

A part of Charles felt a surge of excitement as he analysed this uncanny turn of events. He waited until he heard the splash of the stream of urine. He turned silently, took a smart pace forward, grabbed the rifle in both hands and spun it round hand over hand forming a garrotte which immediately started to strangle his victim. The stream of piss momentarily ceased and then started again with double the force. Krels raised his arms in defence, then they fell back involuntarily. Charles felt the weight of Krels's body come on to the rifle. He looked around for some relief. Behind his left shoulder a small tree forked at about chest level. With all the strength left in him, he pulled the rifle back and passed it through the fork, pinioning the inert body against the trunk of the tree. Krels stood up, instinctively easing the pressure on his neck. The bright red haze cleared and he found himself staring into the eyes of his assailant. The broadly set eyes were familiar, the heavy lids and long stiff lashes, the dark brown irises.

"Bontong, I had to, I had to…my sister Avis, why did you do that to her, you bl…?" Charles had no idea of the meaning of these words, and neither did he care. With a calculated movement, he kicked Krels's feet from under him and watched his weight fall onto the tourniquet formed by the rifle's sling.

Charles turned away and was met by five pairs of eyes, all with an expression of total and absolute disbelief and despair. He was arrested by their stares for half a minute as he orientated himself in the village.

7

He needed to run off the adrenaline, forcing his blood pressure and heart rate to phenomenal levels. He crashed past the five surviving villagers. He desired hard physical effort to burn off the ache he felt down his spine and in his legs. Downhill, at the other end of the village, there was a track much wider and well worn than the path they had come in on. He followed this, still running, until he felt utter exhaustion.

Darkness was falling. He slumped at the side of the track, energy burnt. He had been there about ten minutes and his breathing was calm again when he heard the noise of an engine coming up the track toward him. It was a motorcycle, a large one by its sound, and it was obviously on the track, making for his resting place.

His mind was numb. He had just killed a man in a massacred village. He was without food or water, stranded in unfamiliar jungle. Should he hail a passing motorcycle or hide? It was just like one of those questions that were set in the survival course. They all had pat answers and could be explained logically in the classroom. He could not make the decision without the answer book. He lay there and waited.

The headlamp of the motorcycle came into view, bobbing up and down, flashing randomly. As it drew abreast of him, the engine cut to idle and the machine stopped. The rider leaned over and stuck a black leather motorcycle boot just in front of his face. Charles sat up.

"You all right, mate?" he heard. Australian or maybe New Zealand, female, rough. "Jenny Bones at your service. Christ Almighty, what the fuck are you doing here? Red Cross, eh? You hurt? Where's the rest of your mob? I heard there was some trouble here. Rumour has it there's been a massacre, some small village. If this turns out to be another wild goose chase, I'll be a 'was Sheila.' Haven't sold a story in five flaming weeks. Hey, you know anything?"

"Can you get me out of here?"

"Is there a bloody story or not?"

"Yes, there's a story."

"Bonza, boy. What's yer name? You got yerself a lift. Take me to the village, and I'll get you back to Kinshasa in about three hours. You'll get a flight out of Brazzaville, no problems."

It was only a matter of minutes until they arrived at the village. They rode through, turned, and stopped somewhere near the middle. In the bonnet box, Jenny had a Beam Gun searchlight, which she used to scan the scene. "Yeah, this is the kind of shit I can use. My God, this is the McCoy. What bastards can do this? Look at those women."

Charles thought for a moment he detected some sense of concern or disgust under the delight at finding a saleable story. He was too tired to worry. This was his ticket out of hell, and he was not going to look this gift horse in the mouth.

155

"You stay here with the bike. I'll take a gander." With this Jenny unloaded a long tube, two camera cases, and some small rolls of film from the panniers and assembled her apparatus.

"Tell me what you saw."

"Not much," lied Charles. "I just walked through it and left."

"No worries, pal, I'll just wander through, take a few pickies, maybe write a note or two, and Bob's your uncle. Give me twenty minutes."

Charles couldn't comment; he could hardly stand up. "This is war," Charles realised, "twenty minutes to photograph and exploit the deaths of some three hundred people and the total extinction of their village. Lives lost so a few of the most bloody pictures and a few lines of purple prose can earn a high-flying female globe-trotter a few thousand dollars towards nights of luxury, a supply of film, and a plane ticket to another centre of misery." His thoughts died as exactly on time, Jenny was back.

"Hey, Chas, this is sensational. You'll never guess what I found. You know, I always knew there would be some trouble from the bloody mercs. Up at the end of the village, they must have got one of the bastards. Hanged on a bloody tree. His fat donga was pointing to the sky. Doesn't that tell you something? Big blond bastard, nearly dead. In fact I thought he was dead, but he was gasping, so I cut him down. His throat was all damaged and swelled up. He couldn't say anything. Poor bugger's no use to me, I said to myself; Let the evil sod survive if he can. I probably would have killed him myself if I had a gun. I'll bet the locals caught him raping the girls and their patience was up." She paused for a moment to catch her breath but not to dwell on what she had just announced.

"Eh?" she asked. "What would you do? String the bastard up. Show the world you can't let the white man come raping your women. It's all bloody tribal, you know. Boy, this will make a story. It may be a bit too much for the big papers, but I know a whole string of guys who'll just die to get that picture. It's authentic. He's a *Jaarpy*." she paused. "*Jaarpy* mercenaries. What will Mandela think of that?"

Jenny's exuberance at her scoop was so high, it was unnecessary for Charles to answer any of her rhetorical questions. He remained silent while Jenny put her camera gear in the box at the back of the bike. She seemed to have a bit of trouble fitting an awkward brown object that seemed somewhat familiar into the pannier bag, but Charles was incurious. He did not really care about anything anymore. If Krels, saved by this crazy journo, is eaten alive by soldier ants, no problem. He was too tired to let the remorse that was nibbling at his lower consciousness get to him. The world had gone mad, and this Jenny was another mad player. All Jenny had to do was to give him a lift to Kinshasa and leave the stage with her story.

They mounted the big bike and started down the track. It became obvious that Jenny felt the pressure of competition. She had slipped away from the rest of the press corps and was aware they would soon catch on to the same lead. Charles was inured to the hair-raising speed of descent. After an hour the track became a rough dirt road and after another half an hour the road was thinly tarred. Some of the houses by the side began to have pale electric bulbs under their grey concrete porches. Soon Jenny pulled up outside a white building.

"Red Cross Convent Hospital. I come here for information from time to time. Say hallo to the twins for me. Just go over there, ring the bell, and introduce yourself. Good luck, mate. See you again sometime."

With a loud crack from the twin exhausts, she disappeared down the street, leaving a cloud of dust and smoke behind.

8

Hani spotted Joe as the jungle thinned at the edge of the village and went straight over. He was lying on the ground with the sling of the AK in two turns round his neck. He was not strangling anymore, but Hani could see the man had almost been asphyxiated.

"Joe, boy, what have they done to you? Where's that medic? I never trusted you two together, but I thought you would try to kill him, not the other way round."

Joe couldn't talk. His throat was absolutely raw and he was delirious. All he could rasp out of his damaged throat was, "Bontong, Bontong, Bontong," over and over again.

"Now we're in a fine bloody pickle," said Hani. "We've got two injured men. Man! And where's that Kaffir bastard gone?"

Joe managed to roll over on to his stomach and started waving his right arm, as if pointing. Hani looked in the vague direction of the arm and saw the trail through the village and, for the first time, the massacre. The surviving ancients were wandering up the middle of the road with the silent, naked children. Hani raised his Uzi, but his brief police training stopped him—none too soon—from pulling the trigger on the forlorn little family.

"My God, Joe, are we in Hades or what? The fucking stench! Look at these bodies. We better get out of here or we'll be in trouble, big time. Everyone hates a Jaarpy, man, and they'll nail us for this for sure. Look, we found two of the walkie-talkies still had some power. I'll tell the others to come up here immediately because this road looks like the way out. No chicken stew tonight."

Krels was grunting in reply. Some colour was returning to his face, and although he could not talk except in grunts, he seemed to understand. Anyway, it didn't matter; Hani was talking for his own sake to keep up his courage and organise his thoughts.

"We decided to use our old call signs...Delta x-ray three, delta x-ray two, come in." He went on to tell the others to strike the camp, reduce their packs, and get over as soon as possible. He gave them a compass direction and approximate distance along the path.

And so they got Krels out. It took them all night and all the next day, following the same road taken by Charles on the back of Jenny Bones's bike. And they ended up at the same white building. A nun, a very white, very old lady with a fierce countenance, was out in front with a pair of rusty shears, making an attempt at pruning the hibiscus.

"For the love of God, what do we have here?" she said, seeing the three men with the makeshift litter between them. After a while of explaining with some rather farfetched embellishments, two smiling African nuns appeared.

"Sisters June and July," said the old nun. "Show these men where to take the injured boy to the hospital and give the others some rice."

"From hell to heaven, complete with little angels," said Hani, winking at his companions. She felt his comment begged an explanation.

"They are twins born on the last day of June and the first day of July; nobody quite remembers how many years ago." She smiled fleetingly and after a short pause solemnly added, "Their mother died of the effort of creation and starvation some days afterward."

She paused to appraise her visitors. "This is a kind of clinic and hospital. We can give your injured friend shelter and perhaps some treatment, but for you men, I'm afraid you'll have to be gone within the hour. We hardly have food for ourselves with the uncertainty of supplies. You should be able to make it to Kinshasa by evening, and then you'll have to tell a good story to get out to the outside world."

When they had eaten a little rice and quenched their thirsts with some thin herbal tea, they offered the sisters the rest of their survival rations. They were sick of them anyway and would take their chances with the agent in Kinshasa. They went in to see Krels, but he was fast asleep and snoring loudly. As soon as they entered, he jerked awake, his eyes screaming for attention.

His voice croaked, but the men just made out, "Bag, the bag. Woman!" and what sounded like, "Bitch took the bag."

The men looked at each other askance. Of course, the satchel that was going to make them all rich. Krels, the leader, had nursed it for so long that it had been forgotten by the others. Fokko looked at Hani. "Woman," he said. "What bloody woman?" Krels was asleep.

It was obvious he was not going to give them any more to go on; he could hardly talk and probably knew no more about the woman. They left him snoring and spluttering and turned to leave. They were all pleased to be on the way out, and not very interested in Krels's plan to get rich, not having ever understood what was so important about "certain information," in the precious computer bag.

The old nun came in behind them and spoke by way of a farewell: "He will be seen by the doctor tomorrow. I imagine he will need some sleep and rest after a scare like that. I still can't imagine how he fell out of a tree and strangled himself. It wasn't suicide, was it? He will be needing the priest as well to heal his troubled soul.

"There have been some terrible things happening around here. Only yesterday a young man came through with his friend on a motorbike. He was in a terrible state. He'd seen the massacre in the village up the road and yet we heard nothing of it. I am afraid it's all happened before. All we get to see is the wounded and dying. They bring them to us, but we can't do much."

With their eyes the men signalled to each other to avoid engagement in this conversation. It could only lead to complications, and they already knew what they wanted to know about Charles; he had escaped. They didn't care, not even about the motorbike. He should be ahead of them by two days, maybe three. All they wanted now was to get on out and back home. Their story would be untold.

They let the nuns confiscate their assault rifles and throw them into the cellar, where they landed on top of a few hundred others, rusting in the humidity. They kept their pistols and straggled off down the rough road.

9

The doctor, a wrinkled old fellow with scraggly white whiskers contrasting with his weathered dark skin, carried around his neck one of those stethoscopes, all cracked rubber tubing and a real ivory bell mouth. He came and looked at Joe through sad eyes and prescribed rest. It was about all he could prescribe, given the miserable state of the convent's dispensary.

"I think they have some aspirin here but they reserve it for people with fevers and I don't see any here. Use soap and alcohol on those skin abrasions. I think you may have a cracked vertebra. That is giving you pain but if you lie still for a few days and then gradually increase your movement, you should be OK."

At least the kitchen had something. And a battered old *Deux Chevaux* van dropped off some bags of rice and a couple of boxes of canned meat. The nuns grew vegetables. The doctor passed by every two days from then on. His pretext was Joe, his patient, whose neck he would feel gently and say, "No movement yet, leave it for a few days." But his real reason was more likely the meagre meal of rice and thin meaty gravy.

On Sundays a priest came, and Krels, who had been depressed by his helpless state, began to feel like a celebrity enjoying the continual attentions of June and July, whom he still couldn't tell apart.

"Well, my son, you look a little better today. No, no, don't move, you'll break your precious neck. For the life of me, I cannot believe you're a suicide. The good sister says she thinks you were about to take your own life. A mortal sin, though I have to say, priest or not, I can sometimes understand how the temptation comes about amongst all this violence and conflict." Bright blue eyes shone out of his leathery old face. "You look familiar. Are you the young guard who used to come with those geologists who were to make us all rich?" Krels croaked out an affirmative. "What happened to those boys?"

Krels made the universal throat-cutting gesture to indicate their death.

"I might have known it; the lepers never get anything but promises. God have mercy on their souls."

10

As Krels gained strength and the ability to breathe and speak, his stay came to an end. He managed to get a ride to the city in the old blue van, and following his friends, he persuaded the South African embassy to repatriate him.

He had nothing when he hit the streets of Cape Town. What little money he had, he used up quickly on food. He had to sleep rough. The climate was fine in summer but the patrols were out all night, with dogs moving vagrants on or jailing them for a whole range of crimes. For the whites the jail was not too bad and they gave you breakfast before they kicked you out with a warning. Krels's first job was washing limousines for a rental company.

He found himself a room in a whites-only lowlife boarding house. He was in deep depression and looked for solace in alcohol. He started on cheap sherry and drinking earlier and earlier in the day, until he began to turn up late for work. Then he started showing up drunk until he was let go. He found he could make enough cash to support his habit by washing cars in the suburbs and neighbourhoods, but he became irksome there too and was chased out of some places by angry car owners or security men.

It was about six months after his arrival that he stumbled into the mission. They did soup and a bunk and counselling in the morning after. Breakfast was a thin porridge of *mielie* and a chunk of yesterday's bread.

"You're like a bad penny, Joe," said a gruff voice from the past. Father Driscol was sitting in a small room off the hall behind a school desk on a hard wooden chair.

"Take the chair opposite me, young man. You're looking a bit sorry for yourself. Life in the big city not to your liking?"

"Jesus, Father, what are you doing here?"

"Oh, I'm just biding my time and helping a wee bit while I wait to get my knee fixed up."

"What happened to it?"

"Just old age, my son; climbing up and down those clay pits probably didn't help. I'd suffer the pain, but now locomotion is becoming a tad difficult. What about you?"

"The truth is, Father, my life, which was never anything much, has completely fallen apart. I can't settle, I'm drinking cheap wine, I am unemployable. I guess I am a hopeless mess with no friends, no purpose, no bloody reason. Even hating has gone. I was sustained by hatred. But now everyone has to love one another. I don't seem to have that in me either.

"I mean, those nuns, they wanted nothing, they had nothing. Even you yourself, you seem to be happy or content. I don't get it."

11

"It was not always so with me, Joe," the priest said. "I made a new beginning many years ago and a very dear friend of mine, whom I buried just before I came here to Cape Town, went through a transformation from hate to love, which might be a useful example to you. I'll tell you the story."

Over the next period of days, the old priest rolled out his story. Krels, who had no other entertainment, began to warm to this old man and then to his story, told in the gently lilting Irish brogue.

"You see, my young friend, I came to Africa by default. I think many a white man comes by chance, except if you were born around here."

Krels did not have anything particular to add, so the priest went on. "I was a simple young priest in a small town in Kerry. Do you know where that is? The most beautiful and peaceful place in the world. I had done my initial training and was settling for a holy life tending the needs of simple people in a small rural town.

"To be sure it's a daft story when you think of it. It all started with a girl. All men should fear girls but for priests they can be fatal, or at least shall we say an inconvenience." He smiled. "She started to get my attention when she came to confessions. She was a sly one. Of course by then I'd heard a lot of things in the confessional and was not surprised at any young girl spicing up her sins. But this one was different and

163

she used to flash her eyes at me whenever we met outside. She was a classical Irish beauty, with long, dark, auburn hair and golden hazel eyes. I was twenty-six at the time and she gradually wound me up like a watch spring. You wouldn't know how hard it is for a twenty-six-year-old priest to keep evil or even natural thoughts out of his head when being stalked and provoked by a girl like her. I never found out where she came from originally. She had not grown up in the town but was a newcomer. She had a Dublin accent, rather posh. Her father was a technician at the new feed mill just out of town.

"I went to the parish priest and, without mentioning names, confessed my confusion and even declared that I should leave the priesthood. Well, he told me mine was not a unique case and in fact, it was a very common dilemma for young priests in their twenties.

"You see, there's a terrible lack of young men in the community and the girls are bored and don't have enough romantic or sexual targets."

"His talks were only slightly helpful, and in spite of Hail Marys and midnight vigils, my fantasies became more and more sinful until I was spending all my time either having lustful thoughts provoked by her or in a sweat trying to absolve myself from sins of the mind. He saw the signs and arranged for me to go to a corrective seminary way up north near the border with the provinces.

"Was that a case of being thrown from the frying pan into the fire, as they say? It was a silent order. We all were allocated cells. It was a hot summer that year. The cell had no furniture. You know, the idea being that the supplicant had only a mat to sleep on, and his only possessions would be a toothbrush and some underwear; even this was a concession. But latterly they had decided that we people in a retreat, troubled by problems, might benefit from being able to write out our tribulations and form resolutions on paper as a way of ordering our confusion."

It was as clear as yesterday to the old priest, and he felt the need to tell this young man exactly how it was.

"There was a new, cheap, self assembly desk and a hard wooden chair, old, rustic, and worn. When I pulled on the drawer of the desk it was so short that it came straight out from the plastic runners and spilt writing paper and pencils on to the floor. I felt truly clumsy but as I went to reinsert the drawer, I noticed a thin green file between the drawer and the hardboard shelf under it. It was almost new and tied like a lawyer's envelope with a button and string fastener I picked out the file and looked for a place to put it. It was not mine, so I didn't look inside and, as it was lost, I would return it. It didn't raise the slightest curiosity in me and, anyway, I was still tortured by my experiences at home and was keen to get on with the job of self-purification. I decided to keep a diary on the sheets of paper to record my progress. There were routine silent prayer vigils, self-flagellation sessions and other exciting self-effacing activities.

"Late one beautiful summer evening we were surprised by a visit from the garda. They raided our monastery. They went charging through the place like a herd of mad bulls dragging us from our sleeping mats and chasing us down to the refectory.

"The garda had got word, and it always shames me to say so, that some of our number had been completely overcome by the devil and were engaged in diabolical acts with the boys and even girls at the adjacent orphanage where they taught.

"All of us lined up. We were stripped naked and questioned while the whole place was searched. A big devil of a man called Kevin O'Hara…I try to forget how he was that night, and I have forgiven him and grown to love him since. He was at that time a very bitter man, a priest-hater, and all his hatred was released that night. I was just unfortunate to be in his way.

"He had been one of those turning us out of our cells but had stayed behind to search. It didn't take long as the cells were so sparsely furnished. As he entered the refectory, he was holding the file. I immediately recognised it as he held it high in his right hand. I was not particularly alarmed as the content was unknown to me, but he was pulling photographs out of it. He showed us all the pictures. Well, to be sure, he had found the file in my cell. He called us names and made us kneel naked on the flagstones.

"As he handled a few postcard-size tinted photos he shouted: 'These pictures tell it all, you disgusting scum. You fockin' perverts, all of you going around unnatural, dressed in black fockin' robes with your dog-fockin' collars.' We were all naked except a few who were wearing a specially designed tight undergarment devised in Rome to prevent the deadly sin of masturbation.

" He continued in the same red faced rage: 'We're going to have an orgy but the style will be mine. I'll show you who the abuser is going to be, b'Jaisus. Not one of you shrivelled, snivelling kneelers, benders, and wimps will get out of this without some flagellation from me. Now kneel down and praise the fockin' Lord. Lower, kiss the feet of Jaisus, lick the flagstones. Come on, tongues out; lick.' When we were all kneeling, he kicked our heads with his policeman's boots. Then he walked down the backs of the rows and aiming carefully at the coccyx, kicked from the rear. By now some of the brothers were screaming in pain and begging for mercy, pleading to know what they had done wrong. He tried to get his assistant involved. 'O'Neil, piss on these priest-perverts; wash away their sins.'

"O'Neil was frightened: 'No, sir, I cannot do that. They're men of God. That would surely be a sacrilege,' he pleaded.

"'Right, O'Neil, fock off and make me some tea.' Then he continued, 'Even I am shocked. Can you believe that? Hard man O'Hara, shocked by some pictures taken in an orphanage? Well, now, tonight you will find out what orphanage boys grow up to be.'

"Suddenly the significance of the file became clear. I felt an immediate pain in my abdomen and hot urine on my thighs. The man immediately in front of me evacuated his bowels. I was splattered. O'Hara kicked his head. There was a crack; perhaps he broke his nose.

"He continued: 'Fear! You may well fear. They should bring back hanging for this.'

"Very slowly and deliberately, he walked in front of us, holding the pictures fanned out like playing cards so we could see the images. I had never imagined anything so awful. Mostly boys of around ten or twelve were being subjected to horrible cruelty and sexual acts. Their faces are what frightened me most; the fear, the agony and the despair. There were about thirty of us in the room.

"He ordered 'Look,' as he walked round to each man in turn. It was clear that he was noting very carefully the reactions of each individual. He was sorting out his victims, the ones he was sure were guilty, and the innocent. Occasionally he stopped to match a priest to a photograph. 'Stand over there. You, this side.'

"He sent most to the right, but a few to the left wall of the room. When he came to me, he kicked my head again. 'You stay there, you filth. 'Right, you lot,' he said to the line of shivering men on the right. 'You're guilty by association. If any of you mention anything about this outside this room, you will be dragged through the shit with the rest. It is quite likely that you did not take part. Still, as far as I am concerned, all you fockin' queers and priests are all the same. Take your rags and fuck off and don't breathe a fockin' word, d'y' hear?'

"I don't think he could bring himself to believe that I was involved, because turning to me he said more gently, 'How can a sweet young boy like you get involved with this?' Before I could answer he gave me another kick, this time in the solar plexus. I crumpled completely. My face came down on the smear of excrement left by the man in front, now gone, judged 'guilty by association.'

"As I was wiping my mouth and weeping, I was unable to answer. I was weeping for what? I think as much for the despair of the little boys as much as the despair I was feeling myself.

"And then his litany: 'That's what they say in the fockin' Catholic Church, "Get them young and you've got them for life." Well, the bastards got me. And now I'll get you, you'll see, b'Jaisus.'

"He was visibly completely out of control: in the East they would have called it run amok. His face was bright red, veins standing out all over, and he was shaking. His voice had lost its deep base and was now high-pitched and squeaky. For sure I was in fear for my life. I was the special target of his anger, but suddenly he turned to the others. 'I suppose it's not his fault. I guess you older bastards made him into your

167

bumboy and had him gradually seduced into your filthy sodomy. You shits come to seminaries to learn all the tricks: smooth talk, promises, rationalisation. Seven years of my sweet young life, you bastards beat me and humiliated me.'

"After this tirade he was calmer but had not lost his mission—to punish us, the hated clergy. He could have done it just with words; some of the men were weeping uncontrollably. They had betrayed their God, Mary, and Jesus. What was left was nothing, just empty, morally crushed, voided souls. Two of the five remaining men dropped to their knees and in classic pose, heads turned up and steepled hands to the ceiling, started chanting. They were then treated to the same hard kicks in the solar plexus. They finished up, like me, gasping for air on the tiled floor. It was then that the door was flung open. Two more garda in uniform entered. One was the hapless O'Neil carrying a cup and saucer with the remains of O'Hara's tea slopping in the saucer, the cup nearly empty. The other, by his extra silver braid, was a superior officer who demanded: 'Sergeant O'Hara. What are these people doing here?' O'Hara snapped his heels to attention and stood parade ground style before his senior officer.

'They are the perpetrators. These are the ones involved in the abominations at the orphanage,' he slurred.

'Why are these three on the floor?'

'I would say, sir, that they are probably praying. And the stink, sir, if I may anticipate your next question, is due to them shitting themselves on account of the long time they are going to spend in jail, if there's any justice on Earth, and in hell, if there's any justice in the hereafter. They have been fighting among themselves, sir, each accusing the others of the heinous crimes committed, sir, if you would admit an opinion.'

"The senior officer told him to go home and sleep and not to write up his report untill the following evening.

"O'Hara left, but our predicament did not get any easier. More officers herded us along the passage, where we were given our habits and some rags to wipe ourselves clean, and bundled into a paddy wagon. As we lay on the cold splintery floor, we did not talk or communicate. We could not admit to another human being that we were actually in this predicament.

I did not know who, if any, of my fellow captors were guilty and I was too frightened to want to know. Such knowledge itself would be a taint. It seemed we were all past praying. We were in a worldly situation and God, wisely, was not there.

"Oh, irrationality, my friend; irrationally, having seen the pictures, I began to feel the guilt of an associate. These clerics, I called them father or brother, were my people. Some of them had been in the pictures, horribly threatening in their hairy, rampant, full-frontal poses in juxtaposition to their small, pale-skinned victims.

"My God, if a man must see a sample of hell before he dies, that was my night. The arraignment was simple and straightforward. News travels fast in jails and police cells. As soon as the cage door was closed behind us, we were set upon. Drunks, druggies, burglars, thieves, muggers, buggers, pimps, and ponces punched and kicked us, showering us with frightening epithets until we were just a whimpering heap on the floor. Of course, we were too ashamed to unite against them. None of us wanted to associate with the others, so we took our beatings without resisting until they physically tired of us.

"I think I'm boring you. I've been saying too much, so I have, but I wanted to let you know that you are not the only one to have glimpsed the devil's work on earth."

Joe was sitting wide-eyed. He had never imagined priests to be anything but quiet and boring men leading cushy lives, avoiding work, violence and pain. The fact was he had never really imagined anything much about priests at all, and this was the first Catholic priest he had ever met.

"Well, man, I am lost for words," Krels said faintly. The old priest leaned forward and braced himself on his uncertain legs, raising his rump just off the chair as if to go.

"Look, son, if I am boring you, just say so. The trouble with getting old is you want to retell everything either to justify it or excuse it. Other people may not find it quite so interesting."

Krels murmured, "Go on," and the priest took the cue to continue. "You see, it was the fingerprints on the envelope. Mine were the strongest. They had a fingerprint expert from

169

Dublin. He was at least forty miles from home and with his little powder puff and magnifying glass, he was the one-eyed man in the land of the blind. It was hard to shift the accusation, to be sure. Even for a priest the sentence would have been twelve years or more, and the chances of a nonce living more than a month with vicious self-righteous criminals and bent jailers were about nil at that time.

"Because he was sure of my innocence, my parish priest hired a lawyer with his own money, and he had the brilliant idea of fingerprinting each individual photograph. This showed many fingerprints, some identified as those of other clerics arrested, but not mine at all, at all. Not a single one there, and he managed to convince the magistrate that I had never touched any of them and in high probability had never seen any of them.

"Both the lawyer and the fingerprint man were appalled by what they had been forced to look at. They could not believe any man could be guilty of such depravity. They were convinced of my innocence and wept openly for the small boys and girls in the pictures.

"The day before we were to appear in court, the screw said I had a visitor. It was Kevin O'Hara. He had lost a lot of weight and was looking pale.

'I've come to see you, Father. I think it's an apology I owe you; to be sure, I know I owe you an apology. But of all of them, I was reluctant to think you were guilty. The file being in your room was not proof, was it?'

'I've seen your parish priest. I haven't seen a man so unhappy in a long time. He said you were good. He blamed himself for your troubles. He sent you to that terrible place. He kept saying, "If only, if only," then he looked at the evidence and asked a few questions and realised your dabs would not be on the pictures if you hadn't seen them. That was enough. You'll be free soon. The lawyer has dealt with it all as well as possible.'

"Then Kevin told me how he had been in that very place years ago. How, as a small boy, he had been so full of love for Jesus, how he wept for his wounds, how he glowed when he heard the sermons, and how the miracles were to him the purest truth. Then with tears in his eyes he said, 'The priests took all that away. They bullied us, beat us black and blue, and buggered us until we were bleeding, defeated, and thoroughly dead inside. Our little bodies ached and we screamed, but no one heard. They stole Jesus away from me. There was no goodness in this world, just pain and suffering caused by endless bullying, torture, subjection, and rape.'

"The idea of Jesus had died in his head, he told me, weeping openly: that erstwhile monster, the man I had feared most in my life. Suddenly this powerful great man stopped, reduced. I think he was embarrassed because he was crying, sobbing profoundly, deep sobs as if his heart were about to burst.

"Then he looked up. 'Can you help me?' He drilled me with his eyes, daring me to deny him his deepest need. I was by then confused. I had never seen such a wild change in emotions and I was feeling completely inadequate. He wiped his face with a grey handkerchief. I failed to answer; yes, I failed him at that point.

"He called the screw: 'Thank you, guard, I'm done,' his outward composure restored. Then he turned back to me. 'You have been a good man. Here, this is my address.' He handed me a brown envelope with his name and address typed unevenly on it. 'I need a change of life. A garda's life is not good: too much conflict, too many opportunities to lose control. I'm after coming back from a disciplinary course in Dublin concerning violence and self-control. I am sure I'm a lost cause. I probably can't change.'

"Anyway, after he'd left my cell, there was a kind of emptiness in the place. He had filled it—a large presence but as much as he had arrived small and broken, he left with dignity.

"I should have had to appear in court and plead not guilty, but there was an intervention. A papal envoy showed up, all the way from Rome, would you believe it? He declared the court incompetent to deal with the clergy. The court never heard the cases in the end. None of the priests was punished, so I was not able to show my innocence. Every single priest and brother was cleared by the law, but the whole thing was written up in all the papers, national and local. One of the

171

blameless priests tried to 'clear his name' by telling a reporter of his innocence, but in fact it brought the whole pile of excrement down on us all. Of course I could not go home."

"When I applied for a missionary posting, I was refused anything where I might come into contact with children, women or normal society, except…well…I have been in that leper colony for nearly fifty years, very happy years with good people, wonderful people," the priest said. "They helped me so much when I was young. They smoothed away my bitterness with their simple kindness. Devout and God-fearing, they hungered for a trained and educated priest to minister to them. So after a year or so, I put my complete soul into it. I started their education. Many of my dear people got degrees by correspondence in subjects as diverse as physics, medicine, and arts, one even an MBA, can you imagine? All I had to do was to teach them to read and write English and they did the rest, some with no fingers, some who couldn't walk." The priest, sensing Joe's discomfort, paused. "That was my story."

"I believe you, Father, but does this have anything to with me?"

"Well, I didn't tell you about Kevin O'Hara. You met him at the village. I had written to him at the address on the envelope with half a hope of getting a response. I got a letter from him, not long but what with his laboured handwriting and the vagaries of the postal system, about a year later there was half a page asking for any kind of opportunity, as he had given up the beat and was scraping a living as a general labourer and occasional pub bouncer. By this time I was settled in with my new flock and just beginning to understand how they lived. I suppose more than anything I needed a companion from the old country, so I persuaded the charity I needed a lay assistant, as we had just taken in a new influx of leper refugees from the troubles up-country."

A tear appeared in the old priest's eye.

"That's another thing I remember so clearly about my old friend O'Hara: his arrival. He was wearing a terrible brown pinstriped suit. The cuffs and trousers were frayed and he did not appear to have any shirt at all, just a grey vest. His shoes did not protect the soles of his feet, but perhaps stopped the sun from burning the white ulcerated skin on top. He was carrying a dishevelled cardboard suitcase, which was only held together with twine, the same sailmaker's twine cobbling up a tear in his trousers, no doubt begged from the bosun on the ship. When I offered him food and drink, he did not hesitate. Through large mouthfuls of potato from my garden, he gave a history of his journey. This is more or less verbatim what he said:

"He greeted me in his inimmitable way: 'My God, you're a saviour, to be sure, although I do seem to remember it was yourself who invited me here. I haven't eaten anything but pap and monkey meat since I left that godforsaken ship seven days ago. I'm sure the water has eaten up my guts. These black people are decent enough; we had a good crack on the river. But these last days on the bus—well, Father, I must say Ireland lives in luxury compared with this. But I won't complain; you know, hungry or not, I feel a sort of ease.' And then what gave me the most pleasure was what he said next: 'You cannot imagine how sweet-tastin' this spud is.'

"It didn't entirely surprise me that he seemed to find peace in my little parish. He was away from his origins, violent, disagreeable, frightening as they had been, and yet here for some reason he and I could find peace among an alien race in an absolutely alien environment. A strange bit of psychology; it speaks to us all. What do you think?"

Joe thought he must be mad and exclaimed: "This is Africa and everything is chaos north of the South African border."

"Remember, we were in a leper colony. Peace reigns in such places. Everyone is already cursed and they have humbled themselves to the disease. They all know rejection. They have no chances of 'success,' so all that is left for them after the daily effort of survival and the amelioration of constant pain is kindness to others and thankfulness to God for another day on Earth. I was able to help them at least to fulfil their intellectual need to study, however irrelevant 'discounted return on investment' and 'prion energy exchange norms' may be.

"They loved to sing. Low bass notes from the men and gentle tenor or alto melodies from the women. They would

173

take the words from the bible and put them to tunes they developed as they went along.

"O'Hara and I were the administrators, and he soon showed a skill at keeping things in order. I guess his police training taught him that systematic rules were needed to make a community work. He had a very cheerful disposition and showed enormous patience when a leper would have difficulty in managing a simple task. Most of the people saw a kindred spirit in him and a few began to worship him. One particular young boy called Komo became his slave and proudly followed him everywhere, fetching, carrying, and running errands. On Sundays Kevin would slink away to some quiet place while I conducted the mass and other services. He never spoke of it to me nor I to him. In spite of this, my son, I think that if I am fortunate enough to gain a place in Heaven, I will meet him there.

"I suppose there is something I am trying to say to you and that is that I have been very low; he was very low and had a terrible problem with violence. He became my right-hand man in the leper colony. He seemed to find his humanity again but in a new form. He never went back to the Church, and I will admit that although I remained true to Rome, I have learned that the Roman Catholic interpretation of the scriptures is very flawed. Anyway, after two days of extreme fever, probably malaria, O'Hara died a month ago, and we buried him; it was one of the saddest days of my life. He had forbidden me from carrying out any rites but asked to be buried with his New Testament in his folded arms.

"So the whole colony, now numbering around five hundred, sang a few joyful hymns and laid him to rest nailed down in his coffin with a bible in his arms. There was a wailing and howling, and Komo had to be restrained from jumping into the grave with him."

Part 4: Anwei and Captain Chuck in Limbe

The ugly, orange painted vessel was at anchor, gently rolling as the broken Atlantic swell wound its way through the islands at Limbe, once stockade islands in a harbour for slaving vessels—then known as Limbo and infamous for the long delays as the slaving ships waited for a full cargo and a fair wind to start their voyage across the Atlantic.

Anwei was lying in the one-and-a-half width bed provided for the captain. She did not have work to do until the preparations for lunch started at around half past ten. The cabin was small and battered. The laminated wood-effect furniture was scratched and chipped. Yellowish paint flaked in places from the panelled bulkheads. But the place was a happy place as light streamed in through the brass-framed circular window. She could hear Chuck in the shower unit adjacent as he shaved and washed himself, humming a low tuneless dirge. They were happy together. They had been so for nearly a year. In spite of his age he was an energetic lover, and with him, after so many perfunctory and joyless couplings, she had began to enjoy coitus again. Chuck looked at himself in the small mirror on the cabinet. Instead of the wrinkled, pink, stubbly, aging face he had feared last year, he saw his rugged, creased features, smoothly shaven and blue-eyed with brown curls.

He perceived himself as mature and handsome now, not wrinkled and old.

"We-ell, I ain't done bad for an old roustabout." Then he thought of Anwei. "She may be blacker than an ace, but she's so goddamn beautiful, it almost makes me cry to look at her sometimes."

He liked to verbalise his feelings and thoughts. This was a trick he learned as he, the uneducated tearaway boy, had to learn reading as a teenager and then rules and regulations and techniques as his education progressed in uneven bursts throughout his life.

Life was good, just enough danger to make it interesting. If his New Orleans owners were to find out that Anwei was female, they would go mad and that would be the end of his romantic African adventure. He reckoned he'd paid his dues after all. Twenty-five years he'd worked on deck, anchor handling, towing, cargo running. He'd seen men lost overboard, crushed between cargo or anchors, and lose limbs on the heaving decks as they'd tried to make attachments to five-ton buoys and fifteen-ton anchors in Canada, the North Sea, and during the Gulf hurricane seasons. He'd seen his best buddy whipped away by the loose end of a three-inch diameter chain. Yes, he'd been there breaking his back, pulling out seventy-millimetre wire from quirky old diesel winches. He'd done the eighteen and thirty hour watchkeeping duties, being thrown about the bridge while trying desperately to stop the jumping and jarring tow wire from passing up the side of the crash barriers as it leaped loosely on the horse at the stern. He'd drunk gallons of cheap black instant coffee from chipped and stained mugs and smoked hundreds of thousands of Lucky Strikes until his stomach hurt with the acridity of it all.

And all the time he'd tried to study for his certificates. As he was a latecomer to reading, he was a great enthusiast for learning. His lips moved as he read and he would quote out loud all those important bits of knowledge so the hearing of them set them firmly in his memory. They'd been like a drug to him. While the other students with their arrogant knowledge, acquired casually at King's Point and other smart places, were out carousing, he would be in some dingy motel room, undisturbed by the grunts and squeals penetrating the flimsy walls of adjacent rooms, poring over textbooks and lecture notes, hollering the knowledge into his head.

And now peace. He wiped his face, put down the small towel, and stepped into the shower. He fought gently with the cranky mixer valve—he knew it well and so now did Anwei. She no longer stuck her head round the door every time she showered alone to ask him to turn it on for her. A mixed blessing, a pleasure lost but a chore no longer necessary.

As he washed himself, he took stock of his body. *I guess they'd call me rangey,* he thought as he soaped his thighs. *And that old thing hanging down like a tassel on a drape. Oh boy, he caused me so much trouble in the past, seems to have found a good home for now, though.*

Quite suddenly he changed his train of thoughts and concentrated on the tasks he had set mentally for the day.

He had to gather the crew together for the weekly safety meeting. Among the other business was the matter of children on board. He had been unable to prevent the women, since he had obviously been sharing his bed with the female cook, but he dreaded the day when one of the crew's children got hurt and they made trouble for him. The men were good and they all got along fine, like a big, happy family. The women treated him and Anwei with respect and made themselves inconspicuous, but there was no stopping the children ranging from tots to teenagers from well—being kids.

2

Anwei, alias Stanley Ngowon, had reversed herself on the bed so she was facing the door to the shower. Her chin was cupped in her left hand and her feet were in the air over the crumpled pillows. She knew the effect this would have on Chuck as he came out of the door, towel in hand, wiping the last of the refreshing water from his white skin. It never failed to make him smile broadly and that smile was her prize and stimulation for the rest of the day. Things were all right if she could see that big grin every day.

It had been Chuck's arrival for the first time in Africa. After a half-hour wait a driver who identified himself by a baseball cap with the familiar company logo emblazoned across the high, flat, front came to take him to the hotel. He had checked in , showered and stretched out on the small, hard bed. He'd flicked on the TV, and surfed the channels to find three showing fat black-suited Africans talking what looked like politics in foreign languages. Soon, bored by the four walls, he dressed and made his way down to the reception area to ask if he had any messages. The clerk, shaking her head, said he could go to the restaurant across the hall.

He ate an undercooked steak, French style with sour garlic and vegetables smothered in white cheesy sauces. His body clock awry, he looked around for something to do. Chuck sauntered into the bar, standing with one foot on the toe rail, thumbs in his belt, drawing attention to a big brass buckle. He looked across at the barman's back. "Howdy, friend, could you get me a beer?"

He was conspicuous among the other expatriates, being tall, slender, and dressed Texas style: slim-fitting Wranglers over tooled leather boots with high cutaway heels, and a white fitted shirt with a modest embroidered pattern down the discreet button line. He'd left his hat up in the room and his gold chains in Texas. The other men were generally round and red-faced, potbellied and sloppily dressed in dark polo shirts and blue trousers or shapeless jeans.

Anwei was in a party of mixed Africans and Europeans at a table near the window; the girls were local and the men were expat workers. She was feeling dull and sad but every now and then joined in with an animated "my goodness" or "truly so?" She was down in the dumps because her last adventure with a prosperous local importer had finished in tears that afternoon. It had been a long but not very happy association. She had hung on for the sake of the nice apartment, but it had all finished when his wife sent out a spy to see why his bank showed regular cash withdrawals on Thursdays or Fridays, yet he gave her about half or less housekeeping money on Monday. Although she had been a good obedient wife, she knew her man was up to monkey business away from home and she would make his life unbearable if he did not stop.

Anwei had been partly relieved by the end, but lost her rights to a three-room apartment in a concrete serviced block and the prestige and respect living there.

There were no stools at the bar, so Chuck looked round for a place to go. At that moment one of the Europeans at the table called across, "Hey, Tex, come and join us. Here, get a chair, plenty of space. We are just a bunch of guys going to work and these beautiful girls are with us for the evening."

Chuck had never heard this accent for real before, but he guessed it must be French and his guess was proved right.

"I am Jules, vis is Jean-Paul, Frank, Dino, 'arry, and Marc." As Chuck shook all their hands, he realised they were of different nationalities. "The ladies are all Mimi or Fu-Fu," he joked, causing a giggle of indignation from the girls, who all started to say their names, proffering their hands for him to shake.

After a couple of rounds in the hotel bar, they all decided it was time to go on to a nightclub. The girls suggested th Savour d'Afrique Bar. There would be a famous local band there and a series of singers. By this time Chuck, although some decades older than the others, was relaxed and ready for a good time. They left the hotel and squeezed into two dented Renault taxis. After passing through several roadblocks where they dispensed largesse to the otherwise unpaid police force, they pulled up in a scruffy alley and entered under a crude representation of a giraffe's head animated by flashing yellow neon. The place was just beginning to warm up. With tables and chairs around the edge, a cracked composition dance floor, and a raised platform, the place had a friendly sleaziness completed by the six aging musicians performing with tuneful enthusiasm on battered locally made instruments. The party sat and ordered beer. It came in pint mugs of the dimpled English style with the Lion Lager badge emblazoned on the side.

"I guess I'm not too used to drinking this beer," Chuck said to the girl next to him, who was beginning to pay a lot of attention to him between sips of bright red Cassis, which he thought was probably coloured water. She told him her name was Claire in a French accent. He'd never heard black girls speak in any other than a deep Southern or clipped Chicago slang.

After a while his knees started aching from sitting down so long, and when the music turned to a lively two-step, he rose and taking Claire's hand, led her up to the floor. Soon he had all the crew with him in line with varied degrees of skill either aided or hindered by the booze. They told him they had just come up from Pascagoula in Mississippi and had all become experts in the two-step. The girls were keen to learn and they all had a riotous time. He paid attention to Claire, but he noticed Anwei out of the corner of his eye. She seemed to be interested and her eyes flashed at him on more than one occasion. He smiled at her and she melted into the mess of people around him.

There was more dancing and carousing, and he found himself back with Claire; the other girl disappeared into the darkness and for all their instantaneous intimacy, he realized he did not remember her name. Good sense told him it was time to go. The others were obviously going to make a night of it and he had no idea what was expected of him tomorrow. He said his good-byes and then made for the door. A gentle voice behind him said, "You are going now?" He turned and saw Anwei. "Sure am, and I don't..."

"I am going too, let's walk."

"Just walking, no problem. How far is Hi-Lux Hotel?"

"Not far, no need taxi. We walk, maybe talk."

"Walk, talk OK."

They made their way through the crowd of touts and pimps and small boys selling dope and chewing gum onto a wide boulevard. After while they came to the hotel and the open bar with tables on the forecourt.

Chuck's thirst got the better of him as he was approached by the waiter. "Hey, my friend, stop for a beer or gin and tonic."

Silently they took seats at a metal table.

Unbidden Anwei looked up to the waiter and said, "Coke?"

Chuck nodded assent and then asked, "You got Bourbon whiskey?"

"Jack Daniel," announced the waiter, and Chuck was already anticipating the sharp oily flavour on his tongue.

"I don't drink much alcohol," she announced.

"Don't worry, honey, I ain't going to fall over in the gutter; this will help me sleep."

They were silent until the waiter returned. This pleased Chuck. Anwei was lost for words. She found his accent difficult to her ear, and she was frightened of misunderstanding him. She was also beginning to fear that she was no longer welcome company. The drinks came with a tinkling of ice in the glasses against the near silence of the midnight street. She smiled broadly at him and he returned the smile.

"I'd like to know you. Do you have a cellular?" He handed her the phone the driver had given him.

"Here," Chuck said. "I guess this is mine for now." She took it and dialed a number. A familiar ditty came from her little purse. "I think you look kind," she said.

He downed the Bourbon in one swallow, spitting the ice back into the glass, and stood. "Stay, finish your Coke, and call me anytime." This woman he did not need.

He strode to the bar, signed the check, threw a few coins down on the top, and made his way to the elevator.

Half an hour later, in a sweat, he removed his clothes, piling them neatly on a chair, and lay naked on the bed. *So this is Africa*, he thought, and without much more thinking, he fell into a deep sleep. It was his bladder and the high-pitched buzz of a mosquito that woke him a few hours later. Groping round the unfamiliar room, he noticed his phone flashing. In the bathroom as he peed, he saw on the phone a message. "Thanks a lot, Anwei."

His eyes barely open, he remembered her sudden smile as he had made his parting remark.

Whores! he thought. *Can't they just get to you? This one just seemed a bit special. Why? Who knows?* She stayed in his mind for few minutes after his head hit the pillow—a more agreeable soporific than the usual waves crashing on the beach. At nine his phone rang. He was in the breakfast room trying to make some sense of the local paper.

"Captain, I am Denis. You will be ready in five minutes?"

"Denis, is it? OK, buddy, are you coming to the hotel?"

"Which hotel are you in?"

"Something Lux."

"Hi-Lux, yes, I'll meet you in the lobby. We will go directly to your ship."

"Sounds good."

There was a long pause. "Oh yes, very good, m'sieur."

In five minutes he was ready, packed and sitting on an uncomfortable PVC seat in the lobby. Three quarters of an hour later, after he had stood up and sat down three times and smoked three cigarettes, a man in frayed pinstriped trousers and large black sunglasses entered. "Are you the captain?" he addressed him, the only person in the lobby. "Are you ready to go to your ship?"

Chuck bit his lip to hold down his protest. He was used to the "hurry up and wait" of the oil business, and now he met it again in Africa—in spades.

"We take care of everything with the hotel," Denis said, proffering his bony hand.

A large old Peugeot was carelessly parked at an angle to the dusty street. They got in and François started driving with an air of slick abandon through the crowded streets. Down a steep hill the smell of manioc and timber hit Chuck's nostrils. The roads in this area were smeared with oil and grease from the cargoes. Broken pallets and loose dunnage-wood littered the greasy sidewalks. High walls topped with broken glass hid the activity glimpsed through frequent crude gaps in the block work. In vantage points, on planks or smooth patches, workers wrapped in sheets or sacking slept or lounged, smoking, chatting or just staring ahead. Rusting semi-trailers, with or without containers, were all over the place.

They drove through all this and soon the clutter diminished. They were making their way to the harbour wall.

He saw the ship from a distance as they came out from behind the last shed. He recognised this type of Gulf supply vessel. An open workboat was waiting for him, loosely tied to a rusting ring on the broken harbour steps.

As the boat chugged across the river to the dock on the other side, he saw areas of blue paint showing through the orange topcoat. Change of owner, change of colour, but no unnecessary money spent, a process known as *shine on shite*, which looks quite good if a new director has to visit but lasts about six months.

He was told she had been off-hired because of a fatal accident. Owners were looking for another charter while he was to be the caretaker captain. He would have an engineer and a mechanic, and when they needed to move the boat, he would get a mate and some crew. At the moment he had three deckhands, three engine room hands, and a cook. The manager said he only kept them on as it would cost more to make them redundant, paying them off and dealing with their village chief, who would extract a big fine for not complying with the ad hoc local labour law. He had been told over the phone by the manager he could probably get them washing down and greasing things, but he would have virtually no budget.

The agent told him he had to take the boat down to Limbe, where the anchorage was a lot cheaper. He would call on the cellular phone if there were to be any orders for further movements or voyages. There would be a local pilot, probably more of a passenger who would extract cigarettes and whiskey and give misleading advice. Chuck made his own study of the route through the sandbanks and hoped the pilot would locate the logjams for him. He was told he would also have a chief officer. *What for?* he wondered. But when they turned up together, he realized why. The pilot was a bleary-eyed, wrinkled old man complete with a battered naval officer's peaked cap. His rheumy eyes obviously had little visual ability, and his odour of aniseed suggested absinthe. "My nephew, Capitane Alphonse, will be your chief mate for a week or as long as you want."

The young man looked to be almost competent. "Right, Mister Alphonse, I am the captain."

"Excuse my uncle, he is chief pilot. I am one of the river pilots. I graduated in Marseilles and sailed with the French

Marine Marchande. He did also until about thirty years ago. My mother and his wife are sisters."

The trip was going to be short; with the speed limited by the shallow water on a falling tide, it would take about six hours.

The phone rang in his pocket. "Remember me? Anwei."

"Of course. How are you? Surprise! We are going to some place called Limbe, in the estuary, a bunch of islands in a bay. We go to anchor there out of the way."

"My cousin lives there," she stated. "We have many friends and family there. We can visit you."

Chuck went to silent mode. He was being chased. It worried him and excited him at the same time. After all, this was not a common whore. She was a real person with family and nephews and nieces. A warm feeling of family came over him.

"Right," he said, "be in contact. I will have this phone all the time, so call me and let me know what's happening to you."

She was suddenly unsure. "You don't really want me to, that so?"

"Just do it, honey. We leave here on the tide tonight. We'll be in the bay tomorrow morning. I will tell you about it then."

3

The slaving stockades have long gone, but the natural harbour of Limbe still affords anchorage to foreign vessels plundering the coast. The latest trade is hardwood. Slowed to a virtual stop by the international timber regulations, the machinery and infrastructure remain rusting on the banks. The roads are impressive and an area of flat open storage and corrugated warehouses bear witness to the erstwhile commerce. The Blue Horizon Hotel is a vestige of the prosperity once generated here. While Mister Alphonse was still signed on, Chuck, the bosun and the cook would go into town to buy stores. All three would stay over. The cook and bosun would visit their wives, and Chuck would take a room in the hotel to enjoy an evening of edible food and Anwei's company, which he guessed might be extended through to the morning. She had made it clear she was not to be paid. He thought, *this is the long game. Beware, Chuck Pecan, she'll nail you down.* He did not heed his own warning—what man ever does?

About a month after the move to Limbe, the cook had been given orders to join a ship working offshore. Chuck had nearly puked on every meal and was glad to see the back of him. The cook was overjoyed as his pay would double with the offshore bonus. He wasted no time in leaving. Chuck soon learned that in Africa, it was the chiefs who took most of the men's pay to redistribute among their many wives and children. They acted as agents for the crew. The managers and superintendents went to the chiefs for men.

Anwei had phoned that day and Chuck had thrown her the question, "Can you cook American style?"

"Of course. What kind of woman you take me for?"

"Right. Get your ass down here and you're hired. Don't waste time if you want the job. The chief can't find anyone today, but it won't take him long. If the next cook is twice as good as the last, I'll still be dead from starvation within a month. I just have to get you signed on fast before the chief gets his man down here. By the way, you're a man from now on. Come down dressed in men's clothes—no makeup, no fancy hairdo. Got it? I'll meet you at the hotel at six. I'll make it 'stores day' tomorrow. You'll come with me to the market, and we'll buy proper food."

"My God, you don't give a girl much choice, do you? I might get into trouble."

"Take a chance."

She appeared in the afternoon with a hessian sack in her hand. In it were a scruffy boiler suit, woolly hat, and a rough pair of rig boots a few a sizes too big and well worn. As soon as they were in the hotel room, she tried all this gear on to show him the effect.

"Do I have to wear this all the time? And I owe money in about five shops for this stuff. What do you think? Do I still look sexy or do I look the part?"

He laughed involuntarily, but soon saw his mistake as her face began to crinkle.

"You look magnificent. You have achieved exactly the right effect. You could easily be a male cook, but I know you are a beautiful woman underneath. Maybe they'll think you're gay. You got any fags around here? I was told it's not very common in Africa."

She did not understand the question, but smiled sweetly. The next day, with the bosun driving the fast rescue boat, they went aboard, laden down with the new stores.

"What's the smell here?" she asked as soon as he entered the accommodation.

Over the years Chuck had gotten so used to the smell of diesel and cooking oil pervading all ships that he did not notice it.

"Let's get you kitted up and in the galley cooking and meeting the men. They aren't all from the same tribe, but I have to pay off Chief Osuru whenever I take someone from outside, or he can send his heavies down to throw them off. So you'll have to satisfy them first with the local delicacies we bought today. They won't be getting bush meat and fancy vegetables all the time, but you can impress them on the first day to get them on your side. Here are some chef's whites. There's no assistant or steward, so you have a cabin to yourself."

After he had taken her down below to her cabin, he had grave misgivings. What was he doing? She was black and now she was unmade-up, and in broad daylight he was not sure she was so attractive or sexy. Thinking about it he realised his motive was pure boredom. He had endured a month of shaking down the crew of seven and now could foresee endless months ahead with no activity. The impulse had come to him to make things at least interesting and comfortable.

He was not reassured when he visited the galley. She was there, sure enough but she looked lost.

"Right, snap to, Stanley. Let me just show you round." He demonstrated the cooker, the chip fryer, the disposal unit in the sink, and all the other equipment and the main electrical breaker and firefighting system. She brightened up and then he

186

took her into the fridge, where the shelves were mainly bare. She gasped as the cold air hit her. Although this was the first time she had walked into a fridge, she did not show it, peering at the few items available.

"This is the way to open the door if it closes while you are inside. You must keep the door locked at all times except for access. Here is the key. The boys will steal the food if you don't.

"You better stop smiling all the time. Look bored and pissed like a real cook. Be disagreeable and angry at all requests. Later you can be more friendly.

"That door is to the freezer. Bosun has a key and he stores the fish they catch in there. You won't need to go there as there is nothing else inside right now. If we go to sea, that's where we store meat. It's very cold."

Now bright-eyed, she was absorbing all this newfound knowledge eagerly.

"So where's the food I am to cook today?" The boxes were being unloaded from the fast rescue boat.

And that had been that. The crew soon caught on that she was not gay, but female. Chuck persuaded the chief that the normal ransom should be paid and a little extra bonus. Before long Anwei was a resident in the "old man's" cabin and all settled down. Then the emotions started to kick in. He and she began to be interdependent, admiring and loving. As his twelve-week tour of duty came toward its end, Chuck began to worry about how he was going to square this very tricky situation. Anwei would have to go, he decided, but by now she had gotten used to the pay, which she split between herself, her auntie, and her mother. They were beginning to become dependent on her, and Chuck was aware that he would be causing hardship to a lot of people and children. He would have been careless of this in the past, but familiarization with Anwei and her family situation and a growing fondness now played on his mind.

4

This conundrum was solved when a surprise memo arrived on board with the mailbag. It was from the manager and asked very politely if he would mind postponing his leave. This was a relief for him as he was going to find an excuse to request the same. Then he read the next paragraph.

"Red Dawn Marine is being taken over by a USA multinational company. Negotiations are well down the line. This will be good for all of us as this company has a worldwide presence and has brought together many other operators from all over. The name of the company cannot be revealed for commercial reasons until the deal is completed."

And a week later:

Dear Captain Pecan, you will have had a formal notification that you are now potentially employed by Tidal Marine Workboats of Mobile. As you are of retirement age, you may resign or retire with full redundancy and pension rights. You will receive a package of documents explaining the situation and including the necessary application forms for the settlement you wish to take.

"However, it has been decided that the *Scotfield 2* will not be offered for further charters either long-term or spot. We will be negotiating her sale for local use or scrap. I have arranged to reengage the local chief officer, and the vessel will standby in Limbe until a voyage can be arranged. You will fly back to Houston for discussions with Human Resources.

"Give me your thoughts, my captain, darling."

"She-it, I may as well tell you. Ship's going to scrap. I'm going back stateside. They'll probably put me out to grass."

"Grass, why grass?"

"No, no, they'll make me retire. Younger men are coming along. Less ships. The whole picture is clear. I go home, you stay here. Only thing I can do is give you money to tide you over for a year or so."

"You marry me!"

"Impossible! Bitch at home never let me divorce her. Threatened to drag it through the court until nothing remains. She gets my paycheck now. All I get is the rent from houses I bought without telling her a long time ago. I make a big deal of begging some money off her when I go home so she don't suspect nothing. But the amount she gives me wouldn't keep me in a cheap motel room eating burgers."

"You can live here in Limbe or Douala. We can go on together."

"Look, I give you money. I go back home. I sort out something, then I tell you what to do. Don't worry, I got more money. You'll be OK."

She put her head down in a sulk. Then suddenly she flared like a firework. "Money! Money! I don't want any filthy money. People just give me money. Shit money. I want a person; I thought I had a real man, a man to honour, a man to love. You said you love me. You give me money!" She ran out of steam as suddenly as the outburst began. She buried her face in the pillow. Raising her face just so the words could be heard, she said, "My life is shit. It's always been shit. One wrong turn and all is lost." She went to the small sink and rinsed her face. "You will write and tell me. I know you are my good friend. You may give me money; it will help me to wait for you."

One of Chuck's jobs was to draw money for the wages from the American Express Bank every month in Douala. He had to accompany the agent as there had been a problem with the agent at sometime in the past. He asked about opening an account. It was possible, he was told, to open an overseas account if he had a local address. The account could be operated by a bank card, using a cash machine. He could make transfers from the States. This would work. He could send money from home, and Anwei could take money from the machine in Douala. The charges were high, so he would make the transfers relative large and infrequent.

Chuck had discharged her from the cook's job before the local captain arrived.

Although she maintained her composure, Anwei was shattered inside. She was getting too old for changing relationships. She had a sinking feeling of being a waif without roots, a drifter in her own city, but at least Chuck had promised her money. That would make a difference; she could last out for a few months without having to find some other man to cling onto. She might even try to get a job, but she knew her prospects were very poor. Any job she could get would be virtually unpaid and at her age probably menial. Good jobs went to qualified people. Perhaps she could study. A bit late now, because although she could speak a host of dialects and English and French, she was a poor reader and writing was limited to her name and a few basics after so long without the necessity.

So it was that Anwei found herself at the airport again. She was nicely dressed in African style, beautiful bright colours representing cockatoos with a piled-up headdress. Chuck was very emotional but kept his self control. They held hands and spoke a few stilted sentences in the little separate waiting room in the departure area before he made the long walk through glass-sided passages to the aircraft. Anwei watched his bandy walk in narrow-legged blue jeans and Texan boots from behind with a mixture of pure lust and sadness.

Part 5: Anwei After Chuck Goes Home

All had been well at first, three months ago; it seemed like a lifetime now. She had gone to the bank directly from seeing Chuck off at the airport. Still dressed in her finery to impress the bank people that she was an important customer, she had taken out twenty thousand CFA from the cash machine—enough for settling old debts and buying a few groceries. She then looked for a better place to live. When she told her landlord she was moving, he was pleased as he had a waiting tenant and could double the rent. He still insisted on her paying a month's rent in lieu of notice. She put down a deposit and a week's rent on a ground-floor room in a villa for her and her aunt to share. She felt the deadweight of her relation, but at the same time a familial duty to do the minimum to ensure her survival and get her out of her roadside shack.

Having paid the landlord most of the cash she had, she went to the cash machine for more. She was uneasy. There were some men standing idly nearby. She thought she had seen one of them before, but nevertheless went ahead to draw out money. Before she could do anything about it, the card was snatched out of the machine by one of the men, and then as the money appeared, it was taken by another. They walked nonchalantly away, smiling and joking as if nothing had taken place. When she recovered from the initial shock, she found her cell phone had also been picked from her bag, no doubt to reduce the chances of her calling for help. She looked along the street after the thieves but could not identify them in the crowd. In that single moment her whole life was ruined. Chuck became a memory as there was no way to contact him, no way he could contact her. She went to the building where she thought the ship's agent's office had been to find nothing, just a sign announcing its closure. This possible connection was cut. She had no contacts with the shipping world, and her auntie had no money. She returned to the shack by the road, the only place where they could sleep, and promised to pay the rent to a grizzly man who said he was the landlord's representative. There was no choice. She spent two days cleaning the dingy surroundings and the pallet-wood furniture. Her aunt had never been more disagreeable and nasty. Then on an impulse she decided to go back home to see her mother, whom she had visited three times in the last twenty years.

2

Anwei's mother, Balenga, was dying. It was lung cancer, so common among the poorer women in Africa. None of the earlier dwellings had chimneys to carry off the smoke from their primitive cooking fires, and the danger of smoke was not recognised. Charcoal was a luxury out of reach, kerosene only occasionally available.

Her breathing was shallow and painful and Anwei shared her pain as she attended to her. She had not visited home for some years so it was a surprise to find her mother in terrible poverty and bedridden and to learn that her sister had been killed.

"I must tell you more about your father," she said, her voice weak and croaky. "Bolo Sojenji was not from here but came from a long way away in Congo. His father and grandfather had been from a long line of potters from an area in the Belgian Congo near Cameroon. They made beautiful things from the special clay around their village. Bolo was a refugee from fighting in the area during the troubles in 1960. He managed to avoid the rebel recruiters with a few of his friends by hiding in the mud pits, he told me. But after the rebels had raided the village for recruits, the villagers began to starve as the women and old people struggled to manage without money. He told me several people came down with the sores and rotting flesh caused by leprosy. His father was chief of the village and encouraged him to leave.

"He said he was full of fear of the unknown. But his father just told him to follow the river down to the sea, where there were big cities and opportunities to get rich and start a good life. Your father, just a young boy, wanted to stay to help his family, his mother and two sisters, who were all looking thin and unhealthy. He said things continued to get worse until one day a group of white people, dressed in blue, arrived in white cars. They found several empty houses and some cases of leprosy; the villagers were industrious in making pottery, but there were no young men and no market for the pots in the post-independence chaos. They noted a lack of food and fuel.

"The next thing the villagers learned was that coming on behind this small convoy of white jeeps and strangers wearing blue suits was a crowd—you know, walking wounded lepers. They came from their village fifty miles away. The white people decided that their village of Aku-Agua would become a leper colony.

"His father had no power as chief, even though he had status—the government called it 'évolué'—and he had the rights to the land that was given to him by the government during the National Land Survey of 1945. He had the deed signed by the King of Belgie.

"Anwei. Get it from that metal box under the bed and I'll show it to you. The key is round my neck here."

Anwei put the box on the table and used the key to open it. There were several papers inside and also the goatskin wallet. She opened the wallet, and a piece of paper fell into her hand. They read together the beautifully written French script on lined paper.

"It's there, the deed for the land. That heavy paper."

The document was wrapped in a cured goatskin rolled and secured with a red ribbon. The writing was on heavy cartridge paper about half a metre long.

"Bolo's father and his uncle, the priest of the village, protested. They feared the lepers would infect everyone. The white men did not respect their documents or their rights to the land. Sojenji Sojenji, your grandfather, told his only son, Bolo, to take the documents and find people who would give them proper respect.

"Bolo took his father's advice, so he and his boyhood friend and cousin, Ndoku, set off following the current of the River Congo. But Anwei, your father never had the papers examined. It was pointless. He knew he would not go back to the war-torn areas and he had made a life for himself in Douala and here with me.

"I met your father in Douala. Sunday was his only day off and for me too. I was working in a laundry, hard labour, and he could often work seven days a week as he was in demand from customers for pottery. He had rented a bed in a bidon shack with three other workers when he first arrived. But he was a good man. He saved money and I saved a bit too.

"We used to gather outside the cathedral after the mass. It was there that news from home was exchanged and people made contacts or met up with others from the same village or area." Suddenly her voice cleared and her face became more animated. "It was also here, by way of flashed eyes and hidden smiles, that we might make the overtures to a courting.

"Oh, I was impressed by this young man's smart appearance and the confidence of his bearing. His face fascinated me also. It was different from the local cut of features. Most faces were blunt and coarse, but his features were sharp, with a straight pointed nose and a very square and slightly protruding jaw. As he talked with the other men, I saw his thin lips and beautiful smile and his easy laugh. His colour was black, and I thought his features were handsome. I would think of him sometimes in the week and then one Sunday when I was sneaking a look, he caught my eye and held it until I trembled. I remained back as my friends dispersed. He was in no hurry to leave.

"His voice was deep and smooth. 'I see you looking,' he said. His accent was very French and the words were jerky and difficult to understand, but his smile was wide, displaying fine

194

white teeth and wrinkling his eyes. '*Parlez Francais?*' I asked. '*Oui, oui, facilement, mais l'Anglais, pour mois, c'est très difficile,*' and his face lit up like a child with a new toy. So we made a pact to teach and learn each other's language."

Balenga's voice had strengthened as she rambled on. She was excited by the happy memories of her courtship and her early days with Bolo.

"We stayed in Douala as Bolo was getting good work at the pottery. Soon he had built a small house on a piece of newly cleared land and we were saving money. We married when I was pregnant and gave birth to you. He named you after his boss's wife, a Chinese name, two more girls followed. The junior daughter was dead within six weeks of her birth—I never knew why. She just never seemed to want to live. The doctor said it might be dangerous to try for more children and sent me to a European Protestant agency to explain methods of birth control, really scandalous for a Catholic, but we had no more anyway, although we weren't strict with the methods. I began to hate the city and yearned to go back to my roots up-country now that I had you children. Bolo had saved money and was able to sell the Douala home, giving us enough to buy some land and building materials for a place in Santambo, where my mother came from. He set up his own pottery, buying clay for the fine work and digging out local material for rough water jars.

"He had shown me what the goatskin wallet contained when we were courting. He thought it would impress me. He was a chief of a village. But the truth was, every chancer in Douala at that time boasted to be a village chief; but to give him his due, none of the others had any documents to show for it."

Anwei looked at the other paper in the wallet. It meant little to her except that it was obviously official and important. Loose in the box was another yellow sheet of paper, an original handwritten in French. Anwei was just able to understand it and found the translation typed on a flimsy piece of copy paper.

195

République du Cameroun

Declaration of origin made by Bolo Sojenji at his naturalisation hearing in the Hotel De Ville, Douala. Dated January 3rd 1963

I come from a village called Aku-Agua in Congo. I fled my village because of disease and fighting. I left with my cousin Ndoku. We carried a little money with us to start with and as we moved on we had to work to stay alive. Mostly the people in the villages were ready to hear our story and in spite of all the difficulties of the transition period they were open to giving us employment as their own young men had been taken by the recruiters. We were paid in food and lodging. There was very little money. We would forage for food in the jungle as we moved on. We had set our minds on going to the coastal cities determined to make our fortunes. Of course, we could not follow the river all the way down to the coast but with a mixture of river road and rail routes we slowly progressed towards the evening sun and our destiny. So it was that our path took us into Cameroon, first to Yaoundé. Ndoku was suffering from diarrhoea and dehydration. He died on the street in his own filth. I could do nothing for him, I cried for him but we had no money and in that city nobody cared for a couple of country boys on the street. I found a policeman who without any interest or sympathy called for a truck and I saw the body of my cousin disappear like a sack of garbage. I hated that city and in my misery I heard of another city called Douala.

I arrived in Douala stronger but moneyless and made myself understood in French. I found that my knowledge of pottery was in demand so I was able to secure work, first as an occasional and then as a regular employee in the Ching pottery factory. I have built up a small cache of money in the last three years.

I am now a productive worker in this Nation of Cameroun and wish to be recognized as a citizen.

This document was signed, witnessed and sealed.

Attached was a certificate of naturalisation.

"He had to do that before they would marry us in those days. His birth certificate and my papers are in there as well as our marriage certificate. All very correct.

"This will be yours, and I will give it to you now as I know I am dying." Her voice had weakened again and she sounded breathy and gruff. "You may find it valuable. You are the direct descendant; your birth certificate is there. Are you going back to your life in Douala? You have a husband?"

"A man; we are not married." Anwei yearned for Chuck. She was angry with him but she wanted him more than anything.

"I have much pain now, Anwei. You have not been around me, my daughter. The occasional money you sent was useful. I am thankful. Your sister visited and looked after me. Her husband is a good man. She was killed in a hut fire with my two grandchildren. Her husband is in prison for killing her. He could not have done it. They had a wooden house. He was returning home from a thieving raid on the kerosene store. They caught him with kerosene and accused him of setting his hut on fire. It was revenge or an accident. He was not there. The young gendarme was proud to put his first murderer behind bars." She looked up at Anwei, appraising her belligerently. "Have you made money in the city? I don't think so because you have offered me nothing today. Never mind, I will pass on soon."

That night Balenga died in a terrible bloody coughing bout. After the funeral Anwei took the metal box and walked down the nearly deserted street. The ugly concrete huts were mostly unoccupied, their owners dead or fled. None of the remaining villagers, dull and hungry, acknowledged her passing. She held tight to the tin box on the bus. It represented her being. The contents were her identity, an identity she had not needed before but which now seemed to be an important part of her being. Her fat idle aunt was the only person she had left to connect her to the human race. She was going back.

3

Her feet ached inside the cheap, shiny, plastic, high-heeled shoes. These were the fashion, the sexy thing. She could remember when she had yearned for such smart shoes: the accoutrement of the smart life. But she refrained from dwelling on it. She avoided all thinking, keeping herself in a sort of semiconscious trance, just surviving the indignities of her calling and the burning itch of her calves and shins. Men walked by. She moved almost imperceptibly, exercising the universal body language of sex for sale. The shy near-smile, humourless yet supplicant, eyes wide for a second, a hook to catch a fish, a smile neither of endearment nor of joy. Each man passing was a chance for life, for a new day, the day that would prove better, the day of salvation. She dreamed of a new beginning, back to life from this vertical solicitude. She was aware that only old hacks and naive village girls stood in the shadows on corners wearing bright minidresses and luminous pink lipstick and risked the pain of subjection, humiliation, and dejection from the sort of man who roughly relieved his needs with a few sharp thrusts and grunts, a coarse joke, and a fist of crumpled low value notes.

Jesus had let her go. What had been the point of loving Jesus? He didn't even give her basic succour. Recently, time after time, the encounters were disappointing, frightening, or painful and as time went by, less lucrative. There was no pleasure anymore. The thrill of following a man to a hotel room and the smiles and jokes, the admiration they would show as they beheld her magnificent naked curves: this was lost. The animal pleasure of fingering a rigid penis had become just a chore, no more pleasurable than holding a broom handle. Where had it all gone? Now it was a counterfeit charade and each act more difficult than the one before, a nasty, dirty, malodorous, and demeaning performance of false smiles and faked giggles. Every time she turned her rump to the ceiling for the crude rutting of some half-drunk middle manager, she felt tears in her eyes as she buried her head in a sweat-stinking pillow. Why would life not just finish here and now? Hadn't she paid enough yet? What was the point of knowing great men, nice men, kind men, rich men, if they all in turn found a reason to let you go, ignore you, put you down, and pay you off? And now her best chance of all, the American, had been cruelly taken from her.

She stumbled on a crooked stone in the muddy broken sidewalk. There were fewer men now. She had some small banknotes in her glittery plastic purse. She could kiss the doorman at a little dockside bar and slip in for a late drink to help her sleep, or perhaps, from a sitting position, she could lure a man who would take her to a hotel where she could get a hot shower and a few hours in soft bed. She prayed silently. She could still survive. She was no longer so clear skinned and fresh faced. A few wrinkles here and there, and in spite of subtly applied makeup, she saw daily in the cracked mirror a coarsening of the features.

Her hands were bony due to malnutrition, and the dark brown of her lower legs were spotted with old scars from bites and boils. The few other girls her age were all just competition now. There used to be a camaraderie among them in the better old days when business was brisk and a girl could expect to get a boyfriend who would last a month or even a year—a boyfriend who would be generous, buying nice presents, taking you away for weekends, restaurants, and parties. The younger girls got all these now; showing only contempt for the older women, they'd waggle their bottoms at her as they passed on the arm of some overdressed young blade. So, recently she had started to dread the waking hours, the morning, even after a comfortable night in clean sheets. The rejection seemed more powerful now than in the old days when there was a certainty of another bright encounter soon after. Now her tarnished appearance, the slump in the Cameroon economy, and the threat of AIDS made each morning farewell seem like the final rejection from the human race, which was after all the male race. She thought about how absolutely and completely everything was for the male. The woman is valued only for the instant relief she gives or her ability to produce a string of children.

As she slid into the plastic seat behind the sticky laminate table, she smiled at the bar boy. "Are you well, Simon? Is your girl fine? Has it been busy?"

"Anwei, you look good tonight. What have you been up to? Living in the Meridian?"

"Oh, my God, if only. My feet are killing me. Life is too quiet. What can you give me?"

"Just wait a moment. I can get you something good. Stak is busy with that new girl come in from up-country."

He handed her whiskey and Coke left behind by some Japanese revelers who had moved on recently. It was slightly warm, but as she drank, she felt the alcohol rush through her body, casting aside the pain and stiffness in her muscles. Her smile became less forced. The music began to sound rhythmic and melodious. She had eaten nothing that day. The dance floor wobbled momentarily and the dancers wavered. A white boy staggered slightly as he danced alone, his partner moving free to indulge her own lonely blank gyrations. He came over and peered at Anwei, turning away too quickly and lurching toward the red lit door to the toilets. She had smiled but as their eyes met, she felt immediate rejection as he had registered her blotchy dark skin and dull bloodshot eyes.

She looked around vainly for any of the old crowd, girls she had known a few years ago. Many were dead. A few enjoyed the precarious privilege of being the mistress of a 'big man' with money and some were 'baby mamas' producing a child every year and growing big in belly and bum, like blown inner tubes draped in voluminous cotton finery. Most had faded away back to the villages to marry hapless smallholders or to work in grimy sweatshops making counterfeit jeans or T-shirts, their nights of joyous dancing, giggling, sex and money just fleeting memories to help them pass through the sweltering slavery of repetitive days on the soil or in clattering factories.

At another table a small group of black suited Asian men, coming to the end of a rowdy whisky-drinking session were paying off some younger girls for their time. The men rose together, leaving the girls chattering. She wanted to scream at them, "Get a proper job! Get a husband," but she knew it would be futile. They, like her, were outcasts. Their villages had disowned them. They had nowhere to go for succour. Their lives would be a disjointed and chaotic succession of chances taken or missed. Good men, bad men, luxury, and poverty. Now she saw them taking pleasure in the company of each other like schoolkids, but she knew soon they would tarnish like her and their laughter would no longer be spontaneous and their eyes would not glisten with the pleasure of human encounters.

When the men had left, she wandered out smiling at Simon, and carrying her shoes, picked her way carefully through the filthy street to the mean shack she shared with her aunt.

"What you got for me, little niece?" her auntie squawked as she entered.

"Business was bad," she said disagreeably.

"I'll throw you out, you lying girl. You been having a good time all evening and me here sufferin' an' all. Why you do this to me?" Anwei did not answer. The shack was dark and she felt her way past her fat aunt's bed to the board that was hers. She put her hand up her skirt and hooked her panties off. She felt a relief at the freedom created, and a breath of cool air gave her an ephemeral pleasure as she gently plunged the frilly nylon into a tin can of cold water. Scrubbing them briefly she squeezed them out and hung them on a short line strung between two nails. She snapped the fastener of her tight nylon minidress and shucked it over her head, removed her overstuffed bra, and palmed the diminutive dugs that were the remains of her once-pert breasts.

For a moment she was naked. It never felt bad. Warm and cool zephyrs caressed her, but she was tired and unsteady, so she donned the large grubby cotton T-shirt, her nightgown, and tried to make herself comfortable with a worn cotton towel and an old stained woollen blanket, her bedclothes. The snoring of her aunt was her lullaby and the whiskey her sleeping draft.

Again she revisited the last few months of ruin: her terrible economic loss and her sorry state now.

Always a loser, she thought. *Just as things look rosy, you get slammed down again. Here I am, the lowest sort of whore, standing on street corners.* Weeping quietly with these thoughts spinning in her head, she fell into an uncertain sleep.

4

There were always disturbances, rats, and the occasional dog trying to find morsels to eat: small chance here among the shacks and sheds of the hungry humans.

At three o'clock in the morning, that time when she was just entering the deepest sleep, the crash came. First the door was ripped from its crude rope hinges, then the flimsy walls were systematically bashed with the nightsticks. They escaped holding their arms and their meagre possessions close to their bodies like mothers defending their babies. Shrieking abuse at the drunken soldiers, they stepped over the debris.

They were being told they were due to make another payment to their landlord, who happened to be an army officer with some vague self-asserted responsibility for the policing of the area. Essentially the small-time slum landlord supported by a riffraff of brutal hoodlums.

"Out you get, you wasters and whores," the sergeant, the one with stripes on his arm, shouted. "I have to pay my fucking rent, so do you." Anwei struggled into the road, eyes bleary, brain still asleep, holding tight to her tin box and some hastily grabbed clothes that she quickly donned to achieve some decency.

There was a screech of tyres, a thump, and Anwei went down. When the back wheel went over her ankle, there was an audible crack. The car stopped and four white men tumbled out almost immediately. They were all large, dwarfing the soldiers, who by now had moved a little way on to harass some more hapless tenants of the roadside. Anwei was screaming in a mixture of languages about the abuse and pain and anxiety as to what would happen to her. "How can I live with one leg? Who will love a one-legged woman? You bastards."

The white men came over to her. They saw immediately a massive swelling and the misaligned ankle joint.

"Jesus," said the first, a man of about thirty with a red mop of hair and a half-developed potbelly, "what the fuck do we do now?"

"Let me see," said another well-muscled darker man of about the same age, speaking English with a thick Afrikaans accent. "This looks pretty bad. We better try to take care. She won't have any money for treatment."

"She's only a street tart. Be careful. You start helping, the next thing all the tribe will come out of the woodwork looking for 'compensation.' I'm telling you, man, it'll never end. Whose idea was it to come to this *vrot* haven and gamble our money away anyway?"

"Oh-ho," noted the third, "here comes trouble, soldiers with guns."

The soldiers had taken a few moments to assess the little fracas going on behind them until it dawned on them that they had an opportunity for some action.

Six of them formed a rough line across the road and marched, albeit out of step and in a ragged shuffle, towards the car. They had guns of sorts, government issue. Unbeknown to the South Africans, they were useless, missing firing pins and springs, uncared for except for spit polish on the outside.

The sergeant shouted at the white men. "Arrest, *arêtter*, arrest," a sort of half-French and half-English order. The South Africans weighed up their chances of getting away, accepting that the worst outcome was now inevitable.

The one kneeling by the fallen Anwei turned his face towards the sergeant-looking type and shouted, "We need a bleddy doctor, where's the hospital?"

It seemed the sergeant understood "hospital" and dispatched one of his men to slouch off in the direction of town.

"What now?" The South Africans were standing around looking spare, while the soldiers tried to appear threatening. The sergeant was unsure. He kept his cool, knowing that a wrong move could lose him the chance to make a lot of money.

"How much do you think we have to pay these boobys?" David was on the ground, trying to assist Anwei. He was asking her about the pain and why she had been in the street at such a time. In agony and between weeping bouts, she explained how the soldiers had thrown them on to the street.

"Hear this, Stefan, these bastards threw this lady and her auntie out of their shack at this time of night. Hassling them for some crook landlord."

"Shit happens," said his companion, unmoved, "even here."

A shiny but rather dilapidated old Peugeot arrived at the scene, and a broad-shouldered man in khaki uniform festooned with braid and stripes got out of the back. He'd obviously been surprised by the wakeup call as the buttons of his tunic were not in the correct buttonholes. The soldier had been sent to call him, not the doctor.

"What is going on here?" Seeing Anwei, he raised his eyes to the sky. "Who injured you, girl? You look bad. This is a very serious business," he said, gravely turning to the white men standing around. He returned his gaze to David, who was trying to comfort the fallen woman.

"You ran her over? Careless and dangerous driving, very serious charge. I must congratulate my men for arresting you in the name of the law. You might have killed this dear innocent woman. You are drunk. Who was driving? Open and shut case. That is a hired car. You people come up here from South Africa and think you can make mayhem. Open and shut case," he repeated. "Court in the morning, very expensive for you. Expulsions or even prisons." He puffed out his chest, and the skew buttoning of his jacket became apparent to everyone.

Even so, every phrase he uttered disappointed the South Africans as they realized he was building the case against them for the maximum financial hit.

"You will come to the station with me."

"No, that may not be a good idea for you and your very efficient soldiers and not for this woman. I will stay with the woman until she receives medical attention. I will pay the doctor and hospital and expenses."

"Who was driving?"

Dirk owned up to this.

"Right, you three with me. You can you drive this car?" he said, turning his attention back to David kneeling in the road.

"Yes," said David.

"Put the woman in the car. One of my men will go with you to the hospital. You will take her to a private clinic where she will receive attention. Then you will come to the station."

Dirk intervened. "Officer, we don't need to waste your time with a lot of paperwork. I think this may be a clear case for an 'on the spot fine,' a very serious fine, yes, but we have a system at home in SA. The cops can write out a ticket at the roadside."

A glint appeared in the eyes of the officer. He unbuttoned his tunic, revealing a stained T-shirt underneath, and then re-buttoned it correctly and puffed out his chest again to much better effect.

"On-the-spot, on-the-spot fine. Fine, fine. Definitely a clear-cut case. No need for paperwork. How…" He stopped himself short as he realized he was supposed to set the fine.

"I hereby…" He faltered.

"Look," said Dirk reasonably, fishing out his wallet from his back pocket. "I am a lawyer in SA, and an infringement like this would be about fifty rand. I can pay you in rand here and now."

Assuming rightly there was a bit more to be made of this, the cop did exactly what Dirk was predicting.

"This not a minor infringement even if it is an on-the-spot business. I can insist on a court case and all that. This fine will have to be one hundred and fifty rand on the spot."

"No problem. But I will need a proper receipt with your signature, rubber stamp, and all that."

"Yes, well, perhaps a hundred rand is more better, no signature, but you will have to give my sergeant twenty-five rand for arresting you and his men ten rand each for overtime."

"Twenty for the sergeant and five each for the soldiers." He peeled money out of his wallet, and the eyes of the observing soldiers were popping out from their grimy sockets.

He handed one hundred and fifty rand over.

"So, my good officer, you have done your duty tonight. We will now take the woman to the hospital. I still need one of your men to show us where."

"At this time of night, it may not be possible," the captain answered, smarting at the arrogance of the white man, now in ascendency after the business was closed.

"I think I can make it possible," said Dirk, turning to David.

"How's she doing?"

"She needs to have this fracture set, and she needs some drugs to stop the swelling before it breaks the skin. It's in very poor condition, with lesions, scabs, and the rest of it."

"Can you lift her into the car?"

Then to the captain. "You lead us in your car, officer."

"Yes, you must follow my car," said the captain, trying to regain command and perceiving another opportunity for a bit of squeeze, this time on the hospital staff.

So they started off to the big modern concrete and glass hospital at the end of a road, whose surface was pitted with gigantic potholes, causing agony to the now screaming Anwei. It seems news of their arrival had preceded them, as there was a small welcome committee of a mixed bunch of souls obviously attempting to open their eyes and restore circulation to their limbs.

5

There was a long wait. At about five o'clock the three others left David with Anwei to go back to town to their hotel. By this time Anwei was asleep on a gurney trolley and David was sitting on the marble floor with his back against the wall nearby. A girl in a nurse's uniform was asleep on a ledge, and an orderly of some sort was lying stretched out on the floor.

At about eight o'clock a large man in a full white coat and a stethoscope round his neck came in through the wide double door of the hall.

"Good morning," he said to nobody in particular, looking around the hall at the assembled crowd who had not had a chance to wake up and look alive. Seeing David, he walked toward him, hand outstretched. "I am Dr. Ongonwe. I believe you have an injured woman." The captain had reappeared from nowhere and was approaching the doctor. "Ah, Captain, what has happened?"

The officer made a gesture and led the doctor over to a dark corner near the wide concrete staircase leading up from the entrance hall. They had quiet words; David did not recognise the language from the broken sounds making it to his ears. Now that she was not being moved, Anwei was quiet. The doctor returned and examining the lower leg. "Yes, very serious. We can observe this using the CT scanner. We have the very best Somatom AR Star model. I will look, see what is problem."

"Here?" asked David, amazed.

"Oh, yes sir, we have it. We are most grateful to a big charity in Germany, who financed fifty percent." And we are so lucky that we still have the commissioning technicians on site training our own people."

David looked up for the first time at a large plaque over the wide door at the side of the hall announcing that the x-ray department was paid for by the World Bank in conjunction with a long German title. Apart from their little party, David was puzzled by the lack of bustle in the hospital. He could see through the glass entrance that the building was vast, with at least one more wing and three floors, but no vehicles moving in the driveway and no people milling around. When he looked back toward the gurney, Anwei was leaning on one elbow.

"Are you the one who crashed me over?" she asked.

David, ever the lawyer, did not answer. But then she smiled a very wide smile, completely disarming him. "It doesn't matter. The fault is with these soldiers. They are not real soldiers. No one pays their wages. They are just bully boys in uniform. Are you going to help me?" By now her expression had changed to a frown of need and distress. She was a master of facial expression. It was her livelihood after all, that and body language.

"I will help you," he answered flatly.

"Ah, good," said the doctor. "We can do the scan in half an hour. I need you to pay in advance. Three thousand six hundred rand it will cost."

"Look, I have eighteen hundred rand in my wallet. What can you do? This is very expensive," David said in protest.

"That is no problem. This woman's foot is seriously damaged. Without the scan we cannot know what needs to be done to it. If she does not get it fixed, she may die immediately from gangrenous infection or later from starvation. Where are your friends? At a hotel, the Akwa Palace? You can call them, and they can have the money here in half an hour and everyone will be happy. Here, I have my cellular with me. I even have the number of the reception. What room shall I say?"

David's colleagues managed to get the money for the scan up to the good doctor and the pictures were passed round. The South Africans accepted the doctor's description of the damage and agreed to go ahead with an operation.

"This woman needs a clean place. We have a small hospital here. Not this place. They have no nurses, no staff here. The Banjona clinic is very suitable."

"I am Anwei Sojenji. Not 'this woman'. I don't need an expensive hospital. I cannot pay. My foot is not hurting now, so I will go." She swung herself off the gurney, and putting all her weight on her broken foot, collapsed in a heap on the floor screaming in agony. Suddenly she stopped. David helped her up. The orderly and he put her back on the trolley.

The doctor could not resist a patronizing smile. "Bring her to the clinic. Follow my car. You will admit her, and we will see what treatment she can have."

The Banjona Poly Clinic was a colonial building in town, not far from the cathedral. It is built round a rough courtyard. There were administrative offices, treatment rooms, and an operating theatre on the ground level. Above were the wards, mostly single rooms, but also some multiple bed wards.

She had been issued a cane crutch. "The elevator is being serviced. She will have to walk up."

By this time Anwei was feeling decidedly faint and had to be supported by David and the orderly. The doctor disappeared into the office near the entrance.

"No problem," he said, rejoining the group as they led Anwei into a single room at the end of a short passage. "Eight hundred rand a night for seven nights. Discount: five thousand. OK."

Dirk looked at David as they left the room. "I think we must play the game. You see that bloody police captain is still hanging around for his cut. He can make life very tough for us."

"OK, Doctor, what will happen to her?"

"Oh, I will operate as soon as I can."

"And when will that be?"

"Tomorrow I will operate."

On Friday the operation was done. Dirk stayed with David as the other two had flown home to Cape Town.

Sitting in the bar of the Akwa Palace, they were awaiting news of their rebooked flight.

"How did we get in such a fix? Bleddy black bitch and that doctor and his good friend the captain. What a crew. Don't you feel you've been ransomed?"

"Look, buddy, first, you're out of order. They're Cameroonians. We're in their country. We screwed up and ran over the woman. We pay. What about the insurance?"

"Those buggers aren't issuing receipts for everything, and the ones they do issue are all in CFA. At the official rate— that's what they call it—that is far below the value of the rand. And what is more, the insurance will pay us when they have finished their 'investigation'. Can you imagine when that will be?"

"A write off?"

The barman was approaching. "Telephone behind the bar, for you."

"Our flight," said David as he rose. But it wasn't. It was the matron of the hospital.

"Sir, it is about Anwei. She is very sick. The foot has swelled up and the sutures have burst, and I am afraid the wound is smelling very bad. We do not have drugs here. Can you do something?"

David realized this was becoming a ramp. Everywhere he turned there was another expense greater than the last.

"You must take her to South Africa," said the voice. "You have proper surgeons there and drugs and treatment."

"What do you mean, proper surgeons?"

"Sir, I have worked in South Africa. An injury like this will be treated properly. I cannot say more."

"She needs travel documents."

"I know how it is done. In medical cases there is a special passport. It can be done in one day. It costs money, that's all."

"Who do I go to?" He sighed.

So when the airline phoned, he postponed their journey one more day and added another ticket.

Part 6: How Chuck Gets to Cape Town

1

Chuck Pecan did not kill his wife, Lee-Anne, but her death was so convenient that he might as well have. Their one son, Wayne, was in Alaska. The boy was never interested in his father except as a supplier of money for his upkeep. Lee-Anne had poisoned the relationship as she sought to gouge out the maximum in marriage rather than make divorce possible. So, using a restraint order, she got exclusive use of the family house and 66 percent of his paycheck. Wayne had also abandoned his mother as she got more bitter, sickly and gross, and had gone to make his fortune in the cold wastes of the North.

When Chuck arrived at the house, he found his wife housebound due to obesity. She having everything delivered. Her diet was burgers and fries, donuts and ice cream. The house was full of electronic gadgets and she spent all day watching shopping channels on a fifty-two-inch flat screen. As soon as he entered the house, she started yelling at him until on one visit she went quiet, cried out in sudden pain, and collapsed. Chuck called the ambulance but she never recovered. He didn't even try to find out the medical cause—it was obvious.

Then he drove down to Houston and spoke with the human resources people who offered him three hundred thousand dollars redundancy payment. Before accepting he thought he'd better talk with the operations manager, Fred Muswell, an old friend, to chew the fat and get an angle on where the industry was heading.

"We're negotiating for that boat of yours. We don't want to sell it as a going vessel."

"I agree, Fred, she won't make survey without a rebuild, I mean a complete rebuild. We had to patch the ballast tanks while we were in Limbe. The starboard engine has two empty cylinders and the port engine runs at three hundred and fifty rpm maximum. She's holding together just about good enough for a one-way voyage. You're spot on there; we won't sell it to any legitimate company, maybe not any crook one neither."

"OK, Chuck, I'll level with you. The new management don't care diddly about the peanut money these old boats sell for. They didn't tell me: 'Go and get the best price.' No. All they want me to do is not cost them anything in money or reputation in getting these boats off their books. They don't want them to turn up as competition, so the logic is to scrap them." He paused and looked out of the window at the view of other skyscrapers, preparing himself for an announcement. "The best offer we've got is one hundred and twenty dollars per light ton delivered to India. Barely covers the cost of getting it there."

"Is there a delivery window?"

"Can't say there is precisely," Fred pulled on a thin cigar. "I guess the price is rising in Asia. Delay won't be a problem, but frankly we need to tidy up the junk in our backyard. We got a few more boats we can't hire out after they come down. They gave me the job of sweeping up. We need a skipper to take them to India or wherever: Consultancy, three hundred and ninety dollars a day, door to door. Interested?"

"Might be at five hundred. Got to set a precedent."

"I'll call you. If I do, it'll be at four seventy-five, all expenses, door to door."

So the two men shook hands and Chuck left to meet his son in town. Wayne was easy to spot in his bright plaid shirt, a beefy young roughneck two meters tall among the city workers in white shirts. "Hey, boy, put some muscle on you." They hugged hesitantly, an unfamiliar greeting as they rarely even wrote.

"You bet. How you doing, Dad? You 'bout ready to retire? I came down for Mama's passing. 'Fraid I ain't seen her in a while. Been staying up north in Seattle with my girl, Tracey. She about to have my baby."

"So, you don't tell me I'll be a grandpa!"

"In good time."

"Suppose you want to know if she left you anything."

"I'm making good money, Dad, I don't really need for anything. But we're gonna have to get a place. It'd help."

"Well here's the deal, son: you and me, we weren't very close while your mother was alive. I guess her passing puts a new light on us. I've put the house up for sale; should make around one fifty. That's your inheritance. Should he'p get you a place up north. What do you say?"

"That's OK, Dad. What you going to do?"

"Don't you worry about me. I'll get by."

"Sure you will. Funeral's tomorrow, yeah?"

"Be there, son; pay respect. She wasn't happy. She was a real beauty once and she gave you life and that handsome frame of yours." He paused for thought. "What went wrong? I don't rightly know, but it wrenches at my guts sometimes. But I'll tell you something, my boy: Oilfiel' puts a strain on things. A host o' my buddies done divorced for the same reasons. Too much loose money, booze, and low morals. Women won't put up with it. Time was, my favourite place was drunk in whorehouse, never mind where in the worl', feelin' like a king. You steer clear if you take my advice. Take care o' that girl of yours and show respect. Listen to me! My old pappy used to say the same to me, and I just thought I'd be fine. He used to strum that old Willie Nelson song, 'Mama, Don't Let Your Babies Grow Up To Be Cowboys.'

"Well, Papa was a cowboy or working the carnie when he was sober. But when I knew him, he was pushing tool for Nedco. Stopped raising hell by then and tried to love us kids when we's teenagers. Mama threw him out five times, he said. Then he got God and confessed all his sins and loaded us with the teachin's. Worse 'n any preacher—trying to thump that ol'

213

Bible into our heads. Then he up an' died just when we was gittin' to know him. Jed must a' taken the song serious 'cos he's a lawyer over in Lafayette. He don't talk to me no more. Reckons I'm just oilfiel' trash. He's got a big brick house, pool an' all, pipe-rail fence all round; 'bout thirty acres an' horses. Went up there once. Got near froze out by his fancy wife; kids gone to college. They your cousins. You ever seen 'em?"

"I was there with you, Daddy. He got pissed at you cause o' you gittin' drunk on his Jack Daniels. Mom drove us home in the El Dorado; I got to ride up front while you snored like a hawg in back."

"Only way I could survive that uppity bitch, Loretta, some such." Chuck gave his son a fatherly pat on the shoulder. "That ole jalopy is still there in the front driveway. She thought it was a classy thing to keep, until the tires went flat and the lamps were all shot out by the kids' BB guns. By then she didn't go out.

"Anyway, I got private business to do before this becomes a boozing session. When you heading north again? We'll eat tonight. What you say? Real good Mexi food here in downtown. Guadalajara Hacienda, Katy Freeway, real Mexican. Maybe you been there. Seven OK? My treat. Be a change from seal meat or whatever in Alaska."

He and Wayne cleared the junk from the house, had a huge garage sale, and dumped the leftovers down at the charity mission. They contacted the lawyer to discuss the will. His wife had filled in the spaces in a standard "Will and Testament" from a TV mail-order company ensuring Wayne got everything and Chuck was excluded. The lawyer said he could challenge it. His earlier generous gesture to his son was empty, as the boy got the house anyway. He did not want to argue. Chuck had salted away a small fortune out of reach of the prying eyes of her lawyer and the IRS. He and his son parted on good terms. A week later he went back to the office.

"Well, Chuck, the truth is the new management wants us to release all the older boats in the fleet and they want it done yesterday. They want a new image with powerful new ships ready for a new era of deepwater operations. They want shiny new anchor handlers, dive ships, all dynamic positioning, computerized. You know what I mean?"

"So I'm obsolete and redundant. That what you mean?"

"How old are you, Chuck?"

"You don't need to ask. You got my file right there in front of you."

"OK, let's cut to the chase. How would you like to be our scrapping contractor? You will get good deals on these old boats, and you will get a good profit for arranging the voyages to the scrapyards. I'll make sure there's room for you to come out well in the deals. I've identified five ships for demobilising over the next year, and another six or so of ours and a few from our partners sooner or later in the next two years. I've written up a schedule. You'll see the *Scotfield 2* you left in Cameroon is immediate, then three more come off-hire in three months and the rest later in the year. I'm tasked with having them all scrapped in two years."

Chuck silently digested the information by repeating it to himself in his head.

"Fred, you know me, simple sailor. I'm not frightened to make deals, but administration and the law, well, I might be out of my depth."

"I may be able to help. As we amalgamate these companies and unload these boats, we've got too many port captains or ship managers on the book doing nothing until the new builds get started. We can transfer one or more of these guys to you to do the administration. They're young graduates, mostly MBAs, Texas A&M pain-in-the-ass types, but you can use them for all that stuff you don't want to do. Whatever happens, you will retire from Tidal. I'll make sure they pay you out high. By the bye, Tidal will owe you nothing 'cept your bus fare home, but the new management wants to seem benign, so redundancies are being dealt with generously. It won't last. I know these sons of bitches. They're as hard as nails normally; but right now they're in the business of making a good impression.

"This sort of deal you can handle? Hang loose at the moment and think about how you want to work. Give me a call if you need any help or information. I guess you'll get another five years' work and make a decent profit. If you don't go for this deal, I've got two more captains who might. Wha'd'ya say? No pressure but I want you back here with an answer in two days. I have to meet my new boss with a proposition on Thursday."

Chuck stood and proffered his right hand.

"I 'preciate your offer, Fred. Two days, you'll hear."

Sure enough, in two days Chuck was sitting with Fred and a sharp-suited man from New York.

"The boss got ahead of me, sonofabitch, worked out all the details with Dale here. Let's hear it, Dale."

The deal was for Chuck to buy the first three vessels with a private mortgage from Tidal Marine and then with the profits made he would buy the other boats outright at favourable prices, and his profit would be clear from then onward. He expected to make between fifty and one hundred thousand dollars on each vessel, assured by Tidal as long as he submitted fully supported auditable accounts of expenses and returns for the first three ships. After that he would be treated as a fully independent contractor for the rest of the year, buying the ships at 30 percent discount from the smelter price, and then after the initial year he would have to bid for each vessel in open competition.

The company lawyer offered it to him as a package, no negotiation; sign here or leave the room. Fred was silent. Chuck wanted to ask, "Where's the catch?" but the grim face of the New Yorker and the adrenalin pumping into his system prevented him. He skipped the company's get-out clauses or small print.

"We got a deal. Where do I sign?"

Chuck set up a company in Delaware called Zebra Shipping Inc. to employ the personnel for the final voyages of ships to be scrapped. Fred got the HR department to give him the list of all those being let go, and Chuck signed the contract with Tidal for the purchase of the *Scotfield 2*. Chuck would captain the first few deliveries personally and later he would manage them from the shore. Fred gave him a list of boats earmarked for retirement and the dates of off-hire so he could look ahead.

"We're assigning you a young guy called Steve Roswell, keen as a coyote. I knew his old man; toolpusher got killed trying to shut in the Steer Rock blowout in seventy-six. He'll join you in eight weeks. Look after him 'cos I want him back in one piece. We pay his salary for three months, then you take him as an expense. We get him back when we want him."

2

What with his wife's death and burial, the probate, the settlement with his son, and the setting up of the company, Chuck had been fully occupied as the weeks went by. He'd tried to call Anwei on her cell phone but was unable to get a response. He had seen regular withdrawals from the thousand dollars he had put in his bank account in Douala, so he thought everything must be OK and he had just been unlucky calling her when there was no signal. He did not have time to react to the alarm bells going off in his head when there was not even a short text. She was out of his mind all day, but he worried some at night. Still, he was due to go back to Limbe and he would catch up with her then. He found his heart was in his mouth when he finally arrived in Limbe.

He remembered his first arrival and had hoped to be met by Anwei this time, but he had still been unable to contact her. He had not thought this would have affected him so much. Just another woman who had wandered into his life, made it exciting for a while and somehow wandered out again. Hell, no. This one was different. Well, maybe it was because of the sudden elation he felt as he was now free of the burden of his wife.

He was whisked away by a new agent appointed in his absence. He asked about the old agent and was told in brisk terms that he was no longer available. Further questions led to a stone wall. There was too much serious stuff to discuss. It was obvious the man was in a great hurry to get this business all done quickly with the minimum of effort and delay.

"I have managed to get quick clearance for you even without your signature—very tricky—but I have had to promise to get the vessel out within twenty-four hours. I called the chandler and everything has been bought for your voyage. The fuel barge is available if you need it, but the engineer tells me you have enough fuel for Cape Town, where it is cheaper.

"We have found you some international crew from various vessels around here. We have promised them nothing and they will be coming on board today for you to select the ones you need. You can sign them on. The officials will be there at sixteen hundred, after you have decided. You should be clear by oh six hundred, first light. All right, Captain?" Chuck did not feel all right. This agent had a very dilapidated Renault 4. The metal-framed seats had lost most of their upholstery and the tubing cut into his bony buttocks. He was tired and unusually jet lagged. He was on the point of answering when he realized that this crazy little African was doing his best and did not deserve the stream of abuse that had gotten itself to the front of his mind. He grunted and closed his eyes.

3

The ship was a mess. While he had been away, it was if the children had taken over. Benches had been made and placed in rows on the afterdeck, and a grey-bearded man was conducting some sort of lesson. He counted fifteen or so of all ages. Up by the anchor handling winch was a bush kitchen and some larger mamas at work making pots of the ubiquitous fish stew served by and for everyone. The chief mate met him as he came on board from the open aluminium boat.

"My, Captain! Welcome on board. Our crew welcomes our esteemed captain on board. Please sit down, sir, and the ladies will render you some sustenance." The man was wearing a white shirt with one epaulet, the insignia of a captain of the RFA distinguished by the position of the diamond in relation to the stripes.

"Listen, I don't know who the fuck you are, but you will clear all these people off of here in the next hour, kids and all," Chuck said. "We are not a parish school nor a feeding station for half Africa. You take your ass off with them."

"But, sir, I am Gabriel, your esteemed chief officer."

"Bull she-it, I ain't got need of a chief officer who runs a ship like this. You get all these people off my ship. Get yourself cleaned up and then we'll talk. Got it?"

"Yes sir, now sir, eat, very delicious fish stew. Americans like fish stew. Very special, like gumbo."

Chuck acknowledged that he was indeed hungry and the stew had the rich smells, reminding him of something good, not necessarily gumbo.

He dumped his bag on the deck and found a bench to sit on. "You want to go inside to the mess, Captain?"

"Gabriel, I'm going to set my ass right here and eat some gumbo. You got any beer?"

"Yessir, Lion Lager, cold."

So it was that Chuck rejoined his ship. His mission was new. He was irritated by all these people who had colonized his boat, but he was really more irritated by the loss of contact with Anwei. Where the fuck is she, kept going through his mind.

He relaxed somewhat with the gumbo and a beer inside him, but there was a lot to do. The temporary crew had been told by the agent that they would be paid off in town tomorrow morning, so there was some incentive to leaving. The new crew would come on in the evening, while the immediate task was to get the stores, such as they were, stowed, and fuel and water checked and topped up.

When he was done on deck, he went inside to meet the chief engineer, an old buddy who had spent his time since these boats were new coaxing them into action through phases of spare parts starvation and now nursing them into the extended life of their decrepit old age.

The door from the cabin on the first deck was open. The place was like a bacon smokehouse. The chief engineer and the second, who had arrived the week before, were both chain-smokers. They bought their cigarettes and cigars wherever they were cheapest and nastiest. "Captain Chuck, how y' going, boy? You the new big boss around here, they tell me." He opened the fridge and handed the captain an ice-cold Carlsberg. "What's the story from the top?"

"Cape Town and India. My deal with Tidal ain't fixed completely, but you know I may need some help. Whaddya say, Steve?"

"Well, young Ben here won't be with you. I had to scream at those assholes in Houston just to keep him for this leg. They want him over on a new build in Korea. They only let him stay because he can fly easier out of Cape Town than this place. But make me an offer I don't have nowhere to go just now."

"You'll come to India, Stevie?"

"Siddown, Cap'n. Lemme tell you about this ole rustbucket. By the way I found fuel filters in Douala. Phoned around. Bought them on my own account. Had to get twenty. Originally for some Russian engine but they fit our setup here. Got a shop here in town to try to make a piston, but they made such a fuck-up, I didn't even waste time fitting it. That cost me a bit 'cos I paid them half for trying.

"You're telling me we'll only be doing seven knots."

"Well, Chuck, you're the captain."

"Anything else you need?"

"I've roughed out the fuel we'll use for Cape Town and put the calculation on your desk. Seems we can make it with a little spare—not much for emergencies, but I guess you don't want to take more than you need."

"Can we get more?"

"Don't risk it, Cap'n. You don't know where it's come from. That Nigerian shit is full of water. Get it in Cape Town. We can always go down slow steaming."

"Slower than seven? I'll check it out and call you." Chuck rose and left, relieved to get out of the thick smoke.

There was a lot of noise on the afterdeck as the women screamed at their husbands, now without employment, and the squabbling children. Chuck entered his cabin and saw it had obviously been occupied in his absence. An attempt had been made to clean up, but he sensed unfamiliar food smells under the pervading pine disinfectant. He took a large envelope out of his holdall and deposited a hundred thousand dollars of his own working money in the safe under his bed.

He checked the chief's fuel prediction and found the numbers made sense. Lube oil might be a problem, but he knew this chief would find some somewhere to tide them over.

The chief officer appeared at the door of his cabin and knocked too respectfully for Chuck's more casual expectation. "Come in, Gabriel. How's it all going? Are the families all off now?"

"Most are going off, sir. Only my wife and two sons will stay the night with your permission, sir."

"OK, yeah, that's no problem. Now, I guess you're coming with me to Cape Town. Are you from Cameroon?"

"No sir, from Togo, sir. My family will make it along the coast through Nigeria. My brother and his wife will be travelling also."

"Good man. What ticket have you got? Where were you trained? What experience you got?"

"I am a local officer, sir. West Coast all my life. I got my masters' certificate in Nigeria. Proper examination, passed, all that but had to pay big bribe to get the actual certificate. Nigerians are the worst. But my tutor was a good man, and I finished paying him off two years back. Anyway, no trouble getting around here. No need for radar, sat nav, all that: just compass OK and some sightings of land. I am knowing all the headlands round here, shoals, currents, and by night stars and so on. No problem sir."

"OK, Gabriel, I need a man like you. Do you want to go on the voyage to India?"

"No problem, sir."

"Guess we'll just have to see how we get along. Why don't you get the rest of the tribe off the vessel for the night and you stay up on watch while I get some rest?"

Chuck was unable to sleep. Partly, he knew it was the effect of changing through seven time zones and hanging around Charles de Gaulle airport for five hours in the confusion of the main concourse. The rumbling of the generator was normally a lullaby to him, but tonight it had the opposite effect, irritating him and preventing relaxation. After

221

showering he had lain down on his bunk in shorts and T-shirt, but now at midnight he slipped on his coveralls and went up on the bridge. He found Gabriel in conversation with a very large man with a shiny hairless head and a battered face like a heavyweight boxer.

"This man is called Samson; he's being your bosun for Cape Town leg."

His very large black hand was extended from his tattered grey shirtsleeve held tightly at the wrist by the left.

"Captain."

"Right, Samson, what's your real name?"

"Too complicated, captain. Everyone just call me Samson."

"You got seaman's papers?"

"I'm Nigerian, sir."

Chuck took that to mean "yes, but." Who was he to challenge what the agent had accepted? This was Africa. He was beginning to learn the questions to ask and the ones to avoid. Genuine papers were rare, but if he didn't want to stay in South Africa, the authorities wouldn't check too deeply. He'd have to judge the man as a seaman, not by his paperwork.

"Right, Samson, what sort of ships you worked on before?"

"Everything, Cap, local cargo, whalers, trawlers, tankers, riverboats. Not much I haven't done: bosun, mate, skipper, and even second engineer, a bad mistake—very, very hot, very noisy, kept hitting my head, elbows, knees. 'Humans can't do this, man,' I told myself. 'Leave it to the Scotch men.'"

Chuck looked over the afterdeck as the last few women and children were making their way over the side into a variety of small boats. Gabriel came up beside him.

"I've marked up some charts. Not very much to go on and not corrected very recently. Never mind. I'm used to no charts. But it's safer using charts, don't you think, Captain?"

"You dead right there, Gab. I guess you know your way out of here. I done it a few times but we had a pilot. We don't need one today. This old chart shows the channel. Not much has changed, has it?"

222

"A barge is sunken here." He pencilled a cross on the chart, "and the silt is moving across this way, so we keep to the buoys on the starboard side and make a curved track, not a straight line. Too many buoys are not existing, sir."

"We went close to the island last time."

"Yessir, very steep dropoff there, very safe."

"Good, Gabriel, what time can we get away?"

"All depends on the agent, Cap'n."

"Why'n't you get some rest. The boat is pretty well ready now."

"Right, sir, Thank you, sir."

"Samson can take a look round now, get familiar and then he can get his head down too."

The two men climbed down the companionway, leaving Chuck to contemplate the trip, and to come and stare at the shore wondering at the loss of contact with Anwei. Another relationship dashed. He told himself to forget her and get on with the job. He was going to make a lot of money in the next few years. Women were just a distraction; time for shenanigans later. But nevertheless he couldn't free his mind of images of her smile and her supine body.

"She-it. Goddamn female witches."

Morning brought the bustle of departure. Rusted hinges on freeing ports and watertight covers were freed up. Loose gear was lashed down, the galley and engine room stores were secured. Deadlights for the front of the accommodation were found and secured. Final tank soundings were taken and the fresh water and fuel calculations were checked again.

The chief got the main engines running with the uneven limping rumble of ancient machinery and the dark noxious smoke of half-burnt sulphurous fuel.

"OK, Samson, heave up the anchor," he shouted down to the foredeck.

As the ship swung gently to starboard, Chuck engaged the port engine to take the weight off the anchor. He was happy to be getting underway after so many months of idleness. There was an upwelling of emotion. Was it affection for the old beast now awakening into action?

"OK, Gabriel, you know the way out," he said as he felt the tension come off the anchor and the vessel freeing herself from the soil. "Anchor aweigh, Cap'n," came the deep voice of the bosun over the clatter of the windlass winding in the last shot of chain. Chuck leaned over the bridge wing and said, "Leave it hanging in the water to wash it off, Samson."

Gabriel pushed the combinators forward to half speed on both engines, and with a reassuring belch of black smoke from both stacks, the vessel shuddered and started to gain speed. Chuck watched the echo sounder as the stylus sparked on its successive rotations, laying down fuzzy black smudges on the grey electrostatic paper. The depth slowly increased and the ship began to pitch and roll gently in the increasing swell.

"You OK, Gabriel?" he threw over his shoulder as he lowered himself down the steep companionway to his cabin. From the side windows he saw the small island slide past, identifying the broken wooden stage, once the cause of misery to so many and of great profit for so few.

Their arrival in Cape Town was unexpectedly hostile. Chuck wasn't expecting much of a welcome, but the jumped-up officials were obviously interested in making a meal of this scruffy mixed-up crew. The Americans they could not touch but they made it plain Nigerians were bad news, and the unfortunate Gabriel was only given a twenty-four-hour pass to get a flight back out of the country. No reasons were given for the lack of shore leave permits for the rest of the Africans. Chuck had plans to load up the ship with scrap metal for the Indian Ocean trip to the Far East. He needed to test the market to see where he could get the best price for the metal. The agent did not show up for the entry into port as he and his staff had been too tied up with a cruise liner going south for an Antarctic sightseeing tour.

After a day of being acidly polite to a succession of petty officials, Chuck managed to get a shore permit for himself only.

Part 7 Charles and Joe in Cape Town

1

Another conference. Charles Sojenji had enjoyed the feeling of importance of writing speeches for his professor at various venues for about two years. At a very young age Charles was recognised as one of the most useful research assistants on the world's AIDS problems. He had an incisive intelligence and was able to cut to the quick whenever he was presented with data, medical facts, and laboratory results. Professor DuPree's style was nowhere near as riveting as President Clinton's, whose robust speeches had help the cause along, but when he stood up, people tuned in and listened. They seemed to admire his ability to undermine dubious theories, replacing them with supportable facts supplied by Charles and pragmatic plans resulting from conversations with all sort of other delegates.

What disappointed them both was that after every speech they felt powerless. The money was drying up; AIDS was losing traction as the most urgent world problem; celebrity donors were getting bored with the idea that a cure would take ages and the real solution lay in the grinding task of providing good nutrition, clean water and some palliative drugs to save impoverished Africans. Proposals were manifold but without massive funding and new support, they came to little.

The main theme tomorrow was to be an attack on false or misleading statistics, followed by an indigestible helping of nasty medical analysis. Charles was in South Africa and he had to subtly present the fact that the presidency was a powerful force against progress. Mbeki was going upscale on their list of antagonists, challenging even the pope's supremacy. How the president could not see that the sexual habits of the poor were exacerbating the situation was a puzzle, unless it was Machiavellian. The power of princes was maintained by the distress of the people and the great corporate or political lie. Even the rape cult was an extension of the prince's power base.

225

The subjection of women to a deadly disease worked to keep intelligent women out of circulation.

Perhaps Mbeki was not so evil. Charles was beginning to concede to the argument that all diseases were the result of poverty, and AIDS was no exception. Cure poverty and AIDS will go away. The fact that all aid to the poor was grabbed by intermediaries was not on the president's particular radar. Again Charles forced his mind back to the script. For some reason he was losing his confidence here in South Africa. AIDS was no longer just a disease with chemical or palliative relief. It had become a monster of social ills. An enormous evil imposed on an otherwise beautiful continent—for here in Africa was the worst and most massive affliction—probably by accident or carelessness or negligence of a foreign and more powerful human force.

His brain was boiling. The hotel room was becoming oppressive and he needed to go for a walk. He donned a pair of designer frayed jeans he kept ready for such forays and with a brightly printed souvenir polo shirt tightly covering his excellent physique, he took some money from his wallet, dividing it between his top shirt pocket and the right-side pocket of his jeans. He tucked his passport with the hotel key card into his hip pocket, which he buttoned, and flip-flopped his way down the passage to the elevator.

He did not want to meet any delegates. There were a few at the bar but he avoided looking in. He winked at the porter, who recognised him and smiled broadly, and made his way on to the Harbour Front of the V&A waterfront.

He hesitated. He had not set out for anything more than a walk but the bright lights and the music attracted him, so he sauntered on through the crowd, past the booths selling bric-a-brac. He arrived at a large open sided fish and chip restaurant. The aroma was overpowering and he was contemplating the menu writ high in neon and the other one on a blackboard:

"JUST LANDED SNOEK TONITES SPECIAL OFFER." He saw two men dragging fish boxes over from the wharf. He turned to look at them. It amused him to see one

was wearing the uniform of a paramedic, similar to the ones he'd seen at the hospital that afternoon.

2

The one in uniform stood up straight, and Charles saw he wore a white kerchief high on his neck. The man was blond, thickset, and when he looked up, he was instantly recognisable. Charles was staring into a pair of blue eyes; eyes he had seen before and was shocked to see again.

"Krels," whispered Charles in disbelief, and he turned away just before the other man had time to recognise him. He shuddered in fear. This was truly a ghost from the past. The only man he had ever tried to kill. If he were mistaken, he could not go back for another look. He made a circuitous route around the old warehouses and back to the hotel. His boss's speech and AIDS was now forgotten. He was shaking and totally disorientated. He paced around his room and took a miniature vodka from the minibar, mixing it with the first thing to hand; mango juice. He drank it too fast over the next few paces. By this time his heart was racing; the drink had no effect. He sat on the uncomfortable chair and put his elbows on the desk. He then decided he needed some company. He wanted his own sort, people who would discuss endless minutiae, politics, policies, or even better, rugby or cricket.

He hesitated before descending to the bar. He was grateful that there was a buzz of activity, plenty of talk. He spotted his professor and mentor.

"Charles, so glad to see you. I missed the hospital tour. Actually, I was invited to go to another type of hospital altogether. Let me introduce you to my guide, Miriam. You know James Parker and Olaf. This is his wife, Nora, and Professor Giltman from Holland." Charles shook hands around the circle, and he returned to the space between Miriam and Professor Giltman.

"I am proud to say that I count this young man as my protégé. He has been brilliant in his analysis of the problems here; you must all have heard of him, Dr. Charles Sojenji. He has helped me no end on this tour."

A waiter approached Charles, and he ordered more vodka with mango. He liked the taste and as it was not doing him any harm, he was happy to have another. Charles had met Giltman before, rather a dreary academic who produced dry statistics, the sort Charles loved to challenge after they had been exploited by interest groups. Actually, he often consulted him to get the truth from behind the hype. Giltman had a hard, dry, and cynical sense of humour, possibly a defence against the grim facts he handled. His favourite phrase was, "Now they'll prove AIDS comes from hamburgers. I'm just being used like a prostitute. The real truth is hidden by these people abusing facts selected from my collations." Charles turned to Miriam and was just about to open with a general remark about Africa when his eye caught the badge on her left breast.

[Miriam Krels, Nurse Leader.]

He was momentarily stunned by this coincidence. Krels was not a common name. He looked away and gulped his drink. He thought she had been about to smile as he had looked towards her. His abrupt turn must have seemed rude. He turned back.

"Hi," he said.

"Are you *Mrs.* Krels?" with the emphasis on the *Mrs.* He was staring into a pair of deep, dark-brown eyes set well on her brown, strong-featured face.

"Why?" she asked, and then after a pause and with a slightly strained smile, "Do you know my husband?"

He became abruptly aware of the trap he had set for himself. Should he lie?

"Possibly," he said, instantly regretting it. *Why couldn't I just lie?*

"But you're not from Cape Town, are you? He got quite badly injured in the jungle. He took a long time to recover. But he's good now. He's an ambulance driver. I don't suppose you know him. Are you giving a paper? The professor seems to think you are a bit of a star."

"My job is to prepare his papers. I just help him with his research, especially numbers and stats."

228

The men and women at the bar were dispersing in small groups, the locals going home or to restaurants and the overseas delegates moving towards the dining room. As he was apparently in deep conversation, they did not interrupt him; someone caught his eye and gestured to the dining room. He shook his head. He was in a mental turmoil; his appetite evaporated. Charles seemed to be drawn inexorably to this woman. He looked at her Middle Eastern features. Arab, Jewish…hard to tell because he saw something African there too. She noticed his look and expression:

"Jewish and Malay and maybe something else as well, but African through and through. Now we have won the battle against apartheid, we have AIDS. God has to keep us busy."

Is this the wife of the man he thought he had murdered: the man, if alive, more than any other, he should fear meeting?

"Are you alone?" she asked, "Why not come and meet my husband, Joseph, see if you met him before. He can introduce you to the real Cape Town. I can see you might rather prefer that to the hothouse company here. Get out of the hotel and eat some local fish."

Joseph? His sense of relief was short-lived.

"Oh, he used to be Joaquim, but he hated it. He thinks it makes him sound like a Boer. He had a pretty rough time in the jungle and when he returned he was really low, injured, alcoholic, depressed, and very mixed up about his past attitudes—you know, hard line white supremacist. But we are very quiet and self contained. He came down to find his sister who married my brother."

Charles was already fascinated by this description and puzzled to know how Krels might have survived, but he did remember Jenny Bones's last comment about cutting him down. Miriam's expression became wistful as she went on.

"Well, my brother saw Avis one day near the hospital, wandering listlessly. He saw her from the left so he did not see the terrible scars on the right side of her face. He said he was in love immediately. He's a big old fool, my brother. Anyway, after he'd seen both sides of her face, he didn't flinch and he married her. She saw the gentle giant in him. She doesn't look bad now. She had several more ops, and eventually most of the

229

scarring is gone and the muscles work—just a bit of a crooked smile."

The bar was empty apart from a few stragglers, mostly couples at the tables around the edge of the room.

"Come walk with me. I'm meeting the boys down on the fish quay now this is all over."

Her friendliness had softened him, or perhaps it was the several vodkas.

3

Krels looked up from his work and saw Miriam and Charles coming towards him.

"Red Cross!" he gasped. "Is it you? Miri, what are you doing to me?"

"My God, you're alive." Charles felt light-headed and his whole body felt a hot rush. "My God," he said again.

Krels stood looking at him as if to discern what sort of man he was facing. He took stock of the spotless white T-shirt, the pressed, frayed designer jeans, crisp from the laundry, the flip-flops, thick soled and multi-coloured. These were from a different world.

"Why don't you welcome him, Joe?" questioned Miriam, sensing something offbeat going on between the men.

Charles was tall and very physical but no threat in his fancy threads. Krels, on the other hand, had a slight stoop and a crooked neck. Tears were coming to his eyes. There were some barbeque tables nearby. Charles moved back and sat down, keeping his eyes on Krels as if he thought he might attack. Krels shuffled over and took the bench opposite.

"That's Donny over there. I call him my brother because we were brought up together," chipped in Miriam to break the tension. "I am really a bit of apartheid jetsam. His family adopted me, literally off the street, when my mother was killed in the District Six clearance. I was amongst a bunch of orphans moved to Cape Flats and his family took me in to their house at Kalk Bay, where they kept their boat. We still live there.

Donny has the old house and we live pretty near." Miriam stopped and Joe turned toward Charles.

"Shit! I knew I'd see you again one day. Well, here we are. You, a bloody tourist and me an ambulance man, a paramedic. Well, and I do a few trips in the boat to help Donny fishing."

Charles took a doctorly look at Joe's neck. "I see you still wear something on your neck. Was it a serious injury?"

"We came back to a new world. I survived because that photographer cut me down, after she got her pictures, while I was nearly dead. I lay on the ground gasping for air and water until the others arrived. Jani was good. They made a litter and carried me. We arrived at the nun's clinic after you left. The other boys went home but the nuns thought I wouldn't manage the journey so they kept me on.

"That big fellow, Donny, is my brother-in-law two ways." Charles was speechless. This man he had nearly killed, no, executed for his extreme racism was doubly connected to the big black man who was on the deck of a fishing boat moored nearby. He was stacking boxes and tidying the deck gear.

"I'll get some beer. Join us?" said Joe.

"Here, let me."

"No, brother, I owe you one. What do you want, man, light or dark?"

Donny was coming over. He rolled on nimble feet, wearing yellow ankle boots. He had taken off his soiled boiler suit and was wearing pink and blue Bermudas and a grey sweatshirt.

A girl with big hair and a small face came over.

"Hey, you two can't sit out here. You'll frighten the customers away," she joked.

"You've only got four, and I brought them in for you. Get the beer over here and stop your cheek."

She turned to Charles and gave him a wide smile of approval, then trounced off, giving him the benefit of her well-rounded buttocks highlighted by the white Lycra of her pants.

She was back again very quickly with four frosted glasses of Castle Lager.

They sat in silence, savouring the frozen beer. Charles's head was still spinning. He wasn't sure how to begin. Were these men interested in his tale? Donny was concentrating on his glass.

"Well," said Joe. "What brings you to this neck?"

"AIDS conference," he blurted flatly. Then by way of explanation, "I write speeches for a professor."

Joe grunted. "Miriam's doing a nurse specialisation course on AIDS..." He smiled at her as she took her first sip of the cool beer. "So I get it now. That's where you met."

"I don't treat patients, but I wrote a PhD on the subject. I gave up doctoring as such for academics."

Suddenly Charles thought he'd said too much. He would bore them.

"Hey, I thought you'd make a good doctor. That bugger Jani you patched up is as right as rain. I saw him last year. He's still a fascist supremacist. He can't wake up to the new South Africa. He's living in the bad old days. We don't see eye to eye; know what I mean? He can't forgive me for being coloured."

He gave Charles a surprisingly enormous smile and then turned to Donny.

"Let's all go down to Sea Point for a bite to eat at Khalid's. I can almost taste the kebabs now. What about it, Donny?"

"Ag, man, we have to see if we can get that bleddy old bakkie going again, then we'll all go. Battery's kak."

Miriam stood up "I'm for the metro, got to feed the kids and Vonnie's got night school. Hey Charles, it's been really nice to meet you. You and the men seem to have business. Why not come and see us at the cottage?" She smiled and turned away.

"Hey, Chas, c'mon, you up for a beer and a kebab at Sea Point? It's bit more friendly down there and a lot cheaper and I'm hungry too. I can call you Chas, can't I, Professor?"

"For sure if 'professor' is the alternative." Charles smiled, warming to his old antagonist.

Krels and he held their hands out to each other and almost in unison, they said, "I am so glad to see you."

"Hey Donny, you remember I told you about the man who made me see God...Well, nearly killed me in the process. This is your man. I should hate him really, but no, he's my saviour along with that crazy photographer who saved my body and the old Irish priest who saved my soul." Turning to Charles, he continued. "I don't like to remember it really. It was another part of my life, another life!" He trailed off, embarrassed. This was too personal for their first meeting and the casual open-air setting. Perhaps they'd talk of serious things later when they had a few drinks inside them.

They walked along the quay to the car park and the old Nissan crew cab pickup. It stank of fish, probably more from the heap of boiler suits on the back seat than any actual fish.

"You go in front, Chas," said Krels as if offering Charles a great honour. Charles slid on to the torn PVC seat and reached for the absent seatbelt.

Joe saw his hand searching. "Hey, you don't need a belt. They don't bother a bunch of coloured fishermen. Anyway, this thing of Donny's doesn't go fast enough to hurt anyone. Relax, Chas, make yourself comfortable. Look in the shelf, there may be a few tinnies. Take one and pass me one."

He felt three cans of a four-pack in the doorless glove compartment, greasy to his sensitive touch. He passed one back to Krels and offered one to Donny.

"No thanks, man. I'm driving. That bugger doesn't have any respect for safety." This brought a guffaw of laughter from Joe and they all joined in.

It was a diesel. Donny had obviously done this before. He turned the key and the little coil lit up, fading as the engine turned over slowly. "We only get one chance," he said. "After that the battery won't manage."

The engine turned over slowly and nearly stopped, but then when they all expected a dull silence, it fired.

"We'll park on a steep hill. No problem over there."

They stopped on a hill facing down towards the sea between High Level Road and the Main Road, banging the doors of the battered vehicle. As they sauntered along the raised sidewalk, Charles was pleased to feel the relaxed atmosphere in the warm, soft evening light.

They turned into a shop with sign over the top, "Khalid's Famous Kebab Shop." There was a strong smell of cooking mutton and Charles felt the juices rise in his mouth.

"This old Arab does the best kebabs in town," Donny shouted, nodding at the man behind the counter addressing all who might hear. The man was as big as Donny, with a large Arabic nose, black wavy hair, and a full black beard.

"Donny, Joe, you looking good. Freezer's nearly empty. When you boys going to get me some more fish? Who's your friend? You hiring pretty smart crewmen for your yachting business, eh?" He grinned widely, as anyone could see from his crisp jeans and spotless, bright-coloured polo shirt that Charles was not quite one of them.

"Hey, Chas, meet Khal. He's also famous for his fish curry. Takes a week to make and takes the roof of your mouth off. Eh, Khal, this is Charles from England, famous white witch doctor come to banish AIDS from the Dark Continent." Joe was over his shock, his shyness dissolved, replaced by confused joy.

"Beer first, Khal, longnecks straight from the freezer." Joe winked at Charles as he squeezed behind a small table with uncomfortably upright wooden chairs. Donny touched hands silently with Khalid and joined them.

Nasheed, a pretty girl with the similarly striking features of her father, poured the beers from a few inches above the glass, ensuring ice would form as the bubbling CO_2 escaped.

"She does that better than anyone else in town. I'm telling you, man, go to the Cape Town Palace, those stuck-up waiters in white jackets don't do it that good."

They took their beer. While Charles was savouring the crisp coolness and sharp bubbles and microchips of ice, Joe wiped the froth from his lips "Cross the bleddy continent for that. Eh, Chas?"

"Good," said Donny, and his glass was nearly empty as he put it on the table. "No need to get poetical, man, just keep them coming." Nasheed placed three small bowls of soup on the table with a plate of dusty flat bread.

The soup had a fishy aroma blended with citrus and garlic. There were small lumps of white flesh floating in the bowls. The flavour was just as expected but with an addition of chilli and thyme.

"We taught him this," said Donny. "We used to call it survival soup. All the heads and tails and a bit of wild garlic and lemon grass: almost anything. Khalid's wife puts the fish flesh in for the Arab customers. Good, eh?" He looked up at Charles who had taken his first taste, burning his tongue slightly.

Khalid came over: "Skewers? No, not tonight," he stated. "I got something special for you, sweet as a nut. Killed her myself this morning. Fell off the knife. I ate much raw as I was butchering her. Would have never made a good mama sheep. Bit of a runt, as you say."

They savoured the soup, drank more beer and ate the lamb, grilled undercut and ribs accompanied by a beautifully light and crisp couscous, flavoured with tomato, lemon and fresh garlic. The lamb was exactly as described by Khalid, sweet and tender, completely free of fat and subtly flavoured with thyme, rosemary and arnica. A short round lady entered from the back. She was wearing a black dress and, on her head, a white paper catering hat. It gave her the look of a nun but her broad smiling face and air of propriety made Charles aware immediately that this must be the boss's wife and probably the cook of most of this evening's delights.

"Eh, Fatima," Joe said, standing, "as beautiful as ever and as skilful. The lamb was magnificent. Meet an old friend. He is completely knocked out by the meal, eh, Chas? This is our hostess and the *chef de cuisine.*"

Charles tried to stand, crushed in, as he was between the small table, the rigid chair and the wall. Fatima held out her hand and grinned even wider.

"Good, so you enjoy?" She said looking down at the messy empty plates. "Anwar gave us a special animal this time."

"Anwar is her brother," explained Joe. "He runs a herd of sheep and goats and raises chickens. Most of what he sells goes to these Arab places. They've been here for generations. They got squeezed out by the influx of wine growers. They used to graze the open land. Now he has a section and feeds his stock on vineyard mush and special bag feed. The flavour comes from the grapes. No bad thing, eh? Great eggs and chicken. Bloody superb."

Nasheed brought her mother a small glass of chai, and Fatima sat at the table nearby in silent companionship. Khalid appeared from the kitchen door wiping sweat from his brow. He had been working at the carryout counter on the other side of the wall.

"Busy tonight. Can't complain, a bunch of rowdies from the pub across the road. Six gomgats and their bokies. Kebabs all round and enough chilli ketchup to float a battleship."

"Nice truck though, someone's making money," said Donny morosely, no doubt comparing the shiny vehicle with chrome bars all over it to his battered Nissan.

The meal was at an end and Charles felt slightly embarrassed. "Khalid, that was delicious, absolutely the best. Please give me the bill. I'd like this to be my treat."

Khalid raised his eyebrows and looked at Joe. "No, no, Chas. You don't get it. It's on tick. We supply the most beautiful fish, he feeds us some scraps now and again."

Joe winked at Khalid, who guffawed with a deep laugh. "You call that scraps! And in front of the magnificent lady who cooked it."

"OK, Joe, I've got an early start tomorrow," said Donny.

"What about our friend here? When are you making your speech, Chas?" asked Joe.

"Not me, and not till three for my boss. The whole conference starts at two. There's a show in the morning, mostly pharmas flogging their overpriced pills and potions and justifying their profits to the gullible."

"Right then, nightcap at my place," said Joe. "There's a train back to town at any time if you want, or you're welcome to stay over, Chas."

By now Charles was relaxed by the beer, the excellent food, and the friendship of the man he had feared most in the world. Why would he refuse this latest genial advance? Even the stink of Donny's truck gave him a warm feeling of bonhomie.

"Donny's family managed to hold on to their house in spite of apartheid. It's right on the water's edge. I guess the whites thought it was too primitive and they didn't like the Cape storms." There was a silence. He had read about the

236

regime of H. F. Verwoerd and P.W. Botha and it made sense of what he was hearing.

They climbed into the old pickup and it rolled down the hill, the engine starting with a jerk. The rattling and rumbling made Charles's silence seem acceptable. They continued southward in companionable silence.

"Got to stop for fuel," said Donny as he pulled over to the left on to the forecourt of a smart brightly lit petrol station. "We used to get away with using marine diesel but the cops are on to us now. They caught a man. They took away his boat and tied it up last year. Hell of a row. They gave his boat back but they fined him five thousand rand. He was out of action for six months and the lawyer screwed him for another five thou. Suddenly all of us fishermen became honest customers at the pumps. It was probably those buggers who started the whole thing."

To his great relief Charles noticed there were toilet facilities. "Wait a moment for me" he said as he climbed out. He had to pass through the shop on the way and he noticed they had a special offer on batteries. As he left the restroom he paused and then asked the girl at the counter, "Do you know what type of battery fits that truck?"

She unglued her eyes from the soap opera on the overhead TV and took down a dog-eared reference pamphlet from a hook near the till. The pump man came to the outside window with a few rand notes from Donny.

"Carl, what's that bakkie you just filled up? Customer wants to buy a battery." There was a conference over the catalogue, he paid and then Charles proudly walked out with the battery slung between him and the pump man.

"Here, a thank-you for your kindness." He said to the men in the cab.

"You didn't need to do that, Chas," Donny said, then not wanting to seem ungrateful, added, "Hey, thanks, man. That's good. I tell you what, give me the receipt and I'll give you the money because I can claim it against tax."

"No, Donny, forget it. All you have to do is promise to fit it tomorrow, OK?"

"You're OK, Chas," said Joe, rubbing his eyes. "I'll open my best bottle of Cape Brandy for you. Jump in and let's go."

The house was between the railway and the sea. Access from the road was by a treacherous sloping driveway crossing the railway at an alarming angle. Charles could see the lights of the fishing harbour a few hundred metres across the waves splashing on the rocky shore. They had passed a station half a kilometre before the turning.

The truck stopped on the rough gravel and Joe got out with Charles. Pointing to the harbour, he said, "Donny's normal berth is here but he's got a fishing party tomorrow, from one of the big hotels." And then turning to the open passenger window, "Right, brother, see you tomorrow evening. You won't be in till seven or so. Good luck with the catch."

"Thanks for the ride, Donny, see you again, I hope," shouted Charles over the noise of the engine as Donny backed the vehicle to turn.

4

As they entered, there was a footfall on the stairs above. "Hi, Sugar, I brought Chas back to sample the brandy. I never told you: this is the woman who straightened me out. Literally. She was my nurse and still is."

Then turning to Miriam, he said, "Charles is from one of my previous lives, in the jungle days. I still can't really believe it but this is him." Miriam had reached the bottom of the stairs. She folded her knees and sat on the second step up. Her eyes opened very wide.

"Wow, really," she said. "Forgive me for asking, but...well, the man you told me about was called Charles..." Charles could see fear and confusion in her large deep-set eyes.

"Please," he said, "I was the one. Yes, we were in a different world then. Looking back I can't believe the violence. I guess he's right. The old Joaquim was a bad man." In a very subdued voice, he said, "I thought I had killed him."

238

"You did," interjected Joe, "but the new Joseph was born...a bloody painful business, physically and mentally." With tears in his eyes he followed up with, "You two, well, you two did it for me—stick and carrot, eh? Works every time.." Then after a pause, "Hey, what kind of host am I? Come in, Chas."

He saw the fear dissipate from her face. "Oh, yes," she said, "please, come in here, won't you? The kids are asleep upstairs, all except Vonnie." She turned to Joe. "She's in a big sulk about something or someone, more like. I was just going to bed, honey, my shift is at eight."

They had moved into the room on the right-hand side of the passage. There were two worn leather sofas and a bar with a collection of odd barstools, an array of optics, and two fridges behind. Photos on the walls showed football teams, fishing boats, fairgrounds all populated by a polyglot of smiling people, all ages and races colourfully dressed for fun or sports. He glanced at a big clock set in a brass boat's wheel. It was just past ten.

Charles just managed to say, "I am very pleased I met you, Miriam. Thanks for bringing me to meet Joe. I hope we have a chance to get to know each other better later." It sounded too formal for the friendly setting.

Miriam looked at him again with a bewildered expression. He noticed her eyes were hazel with darkly pigmented surrounds. "Look, I'm really sorry, but I must say good night. Another time; will I see you tomorrow? If you want to stay over, Joe will make up some sheets on the sofa."

"G'night, Miri. I'll be up soon, but I promised Charles some of the Klipdrift Gold brandy," Joe said as he moved over and kissed her. She moved away out of the door and with her went a tension. "Sit down, Chas, that's right, on the sofa." Joe was already twisting the cap off a very smart bottle. "We won this last Christmas at the cannery party. Good do. We supply the grub, and the management provides the booze and one or two of the town's businessmen give raffle prizes." As Joe busied himself at the bar there was an awkward silence. The only thing the two men had in common was the experience they both wanted to forget. The outcome had sorted itself out and further discussion would only open old wounds—a sleeping dog. So they talked of the pictures on the walls and the children's exploits and, as the story unfolded, Charles developed a certain envy for the simple happy life Joe was now leading.

"Her husband, Ray, died in a fishing accident—his boat sank. He was a partner in a big boat going south into the deep ocean for tuna, returning with a good catch. Hit by a tanker. They say it was just a glancing blow, but enough to sink an overloaded tuna boat. Two survivors: Donny and a boy called Tandy tied together a bunch of polystyrene fish boxes. They were picked up by another of our boats. Ray did the same with the mechanic and another young lad. They lost touch in the night. I guess Donny was lucky, as Ray and the others were never seen again. They searched, of course, but nothing was found. Well, that was my luck because Miri took me in hand. I'm just another one of her kids. We only got married a month ago when the firm stopped paying her for Ray's compensation. Just a year: not much for all his years earning money for them. The cannery used to belong to the fishermen, but they got an offer from Fishmarine Corp and well, some say they sold their souls. The Corp built a new shed for the machinery and re-built the slipway and helped to finance two new boats. The offer was too good to refuse."

Charles was taking all this in slowly. He was puzzled as the Joaquim Krels he had known previously did not seem to be the sort of man to settle down with a community of Cape fishing people. He was shy to ask outright so he let Joe ramble on so that by explanation or inference, he might learn how all this happened.

"I moved over here with Miri. She gets the metro to town. I got a job there as well and then joined for a few trips on the boats and, now, I'm getting the hang of handling the fishing and the boat. I really feel at home with this community. Perhaps that's because of Miri but partly it's because I found out it's where I belong."

By now they were settled opposite each other in the comfortable overstuffed sofas, each sipping the fine Cape brandy. "I had my wilderness years, oh yes, man, you believe it.

I came back to Cape Town with a near-broken neck and my voice all screwed up. I could hardly talk. I had no money and was nearly unemployable. I would have gone down and down except for an old priest and my blond hair. I tell you, man, it's a weird world when a few blond curls make the difference between life and death, but I know it to be one of the facts of this godforsaken paradise of a country. I was surviving on handouts and dossing down with all the bums and dronkies the police sweep off the street corners at ten p.m. Something had to be done—was I ready for death? One day I said, 'No, man, pick your sorry arse up and get to work.'

"I was passing a building site that very day and I looked in, straight into the eyes of the foreman. He looked as angry as hell. He asked 'What do you want?'

"I said, 'You got a job for me?'

" He looked up 'What can you do?'

"i looked straightinto his eyes: 'Anything.'

"He scratched his head with his dirty fingers. 'I need a digger operator. I'm sick to death of these stupid Bantu, but it's all the bosses will send me. The last one managed to wreck the brakes and nearly killed everyone in the coffee shack.'

"I was not confident but when I said I had driven one in the past, he practically jumped at me, shook my hand and sent me over to see the clerk to sign on.

"I drove a back-hoe for a bit, you know, a JCB, then a van doing deliveries, then a taxi and then I trained as an ambulance man. I love it, man, the satisfaction of getting there in time to save some poor bugger from a painful death, delivering babies, driving fast through the town with the siren blowing and all the traffic clearing out of the way. Yes, man, I think I've found my place in the world at last."

Suddenly he stopped himself, embarrassed by his enthusiastic outburst. Then more quietly: "Do you know what I mean?" Charles hesitated and before he could agree, Joe went on. "Hey, Chas, you have a vocation. I don't pretend…" He tailed off and held his glass high in a toasting gesture. Charles thought he saw a tear in his eye but the smile was broad and indicated happiness after pain.

This softer side of Joe was entirely new to Charles. He dared to ask now.

"So how did you meet Miriam?"

"She had nursed me when I first came back from the jungle. Then when I hit the street we lost touch. We met again in the yard of the hospital soon after I got the ambulance job. We used to chat a bit but gradually we got to know each other. She, recently widowed, had needs and by God, I had needs. If you haven't lived on the streets you don't know how lonely it is. No one wants to know you and even the *skaarpies* that will talk to you are like scavenging hyenas looking for a chance to rob you or ride you for whatever you've got. All relationships are short, suspicious, mean, phony and…No, I don't want to remember. Even as I was slowly making my way back to normal life, I needed someone, man, did I?"

"And these people?" Charles interjected.

"Jesus, man, you won't believe this. You know I said my sister was married to Donny. Well, of course I met him, and he's this great big coloured guy. Anyway I just thought she has to take her chances like us all and, when I got to know him, I realised he's the greatest guy—couldn't wish for a better brother-in-law.

"We were living happily, I was seeing Miri regularly. We would visit with Donny and Avis from time to time, and suddenly one time at Sunday lunch she says "Joe, I never told you about the box"

"Of course I was pretty puzzled. 'Box?'

"'Yes,' she said, 'the lawyer sent a box-file over about two years after the raid.' There was a short note: '*Krels house. Salvaged items.*' There were envelopes inside marked with the rooms of the house with inventories of the furniture and all the small items collected. The big stuff was in a store.

"I had recognised a few of the familiar ornaments around her house, but I had not mentioned them because I did not want her to think I was trying to make any sort of claim on them. I wasn't interested. Anyway, she says, 'You should have a look through it to see if you want any of the old photos or small items.'

242

"I wasn't keen, but as I left she gave me a cardboard box full of papers and photographs.

"I took it all back to my digs and then looked through it casually when I was preparing for bed. There were a lot of photos of the family on holiday and things like that. You know, on the beach in Durban, waving from the cable car at the foot of the Table Mountain, and with the surfers at Table View where we stayed in a beach hut one summer. All the envelopes were marked with the exact locations where they had been found inside the house; perhaps the police had done it or maybe the lawyer's clerks, whoever. Anyway, there was one photo in an envelope marked 'Bedroom 2 bedside table.'

"I'll never understand how Avis had not removed it before she gave me the box, but probably she'd completely forgotten about it. Well, there we were, Bontong and me, standing naked by the place we called Pig Hole, a dew pond or crater hidden by thick brush. We had killed a baby wild pig there years before. It was a superb place to cool off on a hot day. Bontong was standing tall and full frontal, his magnificent black muscular body dwarfing me, who was standing side on and slightly bent," like a sort of white Neanderthal. We were just about to jump, I guess. The photo was folded back on itself so we could be separated from each other.

"A sudden blush spread from my spine up my back as I realised what I was looking at. This was proof that my sister, Avis, had loved my best boyhood friend, Bontong, as much as I had and this was her little lusty memento. The scene came back to me clear as yesterday, man, we had been peeping Toms on an intimate moment we hadn't really understood at the time and she had been staring at this photo of him naked at the hole. Anyway the tragedy was that I killed Bontong, as he had been urged to rape Avis by his gang of out-of-control youths. If it hadn't have been for the circumstances she might have taken him willingly.

"Well, I killed Bontong, and I also nearly killed Avis and messed up her face something horrible. I cried there and then in my miserable little room, cried like a baby. I couldn't hold the tears back. I don't think I was sorry for myself or particularly for Avis but for the whole bloody human race.

Such stupidity, such waste, such bad feeling and hate and such a mistake.

"Anyway, I pulled myself together, but the cat was out of the bag and I couldn't stop my curiosity, so I went on opening the envelopes until I came to one entitled: 'Bedroom 1, Photos from trunk under bed.'

"These were old photos of the ancestors, Mum and Dad's wedding photos, childhood pictures of them both in different homes, a few teenage photos of them in various poses with friends, posing with cars or motorbikes, prize bulls, football teams and in groups outside college or school edifices. Then there were some faded sepia pictures of people in Victorian dress and men in bush clothes with guns and horses and big dogs. Then a very small photo of an old Hottentot woman, small and well dressed in white lace and black cloth with a little girl of about four. On the back was scribed in a copperplate hand 'Umta and Gertie, 1897.' In a later handwriting I recognised as my mother's, there was written with a blue fountain pen: 'Me and Granny Umta.'

"Imagine that, Chas. I was an apartheid boy. I always believed I was a blond-haired member of the master race. Here was a shock if ever: a Hottentot ancestor. Anyway, I asked Avis if she knew about this, and she said, 'Oh yes. Mother told me when I first went to school because some bitch of a girl with bright blue eyes and a pinbrain under a mass of straight blonde hair started to make my life difficult. Mother thought I could face up to all this stuff better if I knew that I, along with a good percentage of the population, was really mixed and that with apartheid all natural attitudes were buried in ridiculous racist theory and vicious, cruel policies.'

"So as a teenager she knew we were 'pass white,' but what difference did it make out in the country? Mama said Avis could never discuss it with Papa. He would deny it, get angry and possibly even violent.

"I took another look at Avis through different eyes and began to realise I had always taken her darker complexion, green eyes, and loose wavy hair for granted. Before I blasted the side of her face off, she was a beauty and now I saw she used a lot of dark makeup over the whiter skin of the scars.

"This was another relief to me. I am not only a white African, an alien race, but also, at least in some small way, I have real African blood and now I live with these people here, I understand them. The coloured people were always an important part of the community but at the same time despised."

Charles had been riveted by every word. He leaned forward, proffering his hand. "I am glad I didn't kill you. You've become a pretty decent human being. Rough ride, eh?" As they shook hands for the second time that day, Joe added, "So I am one of you lot anyway..." They sat in silence for a few minutes until Joe got up to refill their glasses.

"And the marvellous thing is these buggers down here have taken me into their lives. I love Miri's kids, tantrums, mischief and all; their achievements thrill me every day. We are trying for one of our own. Who knows?" He came back from the bar with two more large brandies.

5

"Now I have to ask you something. It may or may not be important. What did you do with the laptop computer?"

"It's in my room. It's got my research on it. What do you know about my laptop?"

"Is it the one you took from me in the village?"

"No. But I didn't take anything from you that day. After I hung you on the tree, I ran away. I was scared. I was mad with fear. I ran and ran until I collapsed."

"What happened to the satchel and the laptop?"

"I'm sorry, I know nothing about your laptop. What satchel?"

"You know the one I always carried, a laptop case but faded and dirty. Black canvas originally but with mud and so on would have looked brown like the soil."

Charles thought for a moment. "Jenny took it. Jenny Bones was her name, a reporter. She rescued me. She took photos, had a motorbike, brought me out to the nuns, disappeared. Never heard of her since."

"She must be the bitch that put my picture in the tabloids. Thank God no one ever managed to connect me with the pictures but I knew my own face, even covered with a tatty beard. She was cruel. You left me in a very compromised position and this vicious hack took pictures and syndicated them in the gutter press."

"You're right she put the case in the pannier. I thought nothing of it. You were supposed to be dead and I was running for my life, impatient for her to lift me out. Instinctively I said nothing and it dropped out of my mind."

"Right, who is this dyke?"

"Jenny Bones, freelance journo, Aussie or Kiwi, my guess. War chaser. What's the significance of a laptop? They are obsolete and worthless after a few years and you don't look the sort that needs one around the house."

"It's what's on the drive, the hard drive."

"Right, so what is on the hard drive?"

"Look, I may be a reformed character and all that but I am not averse to making a bit of money."

"Right."

"There is a bunch of info on there that I think is worth millions. When we were on our way out of the jungle, that laptop was to be my pension, my salvation. That's why I never let it out of my hands. However heavy or whatever its nuisance value, I kept it slung round my neck. Then your Jenny Bones snatches it while she saves my life."

"What information?"

"It's about minerals. I think it's to do with carbon dioxide and regenerating some sort of fuel or even electronics. The guys were geologists for the mine, but they were interested in energy. They collected samples and stuff from a leper colony nearby. I overheard snippets of conversation. I knew the computer was important. They were killed when the Mai-Mai attacked. I lifted it from Sam, the leader of the team, as he croaked his last. Problem was I couldn't start it. It was password protected. Useless to us unless we could get the password."

"What have you done since? What about your pals?" Charles asked thoughtfully.

"They weren't in on it really. I was the only one who went to the leper colony regularly. The others stayed in the camp, scared."

"Well, now you know the name of the woman with your computer, get it here and I'll see if I can get some sense out of it."

"How can I? Jenny Bones is a common name. I guess there may be hundreds of them."

"OK, tomorrow I'll get on the Internet and see if she's got a Facebook account, website or blog. She's a journalist. She may well have, you know, some sort of presence to help her with leads to stories."

"Well, Chas, you may be right. I promise you these Swedes thought the whole world would change for them if they could get these minerals out. As it happened their world suddenly did change but very much for the worse. They're all dead. But the hostilities are a lot less now. It's not safe but I think the situation is a lot better."

"Are you suggesting we launch some sort of attack on the area and lift the minerals out?"

"Shit, I don't know but we may be able to find some people who'll pay us for the information. If it's really worth so much in real terms, the info must be worth a few grand. Sleep on it. Miri left you all these blankets and pillows. Are you sure you'll be alright? You know where everything is. We'll be up around seven. If the kids bother you for breakfast TV, frighten them away. What a day! I'm bleddy glad we met."

"Me too. I was very frightened of any news of you, more likely from a vengeful brother or one of your band of mercenaries or whatever. Hey man, thanks. I feel a whole lot better about everything—my life, really. Let's join together and solve the mystery of the laptop. Sounds like fun even if there is no pot of gold."

Charles woke up to the chatter of children arguing over Coco Pops, clattering up and down stairs, banging on the bathroom door and generally getting ready for school. His head was slightly muzzy. Joe poked his head round the door of the room where they had killed the bottle of brandy the night before.

"Howzit, Chas? Head OK? Man, we put away a whole bottle. Dangerous, you know my record with alcohol. I can do you some breakfast. What do you fancy?"

"Slow down, brother, my eyes are hardly open. My mouth feels like a disinfected toilet. Let me just have a cup of tea and then if I can, I'll go back to the hotel."

"I'm going to take the kids up to the main road. I'll be back in five minutes. Bathroom's top of the stairs. Have a shower if you like. Miri put a towel out for you." Charles saw a shadow and then Miriam standing at the door.

"Hi and good-bye, Charles, got to get my train. Will I see you?"

"Thanks, Miri, I hope so. Maybe we can go somewhere tonight."

"Lekker, see you."

With that the front door clicked shut.

"Here, kids, come and meet my good friend Dr. Charles." Joe reappeared with a cup of dark tea and two children.

"Did you save his life?" enquired a bright-eyed eleven-year-old while his younger sister hid shyly behind him, gripping her satchel firmly in front of her.

"C'mon, Jan, where are your manners? Say hello to Dr. Charles. OK, Chas, I've got to take these little ones off to the crossing. If Vonnie appears, she'll probably not see you. Like a zombie until past noon. Don't be alarmed."

Joe made coffee for them when he got back and after a couple of slices of toast, Charles caught a Metrorail back to the hotel.

As soon as he plugged his computer in to the Internet, he searched out the name of Jenny Bones on Facebook. Up came about ten responses. Then he thought he might try another approach. He phoned Cape Town's four English language newspapers with a lame story about Jenny being a long-lost friend, and he wanted to know how to find her. He couldn't find anyone to play. There must be a press club. He realized he had to be a bit more imaginative. His conference was attended by journalists from all over the world and local ones as well. He generally avoided them, preferring to release carefully prepared statements on behalf of his professor. But they always wanted conversations. They all fancied they could wheedle out some offbeat confession or leaked idea if they could only interview the researchers or presenters. They hated reading and précising blurb served up to them.

Charles would try to get invited to the Cape Town press club and then extract the information about Jenny from there. It would be a long shot. He changed his clothes quickly and went down to the bar. Pre-lunch drinks were underway. He tried to spot the journalist he needed. There was a small group of types he guessed contained his quarry. They were a mixed bunch of nationalities but all wore nondescript ties, white shirts and loose suits over cheap rubber soled shoe. They seemed to be cracking jokes. One recognized him as he purposely gave the appearance of being slightly lost and lonely.

"Hey, Dr. Sojenji. I guess you're preparing the keynote speech for this afternoon. Any great breakthroughs or surprises? I'm Fred Bogle of the *Cape Argus*. Can I get you a drink? The bar's only just opened. Bit late, don't you think, keeping us all waiting like this. Beer, gin?" Charles accepted a vodka and mango juice, to the consternation of Fred, who was wondering about the orientation of this famous AIDS doctor.

"Nothing I could talk about here, really. Walls have ears, but I may have a few points to give you in advance of this afternoon."

"Look, Doc, it just so happens a pal of mine and I were about to slope off to the Club for lunch. If you don't mind letting the Cape in on the same secrets—we're really sister papers—come with us. He's one hundred percent reliable and it will allow us to get the message into the evening editions ahead of the dailies."

Fred looked across to the bar and caught the eye of a bald, pink-faced man tipping back a stumpy glass with a lemon slice floating on the clear liquid.

The man lumbered over. "Jack, meet an insider for this afternoon's show. Dr. Sojenji, this is Jack Shaw, *Mail and Guardian.*"

Charles shook the proffered hand. "Why don't you guys call me Charles?"

"Right, Charles it is," said Jack with a big smile in his pale liquid eyes. "Very nice to meet you. Can you throw us a few chippies about your speech this afternoon?"

"We need to go somewhere, Jack. I suggested the Club."

"Of course, of course, remiss of me, forgetting my manners in my enthusiasm. My car's in the multilevel. It's near the entrance so we could walk over together."

The brightness of the sun hit Charles like a searchlight as they crossed the pavement to the car park. The white Mercedes had powerful air-conditioning, and soon he was feeling the chill. The club was in a magnificent house from the Victorian era. Colonial in design and set in well-mown lawns with beautiful flower beds overlooking the wasteland that was District Six.

It wasn't long before Charles saw his chance. They had been talking about the new treatment regimes and retro viral drugs coming on to the market when he spotted the information office and, beyond the entrance, the clearly marked toilets. The lunch buffet was laid out on tables in the opposite direction. They all rose together and Charles waited until they had all turned away from the door towards the buffet and, wrong footing them, excused himself.

"I'll join you over at the buffet." He was gone before they could react. At the information desk he paused to see the two men chatting away and starting to help themselves to the magnificent fare laid out on silver salvers on fine white linen.

"Hi there," he said casually, hoping to appear as if he really belonged in the environment. The girl looked up unsmiling, with dyed-blond hair and black eyes, nails painted dark red. "Yiss, sir."

"I'm looking for my old friend, Jenny Bones. She should be a member here. Do you have a list of phone numbers so I can check on her?" It was a slip of the tongue; he meant call her. She didn't notice. "We don't really have members as such, but I may find her in the 'list,' a sort of informal record."

"That's OK, I just want to phone her to see what's happened to her." He saw his hosts making their way back to the table with loaded plates. He waved an acknowledgement to Fred's enquiring look. The girl was clicking away on a battered keyboard.

"This old computer is so slow. Ah, here we go. She came in about a month ago. Left a phone number. Looks like a cell phone. Do you want to take it down?" He wrote quickly and walked back into the dining room.

As he passed the two men, he smiled broadly, and went to fill his plate. Back at the table he explained his quest.

"Jenny bloody Bones! Don't go near her. We don't take any of her stuff anymore. She'd have to have confirmed news of the end of the world before we'd publish anything of hers. She made a specialization of digging for dirt on subjects of the Truth and Reconciliation Committee and caused havoc by exaggerating and distorting the facts. She was like a bull in a china shop, just a bloody hooligan, and screwed up several cases where people were genuinely trying to come clean. She made money from syndicating overseas until she was shut down. She lived around here in absolute isolation. She's supposed to be writing books. She may have emigrated if anyone will have her."

Charles felt it necessary to make a denial. "She's not a friend of mine, but I may have some unfinished business with her. I think she took something of mine."

"I'll bet. She'd steal from her grandmother, that one."

Charles could see they would probably go on in this vein, so he changed the subject promptly before they asked him about the lost item.

"How can I help you gentlemen in return for this nice hospitality?"

"Don't sound so mercenary, Professor, we are simply honoured to have you eat with us. But any little gems in the way of a heads up on the afternoon's presentation would be welcome."

"As you know, there hasn't really been any kind of breakthrough, no miracle cure, and although we can understand more precisely how the virus behaves, it is still as hard as ever to interfere with that behaviour. The really interesting thing some of my colleagues have discovered and my prof will explain this afternoon is that many of the effects caused by the T-cell deficiency in AIDS sufferers are transitory and can be ameliorated by introducing certain chemicals or drugs into the system of patients—nothing very new here, but what is being proposed is that many of these substances are found naturally occurring in the flora, particularly jungle flora in Africa and South America.

"The big pharmas will not like all this to be publicized— naturally enough—because they are looking forward to monopolies on synthetic drugs. The other news is that HIV is not a recent phenomenon. It is thought that monogamy became part of ancient cultures because of retroviruses and that simply restricting cross-infection opportunities kept these diseases under control for millennia."

And so Charles went on, singing for his supper until he thought he had said enough for the two gentlemen of the press to skip the speech and file articles. He added a bit of spice as an afterthought. "A bunch of physicists have isolated some interesting very small particles they call nanotubes. They are working with some medical scientists, and they think they may be able to use these tubes to deliver chemicals in a very targeted manner to particular cells. This includes retrovirus infections. The catchwords are "nano particles" and "nano tubes." Excuse me, gentlemen, but I promised to prime my boss before he goes on this afternoon."

He called the Bones number from the foyer and heard an answer-phone message. This was hopeful. He did not leave a message to warn Jenny of his presence, preferring to try to surprise her later. There would be plenty of time.

He went straight to Kalk Bay after the conference, running away from his inquisitive supporters using the crowded Metrorail with all the returning workers.

"Well, Joe, I'm not sure of it, but we may have tracked down Jenny Bones. I called her number and got an answer-phone message. I left nothing, and as I called from the journalist club, she won't guess we're after her. We may be able to track down her address from the Internet. I think perhaps we should, if possible, go round there and ask her nicely for the computer she's been looking after all this time. She's probably a nasty piece of work so we can offer her a small reward of, say, five hundred rand. Make it seem pretty unimportant, like it contains all your personal e-mails from girlfriend, now wife. You know the sort of thing."

"Don't worry, man, I will look as big and ugly as I can and then go all sentimental. If she knows where it is, she'll split."

The next morning Joe and Charles rode the train back to the city and opened up Charles's computer in his room.

"You know we have to be pretty quick. I go back to UK tomorrow night. As it is, I am skiving a visit to the Pollsmoor Prison Hospital. I would have tried to avoid it anyway. Highest density of AIDS apparently of any place in the world."

"Hey, man, how d'you get involved with all this AIDS business?"

"Drifted into it, really. It just grabbed my imagination as an area of activity where new discoveries may be made. I suppose I had an idea of fame and glory."

"Right, man. How do we find this little wuzz?"

So they set to for an hour and at last came up with an address in Hanover Hill.

"We'll have to give her a phone call first, very friendly, make sure she's home. You could play the 'you saved my life' card. 'Like to buy you a drink and tell you the rest of the story.' She'll go for that. Anything for a story."

"I may have it. Shit, I had this place since the eighties. Never throw anything away—that's how good material can be lost, but I gave up on that computer. You won't be able to use it without the passwords."

"It's my bleddy computer. Password's no problem. Now, be a nice girl, and why not get it? Did I mention a reward? Look, Jenny, I would have lost it without you taking it that day. I got into a hell of a mess after you saved my bacon; it would have been trashed for sure."

"What's on it that's so important you chased me down after all these years? Must be something pretty worthwhile."

"Just private stuff me and my wife did before we got married. Love letters mostly, a few holiday pictures—you know, sentimental stuff, maybe a few intimate pictures of us in a motel. Not really important, you could say. Memories. Trying to remember good times before I went into the bush."

"Mercenary? Rapist? Pillager?"

"I saw the article. Thank God no one recognized me from the picture. A man surprised me as I was taking a piss. He was supposed to be on my side but he wanted to kill me— nearly did until you came along. I was just a low-rank security guard. I strayed into the jungle when our camp was shot up by the Mai-Mai. He ran away somewhere. Never did find him."

"You want me to track him down? He may be the man I lifted out the same day." She paused thoughtfully. "Charlie?"

"I can't be bothered, now I have a good life. All that hatred was just evil and destructive. If I met him now, I might greet him like a long-lost friend, not attack him. Water under the bridge."

"OK, the reward? It doesn't really matter to me, but if I have your computer, I may as well capitalize a little."

"OK, you get it and we'll talk about it. It sounds as if you may have something, but I must see it to know it's mine."

"That's fair. Fancy a beer? Coke?"

"Coke is fine."

Jenny brought in the Coke and the laptop. It was a heavy old thing in the same canvass satchel, which had obviously been washed hard, now a pale-grey colour round the edges. Charles turned it over to see the familiar label of the company logo on the back.

"I have to admit, I tried a few times to access it. Time ran out. I had some good stories to chase and treated myself to a better lightweight model with the bunce from your story. I chucked that in the bottom of my bureau and forgot about it. Should have thrown it away. Well, my friend, what's it worth?"

"You saved my life. I would have died and now you talk about some reward. I owe you everything. No amount would be sufficient, and this little computer is nothing in comparison, nothing."

"No, no, Joe, I take your point. I'm doing OK and don't really need a reward, pleased to be of service." She turned to face him directly. " What do you do now?"

"I've been very lucky. I drive an ambulance and I live down in Kalk Bay with my wife and her kids. But I must make it up to you somehow."

"Just keep in touch, ambulance man, and you may be able to help me sometime."

"For sure. Never mind about the article; no one connected me to it." As he said it became clear Jenny actually had something on him. Surely she was not that evil. Any reward would not make any difference if she wanted to take advantage. Blackmail would be for much more than he was prepared to pay now or in the future. He just had to hope that Jenny Bones had not become suspicious about the laptop's importance.

They shook hands as Joe thanked her sincerely for her help.

Jenny was idly looking out of the window, ice-cold vodka and Coke in her hand, when she caught sight of Joe leaving by the street door and meeting a friend across the road. His look of triumph was enough to cause his friend to embrace him enthusiastically. The two of them were smiling and joking before walking off toward the Metrorail station. Their body language was reminiscent of sportsmen after a good win. A bell rang in her head. Charles! Hard to believe but something about the curly-headed swarthy man was definitely familiar. Always a believer in conspiracies, Jenny pondered the situation. To Jenny any lie was a lead to a story. If Joe had lied to her about Charles, and they were bosom buddies triumphal about separating her from the old laptop, it must contain more than love letters and holiday snaps. This was worth investigating in an otherwise dull patch in the news. She revisited her memory of the original scene once again, trying to reconstruct exactly how it played out to try to arrive at a new interpretation of what had happened.

She sat down and relaxed, drinking thoughtfully. And slowly came to the conclusion that her imagination had run away with itself. She needed a lot more to go on. The country was full of people who looked like these two who were friends or relations. Perhaps she should have insisted on Joe firing up the computer while he was here. Impossible, because the power supply had been lost and she wasn't going to rummage through her accumulated heap of electro junk to find it. Funny, Joe didn't ask for it. He was in a hurry to go after the machine had been found and didn't even finish his Coke. Jenny was also slightly miffed about the reward. She realized she been conned by a kind of psychological reverse logic. She had been induced to talk herself out of maybe a thousand rand—five hundred anyway. It had to be worth that.

9

"What do you think?" asked Charles as they sat down on the hard train seats.

"This is it, no doubt, but how to use it?"

"If I can't solve the puzzle, then I can get some software off the Internet that will crack the password."

"What if there is nothing on it?"

"In that case I catch my flight tomorrow, and we exchange Christmas cards every year."

Charles took it out of the faded canvas satchel and examined it carefully from the outside. The top was rough and scratched, but the underneath he found much more interesting. There were several labels: the usual maker's badge with the serial number and model number, the Microsoft label giving the details of the operating system and in addition a label added by the firm MinInt Analysis SA. Charles knew this required his attention more than the others. It was a typical message, "THIS IS THE PROPERTY OF...," but underneath was written in neat script using a draftman's pen just visible due to fading and dirt: "TOLUENE".

"Let's assume this is a common user computer. The password will be hidden on the machine. I think this word is it. See here: 'TOLUENE'.

"You mean they're stupid enough to put the passwords on the label?"

Charles stopped to think. "That's too simple and Jenny would have tried it. I think it is a clue or a lead. This was before Wikipedia. It would be OK to create a password familiar to a group of people with scientific knowledge and then lay down a clue or lead somewhere obvious. So now with the help of Wiki or some other scientific reference, we can get all sorts of derived words with 'toluene' as the clue. Then we'll probably find toluene has some other significance."

"That's pretty smart."

"No guarantee, my friend, just a hunch. We used a similar trick to restrict the use of computers at uni."

For Charles it was not difficult. He called into a computer shop and bought a suitable power pack. He was surprised at the price but stumped up for it anyway. On his own laptop he made a first stop. Wikipedia yielded a myriad of possibilities but it did not take long. "Toluol" was too obvious; "C7H8" was too short. "C6H5CH3" hit the spot and the operating system started.

Charles opened up the directories on the hard drive and after a few false starts, searched through many official reports on MinInt Analysis forms. The masses of numbers were some sort of code to do with minerals. The directories were all numbered in sequences and named with African names in a sort of regular pattern. Having opened a few of these and finding them incomprehensible, he was able to dismiss all the rest. His eye was caught by a folder called "NANO". Several of the files had similar designation to the ones he had seen in other folders, but when opened up were not on MinInt forms, just plain Excel spreadsheets. Then he was surprised by a file marked "lepers.doc". This turned out to be the target or at least the starting point of the quest. It was a long report in English, albeit loaded with jargon and chemical terms. It was enough.

"Well, Joe, here's a file called 'lepers'."

"Jesus, man, that must be significant."

"Go on."

"It was in a leper colony. In a big hole in the ground that had been made by digging clay for pottery. The pots were a bit special, and one or two arty types had done some primitive sculpture as well. The clay had a sort of radiant quality. They never had to glaze it because it had a finished look to it. The lepers used to sell it to traders, who took it away to market. The traders would bring them food and goods from the town. The Mai-Mai never bothered them. I think they were superstitious and frightened of leprosy. They would take risks with AIDS and most of them suffered with malaria, so the old priest told me, but they were shit-scared of leprosy. That was his theory. The lepers played up to it by having their most deformed people hang around the edge of the village with the typical bell on a stick to draw attention to themselves."

"What about the priest?"

"Irish: talk, man, talk you near to death. But full of good stories, and his own life was a bit of an eye-opener."

"Will he be useful to us?"

"I guess so because he knows the lepers—they nearly worship him and he's pretty clever about most things."

"Now back to this computer."

"These guys were going to make a killing. I listened to their conversations. I was just a dumb bouncer to them and on their side anyway, so they weren't secretive. What they were seeking was coltan, some valuable mineral used in electronics and solar panels. When they saw the pottery they reckoned it was a clue. They tracked down the source and they made little outings to the village. My job was to fend off the Mai-Mai. Of course I had no chance but I had an Uzi and an AK and they thought this was security. I didn't refuse because they paid me and I was bored silly at the camp."

"So you think we can make money if we study all this stuff carefully."

"We probably need a geologist."

"We also need to know what all this coltan stuff can do or who'll buy it and how much it's worth."

"Better read all that stuff on the computer. I think they were well-on with this project. It was getting them very excited."

"It'll take some studying. The big question is; do I catch my flight or rebook? It'll cost me fifty US, but that's not all. I have a job." After a thoughtful pause he continued slowly, "OK, Joe, I'll get this material printed out so we can look at it separately and see what we can make of it."

"Man, I can't read this stuff. I read Wild West adventures and detective stories. A very big book for me is a Wilbur Smith."

"Brace yourself, Joe, I'm not asking you to understand it. Goodness, my friend, I won't understand it technically, but there is also a bit of commercial information. This looks a bit like a prospectus to give to potential investors. You might spot something I miss."

"Well, can I let Miriam help? She's a lot smarter than me, long words and that sort of thing."

Charles left for his hotel room.

Part 8: The Coming Together

1

Anwei was loaded with enough painkillers to knock out a rhino. She remembered nothing of the flight—her first experience of this sort. She was either concentrating on the pain in her foot or dopey and asleep. The men were happy not to have to appear too close to this rather ragged black woman, so although they were sitting nearby and observed her from time to time, they let the airline staff do all the assisting and helping as she was wedged into her seat. She slept through the meals.

In fact she was not *compos mentis* until two days later, when a kindly nurse was leaning over her bed and saying, "Hey babe, wake up. We thought you'd gone to another planet. Snore—my God, a pretty woman like you. Now! What can I get you? There's water there. We have to let you go today, so you'd better take what you can while you can. You had a big infection but it's under control now. The doctors debrided the foot and Mr. Patel operated. You've got a plaster cast on now. Like a great big boot."

Anwei felt a heavy ache in her leg but no pain in her foot.

"Did they take my foot off?" She sat up. "Is this thing what I have now? Like an elephant on one side?" She touched the hard grey plaster. "How can I live with this? I should have died or had my foot cut off."

"No, no, that's only a plaster cast. They'll cut that off later."

"But I only hurt my foot! Cut off at the knee! How will I walk?"

By this time she was screaming through her tears. The strain of everything and the strange surroundings were playing on her mind. She was beginning to wonder if she was actually in heaven or hell and whether she could trust any of her senses. She took the water and was relieved to taste the familiar normal blandness. The bright hospital lights and the clean smell of disinfectant had disorientated completely. This woman seemed to be kind, a white woman; angels would be white, like in all the pictures.

"I am the recovery nurse assigned to you for now."

Anwei looked across the ward and saw the pale face of a really white woman. She wondered if she was in the world of ghosts. Miriam caught her look.

"The wards are mixed now," Miriam said softly, not letting the remark reach the white patients.

Suddenly it was too much for Anwei to register. She closed her eyes and wept silently.

Miriam had seen it many times before: the effect of the drugs, the hypoglycemia, the frighteningly unfamiliar surroundings, and the realisation of their injuries hit the patients all at once. She added some glucose to the drip bag.

"It's all right, darling, you'll be fine. What you need is some food. I have fruit for you—bananas, oranges, or would you like bread or some meatballs?"

"Fruit and water," she croaked. Quite suddenly she shot up into a sitting position. "Where's my box?" she screamed at Miriam. "Who's got my box? My metal box. Is it here?" she asked in a more levelled voice.

Miriam had jumped back.

"Do you mean this?" She pointed to the soiled and dented metal box that looked as if had been made of salvaged cooking oil tins.

Anwei was pleased to see the same string around it and the small label attached by the hospital.

"Anwei Sojenji, Cameroonian, Ward J," read the ticket. Miriam wondered how this one had got here. She had neither money nor relations. She was visited by a young white man who did not want to stay, just to check-up. "When will she be ready to go back?" he had asked furtively as if not really wanting to be associated with her.

"Where will you go when you are discharged?" asked Miriam kindly.

"I don't know where I am now. Am I in South Africa? I seem to remember getting on a plane to South Africa."

"You are at the Groote Schuur Hospital in Cape Town, darling."

"Cape Town," she repeated unsurely. "What happened to my foot? You say they operated."

"We have the best surgeons in all Africa. You'll be dancing again in a few weeks."

But Anwei was asleep again.

"Poor thing," Miriam said to the ward sister back at the nurses' station, "she doesn't seem to have anyone in the world, just that tin box and the mysterious man who doesn't want to see her."

"Decent man, I say," said her colleague, looking up from her paperwork. "He ran her over, they say, and brought her from Cameroon. Big expense. Most of these young slickers would have left her for dead."

"So she has to be discharged with nowhere to go. Typical! Chuck 'em out on the street."

"You're too soft, Miri. Our job is to fix their injuries, not solve their other problems."

"Right, sister."

Miriam cornered David when he visited that afternoon. "She will be discharged this evening. Do you know where she will go?"

"No idea. She has a return ticket to Douala. I will book her on a flight."

"But she needs to visit outpatients after about a week; otherwise, the infection may flare up again. Under the dressing is not healed up yet."

"Can't she get that done in Douala?" he said, trying to put a closure on the whole sorry episode.

Miriam raised her eyebrows, questioning his wisdom.

"Look, how long will it take until she is fully fit?"

"A week or ten days, maximum."

"So, where can she stay?" he asked earnestly.

"We have a hostel: reasonable price, clean, not far from here. You need to pay in advance for a week to get a discount and then daily if necessary."

Anwei was given a taxi voucher and sent over to a small house in Woodstock, where a charity worker met her. On the trip she got a view over the harbour. Glancing across the water, she spotted a rusty orange boat whose lines jerked her upright and twisting to see more clearly. She thought she must be hallucinating after all the drugs she had been fed over the previous days. But no, on second look, she saw it plainly. Probably another boat; the world is full of these ships. Even with this in mind, she made a plan to investigate as soon as possible. Just a chance, but it might be her salvation. She asked the taxi driver for the name of the place. "QE2 dock, they call it. They say the *QE2* came here when she was on her maiden voyage." Of course this meant nothing to Anwei, but she forced herself to remember QE2.

The hostel was nice and clean, and the food was better than Anwei had enjoyed since leaving the *Scotfield 2*. She was hungry and healthy and ate all that was put in front of her. They gave her some crutches and the warden taught her how to use them.

"A man phoned about you," the warden said. "I think it was the same man who paid your account. He credited you with a small amount of pocket money for toiletries, *et cetera*. Actually, I prompted him to be rather generous. You should also be able to buy some clothes. You don't seem to have much."

In the first day she practiced with the crutches and became confident lurching around the grounds. The second day she had to attend the outpatients. This took all day for about five minutes with a nurse, who made her wiggle her toes, puffed some powder under the plaster, and told her how lucky she was.

She was a little more confident on the third day and took some of the money. Opening her metal box, she extracted her seaman's papers. She took a taxi to the harbour, directing the driver down the pier to the ugly orange ship. The security guard on the gate was not fazed by her lack of a shore pass; she was signed on the ship, according to her book. When she arrived her heart leapt as she read the name *Scotfield 2* on the bow. Now she wondered who the captain might be; but no matter whatever happened, she had a fair chance of being reconnected to Chuck.

2

Charles had rebooked his flight and left the itinerary lying on the table while he and Joe went through the information on the laptop. Miriam idly read the name on the paper. She looked up into Charles's face.

"Is Sojenji a common name in Cameroon?"

"I don't really know," he replied. "My birth mother was Cameroonian, but I was brought up in England by my natural father and his wife. They called me Charles Dormand, but they gave me my mother's name for my middle name."

"So why are you Charles Sojenji?"

"Oh, we had a big family row when I was seventeen. I am very ashamed because now I realise I was completely wrong about my parents. The upshot was that as soon as I was old enough, I changed my name by deed poll, removing my parents' name from mine. It was cruel and unnecessary. I accused my dad of abandoning my birth mother and accused my stepmother, who loved me and I loved dearly, of usurping my mother's position. It was what they call teenage angst. Anyway, we forgave each other and now we are pals again."

He smiled remembering the time he had gone back home after his MBBS graduation and taken Sophie and Bertrand out for a gourmet dinner on borrowed money.

After they were home and Sophie had gone to bed, his father had got out the brandy. "Well, Dr. Sojenji, the prodigal returns. You've done very well and I am proud of you."

"Don't rub it in, Dad, I am very sorry if I caused you any hurt."

"It's not me, really, although I can't say I wasn't angry at the time. You have African roots, be proud of them. You'll be judged on your merits, not your name. Your mother was upset. She had always tried so hard to give you equal treatment with her boys and sometimes even better and we were sure you were never angry with them. They looked up to you as their role model and mentor. They never complained when you bullied them and then they felt rejected when you stormed out.

"Let me tell you about your mother, Anwei, a village girl, a most beautiful girl, desirable. I was a young blood alone in Africa. She stumbled across me as I was stuck in a crack in the pavement. Ridiculous! But one thing led to another and you were conceived. I returned to England and married Sophie. Anwei was to be married to a local man. He threw her out because you were obviously not his baby but I did not know any of this. Sophie is the heroine of this story and you owe her your life. We returned to Cameroon by chance and Anwei pleaded with Sophie to adopt you. Sophie accepted. After it was all done, I paid Anwei an allowance. That lasted three years. Then suddenly she closed the bank account and disappeared. I just supposed she married and was frightened to take money from me. I was slightly relieved as it was one complication less in my life. Three children already, as your little half brothers were born by then, was enough responsibility."

"I know you would not have been cruel or callous, but at the time I was a bit lost. I obviously had African blood, yet no human contact with the place. I lashed out. I know I hurt Mum. I'll always regret that. In the meantime I want to go to Africa on a gap year. I've enquired with the Red Cross and MSF, who may have a place for me in Congo. I need funds. I am trying to get sponsorship, but it is not easy."

The look his father had given him said it all. "Whatever you need. You are going into a war zone. You know that. My God, you must be careful. I must not lose you now."

Charles focussed back on Miriam.

"Actually, I did try to find her, a bit half-heartedly," he told her. "What surprised me was that there were really no other Sojenjis on the radar, but then the poor don't make it on to registers and married women lose their names. I gave up at the first hurdle. I was busy making my way in the world I had been dragged into, a better world than a village in Cameroon. The quest suddenly seemed to be pointless"

He paused thoughtfully. "I suppose I could try again. You asked. Why?"

"Oh, nothing really. I discharged a Cameroonian woman today with the same name; coincidence, I suppose."

Charles, concentrating on the job in hand, did not react to the half-heard remark and continued his investigations with Joe.

"We've got everything we need. The exact position coordinates, the method for refining the minerals, the description of the stuff we need. What more, Chas?"

"Come on, Joe, do you think we can just march into the middle of an ancient conflict zone with a GPS, dig up some mud in the middle of a leper colony and become overnight millionaires?"

"Maybe we could buy some pots and extract the minerals from the clay."

"It'd have to be more valuable than gold for that to make us rich. No, Joe, I'm beginning to wonder. We probably need to mount a massive logistic expedition or sell the knowledge to a mining company. We don't have money for the first and we don't know how to deal with the second without being shafted."

The conversation went on while all the time Charles made notes on the information coming from the computer. He was not sure what they would amount to but his education had trained him into the habit of making notes while studying. Miriam disappeared to bed and the men followed half an hour later, Charles sleeping in the tiny spare room after Vonnie had moved her desk and books out of her "study".

As the bustle of breakfast was subsiding and Joe had left with the children to take them across the main road, Charles turned to Miriam.

"Miri, what about this woman?"

"Woman? Oh, yes, Annie Sojenji. No, Anwei. She was rather particular about that. Well, no one likes their name pronounced wrongly, do they?"

"Anwei?" Charles now came wide awake. He calmed himself as his heart pounded. "Perhaps I should meet a fellow Cameroonian. Is she still around?"

He collected the address from Miriam and set off to town to track her down.

The district he had been sent to was a mixture of brightly coloured bungalows, small blocks of flats, corner stores and businesses fixing cars or domestic appliances. The house was a whitewashed two-storey villa. A maid was cleaning the front steps. "Good day, I'm looking for a guest here recovering from an operation."

"Well, that's what we do here. Convalescence. Go through to the back of the hall to the reception desk and ring the bell to talk to the boss lady," she said, barely looking up from her task.

"Anwei went out this morning early. She took a taxi. A bit of a surprise as she really has only a little money. Are you the man who sent her here? You gave her the money? But no, you have a real English accent. He was a local."

"Do you know where she went?"

"Not my business, I'm afraid."

"Did she say when she'd be back?"

"She sneaked off without a word. She's a bit of an odd one. I think life's been hard on her. She's very thin. Eats everything she can get her hands on."

Charles suddenly had an idea. "How old do you think she is?"

"Now, look, I can't start talking about my guests without their permission, can I?"

"Right, thanks. Perhaps I could leave a note for her to call me."

"OK, that will be fine."

So Charles left a brief note: "I am Charles Sojenji. I may be related to you. Please call me at 7887443 any time."

He gave the Krels's phone number but hesitated. He realised he needed to get his own local cell phone. He asked the phone number of the house and left.

3

Anwei had been concentrating on the ship. It might have been a dead thing except for the familiar rumble of the generator. There had been no movement of people for a long time. She stood to stretch her legs and turned away from the heaving vessel towards the dock gate and there in the distance she saw, unmistakable by his gait, the man she sought. Anwei was so nervous, she was feeling quite sick. She was near to fainting as he approached.

She could escape. It was clear he had not seen her and she could slide round the back of the shed and retreat unseen. But her legs would not work. They pinned her to the spot. When she tried to lift one, the muscles would not obey, neither the one in plaster nor the other.

He, it was obvious, had his attention fully on the boat. He looked angry, a visage she had not seen before. She was even more nervous. When she tried to shout his name, her voice was small and weak, so he did not hear it. She saw him climb the gangway and duck down on to the deck and then climb up the outer companion way and disappear into the accommodation. Anwei was shaking and she felt overwhelmingly tired. She sat back down on the concrete sill of the shed. She had been in the shade of the roof all the time and now understood that Chuck would not have seen her from the dazzling light in the sunshine.

She built up some courage and moved over to the edge of the quay and steadied herself on a bollard. A man came out on the afterdeck and busied himself lighting a cigar.

"You, sir," she shouted, "tell the captain I must see him, Captain Chuck."

The man looked up and took in her unkempt appearance and drew his conclusions.

"Captain's ashore."

"No, he just came on board. I saw him."

"He doesn't want any of you whores on board. Come back in the evening and the boys will have a run ashore."

From his voice and now from the long distance, his general appearance, she recognised the man she was shouting at. "You are Steve, you are the chief engineer. I am Stanley. I need some help to get aboard. Can you help me, please, Steve?"

"Well, doggone me, it's Anwei, ain't it? The old man'a be pleased to see you. He was real sad when he couldn't find you in Douala. What about y' leg, it broke or what?"

As he moved across the deck towards her, an enormous fellow emerged from behind the winch.

"Hey, Samson, c'n you he'p the lady on board?"

Samson looked up at Anwei on the quay. His expression gave him away, questioning, disapproving and then friendly. He lifted her with one hand over the brow and down on to the deck.

As Anwei entered the familiar cabin her nervousness was almost overwhelming. Chuck was not there but gurgling noises told her that he was in the *en-suite*. She was going to surprise him in his private space and she thought this was not what she should do, but she could not move. Samson had positioned himself in the doorway, blocking her retreat. He wanted to ensure this was not just a street tart causing trouble and to see what the story was if this was an old acquaintance of his captain.

As he emerged from the shower unit, towel in hand, his face lit up. "My, my, my. Well, honey, what brings you home? This is Cape Town. How the hell..."

"Don't you want me here? I will go. This man will help me back on shore."

"No, no, Anwei, honey. You just stay right there. Samson, it's OK, you may carry on."

A wry smile appeared on Samson's broad face. "Shall I shut the door, Captain?" He pulled it to and lumbered off down the passageway.

They stood looking at each other. Both saw the drawn look of the other, Chuck's through worry about the future and Anwei's through recent experiences.

"I lost everything. Robbers stole my card, my money, and my phone. I could not contact you. I had taken about two hundred dollars; they took the rest."

"Well, how did you get here?"

"Look at this." She held up her leg off the floor. "South African man ran me down, but he was a good man and brought me here to hospital. Now I got this big thing. They tell me my foot is getting better. Another few weeks and it should be mended."

"Wowee. I was thinking you'd be gone. Wife's dead, guessed I thought it'd just be like my luck to lose the one and the other, same time. You want to sign on again? I'm in charge now. No company to worry about. We're going to India. Sell this for scrap and fly back. Take some thinking through. How you been making out?"

"Making?"

"Getting by, making a living?" Anwei lowered her eyes to the floor and could not control herself any more.

"Come here, my little beauty." He held out his arms and she wept, burying her face in his chest.

"OK, I don't need to know," he said, guessing the worst and hoping to be wrong. "Where are you staying just now?"

She perked up immediately. "I have a very nice room in a house in Woodstock." She smiled. "Very nice lady house. Kind people. Maybe a week there and then back to Douala."

"Then what in Douala?"

"Very bad life there. I have nothing there." The smile disappeared from her face, leaving a desperate grimace.

"Well, we better see if you can come with us."

"Chuck, I am not sure. You see, life has been bad for me. I have had to do bad things. You may not..." She could see from his face he did not want to hear what she had to say.

"Do you want to come or not?" he said angrily and then he bit his lip. "Look, whatever you went through; you don't have to tell me. It's great you're here. It's very good. Life starts

271

again today. OK?" She sat back on to the bunk as if the tirade were a hurricane blowing a tree over.

"Chuck, are you sure?"

"Sure I'm sure." He paused and looked at her pleading eyes. "You want to lay down, lay down. I got stuff to do. We need a decent cook. The men are complaining." He smiled at her as he left. She saw the smile as she lay back on the bunk.

An hour later he was back. She woke with a start. "Right, you're hired. I got you a shore pass and you can join in a few days. You are now Stanley again. You've got to wear the galley boots and chef's whites. The old cook leaves in a week or ten days when they can get a flight for him. You come back after he's gone. How does that sit with you?"

Anwei was shocked into submission. This man she adored because he took command and there was no argument. She needed him.

"Right, let's get you back to your place, and I'll sort out this ship. I got to call Houston at six o'clock. They e-mailed the agent here. I don't know what they want."

Chuck phoned for a cab to take him back to the agent and he dropped her off at the hostel.

As soon as she was in the house she went straight to her bed. She missed Charles's letter which the warden had put in a new envelope and stood against the mirror on the small dressing table.

Chuck arrived at the agent's office around six and asked to be put through to the Houston office. He spoke to Fred Muswell, the operations manager.

"Chuck, brace yourself for bad news. Those Yankee cocksuckers have fucked you. They hauled me in and told me to unravel our agreement. They say we should sell these vessels to scrappers here in the States. I bet you they already had this in mind when we spoke a month ago. They say they can't trust them to be broken up if they go overseas, so they'll sell them to their buddies somewhere up in New England. Anyway, you get to keep the *Scottfield 2*, and I released you from the need to pay for it, but you don't get a pension. I guess she's worth more than the pension but you are now on your own expenses-wise. Can you manage?"

"Got no choice, I guess. It'll work. I'm collecting iron and scrap here. There's some good nonferrous. Prices are low here due to lack of refining and industry. Don't get too pissed on my account, Fred. What about you?"

"Pensioned off, but like you I have some resources and I don't want to work for these assholes anyway." He paused. "I've got the ranch and I can get a living from trading some more steers."

A living, thought Chuck. He knew Muswell's ranch business. It was big.

"Well, Fred, leave me to deal with this old boat and maybe I'll come and see you at the ranch when I get back."

"Yeah, do that, Chuck." The line went dead.

Bang go my plans, he thought. *I am just a crazy old man again.* His mind turned to Anwei. Somehow he felt no passion anymore. Losing her had created a great void in his soul and meeting her again did not seem to fill it. She looked haggard and old. She had a beaten-down demeanour, a sort of emptiness in her eyes. It was too late; he had rehired her to cook for the crew. *Wait till she's fit again and the old passion may come back, unless it's me that's just too old*, he thought almost aloud.

He now had a boat to take to India or China for scrap and had to force a hard deal to show a profit. A sudden weariness came over him and although it was lunchtime, he felt he needed to sit out somewhere and forget the whole sorry situation.

He wandered down the quay to the tourist part of the waterfront and sat down looking over the harbour at the fishing boats. A slight girl with big hair offered him the menu with a big smile.

"Just a beer, thanks, young lady," he said.

"Castle? Light or dark?"

"Lager will do, thanks." He admired her pert little wiggle in her white Lycra pants as she went off to get it. Perhaps he'd buy one of these fishing boats when he was done with the *Scotty*. He watched as two men, a stocky blond and a large black unloaded fish boxes from a colourfully painted boat. A couple of fat tourists started a conversation with the men. *That's the life.*

273

Buy a brightly painted boat and spend the rest of my time taking tourists on fishing trips.

4

Charles arrived at the house in Woodstock around twelve. He'd got a very confused phone call from Anwei at about nine o'clock. She was hardly logical, darting from something about a ship's cook, a departure at an airport, a tin box of papers, and a broken foot.

"Please may I visit you there at the house?"

"Oh why, who are you? You aren't going to help me. I have no relations, and I have a chance with my Captain Chuck."

"Look, I can't hurt you. If your life is all together, I just want to meet you. Perhaps we have something in common or perhaps not."

Panic came to her and she banged the phone down.

Charles left immediately for the house in Woodstock. Anwei was riveted to the spot for a few minutes. It was an enormous quandary. To meet this man who might be her son. She was shaking again. The heavy leg stopped her from jumping on to the bed. She caught sight of herself in the mirror. She was shocked.

Her clothes were ragged and her face was thin and pale. She had noticed a cheap boutique a block away. She strode out on her crutches and without hesitating bought herself a simple dress off the rack, some shoes to match, underwear, and some dark lipstick, toothpaste and a toothbrush. She had no more money. Whoever this man was she wanted to look at least human. She worried about her hair which was uncut, unstyled and tangled.

Back at the house she took a shower, gave her mouth and teeth a very energetic treatment and put on her new purchases. Not perfect, but a lot better although she could only wear one shoe. The effect was spoilt by the grey plaster on the other leg.

The warden knocked on her door and took her down to the hall. "You have a visitor, Dr. Charles Sojenji."

Charles stepped forward.

"Hello. My name is Charles Sojenji," he said nervously.

"Yes, and I am Anwei Sojenji. Are you my son? If you are my son, you were born in a village in Cameroon on the third of March 1975. You were adopted by your natural father, Bertrand, and his wife. I loved your father, and he did not know of you when he married his woman. You are very handsome, and I suppose you have a good life. I was right to make them take you."

"So it is true. You have my birthday right and my parents. I dropped my father's name when I was angry with him. I was Charles Sojenji Dormand."

"Your African name is Djarli. Charles was their English way of saying it."

They had said all this standing awkwardly in the hallway, oblivious of the maid and the warden, who were discreetly listening.

"So is this a happy occasion?" asked the warden. "Come into the lounge and sit down."

"I'll get some tea," said the maid.

"This is very exciting. People got separated in the apartheid and reunions happen. Always wonderful times." The warden became effusive.

"So, Anwei, my dear, you have such a handsome son," she added.

Anwei and Charles stared at each other, unable to say more, as if all had been said and no more was necessary. There were questions but they could not be asked in front of strangers. Suddenly the warden rose.

"Janey will bring the tea. I will see you later. Stay here as long as you wish."

"My God, my beautiful boy. Just to look at you is my pleasure. I am satisfied. I gave you to them so you would grow into such a man. They did not abandon me. I broke away from them when I found a man who was to be my husband, a very rich and successful man in Douala."

"What happened to him? Are you married?"

275

"He married me for my looks. We had no children, and he found out I could not provide any for medical reasons. He divorced me. He was generous. By the law he could have left me nothing, but he paid me off with a lump sum."

"Why didn't you contact Dad?"

"How could I? I had betrayed him. I had thrown in my lot with a Cameroonian. It was my life. I was not to run begging to him whenever my luck changed. Anyway, I was having a good time. I was free again and running around with a fast set. Big men came and went. I was a mistress to several and became accustomed to the high life, the excitement, the rich clothes and jewels."

"So what now?"

"You are very cold, my son. Can you not love your mother?"

Charles was taken aback. This was the birth mother he had never known. She was a worn-out African. He knew he was of her blood but where else was the common ground? Yes, he was cold. Although Bertrand and Sophie had been the most loving and supporting parents, they had not been very demonstrative, offering few hugs as he grew from a small boy, through boarding school from seven to seventeen, then college and university. The great feud had barred expression of affection.

He stood and put his arms out to her.

She came forward into his embrace. Anwei felt the muscular arms and strong back of her son and the warmth of his body and his sheer size.

"My dear son, my life is a mess. I have nothing but the promise of a new life from an American pirate. Well, I suppose he is some sort of pirate." She could hold back her tears no longer. She sobbed into his powerful bicep for a minute and then turned her face up to his with a sudden determination. "You must not worry about me. I am doing fine. He has a ship and he's going to make a voyage to India and he'll look after me. I will be the ship's cook.

"Come up with me," she said cheerfully. At that moment Janey appeared with the tea. "Please, Janey, give us both a cup. We are going upstairs." Janey carried the tray up to her room.

"You should know about your ancestors. Perhaps you know about your English ancestors already. But this is your African grandfather and great-grandfather from Congo. You must know about them; it is your heritage. It is very important."

Anwei was thrilled to be able to impart this to her son, the lost son. From under the bed in her room she pulled the battered metal box. "This is yours now. I am an African woman of no account. You are an important doctor." She looked back at him with wide-eyed admiration. "You must know where you have come from."

He took the box and wondered what this ugly, dented thing might contain.

"Look inside."

He wrestled with the untidy knotted string and opened the box. There was a fetid leather envelope and some stained and faded papers.

"Anwei, my mother, what am I looking for?"

"My father was killed in a massacre of my home village. The soldiers were Biafran rebels."

"But they were the good guys, according to my history study. They tried to free Nigeria from the corrupt tyranny."

"All soldiers are cruel. They were provoked. They took horrible revenge. We women and children were saved. I was betrothed to a boy from another village but he went away to Europe and I conceived you with Bertrand. You were born in the village. Your father knew nothing. My mother delivered you, but there was no future there. The soldiers had broken the people's spirit. I ran away with you and we nearly died on the road.

"We were saved by German tree cutters and then I found Bertrand and Sophie. Sophie was happy to take you. She's a good woman. Look at you now.

When my mother was dying, she gave me this old tin box with our history in it. I have not been able to replace the box with a good one. Now I am giving it to you. You can take it to your place and read the documents. You have a noble family. We are not losers but fighters."

She took out her birth certificate, new passport and seaman's book and put the box firmly in his hands.

"These are my present papers but you will find everything there including birth certificates and the death certificates of my parents, Bolo and Balenga. My father left a will to my mother and me, 'the survivor', because of the troubles. I studied it all carefully."

Anwei was suddenly exhausted. "Please come back tomorrow at eleven, but now you must go and let me rest and think. Take this box and read the documents inside. I am truly happy to have seen you, and I do not want to lose you again. I have to talk to my captain." She did not want an unplanned meeting between Charles and Chuck. They would meet but on her terms.

Charles let himself in to the house at Kalk Bay with his key. Just the kids were there. They were changing to go out to the little beach where they would meet their friends. Vonnie had not come home. He sat at the dining table and opened the rusty box. The first thing to come to hand was his grandfather's declaration for his naturalisation and the accompanying papers. Then there was the deed for the land, with the big crest of the Belgian king. As he read on, trying to understand the archaic French, he became aware of something uncannily familiar. It was the numerals for the latitude and longitude. He pulled out the old laptop and waited while it went through the laborious process of booting up. He clicked through the files until he came to the narrative document.

He could not believe what he was reading. The name of the village where his grandfather originated was the same— Aku-Agua. Then he looked at the numerical coordinates. It was extraordinary but to within one mile each way they were the same. He knew from the transcript that his grandfather was a *potier* and the Swedes had mentioned the potters and their special clay. Krels had mentioned the special pottery also. He was having trouble with the French and he was getting more and more anxious to know the meaning of what he was reading. The programs on the computer included a translator call Linguanet Language Wizard. He typed word for word the French version into a Word file and then applied the translator.

278

His schoolboy knowledge of French allowed him to correct most of the obvious mistranslations and in the end he determined that Bolo Sojenji had the title deeds to the land as demarked by the coordinates and by inheritance this would naturally pass to his descendents.

5

He heard Joe arrive back from his job on the ambulance. He snapped the laptop shut and put the documents back in the battered tin box.

"Hi Joe, good day?"

"Two horrible crashes. They drive those old combies too fast and too full and lose control. The police try to stop them but some get through. What about you? What about the mystery woman?"

"She's my mother."

"My God, why aren't you with her?"

"I gave her a big shock and she was tired and she didn't seem to want me to meet her captain."

"What's she like?"

"She must have been a beauty, but she's worn out. I think she's had a hard life but all the same a real life, a bloody African life. She's very thin. She says she's a cook on a ship, so 'her captain' is her keeper. I'm to see her tomorrow."

"Oh good, because tonight I want you to come out fishing with me and Donny. Not too far but the moon is full and we can probably get good catch longlining on the small boat. What you say, man?"

"Would I be able to buy a briefcase of some sort around here at this time of day? She gave me some documents to read in this old metal box. It's horrible. It'll cut my hand one day."

"Does this prove her relationship?"

"Of course."

"Wait." Joe disappeared upstairs and came down with a black canvas laptop satchel with a drug company logo on the flap. "This any good? Miri got it from one of the docs."

"Perfect, thank the Lord for the druggists."

Baiting hooks and hauling the lines was a new experience for Charles. At eleven o'clock after four hours hard work, his back was screaming with pain and his fingers were cut and bleeding but he felt exhilarated.

"Paining, eh, man?" asked Donny. "Miriam will soak those fingers in gentian violet. Sting like hell but you don't want sepsis."

"Bleddy good haul, man," said Joe. "We'll make a fisherman out of you, Chas, no mistake."

As Charles turned over in the narrow bed the next morning, he felt the pain in his back. He appreciated the benefits of the easy life of an academic.

Still aching, with his two index fingers lightly bandaged, he took the satchel and made his way toward Woodstock and his mother. She was looking much brighter and had evidently improved her wardrobe. Another bright dress and some subtle makeup and a haircut with a wave perm gave her a much younger look.

"Captain Chuck came up here yesterday afternoon," she told him. "He has a setback to his business, but he will still make the voyage to India. Of course he's not really a pirate. It was my romantic notion of him. He is actually quite a rich man; all Americans are rich compared to us."

Charles held out his hands toward her and, as she came into his arms, he gave her a real hug.

"You are looking beautiful today, Mother," he said, and he really felt it.

"So what do you make of all those papers, Djarli?"

"Well, really, I want you to tell me. For instance, what did your father tell you about the village and the pottery?" She broke from his embrace and they sat in facing chairs in the small lounge.

"He said it was a dead place: pits in the ground, too many sick people. He and his cousin really never looked back while they were on the road. They were pleased to get out and feared the worst for the people they left behind. When he realised how war torn it had become, I think he just closed his mind to it and got on with the new life. He said he wrote letters and got no reply; then he met my mother and it faded from his mind."

"Why did he keep these papers?"

"His father made him promise to take them to the authorities so they could claim their birthright. His father was the Fon or chief of the village and Bolo, your grandfather, would be the natural successor and the owner of the land. It would be mine now. I don't know whether there is any value to it. What could I do with a few pits in the jungle in a foreign country?"

The more she spoke, the more he hung on her words.

"It says there was disease there. What disease?"

"Leprosy: that's why he and his cousin ran away. Some American missionaries brought the lepers in. When my father spoke of this, he would get very angry."

"Look," Charles said, "there may be nothing to it, but there is a possibility this hole in the ground is worth something. The clay may have valuable minerals. Do not give up. We need to do some research. Do I get to meet your captain?"

"Yes, of course. He's coming here at twelve."

6

So it was that the three of them went for a meal in a Lebanese restaurant a short walk away. The two men seemed to like each other; their age difference did not matter and Charles was satisfied that the captain was going to look after his mother—for now anyway, until he could do so himself. He found out that the voyage was planned soon but that the vessel would remain in Cape Town or Durban while the cargo agent found a load of scrap. They probably had about a week or ten days. The only thing that bothered him was that his mother would have to work hard as the cook.

"Don't worry," said Chuck, "I can't get the cook shipped home from here so he will cook for the crew and she will be cooking for me and the engineers. She does a great Gumbo."

Back at the house Charles found Joe asleep on the sofa in the den with *Generations* on the TV. Joe woke up and switched it off.

"How's your mama, Chas?"

"Looking great! You'll have to meet her. A very weird thing has happened. You know this site on the computer, the leper colony, the minerals and all that. It is pretty unbelievable, but she may own it. She gave me these title deeds, and the coordinates match. I mean, this is like a lottery win or being hit by a meteorite. I want you to look at them and see for yourself."

7

The next day they went to a lawyer in the city.

"*Prima facie*, and I must emphasise *prima facie*, these are the deeds to the land and these coordinates match the ones you have shown me. You will need a surveyor to verify this but these days with GPS, it won't be hard to establish. That part of the world is pretty lawless and dangerous. Having verified the coordinates you'll then have a hell of a job to re-establish title and ownership. But it can be done. You'll need to grease a few palms and dodge a few bullets. Land up there is not worth much unless you find diamonds or gold." He laughed at his joke. "You want to build a holiday cottage, I suppose."

Joe looked at Charles and smiled. "That's right, eh, Chas?"

The sun blinded them temporarily in the street outside, but a voice familiar to Charles arrested them.

"Well, hello again, Joe," Jenny Bones said, with a sarcastic emphasis on the name. "And I was right. You two are consorting. I thought I saw you from my flat. Thick as thieves and emerging from this notorious lawyer's office. My journalist's instinct smells a plot, a conspiracy, and I bet that computer has something to do with it. There's something back in the Congo jungle that is very interesting. I want to be in on it."

"Jenny, nice to see you. We are just friends sorting out some fishing business," said Joe, fishing being the first thing that came into his head, "This is Charles." He hesitated to say his surname.

"So what's the story? Did you two shoot up the village, rape the women, burn the houses? Charles run for his life, leaving his companion to the mercy of the last few villagers alive?"

"Good God! What are you talking about?" asked Charles.

"You know bloody well. I arrived to find you collapsed, having run away, and the mercenary here strung up with his jacked-up donger sticking out. The story seems obvious. Never mind the Truth and Reconciliation. This is stuff for the Hague and the War Crimes Tribunal."

Joe and Charles looked at each other.

"Are you trying to blackmail us?"

"No, no, just wanting to do my duty as a world citizen."

"What you say is not true, so you can't have any evidence," said Joe.

"But I've got the photos, pickies of both of you at the scene and the scene itself. Convincing proof to many a jury. But I don't need the law. I haven't sold a big story in about half a year. This could be made into a Sunday spread and syndicated. I just got a snap of you two coming out of the shyster's office together."

Charles looked at Joe with despair.

"So let's find somewhere to sit and talk."

"I find bars are the best places to go for this sort of conversation," said Jenny. "I drink Riesling at this time of day. Kennedy's is just round the corner."

"Right," said Joe while Charles was getting the drinks, "let's get a few things straight. We, and particularly I, don't trust you. You appear to be holding us to ransom or blackmail."

Jenny put her hand up in a gesture of peace. "Look, I'm just inquisitive. I can't use the pictures, even if I still have them. They won't stand up without corroboration. You could sue me out of the profession, such as it is. But you have some business in Congo and that's my stamping ground. I may be able to help and there may be something in it for me."

Joe's shoulders visibly slumped as he relaxed from his pugilistic stance to one more suited to the convivial Irish pub.

"What actually happened between you two?"

"He tried to kill me. I was going to kill him later, but his chance came up first. The village was a shock to both of us. We had nothing to do with it. We were lost in the jungle and thought the smoke was cooking fires. Chas and me, we're no longer enemies.

"So, Jenny Bones, you've drawn a blank. We'll have a drink and you can go. I suppose I owe you this one for saving my life. Then we'll call it quits. I will just have to trust you not to identify me with the published picture. Howsit?"

"Got yer, blue, I don't want to make any trouble. You got business in DRC?"

"No."

"Just the laptop seemed so important to you both. Not just personal but something more."

"Look," said Joe, "just drink up and relax. This is not a story at all. We're just two chums talking about buying a fishing boat."

She was not entirely satisfied, but she saw that she was not going anywhere with these two men. She would keep a watching brief, see how things developed.

8

When she had gone, Joe said, "Where'd she come from? Is she following us around?"

"She is a very nasty piece of work. I think she could be dangerous if we have anything going on. She's the sort you cannot deal with."

"Yeah, I know; shake hands and check you've still got all your fingers."

"What did we learn today?"

"Do our talking indoors."

"Right, let's go."

On the train Joe could not help asking, "This boat the captain's got, what is it?"

"I haven't seen it, but I think it's a small oilfield boat. The type with a big open deck at the back."

"OK, let's go and see it. Can we?"

It was early afternoon. "Here, give me your mobile, your cell phone. I'll call Anwei. Perhaps we can go today." He was conscious that he had not called her Mother and perhaps would never really get used to the idea.

"Hi, can I speak to Anwei, please?" A few minutes later, he continued. "This is Djarli, how are you today, Mother? My friend here is interested in boats. Could we go and see this ship of Captain Chuck's? When are you moving down there? OK. We'll come right away and give you a hand.

"She's leaving the hostel today and going to the boat soon," he said as he handed the phone back to Joe. "Let's get off this train and get one back to the centre and then a cab to the docks. She says it's an ugly orange ship called the *Scotfield 2*. Horrible name. It's in the QE2 dock, not many ships there."

As they came down the steps onto the afterdeck, Joe cast his eye around knowingly. Chuck came out on to the deck. "Welcome aboard my scrapper, boys. Charlie, who's your friend?"

"This is Joe. Joe, Captain Chuck. He wanted to come and see a real oilfield ship."

"Wrong place, buddy, should'a come thirty years ago. This one's plum wore out. Never go to the oilfiel' again. She'll be razor blades or car bodies 'fore the year's out."

"But why's he painting?" Joe pointed to a big fellow in paint-spattered coveralls carrying a paint kettle, a fitch and a rag.

"Change of name. This is now the *Fenix*. We just paint over the old name.

Chuc continued: "You wanna see the bridge? It ain't a whole lot to see, but mos' people want to go there."

From the bridge they went down to the conference room on the deck below. "You guys wanna drink beer? This is where the fridge is." He brought out a couple of bottles and snapped the crown caps off with a coin.

Joe and Charles sat on a padded bench behind a long conference table. Chuck stood looking out over the afterdeck.

"Y'know, I'm getting a vibe about this boat. This will be important to us," said Joe.

"Where's Anwei?" asked Charles. Chuck put his head out the door and called. She came in, looking cheerful and bright. She sat down next to Charles. "Djarli," she said.

"We went to see a lawyer today. He said you are the titled owner of this tract of land, the village where your father is from. It may have some valuable minerals on it. Minerals needed in today's electronic goods. Coltan, whatever that is. I've been reading up and it could be worth millions or billions for fairly small quantities. Do you want to claim it?"

Chuck perked up and turned to the room.

"Why did you want to visit this boat, Joe?" asked Charles.

"Think about it: diggers, pumps, storage containers, God knows what we need. We need transport. What's the draft of this vessel, Captain?"

"Six feet."

"Two metres," repeated Joe. "Remember the notes the Swedes made. They wanted a whole load of equipment to go to Pointe Noire or up the Congo River to a place called Matadi. A boat this size could easily do that. Then they were to truck it up the main road into Kinshasa Province. Hell of a long way but Matadi has port facilities."

"What are you guys into?" asked Chuck.

"We'd better bring you the whole story tomorrow. Anwei could make herself and all of us very rich."

"Well, I ain't got no objection to gettin' rich, and I'm damn sure Anwei could do with a little money."

They rose to leave.

Back on the train again, Charles turned to Joe. "We must put a convincing plan up to Chuck. That boat is his project and Anwei is *de facto* his woman. I could benefit too as her only heir. I can feel the itch. I will resign from this hopeless quest to cure AIDS and go back to that later when we're broke or wealthy."

"We need seed money, front end. You've seen all this equipment on the list, man. Who'll get that for us?" Joe paused thoughtfully. "You know, that old priest could help us with the lepers. I'm jumping ahead. But we don't want to have to deal with a whole tribe of lepers while we dig up their land. They would trust Father Driscol. I think he'd want to cut them into some sort of deal."

The next day they took all the information and an article from the *New Scientist* explaining the coltan angle and presented it all on the conference table to Chuck and Anwei.

"Well, I guess it'll work," said Chuck thoughtfully. "Not easy but can do. By the way the first thing is upfront money. You want to charter my boat, you gonna buy all this stuff? Have you got a million dollars?" He paused to get their full attention. "Listen, boys, you price all this equipment and maybe I can help you and help Anwei. She's back to being her old self now. She's eating and putting on weight and energy. Get this plaster off her leg and she'll be A-OK. Look at her, pretty as a princess!" He smiled indulgently at her and she and everyone present realised they were an item again.

9

Jenny was sure she would get something out of some unobtrusive tracking of the Jungle Boys, as she had mentally christened them. The "jungle book" or laptop contained something of interest. Observing their movements could be productive. To her surprise they led her to an old oilfield supply boat down at the QE2 dock.

Snooping around she found out that this nondescript vessel was going to India for scrap.

Her careful observation led her to think a little differently. For instance, so many drums, not crushed but evidently containing something important in spite of their rough appearance. In passing casually she noticed detailed mechanical work being done on the "scrap" trucks and some new components being fitted to the old crane.

She repeated her visits and noticed Joe and Charles came down often and Charles would have long conversations with a tall rangy man in jeans and a T-shirt whom she thought might be the captain.

She managed to inveigle her way into the harbourmaster's office and casually asked about the vessel, which had now been renamed *Fenix*, crudely painted on the bow.

"Oh, that old scrap vessel, used to be the *Scott* something. Scrappers pass through quite often. Stop here on their way from West Africa and pick up a scrap metal cargo before going to India or China for breaking. We never know when they are going to leave until the statutory twenty-four hours in advance. Then we call for surveyors from the coast guard to check whether they look seaworthy. They've paid their dues for another two weeks or so. We're not busy so they can stay as long as they like."

She was looking for leverage and had drawn a blank. There was no point in raising suspicions with the authorities. If there was a game going on, she wanted a share of the action, not spoilation. She came to the conclusion that her only option was confrontation. She would have to enter the dock and go on board and try to befriend the Jungle Boys.

The next day she arrived on her motorbike at her favourite observation point just in time to see the captain and Charles speeding off to town in a taxi. She was able to shadow them into the city. There they went in to the office of the same law firm. What she had not noticed as they left the dock was a thin black woman who had been sitting in the back of the cab. She was modestly dressed in a flowered print dress and could have been mistaken for a servant except that she was treated with deference, not just politeness, by the two men.

This confirmed her mental picture that something was afoot. It might be just routine, but the question arose as to what was so important about this plain-looking woman that the men deferred to her as they all entered a big lawyer's office. To many non-journalists this would not have been an oddity, but Jenny was acutely aware of abnormal behaviour because of the potential for a story.

Part 9: The Voyage North

1

The room was getting warmer. An ancient air-conditioning unit under the window was having a private conversation with itself, wheezing, groaning, whirring, and rattling. Historically called the conference room, this was just below the bridge of the rusting orange supply boat now called *Fenix* of Moroni. Anwei was getting beyond her concentration span. She'd said her bit about her father's arrival in Douala all those years ago with nothing but the title deeds to some tract of land in warring Congo, and now she had listened to a load of technical data way beyond her understanding involving something to do with "green energy." When she first heard the term, she had thought she could get more information and assurance from the witch doctor, but when her son, her long-lost and successful son, Charles, had explained the details, she was still not able to relate it all to her experience of life.

The ugly blond man they called Joe Krels was staring morosely at the back of the open laptop computer on the chipped Formica table. Next to him was a giant of a Cape Coloured. *Matis*, thought Anwei—without any judgment, just as an identifier. He was a fisherman, Donny, another seaman like her present keeper, Captain Chuck.

In a heap in the corner of the brown leatherette sofa-seat was the black-clad priest, Father Driscol. Although he was very old and probably harmless, he gave Anwei an uncomfortable feeling. If she decided to confess, she thought, it would take all year. She hadn't been inside a church for thirty years. So much had happened.

"OK, my friends and family, this is the real beginning, at last. You all know some of what we are going to do will be dangerous and possibly illegal in local terms. I think we will use the word *pragmatic* or *practical* to indicate where we are ignorant of the law," stated Charles as a formal opening to the meeting, glancing at the pop-eyed priest.

"We can probably square it all before God, legal or not," the dog-collared man growled. "We're only planning to restore property to its rightful owner and rend it from the hands of the Devil to succour some of God's unfortunates."

"The good father means the land belongs to my mother and we are going to take the minerals and help the wretched lepers now living there," stated Charles seriously.

Charles, who was at the keyboard opposite Joe, looked around at the whole company and continued.

"All the pieces of the jigsaw are in place now. We have worked this last couple of months to establish our legal rights, and now we have to go out and enforce at least part of our possession. Thanks to you all but especially Chuck for bankrolling us and getting this boat together. The last thing we have to get right is the share-out."

The only other woman at this strange meeting lifted her head and stared at Charles, who continued.

"Miriam has come up with a share plan based on the conversations we've had over the last couple of weeks. Like a ship there will be sixty-four shares. As you know, the Anwei Company Limited has been formed in Comoros, and I propose the following split to be formalized in the issue of shares right here and now:

Firstly Chuck, the financier of the trip, gets all the expenses for the boat and the cost of all the machinery paid back at cost. The boat is his property and he is not charging for the charter. We will make one trip lasting about twelve to sixteen weeks and get out before the warlords wake up to what we are doing. Our scoop should be about twenty to thirty million dollars worth of rare earth in the drums. We have two hundred, but we hope to pick up two hundred more drums in Pointe Noire. Of the profit, my mother, Anwei, as the inheritor of the land, has thirty-three shares. Some of these shares will go to me; it is our business how we divide them.

"Joe will get six shares for producing the information. Father Driscol will take six for spotting the location and to look after the lepers. Donny has six for himself and the crew, Miriam gets one, and Chuck will have twelve shares for taking all the risk with finance, the vessel and logistics. Our geologists, François and Patrice, have been paid up front for two weeks of their expertise and that equipment in the steel boxes will be part of the expenses. They have just emailed to say they will be in Pointe Noire sometime this week. Is everyone happy?

"We are cleared to leave tonight. We steam due west into the darkness for thirty miles, and then turn to starboard and up to the north."

Everyone was hyped and fearfully glad to be entering the new phase. Over the last two months, they had settled into a highly productive team, working up to eighteen hours a day getting this old boat into shape and procuring all the equipment they would need. Chuck particularly had had his work cut out to register ownership of the vessel and then equip the expedition for the trip.

The paperwork had been endless, even though he was officially making a scrapping voyage to India. He was now happy with his ship and crew, having re-registered the vessel on the Comoros Registry in a bar in Cape Town, creating all the necessary documentation on the famous laptop with Miriam's help and a printer in the grimy office of the consul. The bribe had been small and the lack of due diligence from the State was more convenient than any other flag of convenience. His first mate, Donny, the big Cape Coloured, had recruited a piratical marine crew all handy with AK-47s and other weapons and hired two fishing-boat mechanics certificated in the Comoros "Embassy" over a beer as chief engineers. He retained his American chief engineer, Steve.

He had kept Samson the Nigerian bosun who had not been allowed ashore because the South African Immigration service was not satisfied with his documents. The South African, Joe, who was practical enough to manage on deck,

291

would operate the earth-moving machinery and train the others on the voyage.

Charles stood up and through the small window was able to see the fruits of their labour on the open afterdeck. During their time at anchor, Joe had scouted around the farms, scrap yards and construction sites near Cape Town to select the earth-moving equipment: two Hitachi backhoes and front-loader tractors, and an American crawler crane with a seventy-foot boom. His purchases also included a couple of mine dumper trucks and one ex-South African Army semi-armoured six-wheel-drive twenty-ton freight truck containing thirty drums of diesel and six drums of good lube oil, all marked "WASTE OIL," and a Kenworth six-wheel-drive twenty-five-ton flatbed oilfield truck. All vehicles were old, dented, and rusty but all mechanically refurbished by Donny's two mechanics. Two hundred used oil drums were loaded next to two battered six-metre containers full of tents and the rough-looking tin boxes containing lab equipment. Two modified oilfield de-sanders and centrifuges and two small diesel generators on skids, all looking more or less like scrap, were tucked up forward near the accommodation by the towing winch. The stowage on the open deck was deliberately disorderly to allay suspicion. He sat down again. "Well, Chuck, have you got something to say?"

A big smile stretched the captain's face, which for so long had been set in a tense grimace as he had navigated his way through the red tape for the shipping company, the banks, the immigration and customs and the port authorities.

"We-ell, this is the craziest venture I ever been on. I've been on a few. Boy oh boy, but here we are. First I got to tell you about this old boat. I know every rivet and bolt, and your chief here, Stevie, they reckon was born on her. Guess he aged two years for each of the thirty-two she's been tramping around the oilfields."

Steve took a long draw on a fat cigar that stank of half-cured tobacco. When he exhaled everyone present was treated to a nicotine fix.

"You all got to know each other but some of you ain't had the chance to get to know this ship too good. There are life vests for everyone. We hope not to use 'em but you need to know how. Before we leave we'll have the usual drill and we'll show you how to launch the rafts. Plenty of guys know what to do but you all need to know how to help them do it. Next thing: We are carrying a whole lot of flammable stuff. Diesel for the vehicles, some dynamite, and most important of all and the most dangerous is—what the hell is it called, Chas?"

"Toluene."

"There you go, well, that shit's lethal. So, no smoking on the afterdeck at all. And that includes our engineers, Steve? We don't want to spoil the trip with a goddamn great bang."

This was going to be an unusual scrap voyage; for instance, what did they need a priest for? An enquiry came from the immigration official, and he was declared the only passenger relocating to another parish in India. Chuck had a fake letter of appointment from the Diocese of Mumbai made out by a clever Indian forger in Cape Flats.

All afternoon the crew was busy chaining down all the various bits of cargo and readjusting the positions of things for the eventuality of bad weather in the coming week's voyage to Pointe Noire in Congo.

At around six in the evening they were ready, the customs and immigration had been down for the final clearance, and they were away, motoring cautiously out of the QE2 dock.

When they were out of sight of land and thirty miles west of the harbour, Chuck cancelled the automatic identity system and altered course northward in the opposite direction from their declared destination in India.

On this new course the vessel took on a gentle motion, which sent everyone except the watchkeepers to an early bed. The speed improved as they got the full benefit of the Benguela current, and the engines, ably overhauled by Steve and his crew, settled into a smooth rumble.

2

Jenny Jones, freelance journalist and adventurer, watched as the *Fenix* left the harbour into the setting sun. She then mounted her motorcycle and rode up the winding road to Signal Hill to get a better view of the disappearing vessel. *India,* she thought, *my arse.* She unpacked her 30X binoculars and stared down to the sea spotting the bright floodlights and the stern light of the battered supply vessel. The ship went neither north nor south but straight out into the shipping lane. Suddenly the floodlights on the after deck were extinguished and she had a hard time seeing the diminutive stern light, now the only clue showing. The powerful binoculars were very difficult to keep steady on the target now it was so small. She boxed them and returned them to their habitual position in the right pannier.

Arriving in her apartment on the lower slopes, she went directly to her desk computer and clicked on the icon for AIS, marinetraffic.com, used all round the world for tracking vessels at sea. She found the ship quickly and read the destination as Mumbai, India, cargo scrap, and other details such as speed and course, which were entered automatically from the GPS. Three hours later, as she expected, the blip on the screen, thirty miles off, disappeared, not to be seen again.

She guessed they had disabled the system on board. Illegal, but these boys weren't too fussy about the law. Their misdemeanour would probably go unnoticed by the coast guard but to her, it was a sure sign that their destination was anywhere but Mumbai.

She studied the map of West Africa carefully and looked especially at Congo. This was the key. That was where Krels and Charles had met. The mighty Congo River disgorges into the sea at a place called Banana. She recalled one of her heroes Henry Morton Stanley had forced his way through the cataracts from the interior to arrive there in 1877.

I guess they are going to the River Congo or possibly Pointe Noire, she thought. *Pointe Noire is a small port in a kind of hooked bay. There is a blacktop road up into the interior and according to late reports it is still mostly in good order.*

It would be a colossal risk for her to go up there without a more certain lead. If her bunch of Jungle Boys were in fact just heading out to sea to make a safer passage round the Cape, she would find herself washed up in a dead-end place in Congo for nothing.

The following morning just to satisfy her curiosity and so she'd know whether the River Congo or Pointe Noire were even possibilities, she went into town to the "Tyneside" Admiralty Chart Agent and enquired about charts for River Congo and Pointe Noire. The clerk gave her a curious look.

"The captain sent you to collect them, did he?"

She made a very quick connection. "Yes," she lied; no risk in a little fib.

"They were actually ready and fully up to date yesterday. We called the captain and he sent a sailor down to fetch them."

"What a cock-up!" she said, thinking quickly.

She left rather awkwardly.

"Flaky bint," the clerk said over his shoulder to his companion.

"She off the *Fenix*? I saw the old rust bucket go out last evening. Girl must have jumped ship." He paused. "She's wiser than you think, Horace."

3

Some sixth sense had led Jenny to the chart agent and now excitement and foreboding rose from her gut. *They* are *going north*. Pointe Noire was pleasant enough. She'd been there as an independent war correspondent five years before. She quickly checked flights to PNR and found it took about fifteen hours via Johannesburg and Brazzaville and she could afford it. This might be another good story, like the blood diamonds or the mercenaries. She booked a ticket and reserved a room in a seaside hotel.

When Jenny arrived in Pointe Noire, she went straight to the Gala Beach Hotel, some two blocks inland from the white sandy beach, but the cheapest her travel agent could find. Natural ventilation substituted for the advertised air-conditioning, and the bathroom was companionable if you did not mind geckos and fat spiders. She drew the mosquito net around the bed and crashed. In the evening after a tepid shower in highly chlorinated water, she ventured to the deserted bar and asked about the dinner menu, which turned out to be entirely ethnic fare she did not recognize and did not risk.

Jenny knew there was a Novotel nearby, so she took a dilapidated Renault Four cab to the safety of their international restaurant. She found the bar was lively with expatriate offshore workers on crew change. Most were going home worldwide, entertained by their managers, who were busy networking, talking shop, and buying plenty of beer. There were a few non-commuters easily recognizable by their less-boisterous behaviour and slower drinking. She ordered a small glass of Fischer Blonde beer.

In contrast to a clique of French resident wives in Paris-styled day dresses, Jenny was dressed in khaki bush shirt and lightweight denims and sneakers. After resisting overtures from friendly but rather drunk roughnecks, she was approached by a clean-shaven man in a French-blue polo shirt and new-looking Bermudas.

"Are they harassing you, these boys? They are going home after six weeks on a rig."

"Oh, they don't bother me. After bushwackers and jackeroos they are real gentlemen."

"So you're Australian, are you an engineer?"

"No, I'm writing a book," came the reply she often used to answer this question. She had learned that journalists were universally shunned and yet "writers" or "authors" were curiosities even to the completely illiterate.

"About Africa?"

"Kind of. I'm researching illicit minerals, not blood diamonds, but the new minerals like coltan."

"Do you know what that is? But that is very dangerous for a pretty young woman, don't you think?"

"I just want to get my facts right."

"And you come all the way from Australia just for this?

"Cape Town. I live in Cape Town."

"Oh, I love Cape Town. You know, outside France, there are only four beautiful cities: Lisboa, Rio, and of course Sydney, and Cape Town. Do you agree?"

She was beginning to feel as if she was the subject of a sales pitch, with all these leading questions. Perhaps it's just the French way. His accent was almost imperceptible, he was rather nice looking and she found his direct manner attractive.

He read her mind. "Let me get you a really delicious drink, an *apéritif*. Do you know *Kir Royale*?"

She suddenly felt gauche and *outback*.

He saw her discomfort.

"Oh, it's very simple and you'll love it. This barman is very good, very careful. He uses only the best champagne, very cold, and then slowly adds the Crème De Cassis. The Cassis sinks to the bottom of the glass and very slowly insinuates itself into the champagne. Not shaken and not stirred." Turning to the barman, he simply spoke his name, "Louis," and held up two fingers and winked.

Jenny was not so daft as to miss the fact she was falling into a trap and the barman was complicit, but she was flattered and beginning to be excited.

"I am Lacroix, François, geologist to the oil industry and anyone who will pay me."

"Jenny Bones." They shook hands. He was infinitely polite; his handshake was exactly right, firm and gentle, not lingering or suggestive. *If I am being seduced*, she thought, *this bloke's a bloody expert.*

Louis brought two flutes of champagne and a bottle of deep red liqueur and with great concentration one-by-one let the Cassis slide slowly down the side of the glasses and collect in pools at the bottom.

"*Voila, madame, monsieur. Santé.*" He put down a plate of salt-free peanuts beside the flutes and left the champagne bottle in a small silver bucket on the bar.

"*Merci, Louis*," smiled François and turned back to Jenny. "*Parfait!* Isn't that beautiful? Watch as the bubbles in the champagne gradually draw the Cassis upward. When the pink is about halfway up the glass, you must take the first sip. You taste the champagne and just a hint of the liqueur; later you get the full flavour of the Kir.

"After this, will you honour me by joining me for dinner? I am delayed here for a few days waiting for a ship and for my colleague to come down from Paris."

She noticed he had fine, long, sensitive hands and used them liberally when explaining.

Her mind wandered. *Long fingers, long…*She gave herself a mental smacking as lurid thoughts invaded her mind. *At least try to be civilized*, she admonished herself silently.

He noticed her attention falter and waited with a quizzical expression on his face until she returned to the conversation.

"That would be chipper, François, you can help me to understand the French menu."

"You like crayfish, *écrevisse* ?"

"We call 'em yabbies."

"Oh, your word?"

"Yes, we used to catch them. Anything we caught in the sea, on the rocks with the binghi children, aboriginals. We used to eat them raw."

"I am sure the chef will not disappoint you: charred around the edges, basted with a little garlic butter."

They continued to drink champagne slowly and deliberately as they ate the most beautifully prepared crayfish followed by red snapper with an exquisite sauce. Jenny was surprised by the quality of the green vegetables—okra, asparagus, and some mild-flavoured spinach.

Throughout the meal they had an easy conversation about places they had been: extremes of beauty and ugliness, calm and conflict, luxury and hardship.

They were in great contrast to each other. He was from a wealthy professional family, partly privately educated and a graduate from the École des Mines de Paris, the most prestigious university for a geologist, and she an outback kid driven by an overriding resentment and grievance against mining corporations. But they were having fun and her instincts told her this boy would yield a story and very likely some very pleasurable nights in the sack.

"You are staying at the Gala Beach Hotel? *Terrible, affreux*, but in the bar, it opens at around half past ten, there is the most superb African Jazz music: a mixture of local talent and musicians from all over Africa. May I take you there?"

Jenny was happy with the direction the evening was taking.

François signed the bill, and they walked the two blocks over to the Gala Beach in the soft tropical night, cicadas and cockatoos the only background sounds, until they neared the hotel, where the heavy boom of the amplified drumbeat drowned out the natural sounds of the night.

They crossed a small dance floor and the front of a wide low stage where about six musicians were in full swing. Many of the rig men had moved over and were grouped around the bar, ignoring the music and slowly getting drunk. The place was big enough for François to take her to a table not far from the stage and away from the rowdiness of the bar.

Their conversation was limited by the music and they sat companionably close, reverting to ice-cold lager.

"I'll put it on my room bill," she yelled. "Dinner was great. It's my shout."

François was beginning to find this odd girl with the freckled face, big smile, and short boyish hair very attractive. He thought to himself, *The old chemistry is working: la charme française. She will be "fun", as they say in English, for the next few days. We cannot stay in this awful place. I will tell her and clinch the evening.*

They danced to the American numbers. He led her, jiving stylishly and handling her so she felt confident doing the quite unfamiliar movements. Then, as the music became more ethnically African, they sat out and enjoyed the complicated rhythms and expressive sounds. The music slowed and there were some smooch classics to which they danced cheek to cheek.

When the band stopped and a DJ started playing CDs, she turned to him and said, "I'm going up now, would you like to come up with me?"

When he said, "My dear Jenny," with a sort of Gallic pleading expression, she thought she'd blown her ploy, but he went on. "Look, this place is awful. You cannot stay here. The mosquitoes can penetrate the nets, *les cafards*, the cockroaches, as you say, are the biggest in the world, the maids are all *putains*, and the coffee is undrinkable. You should collect a few small things and join me at the Novotel, where *la clime* will keep us cool and exclude the local animals. I will order another bottle of champagne and we will have a private party."

"Wait here," she said without hesitation. She leapt up the stairs, nearly tripping over a chambermaid asleep on the landing floor and bumping past an over-perfumed tart giggling as she left the room opposite. She turned the key. Once inside she paused. *This has to be good*, she thought She grabbed her look-alike Louis Vuitton bag and threw in a big white shirt, a small cheeky day dress, her bikini, a couple of pairs of knickers, her diaphragm, a pack of condoms (just in case), and her very minimal makeup bag—oh, and her great big sunglasses (for disguise). She daren't leave her notebook computer behind, so she grabbed the black satchel and shoved a half-read novel into the side pocket. She toed and heeled her trainers, burying them in her suitcase, slipped on some bright-coloured sandals, sprayed her feet and arms with mosquito repellent, and left the room, banging the door firmly. There was nobody at the reception desk, so she dropped the key with its big brass fob in the box and joined François on the front steps. They ignored the taxi tout and walked back through the now quite dark, dusty roads.

François was not a disappointment. He was infinitely polite and considerate, plying her with champagne and gradually seducing her with endearments, undressing her carefully as he progressively discarded his own clothes, and with kisses and caresses, treated her to one of the most wonderful sexual experiences of her life. She laughed to herself remembering her prediction based on the length of his fingers. He was in his element, it seemed. He grinned widely as he thrust his way into her, and they laughed often between bouts of orgasmic pleasure, like abandoned teenagers.

Finally an hour before sunrise they slept, not stirring until it was time for a late lunch beside the pool. The rig men had all gone and a few topless French resident wives and some bored-looking oilfield technicians were stretched out on sun beds reading magazines or paperbacks and drinking beer or exotic-looking *rafraîchissements* with umbrellas or olives on sticks. Faint sounds of Muzak drifted from the bar. They ate Cesar salad and drank rosé, swam a little in the pool and returned to his room for more energetic lovemaking. Pernod *apéritifs*, a fine dinner, and some dancing whiled away the evening before another wonderful night.

Jenny had not completely forgotten her mission but she hesitated to break the spell of this delicious encounter by asking questions about minerals from this delightful companion who surely would be able to give her answers.

"Why don't you move over here and check out from your room at the Gala? You can go back again anytime you wish. There is always a vacancy there," suggested François after the second night. So she gathered up the rest of her stuff and checked in to the Novotel as his room sharer. She was happy to keep things cool, just at the level of a pleasant association but rationalised that moving in for a week was not too compromising for mature wanderers; however, she was surprised when on the third day, it all suddenly ended. As they were lounging by the pool in the afternoon, François was called to reception. He returned with a tall, gangly companion.

"Jenny, may I introduce Patrice? He is the colleague I mentioned, but unfortunately he has very bad news. He has come straight from the airport, and the agent has told him the boat is waiting for us. I am to go now in the car. You may stay here. The room is booked for another three days. It was a package, as you say: seven days *prix fixé* for the price of three, booked in Paris. I regret I must finish this wonderful interlude and go to work."

"What sort of work are you two doing?" she asked, realizing that she had neglected her quest and suddenly run out of time.

"I truly do not know," François replied. "Here, Patrice, stop and have a beer with Jenny while I pack my bag and check out." François disappeared towards his room and Jenny was left with Patrice.

Patrice did not speak any English. Jenny asked him the name of the boat he was joining, hoping to learn something, but it took several attempts before he seemed to understand the question and then he said, "I do not know. Zey tell me nozzing." So Jenny was left guessing. François returned with his large sports bag over his shoulder.

"Jenny, it has been wonderful, these last couple of days, but the best things in this world always come to an end. But here." He handed her an envelope. "We may be able to meet again. This is a local 'pay as you go' SIM card. I have the number. I am going for two weeks' fixed contract. It will be about seventeen or eighteen days with travelling. So if you wish, you may put the card in your phone at that time. I will call that number when I return. If you answer we may meet up again. Who knows? In the meantime feel free to use up the credit."

She thought about asking François to let her go down to the ship with him, but realized this would be clingy. She did not want anything to spoil the magic of their joyous but shallow relationship. Then she considered getting a taxi to follow their car, but that would have been both clingy and extremely rude. So after a brief *au revoir*, the men gone, she went to the reception and asked for a cable to connect her computer to the Internet. Back in the room she immediately went to the AIS site to see if she could find the ship. It was there.

After half an hour the *Fenix* was on the move but the destination was listed as Cape Town. *Bollocks*, she thought. It was plain to her that the destination had to be around here somewhere. They would not have come all the way up here just to go back to Cape Town. But she had no proof that her geologists were even on this vessel; they may have gone to any of the other three in harbour. This time the AIS signal disappeared as soon as the ship cleared the harbour.

4

The trip to Pointe Noire had been restful for them all on board. When they arrived, the agent bustled on board to welcome them. He had the geologists with him, but after the formalities were over, he had bad news.

"You cannot land anything here for the DRC. The border has been closed indefinitely and nothing gets through. They have actually put concrete barricades across the road and stopped all vehicles on the ferry; only local foot passengers, no foreign visas. If you want to get to Kinshasa side, you have to go to Matadi and continue by road. It's a terrible place but we have an agent there who will help you. You can even get visas. I can book a pilot to take you up the river from Banana. You will, please, pay me in advance. I have written out an invoice and the other invoice is for this port stop. If you get away by six o'clock, the harbour dues are negligible for a 'touch' stop but otherwise you will pay the full fee for occupying the berth. We have cleared your two passengers with immigration. So now, Captain, do you have any more business? If not, I advise you to go as soon as you are able. You can be there in the morning. Would you like me to arrange the pilot for, say, seven o'clock tomorrow morning?" Chuck agreed and used the old Tannoy to tell the ship's company of their immediate departure.

The short trip to Matadi was uneventful, apart from an altercation with the pilot, who wanted far more dash than Chuck was prepared to give. "You may want to give me five bottles of Johnny Walker Red Label and five cartons of State Express 555s," he suggested pedantically.

The pilot was not satisfied with Black Label (some sort of taboo), which Chuck had, so Chuck persuaded him that White Horse was far superior to Red Label (which he did not have). As the pilot liked the picture on the label, the toll was reduced to two bottles and three cartons of State Express. After they had tied up at the dock, Chuck took him for a few large nips and a polite conversation in the captain's cabin and made a gift of an obsolete company logo baseball cap and gained a friend for life.

Customs and immigration formalities were dealt with similarly; for a few more bottles and the promise of the Land Cruiser as a present when they left, the customs officer issued temporary import permits for all the vehicles and temporary driving licenses for all the landing crew. All the fees were in cash, but Chuck and Charles made sure all the documents were on government stationery and had impressive rubber stamps.

Anwei, Charles, and Father Driscol took the Land Cruiser and went ahead straight away. They would meet the convoy at Kinshasa after they had done a thorough reconnaissance of the onward journey. The trip by road was about seven hundred kilometres, and they estimated that the off-road trucks would take some twenty hours to cover the distance if the surface was moderately good. Joe decided to ride with one of the two hired artics to make better time, leaving Samson and his crew to manage the rest. Their cover story was that they were on a mission to save the lepers. The deeds Anwei carried with her were to establish her connection with the destination, claiming to be related to the lepers, which of course to some she was, and wanting to help them. Charles showed his medical credentials and Father Driscol put on his best frock and collar as they passed through various roadblocks manned by official government troops.

On the deck and down on the dock, Joe, Donny, Samson, and his crew were busy unloading and sorting the goods. All this work kept them busy, so after the customs settlement Chuck decided to go on a wander to see what Matadi had to offer. Along at the other end of the dock, a small container feeder ship lay alongside.

Chuck made his way up the aluminium gangway to be met at the top by a smart-looking African in khaki shorts and bush shirt.

"Yes, sir, how can I help?"

"Oh, I was just wandering around and wondered if your captain might appreciate a visit from a fellow captain."

"Maybe." He lifted an ICOM VHF radio to his face and spoke into it: "Captain, Chief Officer. There is a visitor here from another ship, the captain."

Chuck heard a guttural grunt from the other party.

"He will come down to see you," said the officer.

A jovial fellow came bounding down the companionway. "Welcome, my friend. What can I do for you? Captain Sid, they call me. They can't pronounce my name, Polish. I can hardly

304

pronounce it myself, ha, ha, ha. Been on this bloody coast so long, I am forgetting my own language. Anyway, I haven't seen a white man in a while. Got some beer in the fridge. Come up and tell me who you are. From another ship? Ha, I see no ships. Oh, yes, the orange one over there."

He led Chuck back up the companionway and up three decks to his suite. "Come in, sit down." There was a day cabin, and in the doorway leading to his sleeping cabin stood a slender young woman.

"This is Grace. This is Captain…"

"Chuck."

"Of course. Grace, the captain is probably thirsty."

Grace opened the fridge and obediently handed them ice-cold bottles of lager.

"So, my friend, what are you up to? Must be mischief in a place like this. No one is on holiday in this forgotten hole."

"We're just looking for scrap."

"Ha, ha, ha, plenty around here. This is Africa, the whole place is scrap." He paused to get his breath.

"I just bring supplies for the fat cats and take away container loads of coffee and cocoa. Bloody train is late. If we weren't subsidized by the government we'd be broke years ago. I bring at least one BMW 7 Series every trip and a container load of Paris fashions, so I am told, and containers full of small arms, vehicles and scrambler bikes for the fighters. My biggest worry is losing end-user certificates and other phony paperwork.

"You didn't come all the way up here looking for scrap. I saw you unloading vehicles in working order, barrels or drums, using the machinery you have on deck. Looks like scrap to the innocent eye, but I am not a fool." He tailed off, acknowledging the discretion of good manners. "You don't have to tell me."

"Your health, Captain," rejoined Chuck to break the tension.

"I don't suppose you need any fuel, do you?" Captain Sid asked quietly.

"Well, who's offering?" answered Chuck with interest.

"A fat Nigerian is in a bit of a bind. You see that flattop barge over there? He's got a thousand tons of good diesel 'bunkered' from Warri. He's stuck. He had a customer here but the police have a new treaty or agreement with the Nigerians. The customer has disappeared. The barge has been in here for a month and can't leave till he pays the harbour dues, and he has to find a tug to get the barge back to sea. If he takes any of the cargo back to Nigeria, he will surely go to jail, because without money he won't be able to avoid it. The cargo is tagged by one of the inspection companies so they will immediately identify its origin."

"Tagged?" enquired Chuck.

"They add a tracer chemical like a DNA marker. If a cargo turns up in the wrong place it can be identified. They are on to him so they will definitely test it."

"What's the offer?"

"Hey, I'm not his salesman, but he may be round for a beer later so you can meet him. I suggest you offer him fifteen cents on the dollar and settle at twenty or twenty-five. It has probably cost him about seventy dollars a ton so far, but he's racking up around three hundred a day to be here and can't pay, so can't move. Have your engineer test it very carefully for water. These Nigerians have some clever ways of watering it down using chemicals."

Chuck's ears pricked up at this news. They had no intention of going near Nigeria, and a couple of hundred tons of good gas oil at a bargain price would be very useful. He did a quick calculation.

Thirty thousand dollars was a lot better than the hundred and twenty thousand he had to budget for. He could afford it in cash and it would be a good investment for the next leg of their voyage.

Every time he made a purchasing decision it hurt, but he kept telling himself, "In for a dime, in for a dollar," - recognition that he was on a ramp and had to pray the final payoff was worth it. As with the whole crew, he was full of optimism, as they had arrived at the destination and had to get on with the next stage.

Before he left the ship, Enno Okwe, the Nigerian, showed up for a beer with Captain Sid, and Chuck bought two hundred tons of his cargo for twenty-eight thousand dollars in cash money, subject to testing by his engineer, Steve. The relief on Okwe's face was profound, and Chuck stayed for a few tots of fine Polish vodka and was followed back to the *Fenix* by his new friend Enno.

As he returned to the ship, he saw Joe and the crew were progressing well with the unloading and preparation for the long road trip up to the site.

The noisy, smokey, old Manitowok crane was a boon. It lifted off the trucks, generators and all the small equipment with Samson or Joe at the controls. They had hired some out-of-work stevedores to help. They took shifts so they were able to work round the clock. Selectively they engaged some of the stevedores for further work up-country.

Steve was dispatched with the water-detecting kit and dipped all the tanks on the barge, which was manhandled along the pier alongside the *Fenix*. Throughout the pumping no water was found. Chuck paid the Nigerian as contracted and threw in a bottle of Black Label and a baseball cap.

The two Hitachi diggers were loaded on to the six-wheelers, now painted yellow with the crude A&Co logo to make them look civilian, so in the end there were six vehicles in the convoy, including four ordinary articulated trucks hired locally, which carried the containers, the generators, and eighty drums of diesel.

Beyond Kinshasa the road to their destination branched off the main arterial route and soon lacked any surface or maintenance. Using the pocket GPS they made their way to the colony with one of the Hitachi machines, using the front loader and much machete work, beating the liana and under bush down to clear the track. The other Hitachi loader was used to transfer the drums from the artic trailers to the military six-wheel-drive and the Kenworth, which were shuttling the loads to the site. The last loads were the freight containers winched on board the Kenworth. The artics were off-hired, as they were unable to venture off the main road.

When Father Driscol appeared at the colony, there was much rejoicing among the lepers, who plied him with food from their meagre rations and sang most beautiful welcoming songs. Some of the men staggered over to the machinery and caressed it with the palms of their hands. The incoming crew looked around for a suitable campsite. There was a flat clearing inside the perimeter just large enough for the tents. Driscol suggested Anwei and Charles should sleep in the church, which they subsequently made into their home, except on Sundays, when they gave it over for mass and other services.

They soon got into a routine with the geologists, using one of the containers as a laboratory and sleeping quarters. Studying the material on the computer and making probes, they marked out the ground telling them where to dig. Joe and Samson and the others started trenching with the backhoes and loading the mine dumpers with the precious black earth. Up on the bank, the two generators provided power for the shale shakers and centrifuges, kept busy sorting the valuable minerals from the basic clay. The clay runoff went to the brick moulds, where the lepers were making the unfired hollow bricks for their houses. At the weekend they stacked all the "green" bricks in a long cave, previously the lepers' finished product store, with a newly made chimney at the far end. They were dry enough to handle but very delicate. Using a hastily made burner bar and a seven-atmosphere air compressor, they started to fire the bricks, sampling them every day. The first batch took a whole week to cure well enough for building.

One of the lepers, who was experienced in making the beautiful pottery, suggested two things for this procedure. First, he added some diesel to the clay slurry to assist the firing procedure, and second, he changed the design of the bricks themselves and the stacking procedure. The new brick design was interlocking and the revised stack gave much better circulation. As if by magic the next batch took three and a half days for a 50 percent larger number, the added hydrocarbon aiding the firing. The time was reduced on each successive firing. Father Driscol was very pleased with the result and set the lepers to clearing the land for their planned housing.

The shakers were producing coltan, dark black in colour and having a specific gravity of around eight, which is about three times as heavy as the clay. The drums could not be completely filled because they would burst, so they filled them to about halfway, an estimated four hundred kilograms. This represented one hundred and sixty thousand dollars per half-drum. If the rate of two a day kept up, it came to over two million dollars a week. Charles did not care to think of it, while Chuck was happy to hear the reports as they came back to vessel in Matadi. He needed most of the first week's returns just to cover expenses.

The second week they produced twenty half-drums and in the third week thirty-two. That was the maximum capacity without breakdowns. At the end of the third week, the first consignment of forty drums arrived at Matadi, driven tortuously down the long road on board the Kenworth flatbed truck. Water became a problem and the job had to be stopped in the third week to dig a well.

The brick making became more efficient. They were able to stack more and more into the cave. The lepers did their best following Father Driscol's instructions and managed to construct the first five one-room dwellings in the second week. The interlocking bricks needed no mortar, provided the ground was absolutely flat and level, a task well suited to the Hitachi, using the small scraper. The lepers able to wield a machete went around the perimeter harvesting fronds, and those with able hands were set to weaving the thatched roofing. All the rooms were three metres square, with three blank walls and a narrow doorway on to the courtyard.

The project went on, creating dry and cool sleeping accommodation which could be made mosquito proof. According to previous custom, cooking was a communal business, and a large kitchen and eating house was built in the middle of the square gradually being formed by the two- and three-room terraces. The mechanics fixed up the old diesel pump. A cistern provided a head of water, and plastic piping was run to two ablutions areas for the males and females and a large septic tank installed for the latrines. The project was on the way to becoming a very civilized communal living unit for the one hundred or so remaining lepers.

The lepers became much more animated and much laughter emanated from their quarters after dark. Still Father Driscol worried about the drugs necessary to alleviate their pain and arrest the development of the awful disease. Charles went into town and begged from an NGO doctor, who gave him some supplies and the information as to how to buy more.

5

Jenny was angry. She was left in Pointe Noire and nobody had told her anything about what was happening. After a week of comparative luxury in the Novotel, she had moved back into the very basic Gala Beach Hotel. There was no Internet connection and nobody to talk to. It seemed that the guests were all either minor politicians or local oilfield workers of various lower orders.

After two days of this isolation, she decided that the only chance of getting near to her quarry was to take the flight back to Brazzaville and try to make a contact. The return ticket meant for a small fee she could change the dates and break her journey. Brazzaville has some excellent hotels, out of her price bracket and some scruffy ones of the type she was used to but resented after her recent stay in comfort. Such was the Hotel Le Blanc. Still, without a story sold she had no silly money to spend. She had lost contact with the Jungle Boys and perhaps would not find them again. She needed to get across the river to Kinshasa.

She went to the embassy of the Democratic Republican to see if she could get a visa. No luck: she could not even get past the guards who, stony faced, blocked her with submachine guns. Her press badge was useless. The doors and windows of the embassy seemed to be shuttered. As she turned to go, one of the soldiers thrust a sheet of paper into her hand. It was a poor quality photocopy of a government notice. On one side was French and the other English.

Democratic Republic of Congo
DEPARTMENT OF IMMIGRATION

INSTRUCTIONS:

If you want to apply visa for Democratic Republic of Congo application form may be submitted wednesday between 15hr and 16hr 30

You will submit: passport, two photos 4cm x 5cm.

Commercial visitor, academic, industrial consultant need submit Letter of Introduction from firm visiting.

Tourist will give address of next hotel and tour details.

Journalist will only be permit from specific accredited publications and will carry document verifying engagement and intended sujet.

You will arrive again on next wednesday between 11 am and 13hr. to collect your successful visa.

Fees: Commercial US$100, Tourist and Journalist US$50 payable in US dolar cash only.

It was Tuesday.

She wandered into town and found a restaurant with some white plastic furniture outside and people in ones, twos and small groups drinking coffee, beer or wine under sunshade umbrellas. She took a seat at a vacant table and ordered a *biere blonde*. She drank the first half quickly and then some more.

311

When her glass was nearly empty, a local man in a loose tropical suit sat down opposite her and immediately started a conversation with, "English?" and a very wide toothy smile. "I am Bobo. I am honoured to meet you."

"Jenny, Australian," she answered, then hesitated as she was not sure where this encounter would lead.

"You like this French-style beer? You need another. I would like one, if you please." He waved at the waiter and ordered two. They sat in silence until the waiter returned with the two thirty-three-millilitre glasses of gently bubbling pale liquid. He drank some and turned back to her.

"Thank you, lady, this is very good beer. I can help you. You see, I am a guide, and I know everything that goes on here. I even know what is going on around the jungle and the Big River. Do you want to visit some tourist sites or know something or go somewhere special? I can get you rhino horn, elephant tusks, marijuana, medicines, special homeopathic preparations for health or sexual excellence. I know where things are happening."

He paused to take a longer draft from the glass. Jenny took a drink from hers.

"Well, I'm looking for some people who may have come into the area to look for something."

"Many people come to Congo to find their souls or erotic satisfaction."

"No, no, they brought diggers and such equipment. They came on a ship."

"Ships don't come here from the sea. Only on the River Congo are just flattop barges, but very, very big."

"I suppose they may have driven up from Matadi to Kinshasa."

"Ah, that is possible. Sometimes oil developers come through there in convoys of many truckloads of equipment. Just a few come now. But Kinshasa is very problem. Border is closed. The jungle route is very dangerous."

Bobo's expression suddenly changed as if he had seen something fearful in the street.

"I advise you to get a visa in the normal way. Then I can help you. What is the big hurry? Thank you for the refreshment. You have been very kind, Ma'moiselle," he said and disappeared as suddenly as he had appeared.

There was nothing for her to do in Brazzaville for the week ahead and what was more frustrating was that she could see the bright lights of Kinshasa across the river.

The next day she took all the necessary documents to the DRC embassy. There appeared to be no hassle. She filled in five forms, which appeared to be different editions of the same form—the same questions in a different order—and was given a receipt for her Australian passport, relieved of fifty bucks, plus fifty more for a service fee, and was asked for a tourism plan. When she said she had not made her plans yet, they said to bring it next week, when they would inspect it and authorize it.

She left the embassy in good spirits and the coming week's wait diminished in its level of irritation. She would occupy herself making a comprehensive ten-day tourist plan written up as professionally as possible. She went straight back to the Hotel Le Blanc and asked if there was any way to get on to the Internet. She was met with general affirmatives but no detail as to how, so she guessed not. She went to the South African embassy and asked if there were any press facilities. They were able to show her into a small room with an Internet connection. This was to be her shortcut to a tour plan of Democratic Republic of Congo.

The main attraction was the Bonobo or pygmy chimpanzee. The trouble was, the only way to get to their habitat was by using an established tour company, probably beyond her means. Never mind; she wrote that her plan was to see the nearest genetic relative to mankind in a planned visit to the reserves upriver from Kinshasa at Nkosso or the Kasai River area. She did not know where this all was or how she could afford it but it made "good copy." The area was strictly under international control, and improved living conditions and jobs as wardens for the locals were used as a bribe to prevent hunting of the natural wildlife including Bonobo.

She hoped that this interest alone would be her *entrée* into Congo Kinshasa. She had money in rand and she hoped this would be acceptable. As a precaution she went to a bank and with great difficulty and at a very disadvantageous exchange rate bought three hundred US dollars in twenty-dollar bills, testing each one ostentatiously, as she was aware of a rash of forgeries. Every day she read more about the Bonobos, going to the library of the British Council in the British embassy, where she found good references in English. Her journalist training had taught her how to become an overnight expert.

She counted off the days and realized it was a full two weeks since she had accepted the SIM card from François. When she thought of him, she had a sudden longing for his close contact and attention. That night, all her tour plan done, she lay awake and fantasized about his great sexual effect on her. She was sweating profusely as her heart rate surged. She took a cold shower and depressed herself by imagining him sitting on a plane to his next assignment, taking off from Kinshasa just as she was about to enter.

She charged her phone and checked that his card was installed. She was not altogether hopeful it would ring on the Brazzaville side of the river, but hoped the signals were the same for both sides or had enough range to cross from one side to the other.

Bobo had been in the habit of greeting her every day, asking her about the visa application. He said her plan for the tour was a good one and he would be her guide wherever she wanted to go. He only spoke to her in the street as she made her way back to the hotel. He never again sat with her in the restaurant.

"I have to go the embassy to collect my visa," she told him.

"I know, I have been listening to what you say. But how will you cross the river?"

"By the ferry, of course."

"OK, I will come with you to the embassy and help you if you like."

"Fine," she said rather too abruptly.

"I think you will need help."

"Right." This smelled like a scam coming along but she was already in a fix. If she dismissed him, she was certain to get

314

into a bind, whether of his making or not. If he was with her, at least he wasn't entirely against her. "Great, thank you."

He did not enter the office but hung around outside.

"You have your plan?" asked the official.

"Yes," she answered, "and I'm so excited to be able to see man's closest ancestor."

"They are not related to us. We are men not monkeys. Why do you people keep telling us this myth? If we are in the image of God..." He trailed off, bored with saying the same thing every week to silly white people with ridiculous theories.

"Go and see the apes fornicating if you want." He planted a big nondescript mess on her meticulously handwritten plan with a large rubber stamp.

"You must have a visa for Angola. You are only allowed in transit."

"Of course," she said, masking her surprise and dismay with a broad smile.

He handed her the passport and she opened it to see another messy rubber stamp with some squiggly signatures and noted it was for twenty-one days transit.

When she was outside, Bobo was waiting. "Need Angola visa, takes another week," he said helpfully.

"Why didn't you tell me before?"

"Because it would have confused you."

"F-damn you. I am confused. I have to wait another week?"

"Ten days. Visas in Angola are Saturday, similar routine. But if I am your guide, it will be possible to go today."

"On the ferry?"

"No problem."

"Legal?"

"Of course. It's just a minor technical itch, as the English say."

"I will check out of the hotel before noon." She looked at her watch. "See you back here at one. Do you want me to go to a different café?"

"Uncle Mac's burger joint. We will eat and then go. The burgers are hygienic and spicy."

315

She packed quickly and checked out in the lobby and then went down the road again to the burger bar. It was clear the proprietor had been to America. The decoration was pure plagiarism. There were stars and stripes all over the place, and the two serving hatches were surmounted by golden arches. There was even a poor replica of the Colonel Sanders manikin with a black face and white moustache and goatee; in his right hand, a white chicken was hanging by the neck and a sign across his chest advertised chicken burgers. Civilization had arrived.

She sat down and ordered Coke. A cola arrived in a glass with ice. The flavour was not quite what she expected. Bobo arrived.

"Here's my tour plan for DRC. If you are my guide, you should know it."

They ordered meat burgers from a boy waiter.

"Our first bus is at three thirty p.m. I have bought the tickets for the ferry. You will pay me for those and for my service as a guide. You can pay me in dollars or rand," he said, laying down ground rules.

"How much? We don't have a deal yet."

"Of course, one hundred rand per day. Very reasonable don't you think, Jenny?"

"Right," she answered dubiously.

"You will pay me seven hundred for the week, and I will pay expenses and charge you later."

The burgers were surprisingly good, served with a green salad that Jenny avoided wisely. *From now on*, she thought, *freshly boiled rice and yams only*.

They fell silent as he read through the itinerary carefully.

"Everything is possible but we will pass through some areas where foreigners are not welcome. Occasionally you may have to play the part of my sick sister. So after lunch we go to a bend-down boutique where you can buy secondhand garments. Don't worry, they are all clean and fresh, but not new. If anyone asks you direct questions, stick your tongue in your cheek and look pained. I will tell them you have an enormous abscess and you have just seen the doctor who gave you pills, and you don't want to try any traditional medicine."

316

"Bobo, how come you speak such good English and know so much?"

"I was in England for six months. I was a student in a terrible place called Reading. I resigned from the course."

"Are you Congolese then?"

"No, Cameroonian, but I left there and came here. I have a girl here and have four young kids. I had a very good job as a guide and host for VIPs, good salary and everything." He did not want to admit he had been sent home from the UK, ran away from Cameroon to avoid being punished by a furious high-ranking diplomat for harassing his daughter and recently sacked for claiming false travelling expenses for VIP clients.

Hearing his story Jenny sensed little bells ring: *Use this fellow but keep him at arm's length and don't trust him more than you have to and expect a cutout at any time.* She wanted him to show her how to get across to DRC. He promised to do so and his price was high but fair. She would trust him thus far but no more than necessary.

"Does Bobo mean anything?" she asked innocently.

"It means cool guy, stylish."

"What language is it?"

"Language? It's just a word. People round here speak pidgin. Maybe it's pidgin, but there're also many languages, hundreds. Pidgin gets words from all over. It's a nickname. You don't need to know my real name."

The phone in her satchel rang.

"Hi, Jenny," François said as if it was last night they had parted. There was a lot of cracking on the line.

"Oh, François, thank God you rang."

"You are still in Pointe Noire?"

"No, Brazzaville. Look, I got my visa to Kinshasa today. Is that where you are?"

"What will you do over here? My next assignment is in Thailand, but I have a two-week break," he said through the crackling of the phone. "Can you hear me? This is a satellite phone. When do you arrive? *Alors*, I am going to stay till you come here to the Hotel Daito, delta alpha india tango oscar. Got it? *Commune de la Gombe.*"

"Got it. See you later. Wish me luck."

317

She put the phone back in her bag and turned to Bobo. "My boyfriend. He's called François."

"French," said Bobo, noticing her change in countenance.

"Well, he's in Kinshasa waiting for me."

6

"Good, we will all go to see the apes," he said, anticipating a better pay rate from a wealthy man rather than this impecunious woman. But there would be no other rewards in kind. He would hit the man for three hundred a day or forty US dollars. Skilful negotiation was required.

"With the man we may have to go first class with protection and all that."

Jenny detected a railroading going on, so she said, "He probably won't want to go. He may have some news for me that will change my plans. Anyway, do you know the Hotel Daito?"

"Very well, very beautiful hotel, first class five stars."

"That's where I am meeting him. After we have crossed the border, can you drop me there and then meet again tomorrow morning when we can discuss plans?"

The crossing was uneventful. As the immigration officer was examining Jenny's passport, he checked the visa and mistakenly hit it with the rubber stamp before he asked about the Angola visa. Bobo caused a minor diversion by treading hard on the foot of the man behind him, and he snatched the passport back. Jenny smiled at the official and Bobo made an abject apology and a contribution to the official's pension and it was all over. They moved on through the crowd of local workers and traders.

Bobo found a taxi and they went directly to the hotel.

"Tomorrow morning then," he said with a big obvious wink that would have offended Jenny had she not been so excited at the prospect of meeting François again.

True to form he appeared as soon as she called from reception.

"You want to check in here?" he asked.

"Where else, you fool?"

Formalities all done they went up to the first floor and in a fever of animal passion reacquainted themselves with each other. At around ten they showered together and descended to the restaurant to have a light meal of local river fish with a fine claret.

"Jenny, I have just come away from the job of a lifetime. Our original fee was about fifty percent above the norm, but in addition, the bonus was double. The guys I worked for were so damn sure they would make a fortune from our work that they went berserk with the money. What Patrice and I found, they would never have seen and yet for us it was too simple. We worked day and night marking out the areas to dig, but it was worth it. So, I want to take you on a holiday before my next assignment."

"What were you doing and where?"

"One condition was a promise not to reveal either the minerals or the location. So I have said enough already."

"I have a travel plan and a guide," she said. "I produced it to satisfy the immigration people. They said I had to get it approved. It's all about the Bonobo chimps. Preparing the plan I read all I could get hold of, and now nothing will stop me from going to see them whenever I can. We could go there and see them. Would you like to?"

"Only on one condition: I pay and we travel first class and stay in the best places. I have been living in a steel container, sleeping on a thin rubber mat in my clothes for two weeks. I had my first shower in clean water when I arrived. Everything in luxury from now on."

"Good on yer. I can tolerate luxury after the hotels I had to use over the river. This place is nice." She had enjoyed the excellent cuisine in the charming surroundings of the dining room with its waterfalls and greenery. When they arrived back at the room, she looked around afresh at the two king-sized beds, good linen sheets, comfortable armchairs, desk, minibar, big flat-screen TV, and *en suite* bathroom. *Yeah, someone has to,* she thought as she shucked her clothes for the second time that evening.

It was a wonderful night for them both as they dissipated their pent-up frustration and anticipation. Although their activity led to a most marvellous relaxation, Jenny found her nerves jangling at ten thirty the following morning when they went down to have breakfast. François was plain exhausted and slightly wobbly on his feet. They did everything in slow motion and were perfectly attuned to the tardy pace of the waitresses.

Sometime after eleven Jenny got a call from reception: She had a visitor. Of course it was Bobo. She told him she would stay at the hotel all day, but could he find a deluxe tour company who would take them to Bonobo country and book them into a good hotel there.

"We would like to meet the tour representative at around six this evening in the foyer."

Bobo was pleased. This was a grand opportunity but it could be fun as well.

When they went back to the room, François asked to see her plan.

"Oh, it's not relevant anymore; we're going to use a tour company."

"But your research, I want to see what you discovered."

As she pulled the three sheets of her plan from the document side of her satchel, the green-striped printout came with it. The front page was showing on top and something caught François's eye.

"The name at the top, Aku-Agua, and those numbers, what are they?" he asked, picking the paper up and studying it more carefully. "Where did you get this?"

"It's something I forgot about years ago. It is meaningless to me."

"OK, but where did it come from?"

"It came from a laptop case I kept for some people. When they asked for it, I gave it back. They were grateful. I had removed that to try to decipher it, unsuccessfully, and forgot about it until I saw it on the floor of my cupboard and packed for this trip. I still don't know what it means."

Suddenly François burst into laughter. "This is what we've been working on. My God, you are chasing these people. Why?"

"I think they are mining here. It's a story, environmental, possibly illegal and so on: a scoop for me, who needs so desperately to get a big story."

"I know about these people. They're legal. There may be a story but I want to take you on holiday. I promised them I would not leak their plans. So we go on holiday and if you are very good, I will tell you about them when we come back."

It did not take her long to decide in favour of a luxurious two-week holiday seeing Bonobos, wherein there was a potential travel story anyway, over the uncertainties and vagaries of a jungle chase in one of the most dangerous parts of the world.

"Deal," she said and rolled seductively onto the bed. François was not slow to respond.

They would have slept through their six o'clock appointment if François had not set the alarm clock. When they arrived, they found Bobo with a portly man of about sixty.

"This is Serge," blurted Bobo. "May I introduce Miss Jenny and Monsieur François?"

After some nodding and shaking of hands he continued.

"This is my boss. Monsieur Serge was a tracker in the hunting days. He made money from tusks, gorilla fists, and the like. He is now a leading conservationist. His agency is one of a few with a license to take tourists to the reserves to see the Bonobo. I am your guide. You will travel first class and you will go to lodges of the five-star type."

"Well," said Serge. "He is right. I have a few guides but you have chosen Bobo. He knows the way; he will guide you. You will have a most marvellous time, the holiday of a lifetime, unforgettable. It will be carved into your heart. You are lovers. You will learn something from the apes—such tenderness, such emotion."

"Mr. Serge, would you like a drink? Bobo?" François asked.

"I got a taste for beer from my clients when I took them on hunting safaris. Too old for all that now, but I can still drink beer. A welcome pleasure for an old man. Thank you."

François hailed a waiter and ordered four glasses of beer without asking Jenny. She was both putout and pleased at the same time.

"Well now, at this time of year the best place is to go to the lodge at the confluence of the Kasai River and then further upriver to my lodge beyond Mbandaka, where the Bonobos often come. It is very peaceful. It is a reserve and there are plenty of trees."

It was plain François was on a spending spree. He hired the very best Land Cruiser available, complete with all safety devices and a camping outfit, and to prevent them getting into trouble, a security guard of the local tribe. The plan was rewritten to include the very best lodges on the way. He told Jenny to buy a windup torch and an adapter so she could recharge her camera from the car. He wanted her to get the best possible pictures, and she rose to the occasion by taking pictures of everything.

Bobo was paid three times the rate agreed by Jenny and was happy. The security guard got nearly as much, and Serge was paid rent in advance for his lodges. Jenny and François went into town to buy new changes of clothing so they would have clean clothes every day. After the third night in Kinshasa, they were ready to go.

At first light they took the road northeast. The dawn was exhilarating as François drove steadily up the smooth road out of Kinshasa. The surface gradually deteriorated until they were slowed to around fifty kilometers per hour, the Toyota's suspension smoothing out the bumps magnificently. After about an hour they stopped to eat their warm breakfast *croissants* and drink the thermos of coffee. There was the faint smell of cooking fires in the cool humid air. The rising sun was fighting its way through puffy clouds, and the dew was glistening on the leaves. Howls of monkeys and parrots broke the silence. In the distance a pirogue was visible on the glassy water—a fisherman paddling home with his catch, perhaps.

Jenny turned to François, tears of joy in her eyes. She opened her mouth to say something but he put his finger on her lips to silence her, then kissed her gently, not wanting to spoil the perfection of the moment. Like so many people with a necessarily tough exterior, she could be caught off guard by sentimentality in such sublime moments.

When Bobo and the guard climbed back into the rear seat, the couple took the cue to do the same.

"How's your driving, Bobo?" asked François.

"Very good; passed test in England and was going to drive a taxi but the immigration got me first. I drive some of my clients here. I can drive if you like but you are enjoying it. Very masculine," he added without mischievous intent.

"With two drivers we can make more miles. Keep an eye on me. We don't want any mistakes."

"Three," said Jenny quietly.

François leant over and squeezed her thigh gently.

There was a deep chuckle from behind. "Four," said the guard in a deep bass voice. "I was a safari driver in Botswana. They used to call me Candoo. Climb mountains, cross rivers, shoot lions, all that."

"Brilliant, Candoo, I am François, this is Jenny. We did not have time to introduce ourselves properly."

It was another idyllic interlude and Jenny began to feel completely captivated by this cultured Frenchman. He treated her with the same courtesy as he had before they were so familiar, and she felt herself losing some rough edges, speaking less Strine and imperceptibly feminizing her body language in spite of the bush clothes. *Is this falling in love?* she wondered, and tried to convinced herself it was just another hit with a stranger, but hoping it was a bit more.

They saw all the things they wanted, including the Bonobo chimps and the wonderful dense forest. They even saw a glimpse of some small forest elephants and some forest people came to the lodge to sell them trinkets. After seven days they returned to the hotel.

"I am very sorry but I have to go to Thailand."

"I know and I am very sorry too but we both have jobs to do." She looked him in the eye and said, "This has been more than just a rumble in the jungle, hasn't it?"

"Jenny, normally I am a very unreliable man. The French are famous for it, as you say. But for me too, this has been a very special time. The truth is you visited me every night when I was sleeping in that steel container. I couldn't get my mind off you. I don't dare say the word, which in the past I have used so carelessly. Don't break the spell. We will meet again and holiday again anywhere in the world, and then we'll see."

"You're right." She paused and then continued, "Your part of the bargain was to tell me about my Jungle Boys."

"Well, you have their coordinates in your bag. Read carefully the numbers at the top. They are laid out in short form: latitude first, degrees, minutes, and decimals as one number without a break, then a comma and degrees, minutes, and decimals longitude. If it were south or west, the minus sign would signify."

"So I can load this on to my Garmin and it will guide me there?"

"Sure. Now I did not tell you the place, only how to interpret some numbers."

"What's there?"

"They are digging for coltan or columbite-tantalum."

"What's that?"

"It's a rare earth mineral used in solar panels, as a catalyst, and lately in mobile phones for very high capacity memory chips."

"And why are they after it?"

"It's worth a fortune, really big money, something like four hundred dollars a kilo."

"So they are raiding a small village, tearing up the environment and dispossessing local people to make a fortune. They are presumably illegally mining."

"I don't know the legal side of what they are doing. All I know is that they hired us, paid us well and are continuing to work there for about another month before they pull out. They may have accumulated about twenty or thirty million dollars worth of minerals before they leave. They have a boat, cranes and machines. It's an operation. They are building new houses for the lepers living in the village. It's a proper brick village from the clay runoff. The villagers are happy to have nice new brick houses."

7

"I need to tell you something," Jenny said. "My grandfather had a sheep station up by Dampier somewhere. Prospectors surveyed his land without his permission and finagled him out of the section his father had staked out fifty years earlier. Granddad was run off his land and the labour force for the new mine ate his sheep. He went on a big drunk with the compensation money and abandoned my grandmother and two kids. She managed to hold on to the girl, we think, but my dad wandered off, an infant, into the bush, lost in the outback at the age of four.

"My name is Bones because he was saved by a mob of Aborigines. He was so thin and starving they called him Bones and he was suckled back to life by a woman called Jenny. He knew his own first name was Jimmy. He was found by the welfare officers playing with the black kids and put in an orphanage. They registered him as Jimmy Bones. When he grew up the only work the orphanage found for the kids was at the very mine on his ancestral land. The English proprietors made themselves very rich while Dad drove a dumper truck for them. Conditions were terrible in the heat and dust. We survived on his miserable wages. Only after the Union got the labour organized did things get better."

She paused. François was listening intently and so she continued.

"My opinion of miners is clackers. This operation you describe is a carbon copy, smaller scale but no less lucrative and with potential to desecrate vast areas of virgin jungle, threaten species and local humans alike."

"Jenny, please don't do anything silly. These people seem to have some legitimate claim. It's not clear what. They are armed but not aggressive, but perhaps if provoked they may turn nasty."

"No, I won't do anything silly but I want to get to the bottom of this and expose anything that smacks of exploitation by diggers, especially if there is anything illegal going on."

"Please don't go and get yourself killed. That would break my heart. I care for you and I don't want to lose you."

Jenny fell into his arms and they hugged for a long moment.

"Yes, François, I will come back to you. Now let's get undressed. You go in the morning."

François explained as he was throwing his clothes on to the chair, "Again, you have the room *en pension* for another week and the Land Cruiser for six more days."

"No," she said, "not the car, but the room will be very useful. Thank you. I will take you to the airport in the morning and return the car immediately."

"As you wish. Maybe you are right. If you went into the area you are contemplating, you may have the car ransomed. I have paid Bobo for another week and told him to look after you. Get your story and go back to South Africa. I will contact you by e-mail."

François told her his assignment would be for four weeks offshore and he would then find her and they would make plans for a longer time together.

8

The following day they found Bobo in the foyer. He jumped in the back seat of the Toyota and came with them to the airport. He was dismayed when after lingering good-byes Jenny took the driver's seat and returned the car directly to the rental company. They went back to the hotel in a taxi and sat in the coffee shop of the hotel to have *petit dejeuner*. She explained what she was hoping to find and the area they would have to search and that they would have to use the GPS to get there.

"I know the area where your people are," he said unexpectedly as the coffee arrived. "And I know the chief of that district. We can contact him and he will let us go to see the location."

"OK," said Jenny. "Who is he?"

"He's a very good politician. He looks after his people; he has schools and places for the sick. He is a very big man around there. If you tell him about these miners, he will want you to help him make a legal case against them."

"Can I meet him?"

"We must go to his village."

Jenny was well equipped for a jungle trek. She had two khaki safari suits, jungle boots, and several changes of clothes.

"I propose we use a motorcycle to travel. It is more useful on the tracks and rough roads. My company does motorcycle safaris."

"We need two," she said, surprising him.

"You are OK on a bike?"

"All my life, Bobo. Try me."

They went to the company's shop downtown and took out two Japanese all-terrain bikes. They had racks and panniers fitted, and Jenny packed her spare clothes and camera, deciding not to take her notebook computer with her. She put her Garmin in one of the large pockets of her safari jacket. *Like old times*, she thought to herself. The journey took all day and into the night.

When they arrived at the village, Bobo introduced Jenny to the chief, Colonel Nkwende Tunde. He was very polite and after they had eaten some pap, meaty gravy, and mashed yam, he showed her to a hut kept for visitors. Bobo and the colonel talked in animated tones in the local language. She slept well after her long journey.

In the morning she awoke to the many sounds and smells of the village coming to life. She was fed and then Bobo took her to see the colonel.

"I believe you know of some foreigners mining on my territory. I am not aware of them. This territory belongs to my people and we will not tolerate incursions. We are civilized and

327

democratic. You have the place on your electronic device. I demand you shown me."

Jenny produced her Garmin with the coordinates loaded and showed it to Tunde.

"This is meaningless," he complained.

"Please wait," she replied. The simple receiver gradually gathered satellite ranges until it had enough to fix their position. As the numbers came up, she explained, "This is where we are now and this line here represents where we have to go to find them. It's about thirty-five kilometres on a bearing of one hundred and sixty-three degrees." She showed him the line on the small screen. The colonel pondered and then using his local knowledge and his experience with maps outlined their route:

"We can go south about fifteen kilometers on a well-beaten path to the village of Konkondo, but then the only path goes southwest. To continue south we must take that path five kilometres, and then the country opens out to savannah, where we go southeast for ten more kilometers where it becomes very hilly and is forest again. That is as far as I know. We have had conflict in that area."

"What will you do when you get there?"asked Jenny.

"We will negotiate, of course. We cannot have such disruption from foreigners."

Jenny was not sure what she had started. She was alarmed by all the men carrying assault weapons surrounding them. She was reassured as she heard the singsong voices of children reciting, "Hello, Mr. Brown, how are you today? Do you want some potatoes? I must catch the bus to town, one, two, three, four, five, six, seven, eight, nine, ten." She looked across the clearing and in an open sided hut, an old man was pointing with a stick to objects on a poster.

"Cow, dog, horse, chicken, tractor." The children were chanting as the teacher moved his stick across the pictures.

"You will lead us to this place. We will leave here in the afternoon. Some foot soldiers will leave now and go down to Konkondo to await us. We have several motorcycles, and we will join them there. We will continue until the motorcycles become useless, then we will continue by foot through the jungle. We should arrive by dawn tomorrow."

"We don't need an army," she pleaded.

"The foreigners are armed, of course. We need to persuade them to cooperate."

The trek south went as planned. Armed men were mounted on motorcycles but she was alarmed to see that all had young boys of various ages on the pillion holding on to two AK-47s and other assault weapons, apparently for the man and boy alike. They made good progress through the jungle paths into the savannah but as it became jungle again at around midnight they dismounted. Jenny could not see the soldiers but assumed the men and the children had also dismounted and were moving through the jungle with them. When they arrived about half a kilometre from the village, Tunde selected five militias and their boys to follow him in. The rest, some twenty more, he posted and told them to follow two hundred meters behind and to keep absolute silence.

"We are going to enter the compound and surprise them at daybreak. This way we will take immediate control and meet with no resistance. There will be no bloodshed." He said this for Jenny's sake as if he really cared. From then on Jenny was obliged to continue to lead them to the position shown on the little electronic screen.

9

Joe was in the habit of making his last patrol of the periphery of the area just before daylight. The village had transformed from a peaceful hamlet falling into terminal decay into a busy mine and construction site. He took with him two leper scouts and a squad of Donny's crew. They looked for sign of trespass. They rarely found anything suspicious and their own incursions into the jungle would have covered the subtle signs left behind by enemy reconnaissance missions. After five weeks of the whole team's very productive activity Joe was becoming paranoid that they were being watched. He reported this back to Charles and the others. They had a small council of war. They took stock of the weapons in their possession.

The most powerful things they had were two RPG launchers and twenty triple grenades. Other than that they had managed to obtain six Kalashnikovs and eighteen boxes of various ammunition including some tracers, some high velocity and a lot of cheap Chinese steel bullets. Not enough to start a war but perhaps sufficient to fend off a disorganized enemy. Joe also had his sniper rifle and ammunition.

Father Driscol was insistent that the lepers be kept away from any fighting. If there was to be any trouble, he wanted them to be evacuated to a safe sanctuary. This meant they would have to find a clearing somewhere in the jungle nearby and build some temporary shelter to hide in if there was to be an attack.

On the fateful day, it was good fortune that Joe and the patrol were on the north side of the compound and heard the suppressed noises of the approaching militias. In silence they shadowed them as they entered the clay pit.

Charles, Anwei and Father Driscol awoke on the thirty fifth day of the operation to find six men and a collection of young boys touting assault rifles standing in the middle of the church square. A very large man in battle dress was at their centre.

"I am Colonel Nkwende Tunde. You appear to be stealing valuable minerals from this area in my domain," his English was clear and clipped. "I am sequestering all this equipment and the entire product and expelling all post colonial raiders from the area. You will be gone by noon or you will all be killed by my democratic liberation commandos."

Charles was surprised to see Jenny Bones who stepped out from behind the self-styled colonel. She was wearing a crumpled safari suit and jungle boots. In her hand she had a camera with a zoom lens. Anwei gasped, "My God, Jason Kalango!" as she recognized a smaller unarmed man in a striped shirt standing next to Jenny.

The next thing that happened shocked them all. There was the crack of a single shot, and the colonel fell dead with a bullet hole in his left eye socket. This was followed quickly by bursts of rapid fire from four other weapons, killing several of the boy soldiers and two of the men. Jenny had flattened herself on the ground behind the body of the colonel and was shooting pictures.

The whole episode took less than a minute. The surviving soldiers ran off into the jungle, followed by sporadic fire from Donny's crew, who were emerging from behind the church, bringing down a couple more boys and one more of the men. Joe strode out and handed his lightweight sniper rifle to the priest as he grabbed the best-looking AK-47 from a dead boy. He and the crew went in hot pursuit, firing short bursts and picking off the remaining fleeing boys and men.

Left in the square were the colonel and Jason, who were confirmed dead by Charles, several more dead men and boys. Jenny, having taken some more extreme pictures, was screaming.

"What was that for?" she shrieked. "For fuck's sake they wanted to stop you from stealing. He asked you nicely or at least they were ready to do a deal. You didn't have to massacre them. Charles, what are you thinking? You at least are supposed to be civilized. Can't you keep that white monster and his apes under control? He's killed boys, just young boys, at least five beautiful young *children*."

She had moved over toward the spot where Anwei had stopped, too near. Anwei stepped forward and slapped her right across her open mouth.

"Keep that stupid mouth shut," she ordered in a menacing low tone, assessing the situation instantly. "You idiot bitch, you brought these fighters here. You nearly got us all killed, and they would have killed you after they had finished playing with you. You would have been raped by fifteen or fifty filthy, depraved, jungle-hardened monsters. You would have been ripped open from your torn and bleeding crotch to your neck. You would have been shot or macheted by one of your precious children as part of his training and left to the ants, dead or alive. *We have saved your life.*"

Her words were strong enough, but her glare had all the harshness of a tiger facing a frightened prey. Jenny melted

331

under the assault and, desperately trying to hold back tears, bent her head to the ground and sobbed the deepest sobs she had ever experienced.

Anwei suddenly changed her stance. She moved over to the dead men. With her toe she turned one over. "Jason Kalango, oh, Jason." she turned to Jenny. "You know this man?"

"He is called Bobo," she answered. "He was my guide and he led me to the colonel."

Anwei stood and suppressed her urge to scream. "He was my childhood sweetheart and my first love." She turned to Charles. "Please, Charles, him at least we must bury properly."

She stood stiffly over the body, then turned away, her feminine grace returning. She put a hand on Jenny's shoulder and consoled her. "Come on, girl, we've got water in the church; you can wash away your grief. Between us we will need a river the size of the Congo."

The shots had all been fired from behind the church, toward the square, catching the warlord and his boys off guard. Joe, Donny and the crew had shadowed the squad for some time and had known exactly when to open fire, when they had clear line of sight. Charles was now worried for them, as they had followed their quarry into unfamiliar terrain. Apart from Joe none of them had any jungle experience. Fishermen do not get much call for it, and anti-apartheid terrorism calls for different skills: violence, yes, but hot pursuit into the thick tropical rain forest, no.

Father Driscol was not fazed by the action. He made the signs of the cross over all the bodies and mourned. "Such a waste. They are hardly out of nappies and should be with their mothers. But Anwei is right, they are all killers and had to be eliminated. So sad. May God bless their souls and bring them salvation in death."

The small group at the church was joined by the rest of the mining crew and some of the more able-bodied lepers.

"If any of them survive, they will join another group and we will be hunted down again," said Charles. "We have to move now. All of us must get out of here. The lepers' village is nearly complete, and they know how to build the rest of the houses. We cannot take our diggers and other machines with us, but they have done their job. If the Mai-Mai want to go on mining the coltan, that's fine. We will leave the fuel up in the village for the lepers."

Joe, Donny and the others returned.

"There were only two of them left," Joe said. "The two men turned and sprayed us with bullets. I was caught by two. One is in my right thigh, the other in my right arm. We killed all the children in the end. They were the most dangerous; two hid in ambush and nearly got us. It was only because I tripped on liana that I spotted them and was able to hit them both with one short burst. That was when the remaining two shot back at us and got me, but our return fire sent them running again. I don't think they were even wounded. These men of ours were good. Bloody fishermen! They can come on patrol with me anytime, but at this moment, Charles, get your tools out and patch up these bloody bullet holes."

"Right, Joe, we are packing up and going."

"Shit, man, that makes sense. Where's that fucking stupid woman, Bones? I'm in a killing mood and she may as well be next."

"Anwei is taking care of her. They're in the church and she's getting cleaned up."

"Jesus, the silly bitch. How do you think she knew where we were to lead those bastards here?"

"It's a mystery to me," replied Charles as he applied iodine to Joe's flesh wounds.

10

Anwei gave Jenny soap and water and a relatively clean towel.

"Do you have any things with you?"

Jenny still felt her voice was unreliable and that she might burst into tears again. She knew she had made some sort of terrible mistake but she was not at all sure how or why.

333

"No, my stuff is in a hotel in Kinshasa," she blurted. "I left there this morning, no, yesterday morning. We cut our way through the jungle all night."

"What made you bring that monster Tunde to this place?"

"He was a politician, I was told, a good man, not a common warlord, someone who cared for the people. I was led to him by the man who called himself a guide—Bobo, the man you recognized. He was supposed to find a local politician who could repossess the minerals of this area presently being exploited by a bunch of foreign thieves."

"How did you find this place?"

"I had the coordinates on a printout."

"What printout?"

"The printout was in the laptop bag. When I was still curious about the contents of the computer, I found it in one of the compartments of the case—you know, a document section. It was a printout on green lined paper with holes down the side. It was nonsense to me. I did not even recognize the fact that they were coordinates. Nor did I know what coltan was, but I read about it in the news just recently and all the bits of the puzzle fitted."

"Why did you follow us? It's not your business."

"I'm a journalist. It looked like a story. It's topical because Congolese coltan has been outlawed by the UN. To those bureaucrats in New York, it's another "blood" mineral fuelling the wars here."

"It is a story, but you are a crazy woman. What do you mean outlawed?"

"There's an embargo. No one can trade without a certificate of origin and all sorts of permits."

"What about Tunde? How could you get on with a man like that?"

"Bobo introduced him as a politician, just what I asked for. He said Tunde was advancing his people. When we got to his compound, all the children were in school, primitive, yes, but they were learning English language and arithmetic from a nice old teacher. I was happy to tell my story, as I was convinced you were about to start some sort of mining operation. I saw all the equipment in Cape Town. I recognized

334

some of it. I thought you must be after gold or diamonds and then I remembered the short article about columbite–tantalite or coltan, and realized this must be what you're after because only this type of mineral would yield enough revenue to justify an operation like yours."

She paused to take a breath and to try to take control of the conversation. "Who are you, anyway, asking me questions like this?"

"My name is Anwei Sojenji, and I am the owner of this land. I have the title deed. My son, Djarli, is the leader of the group helping me take my own minerals to sell before we get killed or chased out of here by jumped-up warlords like Tunde," she stated calmly.

"You own this place?"

"For this minute, yes. We will be leaving soon and be dispossessed or killed," she went on. "Your arrival with that vermin Tunde has shortened our chances, but we have taken enough. Djarli will organise our leaving. We are very proud of the leper village we have built. This place was occupied by lepers who made fine pottery which led us to the coltan. We have built them a village, a hospital and bought them drugs. We have pledged to buy them tons of supplies and drugs for the future. I fear your arrival, and the fact that two militiamen survived our resistance has put the whole project in danger.

"Your interests have clashed with ours and the sufferers will be the lepers. I feel it. Go, look around. They will have taken away the dead bodies by now."

Anwei had tired herself with Jenny. She went to lie down on the makeshift bed. Jenny had been dismissed from the church and had no place to go except out to the front. There was still blood in the dark sandy soil. Some lepers had come down to look around.

"Good morning, madam," said a gnarled and scabby old man with perfect diction with the trace of Irish brogue. "We hope you were not disturbed by the shooting. It is not normal. Normally this is a most peaceful place. Do you want to visit our beautiful village? We have started making pots and cups and plates again. We are firing them in the new cave-oven

Father Driscol gave us. We can use oil fuel now instead of charcoal. It is better."

Jenny was so surprised she could not answer but followed the man as he shuffled up the slope to the new village on the shelf cut out of the side of the pit. The neat, regular pot-brick one, two and three room dwellings were arranged around the square in the midst of which was the eating house. Fires were lit and basic food was being prepared. It was not appetizing to Jenny but she sensed it was nutritious and these people were proud to be preparing it. Jenny must have taken twenty more shots with her electronic camera.

After she had been shown a couple of the rooms, she left, found herself a hiding place around the back, sat down, and finished the weeping fit Anwei had so abruptly interrupted. After about five minutes she felt ready to compose herself and face the others. There was a lot of loud engine noise and crashing of steel going on down in the big pit. She made her way to the edge to see the men all busy loading the big trucks with drums and the old priest laboriously climbing up the sloping path towards her. She got a very atmospheric picture of him.

11

They had winched one of the containers on to the Kenworth flatbed with twelve drums of minerals inside and four drums of the remaining toluene lying on their sides and wedged. This was Joe's idea of a defence strategy. "If the terr's come after us, these could be useful," he explained.

Charles decided it would be best not to sabotage the equipment, though Joe and Donny were ready to remove the injectors from all the engines.

"There is no point. If the lepers or Mai-Mai want to carry on mining, we are not harmed by it. They may be interested to the point of not chasing after us. If they have the diggers and the equipment, they may not see the need to use slave labour."

When the Kenworth was loaded, Joe took command. Hamish, one of the mechanics, took the wheel. Donny and his crew lined up with Joe to shoot in defence. This would be the last vehicle to leave and the one to do any fighting if necessary. Father Driscol and Anwei were allocated seats in the cab of the army truck driven by Saul and, in the back, three men armed with AK-47s were ordered to defend the truck and the valuable contents of sixteen drums of minerals.

The time to leave drew near and the priest, delayed by the burial of Jason, started up to the village to say his farewells to the villagers. As he was climbing the familiar slope up to the new dwellings, he saw Jenny take a picture and then the shooting started. He was able to sense it all from his vantage point behind the wall. Screams and wails came from the lepers as they were mown down by gunmen. With loud explosions grenades blew apart the walls of the village. The priest stood aghast as he witnessed from close range the total destruction of the new village and the whole of his flock of lepers. Smoke and dust billowed toward him. What could he do? Jenny ran down and appeared in front of him, grabbing his hand. "Come on! Run down to the trucks."

Common sense overrode his sense of duty to his parishioners, and he raised his skirts and rushed back down with Jenny to the trucks, now both grinding their way out of the opposite side of the big pit.

Joe was leaning on the open door at the back of the container on the Kenworth, searching for signs of gunmen, when he saw Jenny Bones and Driscol emerge from the smoke and dust of the burning village, running down the slope. Joe raised his rifle towards her. His anger was intense, made worse by the pain he felt from his two flesh wounds.

"No," said Donny, pushing the AK-47 skyward. "She hasn't told her story. We do not know what she did or why. That is not your sniper rifle, but a choppa; you will kill them both. Get her on the truck and we'll find out what happened later."

They watched as Anwei opened the door of the army truck and put a hand down to help the priest up as it inched forward up the slope.

337

Jenny turned and approached the Kenworth. Donny leant down and handed her up on to the flat-bed and Joe spat at the ground in disgust. She clambered over the drums and found a spot to sit down and recover. Donny turned to Joe. "What are we doing with this toluene? We'll all fry alive if they hit us."

"Wait, they are busy in the village. They will then come down into the pit to look at their prizes. Then they may attend to us. This stuff is a barrier between us and them. At the moment we are in danger from it but soon this will be our lethal weapon. Did you load your magazine with tracer?"

"Just as you said, alternate with the steel rounds."

"Good. Where's the box? I need to do the same. This one is serviceable. I seem to have lost the one I started the day with."

The truck was lumbering up near to the edge of the big pit. The militias were dispersing from the ruined village. There were some twenty. Half were children shooting wildly as they struggled to control their heavy and powerful weapons. None of the bullets passed close to the retreating trucks. Their line of sight was soon broken as the Kenworth truck entered the thick jungle track. They were now getting close to the army truck ahead.

"OK, now we offload the drums of toluene," instructed Joe.

They took out the wedges on the first two drums and, as the truck heaved itself over the uneven ground, they let them fall off the back. About fifty metres on they let the other two go. The trucks were roaring as, in the lowest ratio possible and with all six wheels engaged, they forced their way at a slow walking pace through the broken undergrowth toward the graded road.

The first two drums were almost out of sight when the first group of militias came into view. Hearing and seeing the fleeing trucks, they started shooting. Joe turned to Donny. "Here we go." And the two men shot a short burst towards the enemy above their heads. They saw the men duck behind the drums and take up firing positions. The second burst from Joe and Donny strafed from a low angle and then struck home. The steel rounds tore into the drums and white-hot tracers exploded the contents. The lethal footprint would have been about fifty metres in all directions. That squad would all be dead. If more came they could repeat the tactic but they doubted any more would.

Inside the army truck Anwei was having trouble with Driscol. He apparently went into a coma but then suddenly his whole body went rigid and he screamed what sounded like, "Don't kick me! It's not me." His eyes were bright and frightened like a cornered animal, and he then started screaming, "Not the children, no, no, not the small boys!" She did not know what demons he was fighting, but she was worried because his whole body had stiffened and was convulsing. Then as suddenly as it began, it stopped and he went back into a coma.

She tried to make him comfortable but in the cramped and oven-hot cab with its steel bucket seats it was nearly impossible. They ground on for an hour or more at about four to five kilometres per hour with the priest raving every ten minutes. The driver, Saul, was struggling all the time to keep the vehicle moving forward on the overgrown track. They were aware of the Kenworth truck behind and had heard the explosions and shootings soon after they had entered the jungle.

At the metalled road they stopped. It was decided that Charles, Anwei, Jenny and Driscol would take the Land Cruiser, which they extracted from its off-road hiding place. The two trucks would be able to make between twenty and forty kilometres per hour on the improved road. The Kenworth had done the trip several times before, delivering drums of minerals down to Matadi. They were relatively safe from bandits if they kept motoring all night. They were to take shifts at driving.

Jenny wanted to be dropped off in Kinshasa so she could get going on writing up the unexpected story on her notebook. The number and nature of the photographs she had on her electronic camera would be sensational and, if she was quick, still very topical.

Father Driscol did not improve. He was having raving fits on a regular, slightly longer, twenty-minute cycle with a comatose state in between. Jenny said she had seen the Roman Catholic cathedral in Kinshasa. Anwei insisted they take Driscol into the city to find the cathedral. It was a good thing, because on their arrival they were greeted with a high level of indifference from the bishop and the clergy. They had to cajole and coerce them into caring for their brother priest. Anwei was not at all sure they would do much for him after they had gone, so she made Jenny promise to check up after two days. Jenny returned to the hotel from the cathedral and immediately crashed out on her bed. At nine that night she started writing.

Part 10: Anwei's Diamond

Charles drove Anwei on to Matadi, arriving just before the trucks.

They were greeted by a very irate captain. Chuck met them on the dock and had not the patience to hear their story of disaster before he butted in with the absolute bombshell.

"I'm sorry, boys, but our Chinese buyer has sent a message to say he has reneged. The reason is the United Nations universal embargo on West African rare earth and other blood minerals, along with gold and diamonds. Everything must have a traceable certificate of origin. There are no buyers except black-market skinflints who will buy at a possible fifty cents a kilo, two hundred dollars a half drum." He paused to see the effect on the gathered company. "This values our haul at about eight to ten thousand dollars.

"However, I propose we load all the remainder for whatever it is worth and try to work out how we can get a fairer price."

Charles sat on the running board of the Toyota and gripped his head in his hands.

"I would say, Chuck, that we are at the end of a very bad couple of days. We had to fight our way out of the jungle, breaking our backs to get the minerals out and killing dozens of various terrorists, bandits and young boy soldiers. We witnessed our dear friend, Father Driscol, go absolutely raving mad. Joe took two bullets, fortunately not serious, and now you tell us all your massive investment, my mother's inheritance, and seven weeks hard labour have been for a potential reward of eight thousand dollars." He paused and Chuck was unusually silent.

"I think I may go the same way as Driscol," Charles said quietly.

Anwei was looking on. She went over to be beside Chuck. "We still have our lives, the ship and fuel. Isn't that right, Chuck?" she said as she sidled up to him.

"Well, I guess you're right. There will be a market for this stuff some place and some time. It's real hot just now because the UN has just voted on it, but in time there'll be a way. The forgers will be producing certificates of origin as soon as trade picks up again. I've seen it before with other commodities. We'll never get the price we originally estimated, but we may recover more than eight thousand dollars."

They had all climbed aboard and with very depressing thoughts separated to their bunks and went into deep, oblivious sleep.

2

John Jones had a desperate need to put his hard-won theory to work. He was unemployable in academia, untouchable by the chemical companies who might ordinarily have engaged him and unlikely to get support from anyone for his great scientific breakthrough. In his research he had discovered that some minerals available in West Africa— Congo Kinshasa, to be more exact—that would allow him to perfect his technique. Taking some money from the bank account where he had deposited half the proceeds of his house sale, the other half going to his beloved but now divorced Wynn, he bought a ticket to Kinshasa. He found accommodations at the Daito Hotel quite comfortable and he ventured out only tentatively. He was way out of his depth in an alien continent, full of people too busy to give him the time of day, too ignorant to understand his quest and frightening in their behaviour.

On his second day around teatime, he came across Jenny, the only other white person in the bar of the Daito. She ordered a Cuba Libre and told him she had been writing all day, with short bouts of sleep in between and fighting with a very slow Internet connection. She was pleased to have transmitted her copy through to London but with only two usable pictures. Her agent assured her he would sell all of it to a Sunday paper for a very good price and syndicate it around the world.

Now she was in the money again, she offered the Welshman a drink, which he did not refuse despite his chapel upbringing and the early hour. He was interested to hear about where she had been but she was reticent to enlarge upon some fairly generalized statements about child soldiers and minerals. It turned into a very boozy evening during which both revealed more than they would have otherwise. When she mentioned coltan and nanoparticles, he said, "I know about all those things. If you know where they are and I know what to do with them, we could form a company and get rich."

"We couldn't sell the minerals now, because of the UN embargo," she told him.

"Ah but there is value there. You see, always associated with coltan are two vital types of carbon, Bucky balls and nanotubes. Invariably."

As the conversation progressed haphazardly, she suggested if that was the case, he should take a trip the seven-hundred kilometres down to Matadi and find a ship that had a cargo of minerals taken from a leper colony in the jungle.

The encounter with Jenny had been bizarre, but he managed to get a bus down to the port. He found the ship and approached it along the quay, where he found Charles and Joe watching the reloading of the vehicles and drums, now just part of the junk going to scrap.

"Hello, my friends, are you the owners of this ship?" Jones hailed them.

"Who wants to know?" growled Joe, who since his wounds in the jungle, was even less friendly than usual.

"Now look, you see, I've been chasing you people down. No end of trouble I've been through to find you. See, there was a rumour you had some of these nanoparticles. I heard about it from a lady I know." He held out his right hand toward Charles.

"John Jones, PhD. Yes, they used to call me Dr. Jones at Cardiff University, but I had to leave, you see. Very unfortunate accident. But now to the present. Am I right in thinking you are looking to sell some coltan and Bucky balls?"

"I am Charles Sojenji and this is my colleague Joe Krels. We have drums of refined coltan and perhaps Bucky balls and carbon nanoparticles as impurities."

"Mixed? Oh dear. Well, you see, I don't have any money to speak of. It was damned expensive getting out to this terrible place. No complaints, mind you. If you want to get rich you have to suffer, I'd say, wouldn't you?"

Charles did not answer directly, but raised his eyebrows enquiringly. The disasters of the last few days had left him worn and jaded and here was this strange, crazy-looking Welshman in baggy empire shorts and a Harris tweed jacket about to make him some sort of proposition. He had left Chuck and Anwei on the bridge of the vessel planning their voyage to Pakistan to scrap the *Fenix*. Work was slow on the dock as half the crew seemed to be on the point of mutiny.

"So without money how are you going to buy our cargo?"

"I have a very serious proposition. It is not guaranteed but I am told by your friend Jenny Bones that your scheme to make money from coltan has come a bit unstuck. She told me – rather gleefully – if I am to be truthful that it's become an illegal substance. She saw it on the local news – big story in this part of the world, you see."

Charles rejoined, "Jenny knows nothing. She's a dangerous hack. We told her we had no story for her and now it's sadly true. But we do have a saleable cargo. We have had a setback, as our best customer has backed out but there will be other customers."

"And I am your best customer now."

"We like customers with money."

"Don't you worry, Charles, may I call you Charles? You see, we are destined to be partners. Look, I've done my homework. This old ship of yours may turn out to be the other perfect part of my equation."

"What equation, Jones?"

"That's right, be a bit more friendly! My friends call me JJ. Look, are you the boss around here, or are you one of a team in this thing? Are other people involved? You see, this is very complicated. Could I meet the ship's captain, for instance?"

"I suppose we'd better hear you out. What is the broad brush proposition?"

"I can use the carbon particles to make materials that will make you very rich."

"We've been there. We know all about the pharmacists. The quantities are far too small, and we are competing against particles made in their own laboratories. Their price is only just viable or may be loss-making. The truth is, we very nearly all got killed in a raid by bandits."

"I don't need very much. How many drums have you got?"

"Never mind that. Come with me and we'll meet Captain Chuck."

They made their way on board to find the crew engaged in lashing the vehicles and drums to the deck.

John Jones took in the scene and seemed to be absorbing details of everything like a sponge sopping up fluids. They went up to the conference room, which had become the day room for the "upper deck" crowd. They introduced John Jones to the captain, who opened the fridge and handed out ice-cold beer.

"Well, Mr. John Jones from Wales, what can you do to save my ass from this mess?" asked Chuck amiably.

"Diamonds," he stated flatly.

The assembled company all turned toward the small bearded man in the blue tweed jacket.

"Fairy tales," retorted Chuck. "Look, buddy, why not just enjoy your beer and go? You can tell us a story if you like, but don't expect a response. We're rigging down for a scrap voyage to Pakistan. We can sell you drums of mud at two hundred dollars each, cash."

John Jones turned to the other people in the room and caught Charles's eye. "Look, see, Charles, I am sure you're an educated man, university and so on; I'm asking you to read some of my theory. See if you think it's possible. I had four years of rather lonely study in prison. Best thing that ever happened, twenty-three hours to myself every day. So I used the time for thinking. I managed to get my notes sent over from the university and continued from a perfectly theoretical point of view.

"You see, I first trained as a physicist, then I got interested in metallurgy and then in particle physics, but I did not want to discover a new particle. No, no, no, I was interested in practical things. I read all about Buckminster Fullerenes, Bucky balls, and nanotubes and made a lot of calculations. The thing that struck me was that these particles could be the building blocks for diamonds. Other engineers had tried to synthesize diamonds but they always failed. The sledgehammer boys succeeded with enormous forces and very high temperatures, literally bullying the poor little carbon atoms into crystal form.

"Behind bars, my friends, I was isolated from all that chitchat from other scientists. I studied all their methods for growing molecules and realized that before the accident I had been on the right track but I, like all the other experimenters, had missed out on some absolutely critical points."

"OK, Jones, why'd they lock you up?" interjected Joe aggressively.

"Terrible business, terrible. It gives me nightmares still. My assistant was a very bright post-graduate student. Lovely girl and a very good physicist. We were working on electrolysis as the method for growing crystals. We were trying to employ very high voltages in the electrolyte bath, thousands of volts. Well, in the rush to get results, I did not take proper precautions. The HSE inspectors did not understand what we were doing and I have to admit I did not really want them to. To cut a long story short, she put her hand into the

346

hypercharged tank while holding on to the rail and got a belt of about two thousand volts, which killed her instantly.

"Anyway, there were complications. The parents supposed I was shagging their daughter and went for the jugular, and the jury came down with a verdict of manslaughter based on criminal negligence. Eight-year sentence, I got.

"Saddest thing was that I wasn't, you see; she had noticed my interest and one day she said very quietly that I would do well not to get excited about her because she was in love with a girl and preferred to have cuddles and even sex with her. She was a lesbian, you see. Lovely girl.

"My brief said to me that if I wanted to see Welsh anger one hundred times worse than the wrath of God, just mention she was a lesbian in my mitigation statement. I could not possibly use it. Well, I didn't want to really, did I?

"I have not even applied for a job in academia because quite frankly, I see myself a bit more worldly now. Perhaps all those criminals who hanker after riches influenced me. But they all failed at robbing banks, burgling houses or defrauding old pensioners. Of course, I was a social outcast because the *News of the World* made a great thing of my relationship with Wendy, calling me a sex fiend and suggesting I killed her to get rid of evidence of my misdeeds. Oh yes, even the question: was she pregnant? I got bullied to hell inside. You see, I'm not handsome or young or sexy. A bit bald really, slope shouldered you might say, scruffy. They called me a cradle snatcher. I was not a nonce; after all, she was twenty-three. Criminals live in a cruel world. Well, I had in my head the means for a perfectly victimless way of making money." He looked around lugubriously.

"All right, JJ, let's cut to the chase," demanded Chuck.

"Well, you see, quite frankly, I saw something in the *New Scientist* about these carbon particles being found in Congo associated with coltan. I talked to few people after I got out and they said Kinshasa might be a good kickoff place to base myself. Big risk, warlords, Kalashnikovs, AIDS and malaria, but one of the few places where there is an open market in various minerals. I came down and then I met this woman called Jenny Bones in the bar of the hotel. She's an outback girl. Quite honestly, we had too much to drink and we joked about making a fortune as Jones and Bones or Bones and Jones. We were giggling like kids. But I said, 'How can we make a fortune?' And she said, 'Coltan or nanoparticles. We do like everyone else; steal the minerals from under the natives' feet.' Sarcastic she was. 'Can you believe it? I have just witnessed a gang of expats from South Africa taking tons of coltan and nanoparticles from *lepers*.'

"Oh, I said I know all about nano-particles and she said all I had to do was to take a nano-bag and some nano-dollars down to Matadi and find a ship called *Fenix*.

"Felix the cat," I said and we fell about laughing again.

"We were so drunk, we lost each other on the way to the bathroom or bedroom.

"To be quite honest I thought I was on to a promise, but I lost my way in the hotel and couldn't find her room. She had placed the key on the bar, you see, and I took it as a sign. I was probably wrong and anyway I was too drunk to remember the number. Terrible, isn't it, booze? Well, I sobered up and got the bus here."

"So you want to buy, but without money. We need money. We're not a charity for distressed Welsh academics," interjected Charles.

"No, you see, we have to work together. You have all the assets; I have all the knowledge."

"What knowledge? It seems you failed and killed your lesbo friend at the same time," Joe interjected aggressively.

"You are very cruel, you know, my friend. I only told you all that to give you my background. What you failed to grasp is that I will succeed now with the work I did in prison. It's pure physics. It's all to do with energy exchange and energy levels and hyper frequencies of oscillation. Quantum physics gives us the clue. The instantaneous energy levels are critical to the electrolysis."

Chuck moved forward to middle of the standing circle. "Well, look, JJ, you lost me a long time ago. What do you say, Charles? This is going to be a pig in a poke unless you know what this crazy professor is talking about."

"Well, Chuck, I don't understand the details, but everything he's said so far has made sense. Let's take stock of where we are. We just worked out we have enough fuel to take us to Karachi, where we have an open-ended contract to sell this old boat for scrap for a miserable fifty dollars a ton, less than half the world rate. The proceeds will buy our air tickets and a little spending money, then we are all back to square one. You will have lost all your pension money or capital for your next scrapping voyage. Anwei's deeds are worthless. Joe goes back to drive an ambulance and his buddies go back fishing. I look for a career in goodness-knows-what so I can support my mother in her senior years."

Jones butted in. "If my system works, I can produce diamonds that make the Koh-I-Noor look ordinary."

"Oh Jesus, and have you got snake oil as well in your bag?" remarked Chuck with a smile.

"Chuck, listen. JJ may have a point. Anyway, we haven't heard what he wants us to do. Go ahead, JJ."

The old air-conditioning unit that had only suffered the attention of the ship's bashers and kickers but no expert technical care, gurgled approval and squeaked back into life as the thermostat ordered it to counteract the growing heat in the room.

3

The management board was back in session: Father Driscol was missing, with luck committed to an asylum for mad old priests after seeing his dearly beloved lepers massacred by the Mai-Mai. The gathered company missed his growling advocacy, and they all regretted that their mission had lost its moral purpose and had degenerated into a final bid for survival. Anwei had taken herself off to sleep in the next-door cabin. Joe was suffering the pain from his bullet wounds silently, his bitterness thinly masked by a pragmatic acceptance of his fate.

Steve, the chief engineer, had joined them and lit up a disgusting cheroot, and JJ took a pause to stoke up his pipe

349

with some equally horrible non-branded tobacco. They all sat down at the conference table.

"You have what I need," JJ said through a cloud of acrid smoke. "Electric power and machinery, a water maker, chief?" Steve nodded. "Some plastic drums and did I see centrifuges?" Steve nodded again. "Absolutely vital. I'll even bet you may have some platinum anodes somewhere on this ship. You have some transformers and an old radar set with a magnetron, which I can use as a resonator to shake the Buckies and nanotubes apart from the coltan. Of course you won't have a radar anymore. Captain?" He tilted his head toward Chuck.

"Shit, that old radar gives such a dim picture, it ain't worth diddly anyway. Do what you want with it."

"Right. Now, I'll tell you what I have to do.

"I need pure water, so pure it has virtually no conductivity. It has to be distilled three or four times or purified by reverse osmosis. I need Buckies and carbon nano tubes, also pure and microscopically as even as possible. They need to be broken down to single disassociated atoms. This is a multistage procedure. I guess you have started by washing them out with toluene, very good. The centrifuges will be used to drop out the coltan, then we'll use a surface tension method to bring the Buckies to the surface. This fluid concentration we take to the magnetron bath to smash the molecules into smaller and smaller particles.

"The last procedure is the electrolysis basin, which we set up, if possible, in a glass tank. This is the dangerous bit. I will run some transformers in series to create around two thousand volts. I need some diodes, quite a small current. I need to avoid carbon dioxide in the water, which creates carbonic acid. Very low currents with very high potential gradients in the very pure water make for better conditions for growing. Am I making myself clear?"

Charles was thrilling to the theory. His chemistry training for his medical degree gave him a basic understanding of what the scientist was explaining.

"Go on," urged Charles.

"I am hoping that in ten kilograms of carbon molecules, we may be able to disassociate one kilo of atoms using the magnetron and assemble them into a diamond. Do you know how much that is? That's twice the size of the Koh-I-Noor, around two hundred carats. Properly cut, it could be a finished gem diamond the size of the biggest diamond in the world."

His eyes were lit up in a manic expression. Steve coughed once and then surged into a spluttering, coughing fit, threatening to eject his lungs onto the table. JJ came back to earth and drew deeply on his pipe.

"Of course, my friends, that is a vain hope. If we produce anything of that size, it will have to be cut down to allay suspicion." He really had their attention now; they imagined millions of dollars and each looked around as if to assess how many others they would have to share their fortune with.

"Well, we won't be making that because I don't think the synthesis can be sustained for long enough before impurities and external forces start to interfere. But we may be able to make diamonds of five carats or so and these will be saleable on the open market."

"OK, JJ. We get the picture but we would still have a problem selling these magical diamonds," Joe interjected as his interest had been raised above the level of dismissal to amused scepticism.

"Well, when I was drinking with your friend Jenny, I must have mentioned diamonds—no details, you understand, no connection with nano particles. She told me a story about an old Jewish gentleman she knew who had fallen on hard times after challenging De Beers over blood diamonds. She tried to make out she was the hero of the story, being an investigative journalist showing how the cartel was still trading in blood diamonds. Well, it was poor old Levimov who took the hit apparently. I've got a good memory for names, you see. Although I was drunk at the time, I made a special note of this man, knowing that at some time I might need someone to take care of fencing my product. He's not a young man and he was beaten about by the De Beers heavyweights. I can find out more about him from Jenny."

"Don't go near that bitch," said Joe. "She nearly got us all killed."

"Well, look, see, we don't have to contact her or her friend until we have something to sell. By then we may have found another outlet."

"OK, what you need won't cost us anything and we have stores on board and plenty of fuel," stated Chuck flatly. "We even have a cabin available, now old Father Driscol has gone. But I still don't know if we wouldn't be better to sail for Karachi."

"Chuck, we have two options: a dodgy Pakistani; we only know his name is Karamet Ali, but nothing else about him. He says he has a yard breaking ships in the Rahn of Kutch. Do we know anything at all about any of his promises? Not at all. This we have on trust from that shark who calls himself our agent. So we have a choice between Karamet Ali and this academic gentleman."

"Jailbird," said Joe uncharitably.

"You know, Joe, I often wonder how you escaped a long stretch yourself," snapped Charles, turning and glaring furiously at his unlikely comrade. "So let's be polite."

"OK, I'm with you. We trust JJ to haul us all out of this with diamonds," Joe rejoined petulantly.

"Really, it is Chuck who needs to make the decision. He's the one with the biggest stake in this," continued Charles.

"As I see it, we ain't got much to lose. The prof here is going to take the risks with his still and his high current and my busted radar. If he fails, all this junk is still junk or, if he succeeds, we got ourselves a working laboratory or diamond factory. Nobody is to go near this high voltage except him. If he fries himself, we ain't lost much 'cept a month or so. In that time we may find another better deal for the scrap or the coltan. We're burning less than half a ton a day using the genny on deck and we've still got about four fifty tons left."

"You won't notice the extra fuel I use. The actual current will be low," chipped in JJ. "Once we have made the first few diamonds, you won't be bothering about a few gallons of diesel," he added optimistically.

"Right then, Professor John Jones, you tell us what you need. All you have to do is make us some diamonds."

"Captain, I wonder if your engineers could manufacture a few small items for me. Can I take it you approve of that?"

"Go ahead, JJ, Steve here is at your disposal. He loves making things, eh, Steve? The thing we're really short of is ready money. The first opportunity you can, you make a diamond we can sell. We will be on short rations soon."

"And the radar?"

"All yours," Chuck confirmed.

"Oh, I'm only going to take the magnetron."

"To my way of thinking, Prof, that more or less *is* the radar. You take the heart out of a racehorse, you ain't got much 'cept dog meat." Chuck stood to address the whole company.

4

"Now listen up, everyone," Chuck said. "One beer a day from now on. The only thing we have a surplus of is fuel. We will make sure the fridge is kept well supplied with ice-cold water and possibly tea and sugar-water. When the beer's gone, it's gone. We're gonna have to move from here because we can't afford the harbour dues. I have a mind to anchor off Banana in the Congo estuary. When we attract attention, we will move on. I have got bags of flour and plenty of rice, but other items are nearly all gone. Soon it will be boiled rice and bread rolls for breakfast, lunch and dinner. This will not be a pleasant phase but our bosun tells me he will get plenty of fish down in the estuary and there are some wild plants we can gather from the nearby jungle.

"I don't suppose any of them locals wants to leave here in Matadi without the big bonus of success and I don't suppose you guys have any more money than I have. If the prof can't make diamonds, we go to Pakistan or India for scrap and fly out."

JJ did not waste any time in getting his lab together. His first task was to find out what the vessel had to offer in the way of materials and tools. Tom, the most adept electrician amongst the various engineers, was assigned to extract the magnetron and the firing circuit from the old radar.

The deckhands were designated to fix up a battered container to be JJ's air-conditioned laboratory. They positioned it right aft near the stern roller and lined the insides with packing-case plywood and even painted the inside white. A power supply was run from the deck-mounted generator. Tom managed to rewind one of the transformers from the main system so it would produce from five hundred volts to two thousand volts in taps of five hundred volts. This, JJ thought, would be sufficient.

Donny's mechanics were not short of welding supplies and they took steel stock from one section of the shortened crane boom and made laboratory benches and the frames and skids for the other machines.

JJ came to Chuck with an odd request.

"I was looking around upstairs, on the roof. You have a thing up there called an MDL FanBeam. I remember reading somewhere about these things. Is it a laser device of some sort?"

"Yeah. Man, you're everywhere from the keel to the truck, as they used to say, Prof. We had it for our last long contract five years ago. It was experimental. It's a Mark One laser range and direction finder - pretty handy. All the dynamic positioning boats have them now. That one hasn't been used for a few years. I guess it's obsolete. They're probably making the Mark Ten version now."

"Well, Captain, part of my theory calls for a laser beam to add energy to the electrolysis. The photons add to the bosons and can lift them over the disassociation threshold for a few nanoseconds, enough to allow them to reassociate in the diamond crystal configuration."

"It's y'all's if you can use it. I'll get someone to cut it down," Chuck said in complete incomprehension of what JJ had explained to him.

"Oh, and Captain, there's one more thing. Steve said there are some very big diodes for the bow thruster. I don't really know what that is, but he said you hardly use it anymore, now the ship is not running to the rigs. Does that make sense? I need diodes and they may be good for the electrolysis."

"OK," Chuck paused. "OK. I guess he's right."

He was presiding over the slow cannibalisation of his ship long before she reached the scrapyard. These things were "nice to have" items not affecting her general seaworthiness. "You're eating my ship alive, JJ. You better make some good diamonds, or I'll whup your little Welsh ass." JJ grinned and scuttled away down the alleyway.

5

A week later JJ pronounced he was almost ready to make diamonds. There was nothing else he needed, and he was building the final part of the laboratory: the electrolysis bath. They had found two platinum anodes, spares for the raw water pipework protection system. The engineers had made a frame from angle-iron and used glass from the crane cab and some sealant to form a tank about three quarters of a metre long with a width of half a metre and depth almost the same. The top was made of a piece of rigid plastic.

The centrifuges had been rewired to spin faster so he had managed to separate the nanoparticles from the coltan.

"You see, the theory is that we use very pure water with some of these invisible nano particles in it. I will be applying the magnetron to produce an electromagnetic standing wave using the stainless steel reflector plate at the back. By applying the laser, I am going to raise the available energy level so that the electrolytic voltage gradient near the anode exacerbated by the waves allows the deposit of a carbon atom into the diamond matrix. This will happen every ten to a thousand beats of the standing wave. Do you see?" he explained to Charles.

"At that rate we may be able to build about one carat every twenty-four hours. These diamonds should be perfect and completely flawless due to the way they are made. No impurities or inclusions can get in. If there are any impurities in the water, the procedure will shut down. A one-carat diamond of such purity is worth about twenty thousand dollars in the official market and may be sealable for a little bit less on the open market. Here in Congo we will have to accept a heavy discount but it's still good money. Don't you think?"

Charles was not impressed and wondered if they were all wasting their time.

"One thing may be causing a problem here in Banana and that is the ship's motion. Do you think we can stop the ship from moving?"

"I'll have to talk to Chuck," he replied without enthusiasm.

Chuck came down to look at the lab setup. "So, Prof, you want us to stop moving. This is a ship. This is about as steady as we can make her afloat." He paused for thought and continued, "But the hull of this boat was strengthened for going aground on a soft bottom. She used to work in the bayous of Louisiana in her first life. So you may be lucky, my old son. We will go up the creek to the south and find a beach, put the rescue boat out to survey the bottom and find a place where it's all clear, and run her up on the sand. It's more work because the crew will have to rig that five-ton anchor as a kedge to pull her back off again, but it can be done. We'll have to move this container as well. The cable for the anchor will have to pass over the roller there. This thing is in the way. A day should do it. There will be an angle on the deck, perhaps five degrees to the stern."

They got busy with the old Manitowok crane, with its foreshortened boom moved the container to the side and laid out the two-inch diameter working cable from the winch drum, shackling on the anchor. Samson and his crew, directed by Chuck, worked on the deck while Donny and Charles rigged a drag wire from the fast rescue boat and swept an area just off the beach to check for debris, rocks and wrecks. These jobs kept everyone busy all day.

Chuck was beginning to get worried about Anwei. She was always tired, slept for twelve or fifteen hours a day and had developed a nasty cough. She was no longer interested in sex and she no longer showed any interest in what was going on. He asked Charles to talk to her.

Anwei was reluctant to discuss her health with her newly found son, and he had a tendency to ignore fairly obvious signs of illness, dismissing them as symptoms of general jungle malaise. She had a fever so he gave her aspirin from the medical bag he always carried and then, thinking it might be malaria, gave her a strong dose of Novaquin and prescribed it for two weeks. When he thought of the rest of the crew, he was surprised this was the only case. He just assumed they had all been taking precautions as he had instructed and avoided bites.

The next morning, at mid tide Chuck dropped the stern anchor about three hundred metres off and very carefully ran the bow of the vessel up on to the beach. The deck took up an angle of about five degrees as predicted, and the motion stopped. The rise and fall of tide was less than one metre, so Chuck ballasted down and watched carefully to see the boat did not float as the tide rose. Satisfied, he sent Samson ashore with mooring lines from each side of the bow to put around two strong trees bringing the ends back to the winch drums of the windlass to tension up.

JJ was now happy. The container was shimmed up until it was nearly perfectly level, and JJ got ready to start the electrolysis. The nanoparticles were completely invisible in their solution. The water was evaporated by gentle boiling until it resembled a thick glutinous soup. JJ, satisfied by the increased specific gravity, introduced this into the glass tank. He then applied the voltage to the water and raised the temperature, taking care at all times to exclude air. He saw the current rise with the voltage to start with and then gradually the resistance of the water increased as the acidity reduced, until he was applying fifteen hundred volts and getting only a few amps of current and still reducing.

JJ was standing behind a glass shield rigged up for protection, with the control of the transformer in his hand. He knew the next step in voltage was critical. He waited until the current had dropped below a tenth of an amp and then switched to two thousand volts. He knew now that the voltage gradient near the anode was approaching the level he needed to disturb the electrons in the Bucky balls. This would allow the creation of a new molecule of carbon or the birth of a diamond. He applied the magnetron to create standing electromagnetic oscillation and then shot the laser at the site, hoping the photon energy would be just enough to force the atoms across the threshold from nanoparticles to diamond. He knew nothing would appear for several hours and that he had not given himself any method for monitoring his progress.

He waited an hour and then a second hour. He could see nothing. Everything remained in a steady state. He daren't move for the possibility of vibration interfering. JJ slept for the next two hours while the procedure continued. He awoke with a start and noticed bubbles rising from the anode. He immediately stopped the current. It was what he had feared most; the water had started to break down due to its own electrolysis. Oxygen was being produced at the anode, and the carbon was coming off as carbon dioxide. He had cut the current just in time. The acidity of the water had risen and the current with it. In a few seconds the chain reaction would have led to an explosion.

JJ was shaking like a leaf. He dismantled the apparatus and took the anode out of the tank for microscopic examination. Barely visible under the microscope, he saw a dark mass. It could only be a diamond, but again it could only be about one or two points, or two hundredths of a carat. Still shaking, JJ opened the heavy container door to the absolutely black night. He looked at his watch. It was two in the morning; he had been hard at work since the previous morning. He was still shaking with fear and excitement.

The diesel generator must be the culprit; its vibrations were coming through the deck to the container. He returned to the container and shut it down by pressing the big red emergency stop button. When he returned, the silence was stunning. He used his little torch to make his way up the sloping deck to the quarters.

"Hello, Prof," said the duty sailor, looking out from behind the crane. "What happened? The genny stopped. Shall I call the engineer?"

"No, my man, no, no, no. I have succeeded. One small problem remains, but I have made a diamond."

"Right." He paused. "You will surely need some cocoa then, sir?"

"Oh yes, boyo, cocoa it *shall be!* My God, do you know what this means?"

"Well, we got some new stores today: sugar, cocoa, and yams. That very good for us." He paused. "Will we all be rich then, Prof?"

"It means there will be a big payday for us all, young man!"

"Right, sir, there's some hot water in the galley. Wait here, I bring cocoa right out."

JJ sat down on a bollard. It struck him suddenly that he had succeeded and failed at the same time. As an academic scientist, he had proved his theory, but as a man trying to save the "*Fenix* operation," he had a long way to go. Perhaps this crewman was right. He had produced a diamond that on its own might pay for a few sacks of victuals.

He spoke to Steve about the vibration the next day. Steve went away to think about it and came back scratching his head, which he tended not to do until he had solved problems. "I have some rubber bungee, about ten tonne safe working load. It was junk from a drilling rig Chuck had us save. It got forgotten, but it's been in my parts store for five years or so. My idea is to have the genny suspended from the crane. I will ask Chuck."

"I am in charge of a nuthouse, so one more crazy idea from you technical whiz kids don't bother me. Have Joe or Donny check it out and make sure they use guy ropes and suspend it not more than a foot or two over the deck." Chuck exclaimed.

Over the next week JJ did seven more fifteen-hour runs. Each time he made a rough diamond. The biggest one was fifty points or half a carat. They were a bit irregular in shape, being flattened. The largest one was enough to be cut into a small gem.

"I think it is time to send for Mr. Levimov," he told Charles. "How we get him here, I don't know. But I need someone to assay the product. In theory they are near-perfect diamonds, but as they say, the proof..."

"What have you got so far?"

"Six rough diamonds, about two carats altogether. Sold together should be worth about three or four hundred dollars, perhaps."

"No, JJ, we simply don't have any money. You have to make about fifteen hundred dollars worth and we have to sell them to pay for Levimov to come over. You've got to improve the procedure, make some bigger bloody diamonds." He looked at Jones and saw a man near the end of his tether.

"The bloody electrolysis goes unstable too soon. It works for ten or fifteen hours and then suddenly the current goes up and the water disassociates into hydrogen and oxygen, threatening to burn up the diamond deposit already grown."

"Have you any idea what causes this?"

"It may be carbon dioxide from the air. We are not able to seal the top sufficiently. Or perhaps some of the disassociated atoms are finding oxygen atoms and creating CO_2 rather than building the diamond. Then the resistance goes down and a chain reaction starts and there is risk of an explosion. It's not happened yet."

"Any ideas?"

"Well, for safety I am already having a power cut-out fitted. As soon as the current increases the breaker will drop out."

"Good, but does that help production?"

"I have to exclude the air, you see?"

"Oil on the surface?"

"What kind of oil?"

"Ask Steve."

So it was that JJ started to experiment with a thin layer of lube oil on the surface. The result was startling. The rate of growth went up five times, so in twenty hours he produced the first three-carat diamond. But still JJ did not know what to do with it.

6

"You know what they say about Mohammed and the mountain?" he said to Charles after he had separated it from the anode.

"What?"

"Can we send one of the South Africans back with the diamond?" asked JJ. "We get Levimov to look at it and telephone the results to us. He could even sell it and then come up here if he thinks there is a future."

"I'll get Joe to contact Miriam. We are all flat broke. Perhaps she can pay for a ticket. Ten thousand rand is a lot to find."

As it turned out, Joe was ready to go home anyway to get some better treatment. Miri dug into their life savings and bought a return ticket from Kinshasa to Cape Town via Johannesburg. Joe stuffed some clothes in a duffle bag and buried the diamond in the pocket of some dirty jeans. He showed his seaman's papers at the airport and was not bothered.

Joe went directly to the shop and asked for Mr. Levimov Senior.

"Ah, my boy, I've been expecting you. You have a diamond, I think," he said.

"This," Joe replied, handing over the stone in a crumpled bit of tissue. "Why are you expecting me?"

"Right, wait," the old man said, not answering the question, but taking the stone and disappearing into the back room. Three minutes later he reappeared. Joe thought it must be a rejection.

"Very interesting. Synthetic. Molybdenum inclusions in the surface but under that, where I have polished, a pure diamond. Probably flawless and colourless. Do you have more?"

"Perhaps," said Joe guardedly.

"Jenny Bones is interested in you. Are you her friend?"

"Acquaintance." Joe could not lie about Jenny Bones.

"Are you selling?"

"What's the offer?"

"Fifty thousand rand, ten percent cash now; for me it's risky. I have to find a principle buyer."

"A hundred, more like," said Joe, trying to get what JJ had suggested.

"Take it with you, my friend," Levimov said, wrapping the stone back in the tissue. "I don't know anyone who'll pay that, but you can try."

"Meet me," said Joe, knowing he was not up to beating this wise old Jew.

"Fifty-five thousand is very generous, I can do that. If you have more from the same source, come to me and we can maybe give you better terms. I will have to polish this one to assess the quality."

7

Back on board JJ was busy. The lube oil had been a breakthrough. The latest diamond was twice the size and took about twelve hours before the apparatus shut itself down. JJ didn't know why, but he speculated that the molybdenum in the oil was dispersing into the water and acting as an accelerator or catalyst.

"Look, these diamonds make about five hundred to a thousand dollars even here in West Africa. They are worth more. Joe says Levimov liked it and paid more than half its value. Got to be a good sign from a jeweller who knows his stuff."

"I'm paying a full crew. One a day doesn't make sense. Can you increase the yield?" asked Charles.

"There are two ways; firstly, we can increase production and make the procedure more efficient, and secondly, we can get a better price."

"Right. What can you deliver?"

"Production requires better equipment. I've proved the process, but it's not as effective as I hoped."

"OK, so what about price?" pressed Charles.

"Let's get Levimov up here, shall we? I need a diamond expert for two things. First I want to know what we are producing in the way of quality, and also what is the best size for the market. Then we can tailor our production for maximum cash yield. At the moment we are not getting rich, but we have potential."

"I suppose I can leave Joe to recover and fly Levimov up using the return half of Joe's ticket. Joe may not like it. Still, it's the best plan. I'll tell him when he phones; that is, if he is prepared to come."

JJ went back to work. He was under pressure. These people had been good to him, and he had had the chance to prove his theory. It had worked. Production now became his priority. He took a chance on what had been nagging him these last few days. Could he risk increasing the current density by moving the cathode closer to the anode? The risk was breaking the water into component hydrogen and oxygen, burning the diamond, and potentially causing an explosion.

Cautiously he moved the electrodes nearer by ten percent and started the process. He monitored the start-up and slumped down on the rubber mattress for a short nap.

The tedious routine had continued on board until one or two people noticed that JJ had not shown up for any meals or contacted anyone for a couple of days. When they tentatively opened the door of the container they had found JJ on his mattress suffering from heat stroke. Two sailors had hauled him off to the small hospital. Charles had rehydrated him with a saline drip, and he was still sleeping when Donny and the jeweller arrived. Nobody had dared to go near the apparatus, knowing it was high voltage and that JJ's previous assistant had killed herself by electrocution. So they left the electric tank going with the dedicated generator motoring away on its rubber suspension.

8

Two days after their first encounter, Joe returned to the jewellery shop.

"Mr. Levimov, I have a proposition for you. You saw this stone I brought you and you rightly spotted it was a synthetic diamond. I don't know anything about diamonds or the procedure. I am just a messenger. Would you like to be in on it?"

"You want me to be involved in factory diamonds?"

"You are being offered in on the deal."

"You are confident about the stone you showed me?"

"Look, Levimov, if it was crap, you would not have touched it, right?"

"OK, OK. Where is it, this factory?"

"DRC. Mouth of Congo River."

"Am I mad or what?"

"I was told you are interested in diamonds. Life has not been kind to you. Look at this little shop. I bet you sell more copy watches and Chinese trinkets than genuine jewellery and not much of anything. Your son is here?"

"He left. He got a job as a grader in a mine in Brazil. You're not wrong, my friend," he said sadly. "So what is it I have to do?"

"You fly up as soon as convenient. You live on board a ship. You come down to Cape Town with them."

"Do I get paid?"

"It's a venture. Everyone gets paid if you know how to sell the product. If not, we all go broke. Well, I guess you already are." Joe was guessing. There was hardly any stock in the shop, and the old man was distinctly shabby. He had seen what looked like a bed through the door to the back room.

"Is it so obvious?"

"No, no, of course not. I just thought you might like an opportunity. You know."

The old man looked up glumly at Joe. "When do we go?"

"As soon as you're ready, there's a flight at around four this afternoon. I'll make your booking. I'll collect you at one from here and we'll go straight to the airport."

Levimov was shaking slightly; this was obviously both a shock and an opportunity he could not refuse.

When Joe returned in a taxi, Levimov was standing on the kerb. The shop was shuttered with a plain, unpainted zinc roller door, and the man was standing there in a gabardine coat, black trilby, and a small black fibre suitcase.

"Hello, Mr. Levimov. Everything OK? Passport, all that?"

"You may call me Izzy; my friends do. I guess you are my friend if we are to be travelling companions."

"Ah, well, I'm not going. I've just come back. I've arranged for you to be met at Kinshasa by my brother-in-law. He'll take you on to the vessel. You'll be very safe with him. He's about two metres tall and built like the proverbial…"

"Look, what about food? I have to be as strict as possible."

"Don't worry about that. There's not much meat around, mostly fish. You got some money with you? Just buy what you need and keep a note. We'll repay you."

Levimov looked less and less happy, but he did a mental shrug of the shoulders and acknowledged that his fate was possibly no worse than staying at home in a doomed little shop, unable to restock, simply living off the dwindling sales of the goods on the shelves until it had all gone. The premises had been hocked to pay Aaron's fare and the premium to the agent who found him the job in Brazil. His son's last letter said the pay was about half that promised and expenses were high. There had been a small money order in the letter.

At the airport the old man fussed about currency and worried about the exact spelling of his name, to which Joe had inadvertently added an *e* at the end. Then the meals on the flight: "I must have kosher food. Not only for my religion but for my digestion. My juices are not able to cope. The whole of my life—very strict." And then, "What about my tools and instruments? Will they think I am a terrorist?"

Joe finally lost patience. "Levimov, you couldn't be more Jewish if you tried. Jews do diamonds. They are the tools of your trade. Go! And have a nice trip" He almost physically pushed him into the security check.

Donny was there to meet the nervous Levimov as he filtered through the arrival funnel. He was told what sort of man to look for. There was no mistaking.

"They asked me too many questions. I should have had a contract. They don't like people messing with their diamonds. Finally they believed a story I was able to fabricate about having a private client very close to power. They charged me for a seven-day visa and said I would go to jail if I overstayed, all the time poking these stubby sub-machine guns in my ribs. Not friendly."

Donny was puzzled by this dapper little man in the faded gabardine coat and trilby hat. Not the usual attire for a long bus ride through the jungle and then a longer trip in a pirogue. The two made a strange sight, the tall muscular African with the baseball singlet and cap, and the black-clad man about half his size, carrying his suitcase, which he refused to entrust to his minder.

By the time he arrived on board, Levimov was a wreck. His nerves had been tried ever since they left and had to squeeze into a battered and rattling minibus for the sixteen-hour trip to Matadi and then a few more hours in an equally inhospitable Toyota Land Cruiser until they took to the motorized pirogue for the final leg. As it included a good few miles subject to ocean swells as they rounded the headland between the river estuary and their creek, he became violently seasick and dehydrated. He went straight to bed after copious quantities of water and salt fish, which was being served with rice for that day's meal. He did not waste any energy on niceties, introducing himself. He groaned mostly.

When JJ was told that Levimov had arrived, he perked up had a shower and appeared in the galley demanding food. He was duly given a bowl of rice porridge with sugar and salt.

"Delicious," he announced. "Now where's our diamond expert?" he asked, placing a small canvas purse on the table in front of him.

Levimov appeared, looking decidedly unhealthy.

"Are you Mr. Jones?"

JJ smiled and nodded in agreement. "Mr. Levimov, I presume."

"I only eat kosher food. It's my digestion."

"We have rice porridge with sugar. Added salt is a good idea to make it taste better and to take care of heat stroke, you see."

Levimov grunted as the cook put a bowl of the grey slop in front of him.

"You think you can make diamonds."

"You've seen one and I'll show you some more so you can tell me whether they will make us rich or even more broke than we are, if that would be possible."

"I suppose the procedure is electrolysis."

"I like to call it 'enhanced electrolytic transposition'."

"It's what I have been fearing all my life. It had to happen. I am a simple diamond man. Natural stones are my thing. I have worked the trade from the deep mines to the high-class boutiques. My great-great-grandfather worked with Rhodes. We always feared a process that would really work. All the methods so far have been nearly as expensive as mining. So let's see what you have." He paused and wiped his mouth on the back of his hand. "This is very good for simple fare. Just a hint of chocolate. It's not easy to make rice porridge interesting."

"We'll get yams for lunch and fish, if we are lucky. There is what they like to call coffee, if you're thirsty. It's quarter-strength instant with some molasses added for colour. Not bad if you don't remember real coffee. We had powdered milk, but that's all gone."

JJ poured out a cup for Levimov. "Look, everyone calls me JJ, better than Mr. Jones, don't you think?"

"Izzy," said the old Jew, holding out his hand.

They sat in silence for a few minutes, neither quite sure where to start.

"Look, here's a bag of product so far. Not much for the size of the bag. A bit optimistic—the bag, I mean." He laughed nervously at his little joke.

"Why don't you have a glance at those while I go and see how the laboratory is getting on."

Levimov sipped at his drink and gestured agreement to JJ.

The container was so hot inside, JJ could not enter until he had let some air in. The strip light over the tank was glaring down into the liquid below.

The first thing JJ noticed was a gigantic mass at the anode. It was a dull grey and lumpy object. There was no bubbling. JJ noted the voltage was steady. He had no way to know whether the process was continuing or stopped. He paused for thought. The only indicator would be the presence or not of nanoparticles in the water. This could be detected by the density of the solution. This was the first time he had contemplated the procedure running on until there were insufficient particles in the solution. There had been no instability to shut the current down.

For three days while he had been sleeping and then recovering, the electrolysis had been chugging away without interruption. He tried to assess the size of the mass. At first he thought about a hundred grams and started shaking with excitement, but then on closer examination and taking into account the magnifying effect of the parallax, looking from air to the denser medium, he reckoned realistically it could be twenty-five grams. *That'll do,* he said to himself. He hesitated before pulling the breaker cutting the power to the bath. The words "Koh-I-Noor" came to mind.

Very carefully he checked that the bath current had ceased and the high voltage had discharged fully by dipping the heavy copper earthing cable into the tank. He dropped a small glass hydrometer into the tank and measured the density of the fluid. He was right. Practically all the particles had been used up. The specific gravity was about one percent above pure water. The diamond may well have started to deteriorate already. With great precision he lifted the anode out and prized the lump off the platinum rod. On the underside the diamond was bright, but most of it was dull and uninteresting.

Taking a small cloth bag, he dropped the stone in and checking quickly round his workplace, he put it in the pocket of his coveralls and opened the heavy container door to take it to show Izzy.

9

Charles was getting more worried about his mother as the days passed. The fever did not seem to abate with simple medication and bed rest, and he had noticed a few unpleasant-looking patches on the lower parts of her legs. The cough was persistent and reminded him of tuberculosis patients he had been obliged to see during his training. She was now sleeping for sixteen or eighteen hours a day. He went to Chuck and asked about departing.

Chuck said he'd noticed also and he was equally worried. Neither wanted to face the possibility staring them in the face.

"Look, we can bring her back to health if we can get her to a clinic in some civilized place. What about Cape Town? Can we leave now? Even if it takes a week, we have a chance to get her proper attention. She might get better on the trip, but we both want to be sure."

"What about the diamonds?"

"We'll have to stop that operation."

"Just as we have the whole team together."

"What do you mean, the whole team?"

"Well, the old jeweller is here now, and he can tell us what they're worth."

"Bollocks to those two old farts. We should look after my mother."

"To me it was a bout of malaria. We all get it from time to time. Occupational hazard in this area. Mostly it lasts five days, leaves you feeling fucked, and goes away. She's had it before."

"If I'm not mistaken, she has lost weight—not just because she's not eating, but more."

"You're putting the goddamndest idea into my head. The big C or even the big A. Eh, Charles, is that what you're thinking?"

"Get JJ up here. Let's talk to him. We have to stop this nonsense and get to Cape Town. It's bloody urgent. Our thoughts are in the open now, so let's act."

JJ came bounding up the companionway, his eyes alight with a new fire.

"My God, you won't believe this! The biggest blooming diamond Izzy has ever seen and he's seen them all. You can't imagine his reaction. He's visibly shaking. He can't hold it still. I gave him some of our coffee, and he went to his cabin to examine it with his box of tricks. My God, it bloody works. John Jones, I'm a bloody genius. It will be the Hilton from now on, no more beer, champagne all round."

"JJ, shut up a minute," said Charles coldly enough for the scientist to stop in his tracks.

"Oh my God, what will spoil this day?"

"Anwei is very ill and we going to leave for Cape Town now. You have to shut down your operation. We stow all the loose gear and lash the generator down. Your container will have to be brought forward again, and you have to fasten everything for sea."

JJ listened with horror as his dream of untold riches seemed to be evaporating. "But..."

"Do it, JJ. I'll turn out all the hands to help you. Remember, Anwei is the owner and sponsor of this operation. You may save us all yet, but we must save her first," said Chuck seriously.

"You are right," said JJ, looking contrite. He walked thoughtfully down the alleyway and the stairs to the lower deck.

Levimov, a man not given to extremes of expression, said simply, "Well, Mr. Jones you've done it. Whatever your method is, you have produced a diamond perhaps the third biggest in the world and such a shape that can be made into a unique gemstone. It is flawless and perfectly white. Some coloured diamonds would be worth more per carat, but this one may cut to about one hundred carats, and the offcuts will be nearly fifty carats of saleable diamonds of between fifty points and three carats. I can start cutting immediately."

"We are stopping the electrolysis."

"Oh, just when you seem to have mastered it. Just as well, I suppose. The diamonds will threaten the livelihoods of thousands or even millions of people. I always feared the invention of a process that really worked and was cheap."

"Please, Izzy, stop for a moment. Anwei, who is the boss woman here, is very sick."

"What boss lady? Why?"

"All the base minerals for my procedure came from her land. The diamonds are really hers until she chooses to pay us off for our efforts. We are going to Cape Town immediately."

"Do you think I'm upset about that?"

"It will take a week and there is no food except rice. We will have to tidy up the ship now."

"Will I disturb you as I create the finest gemstone I have ever been privileged to work on?"

"Just warning you, rice with sugar, molasses, coffee will get boring."

"Don't worry about me. I could lose a few pounds, and I can digest rice well enough."

There was some fish in the cold store, but the diet was restrictive. No yams or vegetable after the first day. Everything was boiled due to lack of oil or margarine of any sort. The flour had all gone, so no bread. However, many of the crew members were keen to return to urban life, having spent far too long in the jungle or in the confines of this small ship with its tiny shared cabins.

Levimov remained shut in his quarters, emerging only three times a day for his bowl of rice. He was not talkative and gave no clue as to his progress in cutting the gigantic stone. Of course, everyone was interested but nobody dared ask the strange old man who they were told was going to help create success out of their disaster. No one had had any kind of payoff yet, and they had all suffered hardship, danger, and hard work; and now they were reduced to three bowls of boiled rice a day, augmented only by fish in the evening and some soy sauce that had been found squirreled away in the drawer under the chief cook's bunk. They drank a beverage made of water, sugar, and molasses. Some called it Coke and others stout.

A week later at six in the morning, on one of those beautiful clear days when the table mountain sports a white cloth of cloud just to emphasize its remarkable shape, they were about five miles off Cape Town harbour and called for permission to enter.

10

Chuck left Donny in charge, and he and Charles went down to the conference room. JJ and Levimov were there in deep discourse.

"Ah," said JJ. "Captain, Charles. Izzy here has surfaced. He wants to speak to you.

"Shoot, Izzy. We're listening," said Chuck.

"You want I should give you the bad news or maybe the good news?"

"We're not up to games, Levimov," said Charles severely. "Tell us the story. Are we broke or are we flush?"

"You are not broke. You are pretty well flush, but one snag. Are you going to let me explain?"

"Please, keep it short, please, no embroidery."

"I have just cut a gemstone about the size of the Koh-I-Noor. By my rather rough scales, it weighs in at one hundred carats and has cleaved very satisfactorily into a very beautiful flat, round, finest white jewel. It will appear larger than the famous jewel, as it has a more advantageous shape. As predicted the off-cuts amount to about fifty carats, all saleable. The value of the off-cuts is around six million dollars and includes two super ideal at eight and six carats, six very good clear between two and four carat and a handful of mixed gems and industrials of less than one carat. The big stone is priceless and unfortunately that means priceless. You want to get us all killed? Put it on the market." He paused while the import of this statement sank in with the gathered company.

"You want I should show it to you?"

He unrolled a white linen napkin and there it lay.

The others in the room previously unable to judge a diamond from a shard of glass were not impressed at first, but gradually the power of this unique entity started to captivate them. There was silence as they all stared transfixed at the dazzling object on the white cloth. It seemed to grab the light from the windows and reflect it back outward with amplified intensity. Izzy watched with satisfaction as his creation worked its magic on the small congregation. They were gradually becoming overawed. JJ was hardly able to keep his hands under control, wanting to grab it and exert total possession.

"You are looking at an extraordinary object, gentlemen. You think I've ever seen a larger pure flawless white diamond? You imagine I have ever heard of and seen and handled and cut anything like this? Is it sent here by God or *tayri* to tempt us?" He paused thoughtfully, "No, JJ made it. We are all immensely privileged to even see it from such a close vantage point. You must thank JJ for devising a method for growing such a great stone."

JJ looked overwhelmed by the accolade as the others turned to him. "Well, Izzy, what can we do with it?" JJ asked quietly.

"Absolutely nothing in South Africa: I would suggest the only places are China and perhaps Russia, but the risk of getting killed are very real, whatever we do."

"Can you cut it down to many gems?" asked Charles.

"My boy, I could but I won't. Whatever happens, I refuse to reduce this magnificent stone. It would go against all my instincts. I was taught by my father and his father before him that the diamond is sacred and must be cut in such a way to yield the finest gem possible."

"Whoa, stop there, you two," interrupted Chuck. "This stone is Anwei's, and she will decide what happens to it. She'll hear you out, but the final word is hers."

Anwei entered in her grubby nightclothes. "I heard my name and suppose you have something to show me."

"This is your diamond," said JJ humbly. They cleared a way for her to approach the stone on the white cloth. Nobody had touched it since Izzy had rolled it out. She picked it up and held it in her pale palm.

"It's heavy, it's bright. Is it worth money?"

"Perhaps a hundred million dollars US," said Izzy without enthusiasm.

"Quite a lot," she replied dully. "Good." The gathered company listened to this rather surreal exchange in silence. "You have succeeded and the expedition is going to pay you back, Chuck." Her eyelids were drooping, and her face paled visibly. "I am going back to bed. I am weak. Djarli, please come."

When they were back in the cabin, Charles noticed a strange and unpleasant smell. She went straight to her bed and lay down exhausted. "Djarli, I am dying quite soon."

She coughed, making a horrible, hacking, dry sound. "I can hardly breathe sometimes, and when I do, it is very painful. You're a doctor. You must know what the problem is. It's slims and possibly something I got from the lepers. They have diseases."

"We are in Cape Town. You will get good treatment and you'll live to an old age."

"What for? Chuck doesn't care for me anymore. You don't really know me, and I don't want to burden you. Whatever you say, my dear Djarli, I am just a sick old woman. I've had a good life and I'm proud of you. Just let me die quietly. Make yourself comfortable with the money. Look after Chuck. He's not a bad man, just a wanderer. I love him for everything we have done, and I know he loved me and cared for me, but bad stuff happened and a lot of things went wrong. When we met again, I couldn't tell him how bad things had been and why I had not been able to stay in contact. He was angry." Her head flopped back on the pillow and she was almost instantly asleep. Charles watched her for a moment as she breathed deeply and peacefully.

The *Fenix* continued on her course toward Cape Town and waited about half a mile outside the harbour entrance for the pilot launch to bring a pilot and customs and immigration officers to the ship. Chuck was dealing with the boarding officers. The last recorded port was Matadi. The cargo on the afterdeck was manifested as scrap, and the customs raised no particular questions. The fact that the assistant cook was sick was not their problem, as long as she was not suffering from one of the listed diseases to be reported.

Charles went into her cabin next to Chuck's to check. He called her name and gently took her outstretched hand. The hand was cold. He felt her wrist for a pulse and then tried to detect breathing before he feared her whole body was clammy and cold. He knelt on the floor beside her bunk and stared at her placid face. She appeared to have died. He reckoned she must be about forty-eight years old but did not know exactly. After a time tears welled up in his eyes and the woes of the world seemed to descend upon him. It was probable her illness was hastened by HIV. Just at the time when anti-retroviral drugs were becoming available and effective, she had been up in the jungle, undiagnosed, while her doctor son, researcher in AIDS, was too busy trying to organize a crazy get-rich-quick scheme. She had never known wealth or even basic security. Her life had been a constant struggle with interludes of joy. Of course, it was his imagination filling in the enormous gap in his knowledge of his mother. He stayed there for another five minutes while he heard Chuck on the VHF exchanging information with the harbour at Cape Town.

He had noticed that all the time they had been at the village she had felt responsible for the lepers. The whole project had grown on her and seemed to have given meaning to her life. She had wanted to make a difference, even it was just to a small community in the middle of the Congo jungle. They were, after all, her people, some anyway, and she needed a cause. The mission was her undoing. Her compromised immune system may have been unable to deal with the coughing, breathing, and affectionate kisses of the grateful lepers. Her insufficient resistance to the deadly bacteria spreading to her throat meant it had become life threatening. She was only a short trip away from effective treatment of the leprosy, but the HIV had probably already laid her open to a host of other infections that she would normally resist with her natural immunity. All this Charles was thinking as he covered her shoulders with the grey sheet.

Finally he raised himself to his feet and made his way up to the bridge. His sad demeanour must have surprised Chuck, and then of course he got the telepathic message. He raised his eyebrows, questioning.

"I don't know, near to death or possibly already dead. I can't feel a pulse and she's cold and clammy." said Charles as a flat statement of fact.

"Lordy," said Chuck quietly.

Chuck was not unsympathetic, but it struck Charles that he wasn't suffering much for the loss of his erstwhile lover and companion. Charles supposed they must have grown apart during their time in the jungle. Anwei had made the journey back to Matadi a couple of times, but found the noise, heat, and lack of comfort in the big Kenworth truck very arduous. She had kept returning to the village as it gradually grew. Back to her lepers, her *raison d'être* and it was killing her now, so near to proper treatment.

Charles and Chuck were both depressed by this diagnosis. It made sense to Charles, who had already come to terms with the possibility after spending years studying AIDS from an academic point of view. She had admitted her own fears. If a disease was endemic in a whole continent, then anyone leading a normal life could get it and anyone living in the kind of insecurity she had endured was at high risk.

Chuck radioed in for an ambulance to meet the ship and made call to Miriam to get Anwei through the system quickly to a doctor who could diagnose the problem.

Chuck was naturally in denial. Over the last year or so, this woman had been his lover, his intimate companion. Charles tasked himself with persuading Chuck to go to the clinic to get tested as soon as they had arrived alongside.

"Look, if she ain't positive, why would I be? I say I wait until we know what's wrong with her. If she's positive, I'll go."

"No, her diagnosis may be unreliable. In fact all tests are only reasonably accurate."

"Oh, bullsheet, Chas, what a fucking mess." Chuck said very quietly.

"Your fucking mess. Face it. You were a willing partner. Somehow you let her go. Fault or no fault, it happened. Now what are the consequences? You get tested, get medication as necessary, live a long life. Fail to get tested, risk a short life of disability and pain. Your choice in the end, but I want to persuade you to do the sensible thing; this is Africa. It has its own rules."

Charles was horrified by the impending death of his mother, the mother he had hardly known and had not made any effort to get to know while they were together. Awful though the circumstances had turned out to be, he realised now that he had a responsibility to Chuck, Donny, and the rest of the crew. He called a meeting in the conference room for all hands. He made absolutely certain there were no outsiders on board and then addressed the company.

"Our voyage has met with limited success but we have not been able to realise the cash from our efforts. We owe the salvation of our voyage to JJ and to Izzy Levimov, both here now. The vessel will stay alongside for a few days while we try to negotiate sales of our product.

"I must emphasize to you all that absolute silence is required. No one outside this room is to have any suspicion of what we have achieved. As a matter of fact, very few of those present really know what has happened, and I am not about to enlighten you now. All South Africans may go on leave immediately. There will be a payout in three days time. After that we will be paying more until you are all fairly paid off for your extreme efforts and the dangers you have encountered.

"I must repeat, no stories to wives, girlfriends, parents: nobody at all. To answer questions say you went north to find more scrap and it was not a very successful voyage. Nothing about our trip into the jungle, fighting, digging, or anything else.

"And thank you all from my heart for your efforts.

"Finally, I have to announce the critical illness of Anwei, my mother, who has been sick for the last few weeks. Really, we have all been working for her. She is the owner of the mine, and she must benefit from the results."

The hands filed out. Most were distracted by the surprise announcement, not so much of Anwei's illness, but of the fact that she was Charles's mother and the owner of the mine.

The "upper deck" crowd remained back.

Chuck turned to Izzy. "How soon can we have some cash? Can I call the chandler and get some food and stores on board?"

The old man spread his right hand on top of his scruffy lace skullcap in a gesture of thought, "I think it would be best to hock some of the diamonds for some ready money. What do you think if I pawn some of the pointers? As I say, there may be fifty or a hundred thousand rand or so there. Charles, do you want to come with me? Do I still have friends? Only if I bring them a client with gemstones."

"Just before we go," interrupted Charles, "what can we do with Anwei's diamond?"

"Did I not mention?" said Izzy. "It's a major hazard, yet I cannot bring myself to divide it. I can only suggest, misquoting the prophet Jesus, 'Render unto Anwei that which is Anwei's'."

Izzy shrugged in an all-knowing expression of fatalism and said nothing. The implication was clear to them all.

"A hundred million dollars," interjected Donny in a gruff whisper.

Izzy slid out of the room with a sly grin on his wrinkled unshaven face and went to his room for his bag of small stones and his tools.

"He's right," said Charles, "whether she lives or dies, the diamond goes with her."

Lightning Source UK Ltd.
Milton Keynes UK
UKOW02f0502051114

241080UK00003B/112/P